THE PROMISES WE BREAK

BALANCE OF POWER
BOOK 2

BERLIN WICK

CONTENTS

COPYRIGHT

This is a work of fiction. Names, characters, places, and incidents either are the product of the author's imagination or are used fictitiously. Any resemblance to actual persons, living or dead, events or locales, is entirely coincidental.

Text Copyright 2024 by Berlin Wick and Wick Publications.

All rights reserved.

No part of this book may be reproduced, or stored in a retrieval system, or transmitted in any form or by any means, electronic, mechanical, photocopying, recording, or otherwise, without express written consent of the publisher.

<u>A note to the reader:</u>

The book explores themes around sexual exploration and is intended for mature audiences 18+.

Trigger Warnings: Parental abuse, both verbally and physically, talk of miscarriage (not on page or experienced by main characters).

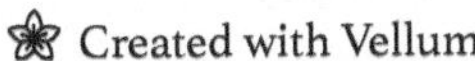 Created with Vellum

DEDICATION

To the quiet, shy one.

I see you, freaky girl.

Playlist

Amber - 311
Iris - Goo Goo Dolls
Bad Decisions - Bobi Andonov
Pony - Ginuwine
Anywhere - 112
Burning Love - Elvis Presley
Love Runs Out - OneRepublic
River - Bishop Briggs
Lose Control - Teddy Swims
Addicted - Saving Abel
No Mercy - Austin Giorgio
Boulevard of Broken Dreams - Green Day
Good Riddance - Green Day
Beautiful Things - Benson Boone
Something in the Orange - Zach Bryan
I'll Be - Edwin McCain

1

HUDSON

"My apologies, Mr. Byrnes. The flight was overbooked and your ticket was canceled. We asked if anyone would be open to giving up their seat in first class, however no one was willing. I'm looking up some other options for you right now."

Pinching the bridge of my nose, I glance up at the poor, probably ridiculously underpaid, woman who looks beyond exhausted, giving people bad news. Her eyes lack energy as she plasters on a fake smile, making quick work on her keyboard.

Looking around the check-in area, there are hordes of people. Some impatiently wait, while others are completely oblivious to their surroundings, perusing their phones, scrolling mindlessly through whatever is capturing their attention.

The woman next to me has her luggage wide open as she transfers clothes and toiletries from one bag to another. She is in a panicked rush as her husband aggressively asks her why she needed six pairs of shoes and enough denim to dress an army.

Why the guys decided to have Jake's bachelor party the first weekend after the New Year, when travel is at its absolute peak, is a complete mystery to me.

I peek down at the name tag of the woman that's helping me, *Ruth*, and when I look back, she has replaced that grimace with another smile. This one tinted with remorse. She's probably in her late fifties or early sixties, close to retirement, and would probably rather spend her days retired with her grandchildren. Instead, she is here, getting yelled at for things beyond her personal control.

As I open my mouth to reply to her, she winces, like she is preparing for verbal armageddon. She's conditioned for abuse.

This poor thing.

"Hey, Ruth. It's not your fault. Please don't stress. I'm not in a rush to get there urgently, but I do need to get there before 8pm this evening. Can you give me my options to make that happen?" Am I frustrated? Sure. But my tone is sincere because, in the grand scheme of life issues, this isn't a tragedy.

Inconvenient? Yes. Life threatening and worth unnecessary anger? No.

Plus, I've just received the most hopeful news of my career, and not even being stuck at the airport during the holidays can dampen that mood.

The breathy smile she releases is both sweet and endearing. Kindness goes a long way. I wish more people could step outside themselves in moments like these and show compassion and understanding.

"Absolutely! I see we have a first class seat available this evening that will get you into Las Vegas around 8pm." She's moving her fingers from her keyboard to her mouse and back again. "Actually, I can get you on *this* same flight, sir. Although the seat is in coach." She leans her head to the left to look past her computer screen, trailing my body from head to toe. "Fortunately, it's in the emergency exit row, so you'll have some extra leg space."

Her once over of me is the exact reason I always book first class. I've played baseball my entire life and my over-utilized upper body muscles are as thick as my shoulders are wide. At least that's what it feels like when you cram me into a coach seat. Like shoving an octopus in a sardine can. My six-foot-four height doesn't help the matter.

"Emergency exit row?" I bounce my head back and forth. It's about a two and a half hour flight. I'll just plug my headphones in and sit tight. Literally—in a water slide tunnel position—for two hours. "That sounds great, Ruth. Let's do that."

"Oh, wonderful, Mr. Byrnes. I will issue a fully transferable first-class credit for you to use at your convenience, and this flight will also be on us." She hands me my boarding pass and California ID back with a beaming smile.

"Have a great day, Ruth. Keep smiling, okay?" I take a step back toward the security checkpoint and she calls out.

"Mr. Byrnes?" I glance back as she mouths. "Thank you."

Showing my Texas roots, I dip my chin and tip my baseball cap at her before heading toward my flight.

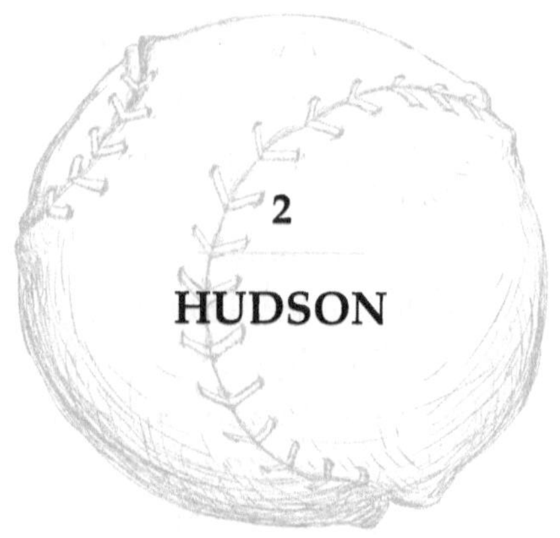

2

HUDSON

s I duck through the entrance of the plane to make my way down the bean pole they call an aisle, I instantly regret my coach decision. The air is as stiff as Marge Simpson's hair and as spacious as a Costco parking lot on Christmas Eve. I'm trying to remain positive, but I hope this isn't a precursor to how this weekend will turn out.

I walk past the seats, and I skim over the aisle numbers for row nineteen. Seventeen, eighteen, ah, nineteen. Here we are.

A quick glance down at the dual lined exit seats has my neck whiplash with a double take. Gorgeous, bright auburn hair, that flows over a petite woman, steals my attention. Her leg is crossed over the other as she balances a crossword puzzle on her lap, nibbling on the top of the pen she is holding.

Sensing my looming presence, she tilts her head toward me, simultaneously bringing her hand to her face to pull the thick cinnamon curtain that attempts to cradle her face behind her ear.

The gaze of her emerald eyes collides with my chocolate ones, and the back draft that flows between them creates a mesh of invisible fireworks that I feel *everywhere*. The once stuffy air is now replaced with thick, dense oxygen, forbidding my body to breathe, and I'm internally choking on the rapid beating of my own heart.

She is the most captivating woman I've ever laid my eyes on.

"Is that your seat?" a gruff voice behind me asks impatiently, ripping us out of our trance.

I turn to look at him, back to the aisle number, then up at the empty overhead bins. I give a simple nod and pick up my luggage to fill the empty space.

I'm terrified that if I look back down at the seat, she'll be gone. Like one of those mystery women in a movie when the character thinks he sees his dream girl, but when he blinks, she has disappeared, leaving him questioning everything in his life, including his sanity.

That's me. I'm that guy.

But when I glance back down, she's still here. Bewitching me. Turning my once confident charm into oatmeal. The same color as the sweater that hangs off one side of her shoulder, exposing her creamy complexion.

I unzip the front pocket of my bag that I've just tucked into the overhead bin to grab my headphones. As I pull them out, a pack of Big Red gum falls out, bounces on the top of the chair in front of mine, then ricochets toward the window seat like a goddamn projectile missile, hitting Little Red straight in the forehead.

She flinches, but still, somehow, snatches the falling gum pack with her free hand before it falls to the floor.

"I am so sorry," I profess. Genuine concern laces my voice as I sit down.

"It's okay." She giggles while handing me the gum. "I have three older brothers. I've had worse things thrown at my head."

The natural pink tint to her lips curl upward in a timid smile and her eyes squint, matching the emotion of her tempting mouth.

She shifts her shoulders away from me to face the back of the seat in front of her, but I'm not ready for this conversation to end. "I have three older brothers, too."

Her head snaps back to me. "No, you don't." An accusatory statement, not a question.

"No, really." I chuckle at her reaction. I pull out my phone, tapping on the photo app to bring up a picture of my brothers from Thanksgiving, from just a handful of weeks back. My parents insist that we always go back home to Texas for *that* specific holiday. In my twenty-eight years on this earth, I have yet to miss a Thanksgiving, and I'm not sure I want to feel the wrath of my mother if I ever do.

I click on a photo and twist the phone in her direction. "This is my oldest brother, Henry, and," pointing to the two guys between Henry and me, "the twins, Graham and Grant."

"And who is this guy?" She points to me, with my arm wrapped around the shoulder of my favorite brother, Grant.

"Oh, *that* guy." I clear my throat. "Well, he's six-four, strapping young man. Born and raised in Texas, but currently resides in San Diego." I instantly hate not knowing where she lives and debate asking her to move wherever I am. Instead of being a complete psycho, I boldly continue with, "he loves baseball, 90s punk music, and recently discovered his weakness for beautiful redheads who like crossword puzzles."

Her eyebrows raise, and an adorable smirk appears over her lips. "He's a charmer, I see."

Oh, I will charm your panties off, little red.

"What's your name?" I ask, holding my hand out.

"Ember." She slides her dainty hand into mine as she gives it a kind shake. Her touch is like velvet on my calloused hand, engulfing me further into her spell. The shockwaves travel down my spine into the uncontrollable appendage between my legs. It forces me to shift in my seat, which is exactly what I don't need right now.

"I'm Hudson."

The captain comes over the speaker, tearing both our eyes and hands apart. He introduces himself and confirms our flight arrival time in Las Vegas.

Two hours will never be enough time. I'd fly to Antarctica in this tin can if it meant I could have more time with her.

3

HUDSON

As I suspected, the two hours on this short-ass plane ride is not enough time. The flight attendant just walked by informing us they will start prepping to land, and I have never wanted to hold a plane hostage more than I do now.

"No, no. I'm telling you we can debate about this all day long, but I'll win. Big Red is the best gum to ever be made." I flip open the top of the same pack that hit the top of her head, offering her a piece.

She throws her head back, half giggling, half eye rolling. "Juicy Fruit all day," she banters back.

"But, how?" I push back. "Juicy Fruit does nothing for your breath, and it loses flavor in like two point five seconds."

"But Big Red? It's like 'oh, I'm unassuming cinnamon gum'." She waves her hands in front of her, giving the gum an extra girly voice, "But one piece, and it's like lightning in your mouth and the sting lasts forever."

Kinda like you.

Exactly like you.

Except the lightning engulfs my entire body, and that everlasting sting will linger everywhere.

I chuckle, shaking my head. She has no idea.

The irony is not lost on me. Not only does she have all the side effects of my favorite ridiculously powerful gum, but she has the same commanding red hair, *and* her name is Ember.

Give me the sting and light me on fire, little red.

Plus, she is stunning, and the conversation has come so easily. We haven't talked about anything too personal, but everything we have talked about is organic and natural. It's been one topic to another, flowing between the two of us like we've known each other our whole lives.

I've avoided the topic of what I do for a living, thankfully. I dislike the judgment that comes with telling people I'm a minor league baseball player. What my oldest brother, Henry, refers to as the 'MLB for the inept'. I'm lying to myself when I use the word judgment. It's embarrassment. I was destined for a long career in the MLB until one injury took my whole career away. I've been working my way back there ever since.

I found out she loves action movies and hates rom-coms. She graduated from the University of Missouri - Kansas City, with a double major in business and marketing.

I was instantly impressed when she told me she offered free marketing services to small local businesses in her town instead of doing fake mockups for her college projects. Thinking like a true entrepreneur and business professional.

Like me, she is on her way to Las Vegas as part of a wedding party. She left from Seattle for what she air-quoted as a 'work thing'. She still lives in Missouri, a small annoying hiccup. When I asked if she travels to Seattle often, she said she hopes it becomes a more regular thing.

She seems anxious to get out of the small town she lives in, or maybe that's just me projecting.

The last ten minutes were spent using the inside of my Big Red gum pack to play Tic Tac Toe. Apparently, she claims that Tic Tac Toe is strategic, and she is proving it by kicking my ass in every single game we have played, no matter what box I started my "X" in.

She circles one of the boxes and beats me in the final game. Again.

"See." She kicks her chin up to me with a smug smile. "Strategy."

"Fine, you've proven your point, but in case you don't realize, my ego is never going to recover. I hope you know this is a core memory, and I'll never get over this emotional destruction."

She throws her head back and laughs. And Jesus, I could listen to that laugh forever.

"Here you go." She tucks the top of the gum pack into the bottom and hands it to me.

"Oh, hell no." I push it back toward her. "Why would I want that now? So I can kill my ego every time I want a piece of gum? No thanks. Consider that your winnings."

She rewards me with another one of those gorgeous smiles before tucking the pack of gum into her purse.

She peeks over at the seat back pocket in front of my seat, and tilts her head to read the sideways lettering, then flicks the corner of the ticket. "So, you got kicked out of first class and have to rough it back here with us in coach today, huh?"

I angle my view to look at the tickets, a first-class ticket with a slash through it and the reprinted coach ticket unevenly peeking out from behind it. I quickly send a silent little thank you to Ruth for this jackpot of a seat. I can't help but smile when I reply. "Yeah, apparently they overbooked the first-class seats, so they offered me this one. But," I lean in close to her ear, "this is hardly roughing it, little red."

I didn't mean for it to come out as sexual as it sounded, but when her cheeks flush with pink, I have no regrets.

"But I am encroaching on your seat here," I touch my shoulders to indicate my size, "which is why I typically always fly first or business class. I try to respect my fellow seatmates."

"Well, thank goodness for your selfless act." Her sarcastic smirk is on full display as she shifts in her seat to face me. "What's the width measurement here, anyway? I'm surprised you made it through the cabin doors." She places her palm over my shoulder and arm, then trails it along the front of my collarbone, using her hand as a ridiculous tool for measurement.

She's hyper focused on her palm, trailing along my chest, as she attempts to take an actual measurement with her hand, her tongue is sticking out between her teeth with how deep she is concentrating, and with every touch, she sends bolts of electricity all the way to my toes.

She's like a little red Magneto.

"You've got to be at least twenty-two inches." She's looking down at her palm, still using her thumb and pointer finger to remeasure her palm as a scale in inches.

When she lifts her gaze to look at mine, my eyebrows are lifted and I'm pressing my lips in a hard line as an attempt to keep my mouth shut while I wait for her to realize what she said.

Her smile fades with a look of pure shock on her face. "No… no, I meant—" Her palms cover her face, interrupting herself.

"Oh no, you can stop and leave it there. I'm fine with this completely distorted measurement." I laugh, pulling her hands down from covering her beautiful, embarrassed face.

With her hands in mine, I turn her hand over so her palm is facing up.

"Your palm is a terrible ruler," I say, using this as an excuse to touch her. I place my pointer finger at the base of her wrist then trace the lines and creases that decorate her hand, wondering which ones are her laugh lines, heart lines, and life lines, wanting to claim all of them. My finger grazes over all of them before reaching the top of her fingertip, and when I glance back up to peer into those emerald gems, her bottom lip is pulled in between her teeth, and she's just as entranced as I am.

I lick my lips, preparing to kiss her. I want to kiss her.

"Garbage?" The crinkle of plastic ruffling rips us out of the moment as the flight attendant walks by.

She grants me a shy smile, then shifts back to face the back of the seat in front of her.

My head falls to the headrest, and I realize the seatbelt sign isn't lit up yet. Needing a moment, I excuse myself.

"Okay, I've got to use the restroom, but when I get back, we're going to finish the other debate," I remind her.

She furrows her brow, tilting her head as her eyes scan the top of her lids. "Oh, you mean the one where you concede to the fact that Die Hard is *not* a Christmas movie?" Her smirk, smug as hell.

"Oh, little red. You're going to be the death of me."

Literally.

She smiles, biting the corner of her bottom lip, both adorable and sexy as hell. I think she likes my nickname for her, and I never plan to stop.

I push myself off the seat and squeeze out of the confines of my tiny space. I glance around, and everything looks so unfamiliar. I haven't once glanced up to see the people around me or even where we are on the plane. All of my senses have been consumed by her from the moment I sat down.

Thankfully, the bathroom is vacant.

Unfortunately, I forgot how fucking miniature these are.

Now I fully understand the meaning of *water closet*. I robot shuffle in a circle to lock the door and finish my robot shuffle back toward the toilet. I lift the cover to expose the metal bowl covered with a thin blue film. The sour stench that radiates from it reminds me how great I've had it sitting next to Ember, who smells like tropical petals and sunshine.

I wonder if it would be weird to ask her what kind of perfume she uses so I can wash my sheets in it. And everything I own.

I wash up and exit the bathroom, turning down the aisle to see a man crouching, leaning on the armrest of my aisle seat. I squint as my feet walk, one in front of the other. When he comes into my full view, I realize he's fucking hitting on her.

Damn, he didn't waste any time going in for the kill after I left my seat.

Since his back is toward me, he doesn't see me approach. I linger a couple of steps back.

"...go out while you're in Vegas?" I hear the last bit of his question.

"Oh," Ember says with genuine surprise.

I don't know why you're surprised. Every man on this goddamn plane wants to ask you out. Court you. Date you. *Keep you forever.*

"That's so sweet, but I have a boyfriend."

What the hell?

My breath is lost behind my throat, her words an invisible punch to my gut. Like this metal tin box for an airplane, my lungs find their own pressurization process, providing me with anxiety I wasn't prepared for.

How did I not ask that question? The chemistry between us was so strong, our conversation effortless. It never came up, and I never even thought to ask. Never wanted to consider.

Of course she has a goddamn boyfriend.

I clear my throat to get the attention of the crouching douchebag here.

He stands up to his full height, meeting me face to face. Well, we do when I scowl down at him, since he is a solid foot shorter than me.

I smile. Close mouthed and sarcastic.

He leaves.

I glance down at Ember as she pushes her purse back under the seat in front of her.

When she turns to face me, it's as if there is a glow around her. A radiance that only I can see and my heart can feel. It fights to not crack open out of the armor that keeps it safe, but feels like it breaks simultaneously.

"What?" she asks curiously.

I just shake my head and joke, because that's what I do when I avoid something I don't want to address. "Those bathrooms are the size of a matchbox."

"Well, I'm sure they are compared to you. You're like the Jolly Green Giant. Except you're not green. So you're just, Jolly Giant. A jolly giant."

She giggles, and it's infectious. Beautiful. My damnation.

I take my seat and we fall into conversation again as the flight attendants make their final rounds and buckle for landing.

Words are being exchanged, but I can only think of slamming my lips into hers. Wrapping my arms around her body, pulling her into my seat. I want to make her straddle me while I explore every inch of every curve of her gorgeous body. Run my hands through the locks of her sunset strands that have entranced me these past couple hours and make her forget there is anyone but us.

Jesus, I want to.

But I follow rules and respect boundaries.

Why? I have no fucking clue. She makes me want to break every rule I have.

The captain comes back on the loudspeaker, telling us we've landed, tearing me from my thoughts. The plane is heading to another city after Las Vegas, so it appears some passengers will stay on and some will get off. He asks that everyone remain seated so that those catching a connecting flight can exit first since our flight was slightly delayed.

I won't do what I want to do and take her in every corner of this plane. But I won't deprive myself of attempting to see her again.

"So, hey." I remove my cap and run my hand around the back of my neck before replacing it on my head. "Why don't we exchange numbers? We could meet for coffee or something while we're here in Vegas?" I sound more confident than I feel.

"Oh."

There's that fucking 'Oh'. The same 'Oh' she gave Crouching Tiger.

"I... I can't."

My eyes narrow in confusion. I know she feels this, too. She has to.

The little boy from Texas, who was raised with good manners, wants to respect what she just said. But the man sitting in front of the woman that has made him feel more alive than he has felt in years. *That man,* I want to unleash on her and see what happens.

My friends are constantly telling me to take more risks with women. Hence, why I'm still single. Actually, I'm single because I believe in more than lust. Sure, I have women that show interest in me. But a woman that sets my soul on fire, I haven't found that.

Until her.

Until today, before getting on this plane thinking it would be an uncomfortable, draining flight. But no, physically and mentally, I'm alive. So fucking alive.

Goddammit.

I'm not letting her get away that easily.

Before I can open my mouth, she tips her chin at the emptying aisle and says, "We're up."

Shit, that was fast.

I stand and grab the bag I placed in the overhead bin as she leans forward to squeeze between me and the seat, brushing her ass against the front of my pants.

"Shoot, I'm sorry."

"Don't ever be sorry for *that*." I wink, giving her my most flirtatious grin.

She returns a playful eye roll before turning around and walking down the aisle. I follow, a few paces behind, to marvel at how perfect her ass bounces with each step she takes. Her legs are thick and her calves are unbelievable. I know that's strange, right? But her small knee and ankle joints add curves to her already muscular legs and her calves... She must wear heels all day or she's genetically gifted. Either way, I want to run my tongue over every inch of her bottom half. Her top half, too.

"Hudson? Hudson Byrnes?" I hear someone say my name, questioningly.

I turn back to the man I just passed, sitting in an aisle to my right.

"Yes?" I reply, just as questionably as he said my name.

"Wow, I'm a huge fan." Holding his hand out for a shake.

"Oh, thanks man, I appreciate that." I slide my hand in his, giving him a brotherly greeting.

"You held the college record for most hits as a catcher. You were lined up to be the next Mike Piazza. You were gonna be so huge, man. Man, it's so cool to meet you!"

The keyword: *were*.

My lips turn down before turning into a tip-lipped smile.

"You're playing in San Diego, in the minors, right? Ever think you'll make it back to the big leagues? Your ankle ready for it?"

Oh, it's ready. My ankle, my body, my heart. They've all been ready. It's the MLB that hates signing players they think are damaged goods due to an injury no one thought I would come back from.

"Yeah, still there. And, one day, hopefully, man. You never know." I hold out my hand one more time, giving him a friendly nod.

I love being recognized, and I love fans. Especially true fans, like he was, *is*. But there are always so many questions about my injury and if I'm ever coming back. I never had hope of that until the last meeting with my coach, which is what brought me here.

Bringing myself back to reality, I look down the aisle of the empty plane. She's gone.

Shit.

I glance behind me to a slew of angry faces because I held up the line for a couple of minutes. I quickly hurry my steps, not just for their sake, but for mine, too. I can't believe she raced off without so much as a goodbye or a wave.

I duck under the entrance doors into the jet bridge and rush my way down the exit tunnel until I pass through the doors into the airport.

There are people everywhere. Slot machines. More noise than my brain wants to comprehend when it's trying so hard to find a needle in a haystack. A cinnamon-haired needle with perfect emerald green eyes and flawless lips.

I tower over most of these people easily, but still shimmy back and forth, pressing onto my toes to stand beyond my full height, shooting my eyes in every direction to attempt to find her.

But she's gone.

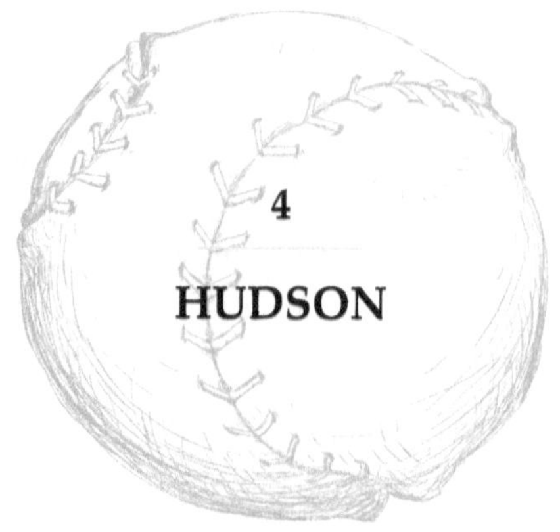

4

HUDSON

I toss the hotel keycard onto the shiny countertop as it slides to the corner, nearly toppling over the other side.

I'm annoyed.

Annoyed isn't even the right word. Annoyed is for people stuck in traffic or picking the express lane at a grocery store when the slowest person in the world is checking out with more items than allowed.

I'm furious that I didn't get more information from her. Like her last name, for starters. Her phone number, home address, social security number, and credit history. So I could stalk her properly.

Now, I'm conjuring up every illegal way to find her and have been since the moment I left baggage claim after searching every single name tag on the goddamn conveyor belt, searching for an 'Ember'.

Fortunately, her name is unique because I had every intention of stealing her luggage and holding it ransom. I never found it, thankfully, because I didn't want to commit an actual crime today.

Jesus, what has gotten into me?

I'm unsure if my behavior is warranted, being that I only spent two hours with her. Well, I know it's not warranted. But, I haven't felt so strongly about someone in so long that it brings a small smile to my face in the realization I'm not dead to it.

Then I remember she's gone, *and* I'm pissed again.

As I take a few meditative breaths to calm myself down, I walk around the well-lit, expansive hotel room.

The room is nice. The guys went all out planning this bachelor party. Well, belated bachelor party.

Jake, our 'groom', for all intents and purposes, got married a few years ago, but they eloped. At first, we thought she may have been pregnant, but it turns out they just wanted to get married without the hassle that comes with the ceremony. Since neither of them have a large family, it worked out, and it was exactly what they wanted. Except for the fact that Jake never got his bachelor party, so fast forward to the present day, and here I am in Vegas with a non-groom-to-be and a total hard on for a stranger I know very little about.

Settling in, I unzip my suitcase, placing my toiletry bag with my shaving essentials in the bathroom. I remove some of the clothes I brought along and eyeball a couple of button-up shirts and my sports jacket, not knowing the exact plan since Seamus took on coordinating this whole thing himself.

Seamus is the most militant guy in our group. Literally and figuratively. He is the most structured routine guy I've ever known, and he's an ex-Navy SEAL. Now, he does something for the government that he apparently can't talk about because every time we give him shit for his job, he says it's classified and drops it. I'd account his systematic routine lifestyle to his military training, except he was like that even as a kid.

He was the first in our group of friends that I met in grade school. We bonded over organizing and color coding our crayon box. I think our parents found us to be absolute lunatics, but a match made in best friend heaven for us. I'm close to all the guys, but Seamus has been through hell and back with me.

My phone rings in my pocket, and I know immediately it's Seamus because he hates texting.

"Hey, Shay. I'm checked into the suite. Great pick, man." I hit the speaker button before throwing my phone on the plush down comforter of the king bed in the bedroom I picked for myself.

"Glad you made it. I was worried when I got your text about your seat being bumped."

"Me too. But I was able to get on the same flight. They just had to downgrade my seat." Except I hit the fucking seatmate jackpot, so it was a complete upgrade in my book.

"Shay, with your, uh... connections. Would you be able to find someone for me? Nothing illegal or anything. Just like a phone number and address?"

"Yeah, easily. Who are you looking for?"

"A girl on the plane. She was... Well, she was fucking perfect. Her name is Ember."

"Oh... interesting. Why didn't you just get her number?" His confused tone mirrors mine. Which I can understand. I'm not shy and have no problem asking for a number. But he also knows I'm never serious about relationships or women in general. I'm not a total playboy, actually not one at all, anymore, and that was a crutch.

I've just never pursued anyone seriously since my last relationship, which was right after high school. So, needless to say, it's been a while.

"Long story, man." I run my palm down my face, scratching at the stubble on my jawline that's beginning to invade too much space on my neck.

"What's her last name?"

"I... don't have it," I squeak out.

"That's a problem." Well, don't sugarcoat anything for me, fucker. We're going to have to talk about his overly factual bedside manner at some point.

"I figured as much. It's fine. I need to shower and shave before we head out. What's the plan tonight?"

"We're going to eat at the steakhouse at the hotel. Then we'll head to a club tonight. Tomorrow night, we're going to *Temptation*." Some background chatter statics through the speaker. "Hud, I just got a taxi. I'll be there in about twenty minutes."

He hangs up. Because he's Seamus and he was done talking.

As much as I'd like to start Googling and stalking a certain redhead, this weekend is for Jake. To celebrate his... well, his pseudo bachelor party. This is the first time all the guys have been back together since our college days. We finally have the chance to give him the bachelor party we always wanted to, and it's either going to be wild and we will either end up in jail or half dead, or we're going to discover how old we really are and retire by midnight.

But I'm doubting the latter.

I walk around the suite that Seamus booked, and it's huge. It has a large living area with multiple couches, a bar, and even a corner area with a stripper pole. A traditional bachelor pad used specifically for bachelor parties. There are four separate rooms, two that have their own bathrooms and another shared bathroom in the living space.

It's far too much room for the five of us guys. Two of them will share a room, or Dane will just sleep on the couch because that guy is the most free spirited one of all of us. He can spontaneously do anything, and I'm not sure he's ever experienced anxiety in his life. He just goes with the flow and doesn't have an opinion about much of anything.

Voices trail in from outside my bedroom door, so I slip on

my shorts and exit the room to see who's here. I'm certain it's Seamus by now, but I have no idea what the flight plans were for the other guys.

Seamus and Jake are reuniting in the kitchen, giving each other a slap on the shoulder and half hug before they look up and see me.

"Huuuuud!" Jake rounds the luggage at his feet and pulls me in for a brotherly hug. "How was your flight?"

Before I can answer. Seamus replies, "He met his dream girl."

Jake ricochets his eyes between Seamus and me with a curious smile. "On the flight?"

So much for the circle of trust with my best friend Seamus.

"Nah, man. I mean, she was great." Rubbing the nape of my neck as I round my head in circles. As content as I was with Ember, coach seating is not built for men like me.

"I think the word you used was perfect," Seamus interrupts. *Dick.*

I turn, giving him the look of death. But I am no match. Seamus is the scariest fucker I know. I'm certain he could John Wick my ass with a pencil.

"Yeah, perfect. She was perfect. But she ran off when the plane deboarded."

Confusion makes way over Jake's face. I usually don't have issues if I attempt to go after a girl, and he knows it.

"I think she had a boyfriend." I shrug. "Looks like I have a habit of hitting on unavailable women."

Jake chuckles because that is exactly how I accidentally met his wife.

"Undoubtedly, the best moment of that night." He pats my shoulder, still laughing, before grabbing his suitcase and heading toward the master suite we reserved for the so-called groom.

"We're eating at the steakhouse downstairs in an hour.

Dane and Kobi will be here in a few minutes, and the car will pick us up after dinner," Seamus calls out, heading in the other direction, toward the room he's claiming.

I grab a bottle of water off the counter and head back to my room to get dressed. My thoughts keep straying to Ember. Damn her for running off. I already liked her, but now, now she's a complete mystery and I don't know if it's the enigma of her or if it's like my father always said. *'When you meet her, you'll know.'*

My parents' fortieth wedding anniversary is next year, and they have been a shining example of exactly what I want out of a marriage. They are truly the quintessential married couple. To this day, my dad still courts my mom. They kiss, laugh, dance in the hallway, and treat each other with the utmost respect. Sure, I see them argue, but in the end, they always support one another and find a middle ground.

They are the reason I'm a closet hopeless romantic, and I'll never settle for anything less than unadulterated, can't live without each other, love. Nothing short of magic, my mom would always say. Of course, I repress those feelings and never appear to be the romantic I am at heart around the guys. Except, I can't seem to help myself with her.

Ember was magic. Her presence was all-consuming, and no one has ever captured my attention like she did. I'm so pissed at myself for not getting a last name or her phone number. I could have stalked her until she broke up with her boyfriend, then went in for the kill or just found ways to break them up.

Christ, listen to me.

I've got to get my mind here with the guys. It's been far too many years since we've all been together.

I flip open my suitcase again and hang up what should be hung in the closet, then I unpack the rest into the dresser drawers.

We're only here for two days, so I don't have much, but I

hate living out of a suitcase. Whenever we travel for away games, the first thing I do is unpack. It makes most hotel rooms feel less stale. Especially the kind of rooms you stay in for the minor leagues. Travel is not nearly as comfortable as what the major league provides and the hotel rooms are typically shared. They are nowhere near luxurious, which is fine. I don't need luxury. I just need it bedbug free, with clean sheets and an extra travel-sized body wash container.

I have to share the news with the guys. They need to know that I can't get into any shit this weekend. I have a solid chance of getting moved up to the majors with the Seattle Smashers. This is the opportunity of a lifetime. I love San Diego and love the guys on my team, but I was built for the MLB. Both my older brother, Henry, and I were raised for it. We ate, drank, and slept baseball. Henry, of course, went on to play in the MLB, with only a short stint of time in the minors, which most ball players do. But ever since my injury, I've had to play in the minors. I've been holding on to the hope of getting signed, knowing my potential is there. But the coaches, they are the ones who steer clear of injured players, especially injuries like mine.

Nope. Not going to risk anything that can prevent this from happening, so I have got to tell the guys. If they get into some shit, I'll bolt. Shameful, but necessary. They'll understand.

I've finished getting dressed and appraise myself in the bathroom mirror. Dark stonewashed denim jeans fit low on my waist, and luckily, the material has enough stretch to give way to my muscular quads. I decided to keep it simple with a basic, but snug, beige colored long sleeve button up. The material is thin and soft and fits nicely over my chest and shoulders. I've strategically rolled the sleeves up just below my elbows, exposing the forearm tattoo I've been intending to turn into a full sleeve soon. I look pretty well put together, considering my brain feels like a jumbled mess.

Seamus bangs on the door as he walks by yelling, "Wheels up," which is stupid because none of us are military trained except for him, and I swear he just likes to boss us around. I'm also surprised he knocked and that I haven't experienced a full-blown invasion of my privacy yet from any of the guys.

As if on cue, Dane busts through my bedroom door without an inkling of a knock, barrelling into me with a manly bro hug.

"Hudson!! I've missed you, man."

"Dane!" I pull back from his hug, rubbing my hand on top of his head, shagging out the long ass dirty blonde hair on his head. "When was the last time you had a haircut, man?"

"Women dig it. Guys, too." He pulls it back in a low man bun, wiggling his eyebrows, and all I can do is shake my head. He has a 'love the one you're with' idea of relationships. I've always thought that he was born in the wrong generation. He's a hippie at heart and could probably live in a VW van his entire life and be totally content with nothing but a backpack full of shorts, t-shirts, and a couple of flip-flops. You would never know that he's brilliant. Literally, the man has an IQ like Einstein with a personality like Bob Marley.

"That sounds like it has a story you'll have to fill me in on." I pat him on the back.

"I will later. It's time to gooooooo!" He runs out of the room, where all the guys are gathered at the mini kitchen island, shots in hand.

"Hudson, hurry your ass up," Jake yells as he hands me my shot.

Kobi holds his fist out to me, since he's the only one I haven't seen yet, and I connect with a knuckle bump.

Seamus holds up the small glass with clear liquid. I'm thankful they decided to go with vodka tonight and not tequila. Not sure that will make much of a difference tonight, but at least tomorrow, the hangover will hurt a little less. "To Jake and his non-bachelor, bachelor party!"

"To Jake!!" "Jakey." "Let's goooooo!" A mix of different salutes overlap each other before the night begins. Hopefully these bastards won't get me arrested.

5

EMBER

"I don't know which one of you ladies was the brilliant mastermind that planned the H2O IV van coming by earlier, but you are the real MVP. If it weren't for that, I don't think I would have made it out tonight," Suzy says as she finishes pressing her lips together, spreading the ruby red color, giving her plump lips a pop against the all white outfit she is wearing. A tight bodysuit donned with a fluffy, short tutu skirt. She looks like a ballerina bride, minus the ballerina shoes. The heels she is wearing are definitely *not* ballerina shoes.

"We couldn't have the bride-to-be only lasting through part one of her 'Fling before the Ring'!" Dana screams out of the shuttle bus window that's currently bumping its way through the strip. Figuratively, by way of the loud as hell speakers, and literally, by way of the incessant bouncing that occurs with every tiny pothole we hit.

Actually, shuttle bus sounds a little too prude here. I suppose I should call it what it really is: a party van. Equipped with alcohol, snacks, incredibly loud speakers, and a stripper pole directly in the middle of the platform of the vehicle. It's built for at least a dozen bodies, far too large for our modest bachelorette party of four, but Dana spared no expense when planning this for her sister. She rented it for the entire night, so we always had a ride to any place we wanted to go.

We are currently on route to *Temptation*, an upscale strip club for both men and women. After Dana thoroughly researched all the options, she decided this was where we were going to spend our last night in Vegas. Yesterday was full of shopping and massages during the day and dancing last night. Tonight, though... Tonight is going to be '*Wet 'n Wild*', according to Dana. And yes, she air-quoted to clarify it would be the same *Wet 'n Wild—girls gone crazy edition*. All of us being born and raised in a tiny Missouri town, we were all ready to let loose.

I've never been to Vegas before, and I've never done anything like this, so I have no idea what to expect. The excitement and anxiety are currently going to war in my head, but excitement is winning.

Last night was fun, nothing too crazy, just dancing. But tonight will be one of the reasons they created the motto *What happens in Vegas, stays in Vegas.*

The girls are already drunk. I've always been reserved when it comes to drinking. I've never liked how it makes me feel. Out of control, aloof, and the next day is always full of regret. Nothing good ever seems to come out of it, so why bother? Suzy insisted I drink, and I buckled under that peer pressure, so here I am, three shots later, and far too tipsy, too early into the night.

Last night, after only one shot, I spilled my guts to the girls about meeting Hudson on the plane. They thought I was crazy running out of the plane like I did but, Christ, he was the sexiest man I had ever met.

In my entire life.

Not that I've had much experience with men in general.

But Hudson. I don't know that I have ever had such a physical response to someone before.

There hasn't been a spare moment where I haven't thought about him and those dark chocolate eyes and perfect smile. At first, I thought maybe he was just a friendly guy, but when the flight was coming to an end and he asked to see me again, I saw a desire in his eyes I've never felt from anyone before. One that mirrored my own, so much so that it scared the shit out of me.

Using the excuse of having a boyfriend to men that ask me out has always been my go-to response to avoid relationships, even when I wasn't actually in one. But when he asked, I couldn't lie. I didn't want to tell him I had a boyfriend when I didn't, not like the guy on the plane that approached me before Hudson returned. For some reason, I didn't want to lie to Hudson, but I couldn't muster the courage to say yes.

I don't want to have casual sex, and more importantly, I won't get into a relationship that will limit my options. I'll be moving soon, hopefully. No, not hopefully. I will be moving. Even if I don't get that job. I'm ready. My time in Weston, Missouri is over. If I have to stay for one more wedding, bridal shower, baby shower, or anything related to marriage and babies, I might actually bury myself under an outhouse and let that be my demise.

All of my friends have since been married, and some divorced, then remarried, since high school. I was fortunate enough to put myself through college and keep my focus there, against the wishes of my parents. Well, specifically my dad. You would think he would support my goals the same way he did my brothers, but to him, my education was a waste of money.

My mom insisted the entire time that I needed to stop going to school. I begged her to help me with the tuition and cost of all the books and supplies, but she took my father's side, as she always does. She informed me, daily, that it was pointless to get a degree when my focus should be on marrying a rich man. *'Why work when you can have a man take care of you?'*

She has always cared more about what he thinks, does, says,

and hardly has a thought of her own. My father grew up incredibly wealthy, and he inherited his father's fortune. My mother's family barely made ends meet. She's confessed more than once she will do anything to keep my father happy because he affords her the life she never knew she could have. That status, that wealth, is what she craves more than anything.

She loves it more than she loves her own children. Her only daughter included.

He provides her the life I know she has always wanted. It definitely doesn't help that all my friends went off and did nothing more than get married and have babies. It's like our little town of Weston stayed frozen in history. Women don't have a life of their own. They are not individuals enhancing the life of their spouses, they are *defined* by their title, 'his wife.' My mother being the matriarch of the town for that exact motto. Being at the beck and call of her husband, my father, the most old-fashioned man in human existence.

I just wish he treated me the same way he treats my brothers.

Instead, they just continued to push my ex on me so forcefully it ended up driving me even further away. Which is why I've applied at every job anywhere in the country. I've been grounded, rooted to an unwanted life in Weston, and I'm over it.

I want so much more than that, and I'm tired of feeling guilty over it.

"I'm ready," I whisper to myself as I look out the window, the Vegas strip's neon lights flashing by.

"Earth to Ember!" Dana screams my way from her inverted position on the pole. Her hair grazes the ground as she floats upside down, her body slowly slipping down the pole, even with her white knuckle grip and leg haphazardly wrapped around it.

"Oh my god, you're going to break your neck!" I launch

myself at her in an attempt to catch her, even though she's not actually falling.

"You are the oldest twenty-three-year-old I know. You seriously need to relax. You're giving yourself permanent wrinkles on your forehead. Get whatever is stuck in your head out of it, because when we step into Temptation, all you bitches better leave all your inhibitions here." She places her four-inch heel to the ground, pulling herself upright.

"Doesn't Temptation only have female strippers, not male strippers?" Sara asks.

Suzy's eyes widen as she snaps her neck over at Dana.

"No, no. It has multiple levels. The bottom level is a sex store, bar, and I hear you can rent rooms. Rumor has it there is a chapel there, too, which is weird, but whatever. The second level is where the female strippers perform, and the top level, the male strippers. We're top level, baby."

Dana was the first to get married. She got engaged the day after graduation to her high school sweetheart, Scott, and officially married before the end of our first summer out of high school. Their love story is the epitome of a small town romance. She was the prom queen, he was the quarterback of the football team, and that's all I need to say about that.

Being that she's been married for the longest, with the most kids, three already in total, her wild side comes out anytime the girls get together.

"We're pulling in," The driver yells from the front of the bus as he flips a switch on the top display above his head. The lights dim softly, changing from one color to another, flowing from the back to the front, then music so loud the windows shake. Ginuwine's Pony starts playing and the girls start hollering.

I guess now is the time to shed those inhibitions.

Joining them, I roll my hips, moving with the music as we glide down the steps into the warm breeze of the desert air.

Even though it's early in January, there is still a warmth to the wind. So different compared to the chill of the air in Missouri.

The host, an incredibly sexy firefighter, but clearly *not* a firefighter, greets us at the front and calls Dana by name. Listing off each of our names, and even without any type of megaphone, the man's voice booms through the small entrance area of the building.

"Ladies, you are our VIP's tonight, front row with top shelf bottle service. Vodka will be served with champagne, along with the mixers of your choice. Each of you get one lap dance with admission, any other lap dances are fifty dollars. It'll be the best money you'll ever spend on yourselves." He winks, handing us back our IDs, then punches the elevator button.

Dana squeals in excitement, doing a small clap jump at Suzy, who's biting her lip, trying to hide her smile.

The elevator doors open, and our host holds his arm out with a small gentleman-like bow. Suzy leads the way in with all of us trailing behind, me being the last.

"Ember?" I hear my name from somewhere behind me. Turning around, I see a group of guys walking up toward the entrance. My stomach flutters, making my breath hitch as his dark eyes connect with my light ones. He's standing at his full height, peering over the top of another guy standing in front of him. "Ember!" Pushing the guy to the side, jutting out in front of the group, but unable to reach us before the elevator doors close.

"Holy shit." Suzy turns to me. "Was that him?"

"Who?" Sara asks in unison, with Dana asking, "Who the hell was that?"

Hudson.

Panic blankets every inch of my body. I shift uncomfortably and turn to the girls, then back at the closed doors. The feeling of lust and anxiety blend like oil and water as my body stutters to react. I open my mouth and close it. Words have completely escaped me.

"Wait. Is he... that group of guys... Are they coming up here?" I turn, grabbing the jacket of the firefighter attempting to turn him toward me. Instead, I just end up exposing more of his torso and chest as his jacket flies open with my aggressive grip.

"Oh, um. Sorry," I say, while he chuckles. I pull his jacket forward again, trying to close the front with a small awkward pat, but he adjusts it himself, leaving his abs open and on display.

"That's probably the group for the second floor. There's no access once you are on the floor to move. We have it set up so you stay on the floor you pay for."

"Oh, good. Thanks." I'm relieved. Right? Ugh. Why did they have to come here? Why did we have to come here? What are even the chances we would run into each other in Vegas? There have to be a million people in this city.

"Good? Girl, that is not good. I don't care if it's a Vegas fling. You need to let that man do *something* to you." Dana circles her hand at the elevator door.

Shaking my head in short, frantic movements, "I can't handle the temptation that is Hudson."

Dana leans in to me and whispers in my ear. "Inhibitions are on the bus, remember? Plus, this *is* Temptation."

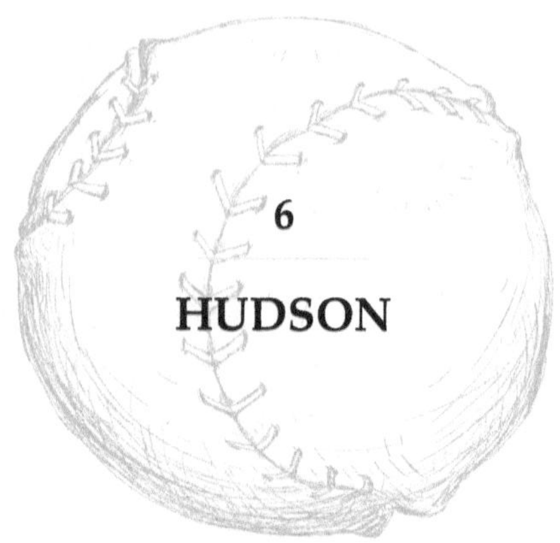

6

HUDSON

"**W**as that her?" Seamus pulls my arm back before I cross over the threshold where the host stand is.

"That was her." Flustered, I run my hands through my hair, resting them at the nape of my neck as I look up toward the sky. Okay, she was already in the elevator, but why is she running away from me? She could have stepped out. She saw me and just stood there.

I thought maybe she was just running late and ran off at the airport, not that she was actually trying to avoid me. At least, that was the excuse I was telling myself all day yesterday.

Clicking on the pavement catches my attention as a woman, with heels larger than my condo and a skirt shorter than my fingernail, appears behind the host stand. "Seamus Matthews," she calls out, her seductive gaze bouncing between the five of us.

"That's me." Seamus steps forward. "Can I ask where the group before us is going?"

"Bachelorette parties are typically on the third floor with the male dancers. I'll be showing you to the second with our female entertainers. We don't commingle the floors, and we'll take you up and back down. There is no public access to either floor other than this elevator, so don't worry, the girls won't know whatever you guys end up doing tonight." She winks, clearly not understanding that we are actually trying to stalk them, not hide from them.

Seamus shoots me a knowing look. I'm certain if he had time to plan, he could find some emergency exit or security access easily, but he would be going in blind and we would end up suspiciously looking around the floor and, more than likely, end up getting kicked out.

"Can I just go up to that floor to see someone? I... I saw an old friend head up that way, and I just want to say hi." Usually, I'd be more charming, but seeing Ember put me in pure panic mode and I have a desperate need to get to her before she disappears.

"No, sorry." She shakes her head, pulling up a sheet on the clipboard she is holding, inspecting it thoroughly as she squints beyond the mile long lashes gracing her eyelids. "Well, actually, we have the other VIP table available. It's opposite the stage to that bachelorette party on that floor."

"Can we switch floors?" Jake chimes in, and I snap a confused look toward him. There is no way I'm allowing a switch to the male dancer floor on his bachelor party.

"Hell yeah, can we switch floors?" Dane adds. Of course he does.

"It's too late to cancel your VIP table with our lady entertainers tonight. However, you can pay for the VIP table service on the third that includes admission, a lap dance for each of you, and two bottles of liquor. Unfortunately, I can't do anything about a refund on the other floor."

"Fuck it." I reach into my wallet to pull out my credit card. "You guys head up to the table. I'm going to go to the third, and I'll meet you after I find her."

The guys glance at each other. Dane has a smile plastered on his face. Seamus is pinching the bridge of his nose, and Kobi's smirk says everything.

"Hell no. We're all going." Jake laughs, patting me on the shoulder. "This is going to be interesting."

The elevator door expands, and the previously muffled music blares through the small space with clarity. Miraculously, five large men and our very confused hostess, dressed as Rainbow Bright, are able to fit in it. She steps out first, and I'm still amazed she's able to walk in those platform heels. Or boots or stilettos or ankle breakers. I'm not quite sure what category they fall into. Probably all of the above.

I follow behind her, with the guys trailing behind me, as we shimmy in between loads of people and the tables that are placed closely together throughout the open floor. She continues to guide us toward the side of the stage, all the seats front and center. Nestled between the seats is a small table with a huge bottle of vodka and some other carafes of what looks like cranberry juice and soda.

"Here you are, gentlemen. Enjoy the show." She smiles, as she should. She just sold us a two thousand dollar table that would have otherwise been vacant and still got paid for the VIP table on the other floor. But I don't care about that at this point. All I can do is scan the room, looking for those gorgeous cinnamon locks and sparkling emerald gems I've been dreaming about since yesterday. Anxiety sets in as I skim the room and can't find her.

"I don't see her." I lean in to tell Seamus.

Crossing his arms over his chest, he tilts his chin down and his face forward as he scours the room. His eyes are pressing to the tops of his lids as he performs his own scan with whatever weird built-in military x-ray vision he has. I watch him as his eyes bounce around the room, and a small squint has my neck snapping in that direction.

There she is.

I stop breathing. She quite literally steals my breath away, and I can feel her presence all the way to the marrow of my bones.

God, she's beautiful.

There is a glow radiating from around her as the ceiling lights float around the room. The diamond sequined disco ball flickers bits of light over her face and body. There's a man-made fog machine, somewhere. It's permeating the air, transmitting a translucent glow around her, and that does nothing but highlight the perfect features of her face, which are on full display as she crosses the room, landing across the stage opposite our table.

Suddenly, the lights dim completely to dark and a figure, introduced as Kilo, appears on stage. *Knockin' the Boots by H-Town* blasts through the speakers as the spotlight beams down on the guy, center stage. He rolls his hips, popping his legs as he begins to walk around the stage. Kilo looks out toward the crowd, down at us, then back at the girls. He skirts along the border of the stage, calculating and slow, like a predator hunting for its prey.

He stops in front of Ember.

Motherfucker.

Everything in me tenses. Hard. The agitation seeps out of my pores as Seamus turns toward me.

"Don't." His brows narrow at me.

I can only see her silhouette. She's standing next to a woman, who I assume is the bride, with the silhouette of an unusually large ruffled tutu and veil.

The crowd hoots and hollers loudly as he takes a step off the stage. He sits on the edge, facing the girls, shifting slightly to the left side, grabbing the bride.

Thank god.

My fists relax, although I was unaware that they were

clenched until after the relief of tightness spreads through my knuckles.

Spinning the bride to face away from him, he pushes her upper back forward, bending her at the waist. Kilo's fingers latch onto her hips as he grinds her from behind. One of the girls whoops loudly, putting a few bills in his waistband as he continues to knead his groin into the bride.

I can only see Ember's shadow, her hand is covering her mouth, and I can imagine a blush unavoidably gracing her cheeks.

Pulling the bride back up gently by her hair, he flips her around, nipping her chin with his thumb and forefinger, as he helps her step back to her seat.

In a move so goddamn fast I barely register it, he shotguns his arm out, wrapping it around the back of Ember's neck, pulling her close to him as he nuzzles into her neckline. His tongue traces an invisible line from the base of her throat to the shell of her ear.

"Fucking…" I step forward, but Seamus steps in front of me.

"It's a goddamn strip club, Hudson. It's a bachelorette party. What the hell did you expect?" His hand presses into my chest. "You've never been like this before. What has gotten into you?"

Fuck, he's right. Goddammit. I don't even know what I'm doing. And I've never responded so possessively to a woman. She has a hold on me—over me—and I have no idea why I'm acting like this. I came here just to talk to her. Actually, let's be honest with myself here. I paid a lot of money for a VIP table at a strip club in Vegas to talk to her. But all that has gotten me is a view of her getting groped by male strippers.

What the hell was I thinking? I just need to get her number and get out of here.

Or grab her and carry her to my bed.

Dane steps toward the front of the stage waving a handful of bills while Jake laughs because Dane is clearly happy and excited about our change of plans. But also, knowing Dane, he's trying to create a diversion, which seems to be working because Kilo changes course and releases Ember.

The spotlight shifts as he heads our way. The disco ball comes back on, providing us some flickers of light, and Dane comes into view of the spotlight as he stuffs the bills into Kilo's too tight boxers. In true male entertainment fashion, Kilo grabs Dane's head and presses his crotch straight into his face. The crowd goes wild again. Bills are flying to the stage and all the guys are cheering for Dane, who looks like he's living his best life. Kilo releases Dane then pushes himself back toward the middle of the stage. He slides his body onto the floor. The radius of the light in the room spreads and she comes into view again.

A genuine happiness exudes from her as she laughs with the girls, and they toast before taking back a shot. At the same time, the guys hand me a shot, which I shoot back without turning my eyes away from her.

Grimacing, she hands the shot glass back to her friend and peers past the stage. Her eyes land straight on mine. And just like when I first saw her on the plane and a few minutes ago outside, the fireworks explode behind my ribcage. Her smile slips for a brief moment, but then she bites her lip and her shy smile beams back at me. I can't help mine either as it broadcasts across the stage like an invisible airwave, and for a moment, it's just us again.

Until Kilo takes her hand and pulls her onto the stage.

7

EMBER

Holy. Shit.

He's pulling me on the stage. He is *pulling* me *on the stage.*

Wide-eyed, I glance back at Suzy and the girls, void of an external freak out, conflicting what is actually happening inside my head. Unsure if it's because the dancer, known as Kilo, is pulling me on stage or the fact that Hudson is here?

Why is he here?

My head is already fuzzy, and I'm confused as to why a group of guys would be watching male strippers. Unless his bachelor party is for a gay groom? Maybe that's the case.

The guy with the dirty blonde hair and huge smile is certainly happy to be here. Maybe that's the groom. Two other guys are toasting a shot to each other, and they are far too handsome for their own good, as well. Although the area is dim, I can see one of them, with his razor sharp jawline and gorgeous smile that would make any woman's ovaries scream. The other is some kind of an exotic mix and absolutely breathtaking.

Jesus. Hudson travels in a pack of hunky men.

Regardless, none of this should be happening. Hudson should, most definitely, not be on the opposite side of this stripper stage, and I, most definitely, should not be in the middle of it.

Somewhere between the vodka shot and my shocked, hypnotic gaze at Hudson, a chair was placed in the middle of the stage, which I'm now sitting at.

The dancer, with his chest of steel and washboard abs, circles the chair like a vulture. If eye fucking was a real thing, that is happening right now.

I steal a glance at Hudson. His jaw is clenched, and he looks angry. Nothing like the easygoing, playful man I met on the plane.

Another shadow appears in my periphery as a second chair scraps along the stage, the legs screeching over the music. I look down at the empty chair and my eyes slowly roam up to see a second dancer, larger—much larger than the first—staring down at me.

Oh. My. God.

My eyes bulge and my jaw drops.

This man is huge. His skin is smooth and dark, and really, really oily. His legs are the size of tree trunks, and his midsection the width of a goddamn refrigerator. Every inch of his body is hard ropes of muscles, in areas I had no idea muscles were supposed to be. He is wearing a neon green g-string that covers nothing. Nothing. It's like a mini sock for his not-so-mini penis.

Holy shit.

Holy. Shit.

When I am finally able to tear my eyes away from his body and look at his face, I'm stunned to discover he has the kindest baby face I have ever seen, contrasting his hard body. In the background, the music fades and a loud booming voice introduces the man as Bear.

Fitting.

Nerves get the best of me, and I whiplash my face to the floor. I stare down at the ground to avoid looking at him. There is a crumpled one-dollar bill that has caught my attention and I hyperfocus on it. I wonder if you shine a UV light on it, if it would light up like Times Square.

Bear's foot lands on top of the poor abused dollar bill. As it splays out under his foot, a small corner peeks out from underneath his big toe. I'm too focused on that to notice Bear's crooked finger touch my collarbone and trail upward to my chin, lifting it slowly. His hips are at the exact level of my face, so I have a front and center view of his crotch. All I see is green. Bright, bumpy, and blinding neon green.

Mortified, I cover my face with my hands to create a barrier between his monstrosity of an appendage. But because I'm human, and can't look away from a pending car crash, I spread my fingers and peek through the slits to see Kilo come up to my left and Bear step ever so slightly to my right.

Oh. God.

I can't handle one of these guys, much less two. Letting my hands slip from my face, I lean my neck back to look at the girls and point to the chair next to me, mouthing 'Get your ass in the chair.'

They are drunk. Screaming drunk. Laughing and happy as can be, waving their hands in the air, egging on the dancers.

I am going to kill them.

Dana's face scrunches up as she ducks to look in between one of the dancer's rooted legs, which catches my attention, forcing me to follow her line of sight.

Opposite the stage is Hudson. His body language is frantic, and his arms are flailing all over the place as he talks to his dark-haired friend, who looks like he could murder someone with his pinky finger. The dark-haired friend shakes his head, grabs Hudson's bicep with one hand, then splays out his other hand toward the alcohol table. Hudson clearly hates whatever idea he's suggesting because, instead, he plants his hands on the stage, pushing himself up onto it.

What is he doing?

As his feet touch the stage, his shoe lands on another stray one-dollar bill. His foot slips from underneath him, slamming his chest and chin into the stage. His face scrunches up, and I can't help but wince and do the same, because Jesus, that looked painful.

Ouch.

Kilo and Bear hear the collision and turn around just in time to see Hudson recovering as he pushes himself upright in forward momentum. His legs roadrunner in front of him, stumbling over each other, before plopping down in the seat next to mine.

Concern, confusion, and relief are mixed into one all-encompassing facial expression as I turn to look at him. By instinct, my hand lands on top of his thigh, which feels like a comfort for both of us at this point. He glances down at my hand before his gaze meets mine.

"What are you doing?" I scream at him over the music.

He leans in closer to me, sliding his hand over the top of mine.

"If anyone is touching you tonight, it's me."

Then shifts forward in his seat, facing the crowd with his spine ramrod straight, still holding his hand over mine.

Bear appraises us. Looking down at our connected hands, then to our faces that are still staring straight ahead, avoiding all eye contact with anything, then back at Kilo in a systematic routine. He steps back, pulling Kilo with him, whispering something.

The alcohol is starting to kick in, as the sounds around us

aren't nearly as overwhelming as they were before. I know there are a ton of people in the crowd tonight, but from the lit up stage, it's hard to see everyone clearly. Or maybe that's the alcohol too.

At least I'm not feeling as nervous as I was earlier. Actually, that is probably the alcohol as well.

Kilo grabs a microphone from someone at the side of the stage and pauses, giving the crowd a bit of a tease. Putting it to his mouth, then pulling it down, smiling before repeating. The crowd is screaming and way too excited and I wish I had any clue as to what they are doing. I'm assuming we are both getting lap dances, on stage, in front of everyone, which brings another heatwave to my cheeks, making them blush further. They will probably hold nothing back, especially with Hudson.

Dana slides two full shot glasses across the stage that stop just shy of my left foot. Pulling my hand from Hudson's tight grasp, I lean down, pick them up, and then pass one to him.

This is the most liquor I've ever had in my entire life. But if people are watching me get a lap dance from either one of these men, I'll need to drink the rest of that bottle to get through it.

We stare at each other for a brief moment, neither one of us believing this is actually happening, and for some reason, neither one of us can hold back a genuine smile. We clink our glasses together with a silent toast before shooting back the clear liquid. The burn doesn't feel so bad anymore. Not surprising, since my entire body is already on fire, thanks to the man sitting next to me.

I snag the empty glass from him, toss both back to Dana, then sit upright and face forward. Hudson does the same, except reaches over and grabs the top of my hand, interlaces his fingers between mine, then places it back on top of his leg.

Just then, Kilo screams into the mic. "Amateur Night!" Accentuating the word 'night' into a long, breathy word.

And our faces drop. Hudson's eyes widen, as he gives himself a neck fracture, turning to look at the dancers, who are throwing their hands up and down in the air, trying to get the crowd even rowdier than they already are.

Placing his fingers on his forehead, he massages the area before running his palm down his face. Over his eyes, his nose, then landing on his mouth. He's deep in thought, his eyes bouncing between the crowd, the dancers, his friends, then me.

And he just stares at me.

Into me.

Through me.

This desire deepens in his chocolate pools, turning nearly black with flashing emotions of fear and lust. A determination that wasn't there before shines through.

The lights dim and *Anywhere by 112* begins to play throughout the open space.

Suddenly, he stands up, kicking his chair, and it goes flying back toward the side of the stage. He wraps his arms around me, gripping the back of my chair, swinging it around so I'm facing the back of the stage.

Radiant colors stream from the small sources of light that remain, bouncing off the small windows, and I can see the glass vibrating with the beat of the music. The slow sensual sound makes my pulse raise and heart bump harder than the rumbling of the bass.

I quickly realize that my strapless pantsuit was the best outfit choice tonight as opposed to the skirt that Sara wanted me to wear, because Hudson pulls my hands away from the tight grip they had on the chair before sliding his face... into my lap. Then he places my hands on the back of his head as he spreads my legs open and nuzzles into my center. Although the back of my head is facing the crowd, I can't help but tear my hands away from his hair to cover my face.

"Oh, no you don't, little red."

He looks up at me, taking a hold of my wrists, then pulls my hands back down. A playful smile crosses his face, and as he drags my hands down, his body, slowly—so sexually—transcends up. His lips are now a whisper away from mine. There's a hefty pause as the music beats through us and his eyes flicker down to my lips.

My heart manages a flutter, somehow, between the heavy thumping against my ribcage.

I don't have a ton of experience with men, but I know he wants to kiss me.

He releases a long breath before abandoning that idea.

"Hold on to me." He swings my arms on either side of his head, and I grip his shoulders and neck. Grabbing my hips, he easily draws me up to him, and naturally, my legs wrap around his waist. His touch is gentle, yet assertive, and when he pulls me flush against him, I instantly feel his hard length.

My eyes widen as does his smile, and then he freaking hip bumps me with a wink.

Spinning us around, he sits down on the chair that still faces away from the crowd, forcing me to straddle him. Fortunately, it's still dark, and as I peer over his head, I can't see faces, just silhouettes of people. So many people.

"Now, ride me," he growls in my ear.

Squeezing my eyes shut, urgently shaking my head as I nuzzle into his neck, feeling shy and exposed. "I can't," I whisper.

Removing his hands from my hips, he places them over each of my ears, stifling the noise, causing me to open my eyes and pull back to look at him.

"Ignore them. It's just me and you." I peer into his passionate, lustful eyes as they swallow me whole. "It's just us," he whispers over my lips before crashing them together.

Oh, God. He tastes like cinnamon, cranberries, and sin. I

moan into his mouth at both the taste and the touch of his tongue running over mine. My hips take on a mind of their own, rolling into him, back and forth, circling in a punishing rhythm.

"Fuck, yes. Keep going," he moans into my mouth.

Jesus, this pantsuit was far too expensive for the fabric to be so goddamn thin.

I feel everything.

The bulge in his pants is even larger than before, as my hips rock back and forth over the denim covering his length, creating friction between my legs that feels far too good for me to stop.

In my defense, I keep telling myself to stop. But I can't. Instead, I just circle my hips deeper and harder, rewarding me with a guttural groan from Hudson that spurs me to grip his hair and retreat away from his kiss so I can see his face.

Desire, passion, and desperation engulf his face, and, Jesus, it's *so* sexy.

His hands inch back behind my head, pulling my hair back, exposing my neckline to him. His tongue finds my pulse point and massages my skin as he trails kisses to my jawline back toward my ear.

"I want to be buried inside you. To feel you flutter around me as you scream my name."

"Holy shit." The breathy whisper comes out as I moan.

"Hold on to me," he demands, as he presses into his feet, standing us upright. My arms and legs tighten their hold as he takes a few steps away from the chair. Kneeling, he plants one knee down, followed by the hand that's not wrapped around me. His strong body holds me, as I cling to him, before he gently lays me on the ground.

He's hovering over me, his broad frame covering almost everything in my line of sight. He lowers himself, crashing our lips together, and now it's his turn to roll his hips into mine. Encroaching between my legs, he nips and sucks at my ear, neck, mouth, and I feel him in places he's not even touching.

The tingling sensation in my core is building with every touch, and I'm confused as to how we're both still fully clothed and yet he's making me feel more aroused than I've ever been in my entire life.

He looks at me behind hooded eyes, licking his bottom lip, and a gaze as punishing as the rolling of his hips.

"Hudson..." I whimper, desperate for more.

He throws his head back, closing his eyes before dipping his chin to look back at me.

The determination in his eyes is unwavering. He leans back and begins to unbutton his shirt, and I see the ink lines that decorate the top of his chest. I reach up to trace the lines with my finger when the music fades, and the entire building erupts in hollering.

We're ripped out of the bubble we were in, as I see money flying over us and next to us. The lights are flashing and people are screaming. I'm shocked that my sheer focus was purely Hudson, and his for me.

Without lifting my head off the ground, I turn to face the crowd, seeing my friends combined with his friends, high-fiving and fist pumping each other.

Hudson leans down and whispers in my ear. "I'm not done with you yet, little red."

He pushes himself up, taking my hand with him, as he helps me to my feet. I sway, instantly lightheaded, and fall into his arms, grabbing his unusually large bicep to steady myself.

"Come on." He kisses the top of my head before leading us off the stage and toward the elevators.

Our collective group of friends are still cheering as the elevator chimes to allow us entrance.

I remember bracing myself on the elevator wall before

Hudson collided his lips into mine. I recall the power behind his kiss and the ache in my core. Followed by the faint sounds of music, the voice of Elvis overlapping with ringing bells and the promises of, "I do", just before the taste of cranberries and cinnamon hits my lips.

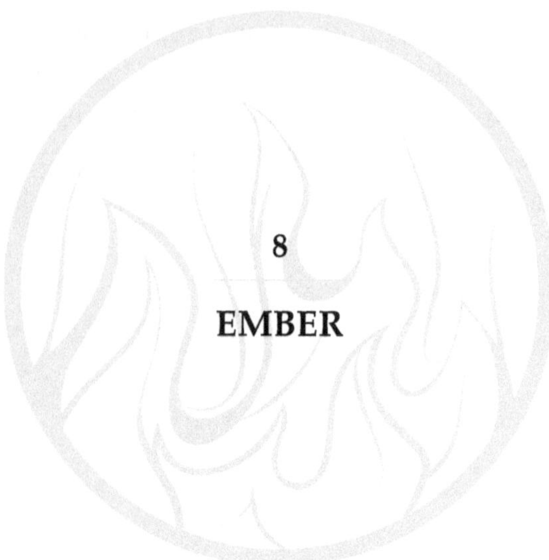

8

EMBER

O h, God. Everything hurts.

The incessant pounding in my head matches the sound of my heartbeat as it pulses through my eardrums. I don't know how much we ended up drinking last night, but I'm certain by the way my eyelids are protesting, it was far too much.

I wonder if Dana can have that hydration IV truck come back today. I didn't need it yesterday. I, for one hundred percent certainty, need it today.

I roll from my side onto my back as the blanket lowers, exposing more light than my closed lids desire. So, I continue to roll onto my other side, curling up into the pillow next to me.

Except it's warm. And hard. And muscular.

My eyes flip open, and the instant jab to my irises is like lashes to an open wound. My brain chastises me for it before I squint, turning my face into a pillow that smells like cranberries and spice.

Cinnamon.

Giving my abused eyes a moment to adjust, I slowly open one lid and glance at the corded muscular arm that takes up the center of the bed. I trail my eyes up the lines that ink his light olive skin, following the intricate design and colors that collide on his shoulder and over his collarbone.

I follow the rise and fall of his chest, as he takes in slow relaxed breaths, before trailing my eyes up the column of his throat. I can see his pulse protest through his skin in steady beats as mine begins to race.

Oh. My. God.

For the past two days, I couldn't stop the perpetual memories of our flight invading my mind. I left because I had to. He is *so* dangerous. To my willpower. To my resolve. But now, I've ended up in his bed, proving both of those characteristics in me totally suck. I slam my face back into the pillow with a groan.

Slowly rolling out of the bed, I'm unaware that I am completely naked until the frigid air of the hotel air conditioning hits me with the power of a pressure washer.

I. am. naked.

I pull the comforter from the bed, yanking the fabric that's fighting to stay glued to the goddamn bed frame. Finally, it frees, and I slide it off the bed, separating it from the sheet that was covering Hudson. Also, the thinnest sheet in the entire world, that now only covers Hudson's hips and thighs, but partially see-through as it frames his impressively sized dick.

A flashback of a neon green g-string covering another enormous piece of meat glints through my mind, and I cover my hands over my face in absolute horror, recalling being pulled onto the stage by Kilo.

Another wave of cinnamon hits my nostrils as I pull my palms down to investigate. Realization dawns on me that I probably never washed my hands after the strip club.

So gross.

The wave of nausea that hits me is not from the thought of questionable germs on my hands, but from the small, shiny tinfoil wrapped around the ring finger on my left hand.

I squint as I examine the foreign band on my finger, flipping my hand back and forth, back and forth.

The stage. The dance. Cheers and people shouting. *Elvis.* Wedding bells. And Big Red gum wrappers that we magically turned into origami sheets to make wedding bands.

"What the hell!" bellows out of me unexpectedly. I not only scare myself, but Hudson, too; his arms fly up over his head, like he was preparing for an incoming attack.

I grab the comforter that's wrapped around me with my right hand as I wave my left hand in Hudson's direction.

"We got married?!" I scream as both a question and a statement.

Hudson looks around disoriented, one eye squeezed shut, the other hardly open. Then he brings the base of his palms into his eyelids with a long breathy groan. Another memory hits me as the sounds of Hudson's voice seize my brain.

"I've thought of nothing but you since I saw you on that plane."

"I can't wait to have your tight pussy wrapped around my cock."

"You look good in my bed."

"Come for me, little red."

My breath quickens as panic truly sets in. I take a few unsteady steps back, hitting a wall, and I slump down into myself. Wrapping my arms around my legs, pressing them closer to my chest, and I drop my head down to my knees.

The rustling of the bedsheets doesn't lift my gaze. Only when I feel his hand cup my cheek do I peer up to look at him.

"Hey." He tucks my hair behind my ear and lifts my chin. His hair is savagely wild, and his jawline is peppered with a stubble that wasn't there yesterday.

"We'll figure this out," he says softly. His brows pinch together, painfully, probably from the looming hangover that proceeds us both, as well as the devastated redhead currently freaking out in his room.

I give him my best and forced, tight-lipped smile that lacks conviction in his statement. A slight squint meets his eyes before they widen.

"Your boyfriend," he whispers out loud, closing his eyes as regret blankets his face.

"Who? Huh? My—What boyfriend?" My reply is defensive and abrasive.

"Fuck. We'll fix this. We'll fix this today." He stands, grabbing a small decorative pillow to cover himself. He turns around, the hard round globes of his ass cheeks on full display, and so goddamn sexy, I might add, as he walks toward the en suite.

Pressing into the wall, I push myself up to stand.

"I don't have a boyfriend." I say it like it's a disease. Why would he say that?

He stops and looks over his shoulder back at me. Which is really dangerous because now, I not only see his handsome face but his gorgeous, incredible ass, as well.

"You told the guy on the plane you had a boyfriend. *You* said you had a boyfriend."

Realization hits me that he heard that conversation.

"I was trying to turn him down nicely." His eyes narrow and look downward, blinking a few times, then returning to look at me.

He takes a step toward me.

"But you didn't tell me that."

Another step.

"You told me, *'I can't.'*"

Another step.

"Why did you tell me that?"

He stops in front of me.

"Why didn't you turn me down nicely?"

I swallow hard enough my ears pop.

"I didn't want to lie to you," I admit.

"And you didn't want to go out with me?"

A small quick shake of my head naturally responds.

"No, you didn't want to go out with me? Or no, that's not right?"

This is definitely how miscommunication happens.

The constant hum of the air conditioner sounds like a foghorn through the silence.

Because you are a dangerous distraction, and I don't want to become my mother.

I bite my lip, pulling the soft flesh in between my teeth. His eyes bore into me, demanding an answer that refuses to show up.

Reaching out, he grabs my left hand with his and gently rubs the foil that's wrapped around my ring finger. A long breath leaves his lips as he turns his hand over to reveal his own foil band wrapped around his finger, taking a moment to inspect our matching makeshift rings.

Everlasting sting.

A lopsided grin graces his face as he turns his eyes up to meet mine, and I wonder if he's thinking the same thing. Leaning into me, he kisses my temple, then smacks my comforter-covered ass.

"Come on, *wife*. Let's get you some breakfast."

9

EMBER

Since I didn't have anything to wear, and a strapless pantsuit isn't ideal for breakfast, I walked out to the dining area of Hudson's hotel wearing an oversized T-shirt from one of his drawers. I only recognize the large "UH" symbol as the University of Houston, because my alma mater played this university many times during both football and baseball season.

When you are an only sister to three brothers, with a sports fanatic father and a mother that lets him incorporate every game of every sport into his daily life, you get familiar with the teams.

I glance around the grand hotel room. This has to be one of the hotel's larger suites; it's absolutely gorgeous. It's modern and everything is neutral, with strategic splashes of color. The floor to ceiling windows have a perfect view of the strip, and we're on what appears to be the top floor. The expansive living room leads into a dining area, with a kitchen island adorned with six barstools evenly placed in front. Although there is only a small kitchenette area, it is next to a full bar, so this beautiful, thick marbled island is probably better suited for drinking games than for breakfast.

I round the island and open the refrigerator, grabbing a small bottle of orange juice off the middle shelf.

This will definitely make me feel better.

I screw the top off and press the opening to my lips just as Hudson walks out from his bedroom door into the living area. Shirtless. Barefoot, wearing tan joggers that hang just below the V line of hips. His hair is identical to when he rolled out of bed, wild and unkempt, with stubble that makes ovaries go feral.

The orange juice picks a fantastic time to go down the wrong pipe as juice comes flying out of my mouth, the orange liquid splashing against the white and gray speckled countertop.

I snatch a towel from the opposite countertop and cover my mouth as I catch a glimpse of Hudson silently chuckling.

"Went down the wrong tube," I say, as I begin to pat down the mess. "You know, topless men are illegal in some countries," I point and swirl in his direction.

"I would have worn a shirt if someone hadn't stolen mine." He shrugs, sauntering toward me in all his nakedness before grabbing the handle of the refrigerator and reaching for his own juice. "Looks better on you, though." He winks, taking a sip of juice, not choking on it.

He doesn't take his eyes off me, and I don't know if he's trying to seduce me or just figure me out. A long silence passes us as he rounds the island and pulls out a stool to sit down across from me.

As I appraise him and glance around the room, a feeling of absolute dread weighs on me. I married a total stranger. I have never done anything so careless in my life. Where the hell were my friends last night, and how did all of this even come to happen?

I was a straight-A student all through high school and college. I never snuck out of my parents' house when I was a kid. I've never broken a law, or even gotten a parking ticket. Yet, my first trip to Vegas and I get blasted drunk and end up married.

My parents should be so proud. Sadly, they would probably be more supportive of this rash decision than my choice to get my degree. If they would have known about the wedding, they both would have shown up in support, unlike my college graduation. My parents would be happy that I'm married and my sole purpose in life, as a housewife and mother, could be fulfilled.

"You *really* like Elvis." Hudson's comment strips me from my thoughts.

I do. I have been obsessed with Elvis since I was six years old.

I open my mouth to protest when the memory of Elvis hits me. We saw *Elvis* while we were leaving the club. He was heading into the first floor entrance as we were exiting the side entrance from the floors above. I insisted to Hudson that we go say hi, and I think I genuinely thought that was the real Elvis.

"I really thought that he was the real Elvis, didn't I?" I ask Hudson.

"Yup." His brows are hitched as he gives me a lengthy nod while pressing his lips together.

"I asked him to marry me, didn't I?" I lean my elbows onto the island and press my face into my hands for support.

"It was the most adorable proposal I've ever seen," he says, trying to comfort me.

I remember now that the first floor had a chapel and Elvis must have been there to officiate. I asked him to marry me, and when he turned me down, I... Oh, God. I gasp. I lift my head to look at him. "I actually asked you!"

"It was more like begging. Something about how epic it

would be to get married in front of Elvis, so yeah, something like that." He can't hide his smirk as he takes another sip of his orange juice. "I couldn't say no, and I realized last night that you are definitely a woman who always gets what she wants."

That included multiple orgasms that I recall begging him for, too.

Ugh, really Ember? I silently scold myself.

"Elvis married us," I whine, coming out as both a fact and a question.

"You got married?" Two men halt their steps as they appear in the living room. A third man, who I had no idea was in the living room, peeks out from over the top of the couch.

My spine snaps upright, and I stand to my full height. Hudson uses the corner of the island to push himself around on the barstool and turn toward the guys. He's calm as a clam as he looks at his friends, who are frozen in horror, then circles back around, still sitting on the barstool.

"Ember, these are the guys. Seamus and Kobi," he points to the guys still frozen in step, "and Dane." He points over his other shoulder to Couch Guy.

"Guys, this is Ember. *My wife*." Unable to hide his smug as shit smile that only I can see.

Their jaws are slacked as they share looks between each other, the back of Hudson's head, and me.

"Temporary. It's temporary," I spit out. "I gotta run. I'm just going to... get dressed." I hike my thumb over to Hudson's room before side stepping a few, then shuffling my feet faster toward the room.

I quietly shut the door and tiptoe, like an idiot trying to hide, even though they clearly know that I'm in here. I strip off the shirt and throw it onto the bed, step into my pantsuit, and slip on my shoes. Grabbing my phone to get an Uber, I see that I've missed a load of text messages from my friends, as well as a missed call and voicemail from an unknown number.

I click on the Uber app and pin my location before confirming the car, and it gives me an ETA of eight minutes.

That's so fast.

In Weston, you have to schedule your Uber a day in advance.

Pulling the hair tie from my messy bun, I shake my hair out and click on the voicemail button, placing the phone between my ear and shoulder.

Good morning, Ms. Riley. This is Rowena Sutter from Ford Enterprises. My apologies for calling you on Sunday, however I wanted to share some great news. Please give me a call back at your convenience.

Oh my god.

Dropping the phone back into my hand, I hit the green phone symbol and dial the number back immediately.

"This is Rowena."

"Hi, Rowena, this is Ember Riley. I'm returning your call."

"Yes, thank you for calling me back. I do apologize for calling you on a Sunday, however the executive team has made their decision to bring you on as the new Technology and Marketing Manager and wanted to share with you immediately due to the timeline of the upcoming project."

I bite into my fist to prevent myself from squealing. How I manage to stay quiet and maintain my excitement is beyond me.

"That is great news, Rowena. Thank you for letting me know." My excitement is evident, but I maintain my poise. A complete miracle.

"You mentioned in your interview you were in the process of a move, and I wanted to confirm there wouldn't be any challenges with starting on Wednesday. That was a concern during the decision-making process."

"This Wednesday?" I swallow hard. Christ, wow. That is fast. I have two days to get home, pack, then drive to Seattle. I'll never make it. Maybe I'll fly then go back to pick up my car on the next long weekend. But, I would need longer than a weekend. Okay, I'll just need to fly and be without a car until I figure things out. I'll stay in a hotel for the first few days until I find an apartment. I have a small, *really small*, savings account I can tap into.

As I continue my overthinking, Hudson walks into his room that I've been pacing for the last few minutes. He is still shirtless. Damn his pecs, still on full display. And frankly, there were way too many pectorals out there. All the guys were shirtless, like this is some Vegas male topless bar. What is that nonsense?

Rowena asks me if I'm still here, reminding me she is still on the phone and I never replied with my no-brainer answer.

"That's not a problem at all. See you on Wednesday. And thank you!" Pressing the *end* button, I glance at Hudson, my newlywed husband, and begin to panic. I can't afford the mistake I made last night. Not only can I not afford to pay for it, but I have been working far too hard to get an opportunity like the one Rowena just offered.

How could I be so stupid?

I grab my clutch and open the pocket to slip my phone inside. The Big Red gum pack sits tucked inside and I pull it out, tossing it onto the bed. It lands upright with the flap open. Our Tic Tac Toe games reveal themselves, reminding me of how much fun we had in those two incredibly short hours and just how easy everything was with him.

Hudson looks down at the pack of gum, then returns his gaze to me. He senses more urgency in me. The same flight or fight response I had on the plane, and he's not moving from the doorway. Which he happens to take a majority of the space in.

"Stay. At least for breakfast," he offers subtly.

Staying means giving up the promise I made to myself. I was with Elliot for so long during high school and college, I felt like I lost a piece of myself. It took me long enough to get out from under the prison of that relationship that was so heavily guarded by my parents. It was like breaking up with them when I broke up with him.

"I can't," I reply. His eyes slowly close, and he throws his head back, placing his hands on his hips.

"Are you going to run on me?" he asks, and I bite my lip and shake my head in response.

"No, I just have to go." My phone beeps inside my clutch, and we both look down at it, like it's a ticking time bomb.

"My Uber is here." Closing the clutch, I step toward the door.

"How do I get in touch with you?" he says urgently, as he shifts so his body is now fully blocking the doorway. "The paperwork for..." He waves his left hand in the air, the aluminum foil still wrapped around the base of his ring finger.

"Right..." I can't avoid this. "... give me your phone." I hold my hand out. He places it in my palm, and I plug my first name and phone number in as a contact.

Handing the phone back to him, my lips thin as I press them together, showing more nerves than I'd like. He looks down at the entry and frowns.

"What's your last name?"

"Riley. Ember Riley," I reply, knowing he'll probably try to find me if I ignore him.

He types in my full name, then presses the message icon and sends me a message that beeps from my clutch.

He smiles, satisfied that I didn't give him the Pop-Corn phone number, then steps aside to let me through, but my feet are planted. Damn my feet to hell. I need to leave, but leaving him feels so much harder this time.

A flashback from last night flips through my mind. The kissing and laughing. The feeling of his tongue on my skin and his breath on my body. The way he touched me and held me like he never wanted to let me go. My heart hiccups in my chest.

I need to get out of here.

I look down at my shoes, the ones rooted into the ground, urging them to move. They shift up onto their toes, giving me enough height to plant a kiss on his cheek. He inhales deeply and his eyes close. When he reopens them, he palms my cheek, then swivels my face so my lips meet his.

His kiss is soft yet demanding, and it swallows me whole. It's consuming in ways I never knew a kiss could be.

The taste of his cinnamon spice and citrus linger on my tongue as I pull away. He presses his forehead to mine, and I avoid his gaze as it attempts to find mine. That will be my downfall and crush my resolve. Urgently, I turn away and step through the door, rushing to the front of the hotel room.

Dane is now sitting upright on the couch with an ice pack on his forehead as I pass through. A third guy I was never introduced to is now in the kitchen drinking coffee with Seamus and Kobi.

"Does he know you're leaving?" Seamus asks, as he jumps off the barstool and begins to follow me like it's his sole purpose in life. I remember him from last night. He's the scary one with all dark everything. As I glance back at his domineering form trailing behind me, my eyes are drawn to a large but faded scar that crosses over his chest, and a smaller scar in his lower abdomen, which just adds to his broody and frightening demeanor.

"He does. We're good. Great to meet you guys." Seamus stops, thankfully, and I wave with a half smile back at them as I grab the door handle and exit, heading straight for the elevator.

The doors are barely open enough for me to shimmy through before I'm punching the lobby button, and when the doors finally close, I blow out a hefty breath. Pulling out my phone to check my Uber, it's only a minute away, which provides another sigh of relief, knowing my getaway car is nearby.

I click out of the app and into my text messages. A single text message from an unknown number pulls through. I know it's Hudson, and when I open the message to see two simple words, they weigh down on my already heavy heart.

Unknown Number: Don't go

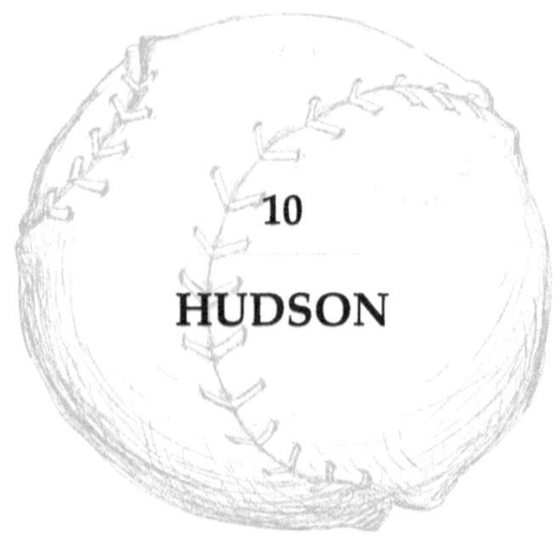

10

HUDSON

It's amazing. Time.

It's the most deceitful scientific measurement of reality. Quantifying your irreversible timeline in seconds, yet somehow our own awareness of time can easily alter its basic mathematics.

How is it that something so scientific, so matter-of-fact, can feel so different in defining moments?

Two hours on a plane with the most captivating woman I'd ever met felt like nanoseconds. Two hours on the plane flying back home, every minute getting further away from her—both physically and mentally—felt like a life sentence.

And in the last three days, the minutes have gone by painfully slowly, even though the days have felt fast.

Before flying to Vegas, I got, potentially, the most exciting news of my career. I flew to Seattle for a meeting with the Smashers' coach. Apparently, something came up, and he had to cancel. That sent me flying directly to Vegas with only a sliver of hope that a trade could happen.

Leaving Vegas on a dreadful, and terribly boring, plane ride with a seatmate that held no comparison to Ember. I finally made it back home, just to be told by my coach that he booked me a plane ticket back to Seattle for a rescheduled meeting. That would have been the highlight of my week, if not for meeting Ember.

So, I went home, packed a majority of my belongings and jumped on a flight back to the airport where I had first laid eyes on her.

I didn't need to pack everything, but I couldn't help but hope that I was leaving San Diego for good. Not that I dislike San Diego. It's one of the best cities in the world.

But I've been ready. Ready in all the ways I could ever be ready for this change.

I could get traded back to the major leagues. *Finally*. Something that I've been waiting for, for what feels like forever. Years of training, growing, rebuilding, and dreaming for an almost impossible opportunity. Along with years of dread that it may never happen. And now? Now, I have a chance, and it feels like my injury was yesterday. I can't recall anything I've learned or healed from during that time.

Again, *time*—the best magician in the world.

Fast forward to today, Wednesday, the day I meet Coach Raymer. He's the coach for the Seattle Smashers and has the reputation of a total hardass. When I flew here before the bachelor party, I was a nervous wreck. So, when I was told something came up and he had to reschedule, it was devastating. I believed he truly had an emergency and wasn't just being a jerk. But I have to admit, there was a small part of me that felt discouraged, like he changed his mind about meeting me and I missed my opportunity. So, needless to say, I'm glad he actually rescheduled and I'm here now. Nerves completely faded. Confidence on full alert.

My coach said this is truly an interview, that he wants to meet all the players he was considering before making his final decision. But I refuse for this to turn out any other way than me leaving as a new catcher for the Seattle Smashers.

I take in a commanding breath as I sit in the cab of the truck I picked up yesterday, leaning my head against the head-rest with my eyes closed and all my insecure wounds open. I always thought I was good enough, until one day, I just wasn't. In the blink of an eye, my injury defined my life and everything changed.

Another amazing fact about time. They say "time heals all wounds", a common misconception. Time doesn't heal, our memory of the situation just fades over time. It doesn't hurt as much, but the pain is engraved in your subconscious, questioning your own perception of yourself and your trust in others.

Time fades pain, yes, but people heal themselves. If they allow it.

I guess I'm still working on that.

Treating this moment like the biggest game of my life, I open my eyes, take in the stadium that *will be* my future home, and exit my truck. I straighten out my tie and button my suit jacket. The fancy getup isn't required, but I'm here to impress and take back what I lost.

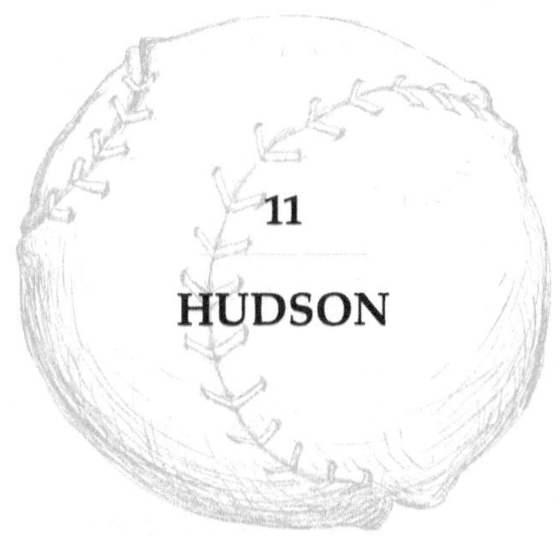

11

HUDSON

"**C**oach Raymer, Hudson Byrnes is here, sir," the assistant to the head coach says into the wireless headset attached to her ear that is truly, completely handless. She never once picks up the phone; she just tilts her head to one side to call, speaks into the headset to call Coach, when finished, she tilts her head to the other side.

This stadium is one of the newest in the country, and everything is modern and built around the most advanced technology. Even the parking lot is automated for the players and coaches. It has built-in vehicle lifts that park your car and bring it to you when you call for it on an app.

I didn't use it since I'm not a player... *yet*. Plus, I'm not all that comfortable with a robot parking my overly sized rental vehicle.

"Have a seat. He's just finishing up a meeting." She gestures to the plush leather seats in the middle of the room.

Glancing around the room, there are posters of baseball's greatest lining the walls. Trophies, plaques for charities local to Seattle, team emblems, and shadow boxes full of memorabilia.

Some recent, for celebratory reasons, and some original items, that are truly priceless.

Before my injury, I thought I would play baseball my entire life. Hell, even after my injury. I was so determined to come back, join my team, and keep going. My ankle had other ideas. The doctors said when it broke, shattered really, the bones could never fully heal properly. Today, it's better than ever. My movement is no longer restricted, and I trust it again. It's taken years to feel like I can completely rely on it without doubt.

It's myself I doubt on the bad days.

When the doctors said I was ready to come back, the team already had a full roster, and it didn't make sense for them to add me back in. I was limited on playing time, and for them, I was a liability. So, they gave me a choice; play for their minor league team to gain back my ankle strength back or become a free agent. Being that I'm a catcher, I needed the practice and time to rebuild my strength. I knew I needed it. I didn't want to become a free agent and risk no one picking me up. I couldn't blame them for not bringing me back, but I can't say the fall from the top didn't hit hard.

As much as I've been trying to stick it out with them, in hopes of getting moved up to the majors, my time there has an expiration date. I know it, my coach knows it, they won't consider me for majors again.

I want this so goddamn bad.

I need this.

"Mr. Byrnes, he will see you now."

The nerves I pushed aside come back full force in an instant. My brain is frantic, thinking of all the ways I need to make this happen. A storm of chaos bellows in my stomach, and I need this to end better than last weekend, when Ember walked out of my hotel room, never looking back.

I walk into the coach's office, holding my hand out with confidence and enthusiasm. "Coach Raymer, it's great to—"

"Sit," he grunts out.

I halt in my step, jarred by how blunt he is. He's known to be a hardass, but he's verging on rude, being this is the first time we've ever met. But before he can say anything more, I sit.

"I understand you flew here last week to meet with me, but a scheduling conflict on my calendar prevented that from happening," he starts as he shuffles through a couple of papers.

"Yes, sir."

"I'm glad you're taking this opportunity seriously." He peers up from his glasses to appraise me.

"I am, sir." Less is more with this guy.

"I'm a straight shooter, Hudson." He leans into his palms, rising to his feet. He's hovering over his desk like he needs to yell at something, and I'm totally unsure why he seems so damn angry. "Your stats speak for themselves, but you're a risk and I need a reliable player."

I say the only thing that comes to mind.

"I'm better than ever, coach. Mentally and physically."

He peers down at me again, a small squint in his eye. Releasing the papers he had in his hand, they float to the desk as he sits back in his chair. He just stares. He should intimidate me, but he doesn't. I want this more than anyone else he is considering. So, I tilt my chin up, showing the confidence I have in myself and what I just said.

"I have a lot to offer. And I'm ready." It's not cocky, it's realistic and honest.

"I like your stats. They outweigh the risk. But you're also a known playboy. I've heard about your 'ladies' man' reputation. I don't like that wild shit running around my team. It's distracting. The media thrives on making a mockery of it, and I can't have that here. That's a huge risk to the image I'm trying to preserve for my team."

My first year on injury reserve, I used women and alcohol as a crutch to get by. I was the instigator of every party and probably every problem that had to do with the media, but over time, I eased up. Somehow, it has stuck with me ever since, even though I had no reputation before or after that.

Hiding my internal frustration, I close my eyes and see a blanket of red. Not the violent red caused by rage. The kind of red you see when the sun hits the hills of the horizon, after the blending of yellows, oranges, and reds, that causes a chain reaction spreading through the sky, before taking your breath away.

My little red.

I'm not sure what comes over me because I'm unable to stop the next words that come out of my mouth.

"I'm married, Coach, and quite obsessed with my wife, actually." The shock penetrates his face as if I physically attempted to punch it.

Mine, too. I just hid it better.

Usually I'm a terrible liar, but neither is a lie, technically.

His neck snaps over to look at his assistant coach, who seems to be sifting through papers, like that was partially a deciding factor that they missed.

My eyes widen as I silently scold myself. I look down at my shoe to avoid them seeing the horror that is written all over my face and shift uncomfortably in my seat.

What the hell was I thinking?

"Well..." He clears his throat. "I wasn't aware, but I'm very happy to hear that. The last thing I need is some philandering womanizer running all over town when he should be making *this* his first priority."

It's unbelievable. You can live your whole life doing the right thing, uphold a standard code of normalcy, and never get into any kind of trouble. A few short-lived mistakes during a rough stint of time and your reputation becomes that and only that.

People do not forgive easily and they sure as hell don't forget.

I don't have the energy to defend my actions, nor do I feel the need to. But I do need to stand up for myself and fight for this.

"I've made some mistakes in the past, sir. I know this. But that was then. I'm here now, and I'm invested. I'll be the first one here and the last one to leave. I guarantee you, if you give me the opportunity to bring what I have to this team, I won't let you down."

He sits back in his chair and inhales so long, it's abnormal. Finally, at its peak, he huffs out an exhausted breath, crossing his arms over his chest. He stares through me, being his own personal polygraph, pausing for what feels like a light-year.

"I've always gone with my gut, Hudson. In my role, you have to. I'm gonna sign you. Don't make me regret my decision."

Holy shit.

This is it. My second chance.

Trying to hide my shock but show my genuine excitement is a balancing act I was not prepared for.

"Sir, I'm beyond honored." I smile and stand, throwing out my hand to him.

He stands, sliding his hand into mine. He's still stern as hell, but not even his sour face can erase my smile.

"I'll get you set up in one of our leasehold estates, effective immediately. We have condos across the street from the stadium that all our players stay in.

"Practice doesn't usually start for two more weeks, but I'd like you here, starting now, so the coaches can work with you on a few things before pitchers and catchers report for the season."

"You got it. Not a problem, Coach," I reply.

"What's your wife's name?" he asks.

"Ember." Just saying her name makes my stomach drop, remembering my lie. Well, non-lie. Half-lie.

"Ember *Byrnes*." Chuckling to himself as he accentuates her last name. "Wow, she probably hated the idea of marrying you."

Neither one of us remembers it much.

"I'll make sure both your names are on the agreement. She'll need to be here to sign it when it's ready. I'm looking forward to meeting her." He finishes shaking my hand, releasing my grip.

The realization of the seriousness of my lie hits me and bile rises to the back of my throat.

She lives in another goddamn state and acts like she's allergic to me. I have no idea how I'm going to pull this off.

"Thank you, Coach."

I exit his office and urgently walk to my car. I'm not sure if I'm running from the blinding white lie I just told or running as quickly as I can before he changes his mind.

Jesus, what the hell was I thinking?

I want to call Ember. Demand she come here. Frankly, I want to demand more than her just coming here because where she is concerned, I'm greedy. But with her, I need to be persistent, not pushy.

I could ask her here. Maybe she'll pose for me for a day, but her constant "I can't" response gives me PTSD I didn't realize I had until now.

I need to figure out how the hell I'm going to get myself out of this.

I hop into the truck I rented, dialing Jake before my phone even connects to Bluetooth. Since he lives here in Seattle, it just felt natural to call him first.

"Hey, Hud. How did it go?" His voice comes through faintly in the background from the small speaker of my phone instead of the speakers of the truck.

"Hold on." I press *connect* on the touch screen.

"Hello?" Jake's voice blares through in echoing waves as it finally syncs.

"Jake. Man. I messed up." I run my hand through my hair, attempting to tame the crazed strands making my appearance just as deranged as my lie.

"What happened?" he asks curiously.

"I got it. He's signing me, but he kept bringing up my 'playboy' reputation. It was a concern for him." I chipmunk my cheeks, pushing air out of my lungs. "I told him I was married."

"That's not so bad, right? I mean, technically, you are." Jake's tone is uncertain.

"He asked for her name to put her on the lease agreement. I gave him Ember, and now she's gotta be here to sign in."

Now his full, accentuated grunt sounds like he partially choked on his own spit.

He recovers easily, avoiding a laughing stint as a favor to me, I'm sure.

"Married and buying a house together, all in the span of a long weekend. You're a busy man."

My silence says it all.

Clearing his throat, "I'm at the Ford building downtown. Chris and I are taking Elena out tonight. Come by here and let's figure it out. We can all go to dinner to celebrate." Leave it to Jake to always stay calm in every situation.

I mean, I'm calm. On the outside.

Inside, my stomach wants to barrel through my esophagus, my heart wants to palpitate out of my chest, and my brain wants to kick my own ass to the next planet.

"See you in a bit." Hanging up, I press the *Push Start* button on the truck's ignition and head in the direction of the Ford building. Normally, I would plug the address into GPS, but it's the tallest skyscraper in Seattle and you can't miss the damn thing. It's a glass fortress that towers over everything downtown.

Elena, Jake's wife, is the one who inspired us to throw Jake a belated bachelor party. Christian Ford is *their* significant other.

I think. I'm not quite sure what his label is. At some point, they opened up their marriage and Christian met Elena through a work contract. Things escalated over time, and now they are in a poly style relationship together. I think they all pretty much live together when Christian isn't traveling. He's Seattle's local billionaire, philanthropist, and entrepreneur. No big deal.

When Jake first told me about their unique relationship, I initially thought that would never work, but I have never seen Jake so happy.

I'm not sure how Jake does it. I could never share Ember. Just the thought of her with another guy makes my body tense, gripping the steering wheel of this Chevy truck so goddamn hard I could snap it off. Even more so, a deeper jealousy blankets over me, thinking of someone else getting her days, her time, her moments. The special ones. Her excitement, her joy, her love.

Fuck.

I just need to get over it. Get over her. It was one goddamn night. I need to get settled here, send her divorce papers—annulment papers—and just move on. I have so much to focus on with the Smashers now, and I need to be present. Invested. Having her at the forefront of my mind is the exact opposite of what I committed to my coach.

I also told him I was fucking married. To a woman that doesn't even know my last name, lives in another state, and runs from me every chance she gets.

As I pull into the parking lot of the Ford building, I park the truck and stare at the ignition button. *Push Stop.* If only my emotions could be that easy.

I press into the button, allowing the engine to cease, and will my perpetual thoughts of Ember to do the same.

12

EMBER

My relationship with Elliot might as well have been arranged with how much they are pushing him on me. I know my father wants Elliot to work for him throughout his campaign, but I don't need to be married to him for it. Although my father, Robert Riley, Governor candidate, and his right-hand man, Elliot Jones, his son-in-law, appears to be so much more prestigious in the eyes of an antiquated community.

The chokehold they've had on my life has only gotten stronger the closer he gets to the campaign, and even worse, the more I pull away.

Even the rotten tone of my mother's texts and archaic thoughts of Weston, Missouri can't shed the smile off of my face as I look around my new boss's office.

We've gone through the full day of orientation, meeting the teams and going through the expectations she has in my new role at Ford Enterprises.

"I see you also applied for the New York office. Did you apply for the location or the position?" she asks, handing me a few folders of current projects I need to familiarize myself with along with my brand new iPad, already set up in a case ready for use.

"Both actually. The position sounded amazing, but the fact that it was in Manhattan was a plus. It's a bucket list item for me… living in New York," I say with a smile.

"Well, maybe one day, but for now, I'm glad we snagged you for our Seattle operation."

"Me, too. I couldn't be more excited. Today has been a dream," is all I can muster to say to the amazing woman that saw something in my resume, in me, to give me the experience I am currently having.

I am the newest, and I think youngest, Marketing Manager for one of the most well-known companies in the US. The need to pinch myself is real.

Not only is the company amazing, but my new boss is one of the coolest women I've ever met. She's smart, driven, and easygoing, yet I know she has expectations of me because her intent is clear. The moment she walked into the HR office, her presence alone was commanding. But one smile and introduction of herself and I felt instantly at ease. Like my mind and body felt comfortable, but I had no choice but to automatically respect her. She demands it by way of body language and a smile, and giving it to her is easy.

I strive for that kind of presence one day, so getting to learn from her is going to be literally life changing.

"Your credentials speak for themselves, Ember. I knew immediately when we met last week you were the perfect person for this role. Everything about you completely aligns with our image, what our company represents, and our goals." The tears are looming, but I somehow manage to push them away. The fact she believes in me more than my parents ever have is a realization that I will probably need therapy for sooner than I'd like to admit.

It's the end of the first day and I wish it didn't have to end. Who wants that? I don't want to leave. I want to work, plan, schedule.

Although, as much as I'm dying to find an excuse to stay in the office, I do need to get back to the hotel to get my luggage. Everything moved so fast that I just booked the closest hotel to work. It's the nicest hotel in the entire downtown area, and I could only afford one night, so I checked out this morning and left my bags at the front desk.

I have to look for an apartment, but until then, I was able to find another hotel for much cheaper. After booking it, and paying the same amount for two weeks that I paid in one day at the hotel across the street, I found out—according to Google—it's in the most dangerous neighborhood in Seattle.

Lovely.

It's temporary. Which is the same thing I've been telling myself since I arrived yesterday. The first few weeks will be a lot, but it *will* get better.

Plus, it can't be worse than staying with my parents in the smallest town in America, listening to them tell me how I'm wasting my time and energy climbing a corporate ladder when

I should be changing my name to *Mrs. Elliot Jones*, to become the wife to the boy next door.

Literally.

"Okay, let's call it a day and meet in the morning. I have a few people to introduce you to before our first client meeting." We gather a few things from her office and make our way out through the expansive floor to ceiling glass doors.

"Sounds great and thanks again, Elena. I'll see you—" My words are cut off, certainly by lack of oxygen to my brain, due to a certain broad-shouldered, dark-haired, brown-eyed, Johnny Bravo jaw-lined god, standing in the middle of the lobby.

My *husband*. Who is dressed in a goddamn suit and tie like he owns the goddamn building.

Oh, god. Does he own the building?

He's mid sentence talking to another man. *Shit.* The Vegas groom.

Shit. Shit. Shit.

Somehow my body channels Gumby at this exact moment. Everything in my hand falls to the floor, and I falter in my step, tripping over my own heel before my hand finds the leather surface of the lobby couch and I'm able to grow my bones back.

The moment everything hit the floor, both guys looked our way. Hudson's arm juts out to his side, his palm and forearm landing on the groom's arm while his other hand flies over his own chest, like he might be having a heart attack.

Hudson is just as shocked to see me.

"What the hell?" comes from someone. The groom, I think.

"What is he doing here?" *My voice*, a whisper to myself, or so I thought until Elena speaks up.

"You know him?" she asks.

Know him? Barely.

Married to him? Yup.

"Yes." Another hardly audible whisper.

Gathering myself together, I pick up my binder and iPad off the floor. Fortunately, the case protected it from any damage, which I'm so thankful for, considering it's only day one. Standing tall, I turn back to Hudson and silently beg, with every form of body language I have, that he doesn't say anything.

"Hey, honey." Elena sails past me into the arms of the groom as he plants a kiss to her lips.

You have got to be kidding me.

"Jake and Hudson. This is my new marketing manager, Ember Riley."

"Ember Byrnes. Her last name is Byrnes," Hudson says, barely letting Elena finish the introduction. "My wife."

Elena's eyes bounce back and forth between the two of us, then back at her husband.

"Oh." Her lips purse and form a very large "O" as realization hits her.

Wait. His last name is Byrnes? I couldn't have accidentally married into a worse last name for myself. *Ember Byrnes.*

"We'll let you two... catch up," Jake says, grabbing Elena's hand as she looks at me with the same facial expression you give a dying dog, and I immediately know she knows everything.

Great. My new amazing boss knows I got drunk-married in Vegas last weekend.

Awesome.

The moment they step away, I shift my gaze to Hudson, who is still in only what can be described as shock.

"What are you doing here?" I whisper-yell at him.

"ME? What are *you* doing here?" he whisper-yells back.

How we're both mad at each other, when this is clearly the most odd coincidence to happen in the history of coincidences, is beyond me.

"I just started this job today. I moved here yesterday. I can't have anything ruin this." He flinches, like I attempted to stab him.

Palming my face, I exhale into my hand. That was the wrong thing to say.

"I'm sorry. I'm just surprised to see you, and it's been a wild couple of days."

In the span of three days, I flew from Vegas, to Missouri, to Seattle. I somehow managed to pack up everything that means anything to me and my necessities, which sadly fit in two medium-sized pieces of luggage. I moved to an unknown city, where nobody knows me, or so I thought, completely alone and against the wishes of everyone in my entire family. And when I say against, I had to outright lie in order to leave the house with my luggage.

You would think they would be proud to have an ambitious daughter. The only future they see for me is a day of me wearing white, then immediately having more kids than I do fingers. So lying to them and telling them I met someone in Vegas that I was going to visit for a little while because I needed some time away from home, that was just easier. I would have never gotten out of the house if I were permanently moving or, god forbid, for a job.

But really, what *is* he doing here?

"I thought you lived in San Diego? Are you here with..." I glance over to where Elena and the groom disappeared to, because I don't know his name.

"Jake. The groom." He air quotes. "Sort of. I flew home first, then here. I live here now, too."

My jaw loses all its elasticity.

Hudson just chuckles. "Don't get too excited."

I've had a couple of boyfriends; nothing that turned too serious, for me at least. Elliot proposing to me was more my parents pushing him to do it than either one of us, but he definitely wanted more than I did. Somehow, a few short minutes with Hudson makes me feel more excitement and butterflies than Elliot ever did. Which is dangerous for me.

But living near him, that is another level of danger I can't even begin to decipher.

"Where are you staying?" he breaks the silence.

"Across the street. Well, I was. I'm heading there now to pick up my luggage and check into a different hotel for a couple weeks."

I hardly finish speaking when he blurts out, "Stay with me." His hands run through his thick, dark hair. It's clean cut, yet the longer strands on the top are slightly disheveled, reflecting how I'm currently feeling. "I mean, I have a hotel tonight, but I'm moving into a condo near the water tomorrow. You should... you should stay with me. It'll be easier than being at a hotel."

My lips thin as I suck in my lower lip.

"I... um, I can't." Hudson opens his mouth to reply, but I interrupt. "I mean, I've already paid for it." I shrug with a smile. "I should go."

His brows furrow in disappointment as he gives me a heavy nod.

I walk toward the elevator, and I can sense him following behind me. The pack of Big Red I picked up at the airport falls out as I pull my phone out of my purse, landing on the floor in between us as we wait for the elevator. Embarrassment floods my checks because it's a new, still in its original plastic, pack.

So what if I bought it because it smells like him?

He reaches down to pick it up, then hands it back to me, his shit-eating grin on full blast.

"Thanks." I ignore his smug-as-hell face, placing it back in my purse, shoving it all the way to the bottom where it belongs. That treacherous, traitor pack of gum.

Pressing the down button, the doors immediately open to an empty elevator, and he holds his arm outward to allow me to walk in first.

A few flashbacks of the last time we were in an elevator come to the forefront of my mind. We couldn't keep our hands off each other. It's amazing what the mix of alcohol and zero inhibitions will do for you. Without them now, the tension is thicker than wax.

As we step out of the elevator, I tap on the Uber app so I can order a ride as soon as I have my bags. It's barely loaded on my screen before Hudson speaks up.

"I'm taking you to your hotel." I look up to see him, fucking gorgeous by the way, staring back at me. His eyes are a deeper color brown than usual. The playfulness is replaced with what looks like frustration, maybe.

"You don't have to do that." My reply is quick.

He reaches out and gently tugs on my arm, halting my steps toward the rotating door that leads outside.

Stepping in front of me, his eyes rip straight through me. A slight squint in his chocolate eyes, that flood with a need. A need I can relate to because they're laced with confusion, just like mine.

"Stop running."

"I'm not."

"Not physically."

I open my mouth to reply, but nothing comes out because he's right. I may be rooted here, but everything else is pushing him away.

I huff, then simply nod. Grabbing my hand, he leads me to the large, glass circular doors on a painfully slow automatic turnstile. Allowing me to step in first, he wraps his arms around my waist, pulling me closer, as we use the same small triangular space and shuffle through the door.

His hard body feels like the softest comfort blanket, and a part of me feels relaxed for the first time since waking up next to him in that Vegas hotel.

The crisp air hits my cheeks as we walk through the courtyard of the building and across the street to the hotel. I love the smell here. The dampness and slight saltiness to the air fills my senses with another comfort I didn't know I needed.

I quickly head into the hotel as Hudson goes to the parking lot to his car. I can't say it doesn't cross my mind to grab a quick Uber and take care of everything myself, but him calling me out on running, both mentally and physically, has me questioning myself.

As I roll my luggage to the sidewalk outside the hotel, I see Hudson in a truck that pulls up to the curb. He jumps out and grabs the luggage, placing it in the back, before opening my door for me. Holding my hand, he guides me to the open passenger door. I press my heel to the running board of his truck, pushing into it to hike my body up to the seat. He grants me that stupid contagious smile of his, then closes the door. I see him jogging quickly around the front of the truck, and I decide at this moment to just allow whatever this is to happen naturally between us.

Stop running.

He's starting the truck when he turns to me. "Where's your hotel?"

"It's off of Pine Lake Way, I believe." Reaching for my phone to get the address.

"Pine Lake?" he says with disgust. "No. You're not staying in Pine Lake."

My head whips his way, and his face matches his tone. "What?"

"No, no way in hell you are staying there," he behests.

"It's what I can afford right now. It's already paid for," I punch back.

"It's dangerous." His tone is softer but still demanding.

I just tilt my head at him, annoyed. So annoyed.

"Fine. You want to go to Pine Lake? Let's go to Pine Lake."

He puts the truck in drive and begins to drive without the

use of GPS, and it makes me wonder how he knows the area so well.

Somehow, he reads my mind and answers my silent question. "Jake's lived here a long time. I used to come visit him a lot, and I spent some time here when my brother went to school here."

"Your favorite brother, Grant?" I ask with a smile.

He looks at me, blinking a few times. "Yeah, him," he replies quietly.

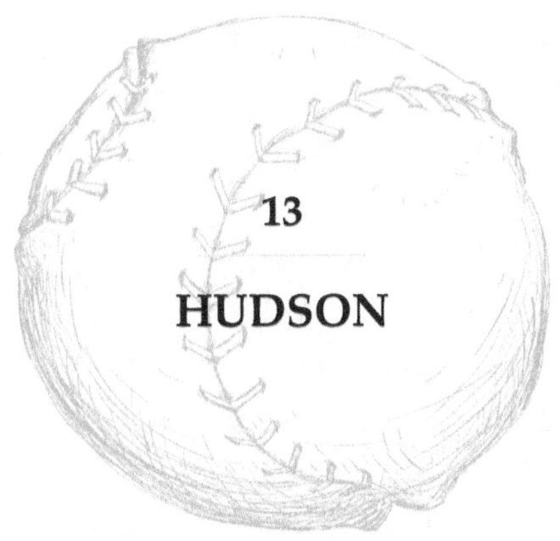

13

HUDSON

She remembered.

She remembered who my favorite brother was. She has an unopened pack of my favorite gum in her purse. The gum she insisted was inferior to all other gum.

And she's fucking here. I can't decipher the floating sensation in my stomach. The one that causes a natural quirk in my lips as I fight a smile.

Although, I'm not fighting half as hard as she is. She is beating her feelings down like the next upcoming UFC fighter battling for the top spot, fortifying herself with platinum steel, and I have every intention of breaking down those ridiculous, unnecessary walls.

We ease into the type of conversation we had on the plane, and it makes me feel exactly the same. Like she's absolutely perfect. Everything between us is so easy and natural—when she's not wrestling with her feelings and beating them to a pulp.

"So, what's with the sexy suit?" Her eyebrows lift to her hairline.

"I had a meeting with my..." here goes nothing, "coach."

She squints, looking back down at her phone. "Coach? What kind of coach?"

"I got called up, well technically, it's a trade, since I was with another team, but I'll be starting as the new catcher for the Seattle Smashers this year." I shift my gaze to her as her eyes meet mine.

"You play professional baseball?"

"I do, now," I reply with a smile that I can't hide because I'm so goddamn excited. "As of today, yes."

"Congratulations!" She grabs me, pulling me for a genuinely excited hug. I reluctantly keep one hand on the wheel and release a small grunt when she squeezes a bit too hard.

"Sorry." She releases me. "I got excited for you. I know you mentioned you played baseball, but I thought you meant for fun, not professionally."

I can't help but chuckle. She's so adorable.

"Your team has to be pretty pissed about our 'marriage'. If you're a big league player, I can imagine that's a total media nightmare for you, right?" she asks.

She is so carefree and light when she's not holding back. I love it and will do whatever it takes to keep her in this space.

"Actually, I need to talk to you about that," I reply, and turn to her, since we're stopped at a red light. There is a small squint in her eye as she gazes back at me with her head tilted to the side. I'm hesitant to start this conversation right now, since we're around the corner from her hotel, but I need to figure this out.

Just as I'm about to talk again, a banging on the side of the truck rips us from our conversation. My head snaps in the direction of the banging as Ember jolts forward, belting out a startled scream.

There is a guy, a very unstable guy, pressing his face against the passenger side of my truck. You can see the track marks on his arms, and he's a few too many notches from sober, and a little too desperate for his next fix to be predictable.

The light turns green, and I step on the gas, leaving him behind. Ember's safety is first, and he was completely unpredictable.

I take a right on the next corner. The Pine Lake Blvd. sign half hangs off the light post. The green reflective surface is weathered and dull from age, and you can barely read the words with the graffiti painted over the top.

This must be the dirtiest street I have ever seen in my entire life. There is garbage all over the sidewalk; the wind ominously carries plastic bags and other trash particles throughout the street. There are broken bottles scattered along the curb, bars on every single window, and more questionable people wandering around.

I couldn't have paid for a better set up to get Ember to agree not to stay here.

There are three guys standing in the walkway next door to the hotel. As I pull up to the curb, one of the guys, with a hoodie over his head and a cigarette hanging from his lips, stares directly at Ember. I can see the whites of his eyes through the smoke that is levitating from the end of the lit cancer stick.

Naturally, Ember's body shifts closer to mine, attempting to further herself from the passenger door. Her hand finds my thigh, and just her touch sends lava flowing through my entire body.

"Here we are," I say, with a big fat smile on my face.

She turns to me, her eyes wide with a slight shade of horror on her face.

"Right," she whispers.

She slowly reaches for her purse, and I'm now worried I'll lose this battle to her extreme stubbornness. I was waiting for her to change her mind on her own accord, because there is no way in hell I'm letting her step one goddamn foot out of this vehicle. If I have to kidnap her so she doesn't stay here, I fucking will.

"So, where did you say your place is?" Hesitation laces her tone.

"About five minutes from your office." I state facts only.

"Right," she says again.

She takes another glance around, then turns to me. "If, um, you're okay with it..."

I don't allow her to finish or give her a millisecond to change her mind. "I thought you'd never ask, little red."

I shift back into drive and pull onto the street, driving us straight to my hotel, wondering how the hell today worked out like it did.

14

EMBER

We pull into the parking lot of a very luxurious hotel, right into the valet area in the front of the lobby. My heartbeat is finally back to normal after stopping at *my* hotel. Well, my hotel that I'm never going to stay at. Ever.

I can't imagine walking to and from the bus or train station everyday for the next two weeks in a place like that. I know I'm not well versed in travel, but it doesn't take a genius to spot a perilous situation like that one. It was immediately clear, no tourists were safe there.

Now I understand why Hudson was so forceful when I first told him where I was staying. I was angry with him at first, putting him in the same category as my brothers and parents, always preventing me from doing anything I wanted to do. But his reaction makes complete sense now.

He exits the car as I reach for the straps of my purse. I'm still a little jarred from the sight of the hooded guy with the crazy eyes, as my door opens and Hudson holds his hand out.

He's truly a gentleman, and I have no idea what I would

have done if I would have Ubered to my hotel tonight. I step out of the truck and reach for my oversized suitcases that have the handles up and ready. He pushes my hand away, grabbing both, pulling them behind him without giving me a second thought.

"Hey, I can take a bag. Give me a bag." I keep pushing because I hate when people do things for me.

He stops, pulling the suitcases to an upright position, then concedes.

"Fine. But we're trading." I squint, unsure of what he means exactly. What is he going to do, carry my purse? But he steps aside so I can grip the handle of one bag, takes a step forward, then holds his now free hand behind his body, blindly searching for mine.

I roll my eyes, shake my head with a smile, then slide my free hand into his.

As we walk into the lobby, which is all marble, glass, and absolutely gorgeous, he steers us directly toward the elevators. We step inside the doors, which are already open and waiting. He slips a magnetic card from his wallet, pressing it to the reader and pressing the twentieth floor.

The top floor.

"You must make a good living playing in the minor leagues?" I smile at him, tipping my chin at the floor panel.

He purses his lips, and a brief expression of sadness crosses his face. "My brothers and I inherited some money when my grandfather passed away. It's the only reason I've been able to support myself while keeping my focus on my baseball. He was my biggest supporter my whole life. Physically, when he was still living, and even now by how he set up our inheritance. If it wasn't for him, I would be on a totally different path."

"I'm so sorry." I was not expecting that response at all. I figured he really did make a decent living as a baseball player, but I have no idea what the minor league would typically pay out to their players.

We ride the rest of the way up in silence, as his thumb caresses the top of my hand, making a circular motion that oddly comforts me, him too, I think.

We finally make it to his suite, and when the door opens, I'm in shock. It's beautiful. A large, open, expansive living area with couches that overlook a large floor to ceiling window, and a small modern kitchen on one side. The other side is adorned with two french doors, leading into one large room. With one large bed.

"Is this your room?" I ask.

"Our room, little red. Our room." His answer is as factual as that view is beautiful.

"I can sleep on the couch." My reply is just as certain. I may have asked to stay here for safety reasons, but I'm not about to burden him and take half his bed.

He huffs something inaudible and shakes his head.

"It's only for tonight. The condo will be ready to move into tomorrow. It's fully furnished, so you'll just need your personal stuff." He's rolling my suitcases into his room, clearly deciding they belong there.

"I can find another place by tomorrow," I say, putting my purse down on the coffee table between the couches.

He stops. Like a dead stop. His head dips down, like he is staring intently at his shoes.

He turns, taking two large purposeful steps toward me, crowding me instantly. Cinnamon and woodsy spice overwhelm my senses as he stands directly in front of me. Lifting my chin to look up at him, his dark chocolate eyes sear into my green ones. It's so intense, I feel the need to look away.

His grip on my chin stays firm, disabling that thought.

"Stop running from me." He tilts his head to find my wandering eyes.

"This is simple. We are simple. Let this happen, Ember." His statement is a plea.

A fucking terrifying plea. I have no idea how to let this happen without allowing it to break me. He could break me.

I pull my nervous lip between my teeth, tugging on the sensitive flesh. He looks down at it, then back up to my eyes. His Adam's apple bobs as he swallows thickly, and I know he's holding himself back.

He's going to kiss me. Do I want him to? I don't know. I think so. Probably not. But, yes.

Shit.

Just when my brain gives in, he steps back, releasing my chin. He walks back to the room, past the French doors through the bathroom door, closing it behind him.

My breath gives way, and I stand in the middle of the living room with more emotions than I can decipher, aroused being well at the freaking top.

WE ORDERED PIZZA FOR DINNER, which was better than any pizza I've ever had, and ate lazily on the couch together. I haven't had that much fun eating in, since, well, I don't think ever. Most dinners at my parents' house were formal, at the dining table, no matter what kind of food it was.

So this was a breath of fresh air.

We sat in every odd position, sometimes me leaning back with my feet propped up on Hudson's lap as he attempted to throw sliced olives in the air and catch them in his mouth. He succeeded on every occasion, which makes him far too talented for a random show. Which led me to giving him shit for, more than likely, practicing alone with his previous pizza nights.

I glance at my reflection in the bathroom mirror as I recall tonight and the moments since we met. He's right. Everything is simple between us.

Simple and scary as hell. One night with him, and I want all of them to be like this. But I have a job to focus on. A career. And he has his baseball and his new position on a new team to worry about. We have goals, and I'm not interested in anything more than a friendship at this point. With anyone. I spent too long trapped in a relationship I didn't want to be in, and I have no desire to waltz back into another one, as *simple* as it may be.

I've had a few straying thoughts about the whole one bed thing. It's a little daunting, even though we've already had sex, only making this a tad more awkward. Although I only get flashbacks of our night together, each one is like reliving the best porn clip I've ever seen. And of course, the wet dream I had the first night I came home was a whole other experience.

Actually, are women's sex dreams called wet dreams? I'll have to look that up later.

I finish up in the bathroom, carefully setting my things in the corner of the bathroom sink, so it doesn't take up too much space on the counter. I'm dressed in my silk pajamas as I walk through the door into the room we're now sharing. The tank top's thin straps rest over my shoulders, and the top stops short of my belly button, exposing a little bit of my stomach. The shorts, if you can even call them that, are more like underwear, but this is normally what I sleep in. I don't really have other options because I didn't anticipate having any kind of sleepover.

He's facing the other direction, plugging his phone into the charger built into the nightstand. Black boxer briefs fit snug against his perfectly shaped ass, which is all the clothing he currently has on. His broad back on full display, ink lines his perfectly smooth skin, the charcoal shades crossing over the top of his back, shoulders, and down the middle of his spine. My eyes trail down again, and I've decided here and now, this man has officially turned me into an 'ass girl'.

I don't see his face turn in my direction until I hear his phone fall onto the nightstand.

Glancing up, his jaw is slacked, and he's running his hand through his still damp hair, looking a shade darker than usual.

"Holy shit," he whispers loud enough for me to hear.

I look down at myself, slightly uncomfortable with my outfit considering the circumstances, and cross my arms over each other, covering my bare tummy.

"Don't you dare cover yourself." He's shaking his head with his demand.

I automatically release my arms as they fall to my sides, like I don't have a mind of my own.

He stays there, studying me. And like his hair, his eyes are a few notches darker. Maybe it's the dim lighting, or the fact that his gaze is plowing through me so deeply, but it's turning my body into jello.

I've never had anyone look at me like he's looking at me. Like he needs to own me. Like his body needs me to survive.

My backstabbing body responds easily to him. My nipples pebble and harden, piercing through the glossy fabric.

I know he knows immediately when his eyes drift down to my chest and he lets out a heavy breath. My hips shift of their own accord, attempting to combat the tingling sensation building at my core.

Can someone eye-fuck you into an orgasm? I think it's entirely possible at this very moment.

I attempt to ignore my body's desperate need and walk to one side of the bed, opposite him, as he turns to face me.

He stands there for a second—a year, maybe—his eyes never leaving mine.

"Which side do you like to sleep on?" I ask.

"Whatever side you're on." He lunges forward, his knee dipping into the middle of the mattress. One swift move, and he's pulling me toward him and I'm wrapped in his arms as he slams his lips against mine.

My lips part immediately for him. His tongue invades my mouth and the same comfort his kiss brought me, since the first time he gave me one, engulfs me. My rigid frame softens into him, and everything I've been fighting against melts into nothing.

"Do you know I only have one regret about that night?" he says as his lips trail over my jawline toward the shell of my ear.

I don't reply because I only need one guess to answer that question, being that he married a complete stranger, with no prenup, by the way, because apparently I asked him after being rejected by Elvis.

"Knowing that you don't recall every minute of that night, when I had you in my arms, my lips on your skin, and my cock inside you, is a special kind of torture I wouldn't wish on anyone, and I'll spend all fucking night reminding you of how perfect it was."

I breathe out a small gasp from the shock of his answer. A bigger gasp, mixed with a groan, falls from my lips when he grips the strap of my top, pulling it down and exposing my hardened nipple before sucking the peak into his wet, hot mouth. White hot flames swarm over my body, licking inside my veins.

In an instant, every part of his body has a complete choke-hold on me. One hand gripping my ass, the other pressing my arm to my side, rendering it useless against the punishing lapping of his tongue on my nipple. Not wanting to let go of his grip, he moves toward the other nipple, sucking it over the thin silk. The sensation is teasing and I'm in dire need of more.

He leans back on his heels, his knees bent in front of him. The black boxers are now so tight against his growing cock, the waistband is pulling away from his skin, giving me a barely there view of his pre-cum laced tip, which is just teasing me further.

Spreading my legs over his, I straddle him, centering myself perfectly over the length of his cock.

God, he's so hard. I roll my hips over him, creating the friction my body is in desperate need of. He groans into my neck as I nuzzle into him, nibbling on his earlobe, licking his jawline and pulling on his hair.

"Fuck, little red." He pulls down both the straps fully, exposing my breasts now, as he slowly licks over each tight bud.

"I need you. I've needed you since the moment I laid eyes on you." He licks more, lightly sucking, as I continue to ride him just like I did that night on the stage. "I want to fuck you, but I don't want this to end."

I don't have all that much experience in bed, only having one past lover, *Elliot*. Everything with him was so plain. Vanilla, I guess you could say. He said he didn't like blowjobs, so if I ever tried, he stopped me. It only happened a couple times, and each time, the rush I felt of the control I had was indescribable.

I shimmy off his legs and place my feet on the ground, pulling myself from Hudson's grip.

"I didn't mean to stop." He urgently follows me off the side of the bed. He's standing now, giving me easy access to his waistband. I grip the sides and rip them down, and his cock bounces out between us. His eyes widened, shocked at my sudden display of authority.

If a cock could be perfect, this would be it. A display worthy cock, that should probably be molded for a shrine.

I lick my lips to contain my smile and begin to kneel in front of him. His mouth drops open, timed with my descent, and by the time my knees touch the ground, I have the tip on my tongue with my hand wrapped around the base.

He grunts, throwing his head back, then quickly looks down at me again, not wanting to miss the moment when his cock disappears into my mouth. Still gripping the base with one hand and grabbing his hip with my other, I pull him closer, sliding the length of his cock over my tongue, and bob back and forth. I taste the sweet and salty mixture of his pre-cum and moan because that's so fucking sexy.

"You look so fucking beautiful on your knees, taking my cock like that."

God, he's got a sexy, dirty mouth. His words just encourage me to push him deeper into my mouth, testing my gag reflex with every thrust.

I surprise myself when I get used to his size and start breathing through my nose, timing it perfectly with the bobbing of my head. I'm taking him down my throat, then licking him up and down, going back and forth between licking and sucking. His hip movements are completely erratic, and his moaning is deeper and more desperate.

"Ember. Fuck. Mmmm. Your mouth." He groans between every word. "You make me lose all control."

Not only is he a dirty talker, but also a moaner, and I can't get enough of it.

His hand cups the back of my head and he begins to thrust harder. My eyes peer up at him, a twinge of worry behind them, as he takes more control.

"That's my girl." His perfect tempo barely avoids my gag reflex, as he takes what he needs. I think he's ready to come when he urgently pulls away.

"Fuck." He squeezes his eyes shut, huffing out a weighty breath. When he re-opens his eyes, he leans down, grabbing my top, using it to pull me to a standing position, then yanks it up over my head.

We shift, moving together as we switch positions, and I'm closer to the bed. He nudges me back a step until the back of my knees hit the side of the bed, falling on top of it. My hips lift naturally as he grips the sides of my shorts, pulling them down, and I'm completely naked in front of him.

Although, it's not the first time, it is the first time that I feel this exposed in front of him. I typically hide, cover myself up a little more, but the desperation in his eyes, the lust dripping from every ounce of his body, has my confidence skyrocketing.

"It's my turn," he growls.

15

HUDSON

It's my turn."

Fuck, it took everything in me to pull her up off her knees.

Not only am I recovering from the shock of how unbelievable her mouth felt on my cock, I'm still in shock as to how it happened. I've been so used to her running, I fully expected her to bolt out of the room when she stepped off the bed.

Instead, she dropped to her knees and wrapped those gorgeous lips around me and blew my mind, in more ways than one.

Now, she lays in front of me, completely at my mercy.

So, yes, now it's my fucking turn.

I grip the back of her knees, pulling her closer to the edge of the bed. Kissing the inside of her thighs, granting me a small moan as I continue to tease her. I slowly graze my lips over her smooth skin, getting closer and closer to her pussy. Her lips glisten with her arousal, and I can't wait any longer for a taste of her.

I fucking need her.

Before I'm able to make contact, she pushes her hands down onto the top of my head, pushing against me.

"You don't have to do that," she tells me, as she attempts to pull her legs back.

I lift up, meeting her gaze, and I can see the stress in her eyes. I can't help but tilt my head and stare at her, confused, questioning her reaction.

"I know guys don't like... doing that." She makes a hand gesture in between her legs, in which my face is mere inches from.

What the hell kind of *"guys"* is she talking about?

That is not fucking happening, ever.

I press into the mattress, holding the weight of my body as I climb over her, meeting her face to face.

"I'm not *guys*. I'll never be fucking *guys*. I'm your husband, and a husband devours his wife's pussy whenever he fucking wants." I graze my lips over hers, caressing my tongue softly against them, and she welcomes it. The feeling of her letting me in opens me up and makes me feral. I retreat, reluctantly, because I want my mouth elsewhere.

"Now, nod that you understand."

She pulls her lip in between her teeth and nods softly.

Trailing my body back down hers, I press my hand into her low belly, holding her in place.

"Open your legs."

She obeys as her knees fall open, still biting that goddamn bottom lip. I press the tip of my tongue between her slit, easily finding her hardened bud between them. She gasps loudly as I flicker back and forth, teasing her with the lightest touch of my tongue.

"Oh, God... Hudson." My name on her lips, with that needy goddamn whine, pulses in my cock, hardening it to rock hard steel.

She tastes so good, too, like sweet honey and my new

favorite dessert. I flatten my tongue, providing more pressure over her clit, and I keep moving. Mismatching my pace, edging her a bit. She's so goddamn sexy, writhing underneath me. I could do this all fucking night.

"Hudson, please. Please." This is exactly what I need. Her begging for me. Remembering how she needs me. So she doesn't default to running.

Using my fingers, I press into her mound, forcing her lips open a little more. I suck on her clit, then loosely wrap my lips around it, flicking my tongue back and forth. I peer up at her face. She's biting her lip, and her fingers are gripping the sheets so forcefully I can see the whites of her knuckles.

"Oh my god!" she screams, followed by a whisper, echoing the same. She almost sounds like she's in shock.

I lift my head up so I can see her face. Her eyes are squeezed shut, as tightly as her grip is on the sheets.

Realizing I've stopped, she opens her eyes and narrows them at me. My lips graze over her skin, as I move them slowly over her hips, belly button, and down closer to her clit. Torturing her. Maybe this is my way of payback for how tortured I feel by her.

Pressing her back into the mattress, her hips lift naturally, a feeble attempt to get my mouth where she wants it.

"You taste so fucking good... I want you to scream my name when you're coming on my tongue." I flick it in between her slit, teasing her again.

"I've... I've never..." She trails off as her head falls back against the bed.

Is she saying what I think she's saying? I give her a curious squint and a facial expression, begging for her to continue.

"No one has ever made me come... that way." Her confession is my fucking undoing.

"After I'm done with you, there won't be any part of my

body left that hasn't made you come all over it." Not giving her a chance to respond, I devour her.

My tongue and lips begin lapping over her clit, alternating between licking and sucking. She tastes so sweet, like my own personal addiction, and I have no idea how I'll stop.

I press my fingers into her entrance, motioning them in and out in pace with my tongue.

She writhes underneath me, moving between lifting her head to watch me and palming her face. Her hands run through my hair then grip slightly, then she releases, like she's not sure she has permission to do it, so she stops.

Lifting her head up, she watches me as her body begins to tremble. She's biting her lip and her eyes squint, then widen at the same time her lips part to gasp.

Her head flies back on the bed as she screams, and her clit throbs over my tongue.

"I'm..." she groans. "Hudson..." gasping, "I'm coming." She releases.

Christ, she's fucking beautiful when she comes. I continue moving at the same pace while my eyes never leave her face. As she finally starts to come down from her climax, I reluctantly retreat, even though I could live there and die a happy man.

Pushing myself up, I pick up my wallet and pull a condom out, sheathing myself in it.

I line myself up, pressing my thumb on her clit, hoping I can ride out her high a bit longer.

"Oh, God." She jerks up, her hips pushing down onto my cock, and she's so tight I hiss as I plunge into her until our hips are flush together. I rub over her sensitive clit and begin to thrust in and out. She's perfect. Everything about her is perfect. Her gorgeous face, her unbelievable mouth, her tight pussy that has a complete chokehold on my cock. Her body. Her soul.

"I need one more, red." I piston into her; my dick grows

thick and hard as I plunge deeper into her. "You're so fucking beautiful when you come."

I continue to rub her clit, and she moans through another orgasm, or maybe just an extension of the first one.

"Fuck yes. Fuck," I repeat, as my own release begins to barrel through me. I'm either low on oxygen or high on Ember, because my skin starts to tingle everywhere. A guttural sound escapes me from somewhere in the middle of my chest as I come harder than I ever have.

"Jesus." Falling forward, I rest my forehead at the center of her ribcage.

"I hope you know we're doing that again." My preemptive attempt to remind her she's not running.

She attempts to hide her giggle, but her chest vibrates slightly, and I just hope that she's just as enamored as I am.

16

HUDSON

We wake up the same way we did in Vegas—naked, wrapped in each other's arms. Except this time, I remember every single moment of the previous night, and it's now branded as part of my soul.

She's perfect, and it's absolutely terrifying because she's a loose cannon and I have no idea if she's just going to disappear on me.

I'm up, showered, and ready to get to the stadium. I order breakfast for both of us to eat before I drop her off at work.

This feels very domestic, which I don't mind so much. It's Ember that I think does. She has a strange outlook on relationships. It's clear she doesn't want one, for reasons I haven't been able to figure out yet, but she feels something for me.

At least I think so.

Speaking of relationships, I need to figure out my... situation. I didn't bring it up last night, but I can't keep avoiding it.

"So... I have a predicament. I... sort of, need some help with..." I mention nonchalantly as she walks out of the room into the kitchen, where I have placed some fruit and pastries.

She climbs up on the kitchen barstool, eyeing the layout of the food I've put out. "Really? What kind of predicament?"

I slide a cup of black coffee her way, placing it next to a small saucer with cream and sugar packets. She wraps her hands around the coffee cup, holds it just under her chin, as she closes her eyes and inhales, then takes a slow sip of the dark liquid and happily moans. I have no idea why discovering her being a straight black coffee drinker is a turn on for me.

But everything she does is.

She is leisurely bringing the cup back to her lips to take small sips, but stops dead on route when I tell her.

"I sort of told my coach I am married, and he wants to meet you," I say, popping a grape in my mouth like it's no big deal.

"Why?" Her brows are pinched together.

I chew on the inside of my cheek and my lips purse out a bit as I debate on how to say this.

"He thought it would help with my image. He wasn't as interested in the trade if I was single." I leave it as generic as possible.

"Mr. Byrnes..." elongating my name. "Did you have an issue with your *image*?"

I roll my eyes. "No, he just associates bachelors with partiers."

She drapes her head to one side, like she knows better.

"My first year in the majors, I got injured, and I was injured for quite some time. They moved me down to minors, and my behavior during that time was not the best. That lingering reputation is still thought of at times, even though I haven't been reckless in years," I admit. "I've been waiting for this opportunity and... I just really need it." The admission feels too vulnerable and desperate for my liking, but she needs to know how badly I want it.

"So, can you just stop by the stadium today? Pretend to be a doting wife for a day?" I smile, raising my eyebrows, silently begging.

She stares at me, with a sexy pout and a curious squint.

I'm not sure why she fights this so hard. I need to be persistent and show her what this could be and that she doesn't have to keep hiding from it.

"I'll get the keys for the condo, and we can move in. You can stay until you get a place in order. So, it's like an exchange of favors." I lean back on the counter, crossing my legs with my coffee in hand.

Still holding her mug, she places it in front of her and then turns her head to gaze at the sunrise through the balcony windows of the hotel. The sun is still low on the horizon, making the red and orange rays of the sky glow within the apartment walls. It highlights her natural color and brings out the green in her eyes, that look like perfect uncut gems.

When she turns her eyes back to mine, they look lighter than I've ever seen. I hope I had something to do with that, and it's not just the sunrise.

"I'm in a little *situation* as well." She bites the corner of her mouth.

"You don't say." Slowly, I smile because she needs something, too.

"Don't do that with your smug face." She throws a strawberry at me, then grabs some other seedy item, tossing it at me.

"Okay, okay. Stop, fruit ninja," putting my hands up in surrender. "What can *I* do for you?"

She pauses, taking in a deep breath.

"I had to tell my parents I was just visiting here. I told them it was a friend I met in Vegas. But I'm going to be here a lot longer, and I have to go home for an event in a few months. It would be better if I brought that someone with me, so they think I'm in a relationship and not moving back home." She shifts uncomfortably in her seat. "It would look better if I got into a relationship, then I can tell them I'm officially moving here."

Every chance she gets, Ember distances herself from me, and it's clear she doesn't want a relationship, yet she lied to her parents about moving here because of a *friend* she met in Vegas.

I'm fucking confused.

"I don't get it," is the only reply I can think of.

"They were more accepting that I was visiting a friend for an extended period and taking some personal time for myself than moving here for a job."

My brows pinch together, still trying to understand.

"They have never been supportive of my desire for a career. Even after I put myself through school, all they wanted was for me to give them grand babies and marry Elliot." She says that guy's name like it's a plague, which makes me quite happy, I must say.

But who the fuck is Elliot?

I take a step toward the counter and lean closer to her.

"Let me understand. You knew your parents wouldn't let you move here for a job. So you told them you met someone, in an entirely different state, and they were okay with you leaving? Alone?"

"Yeah." She chuckles shyly. "Ass backward, right?"

"It's not Elliot specific?" I ask.

"Nope, not for me, at least. I mean, we dated, and my parents think he's God's gift to... well, everything. He was my boyfriend during some of my college years and my next-door neighbor. He sort of works for my dad, and my dad has been pushing Elliot to propose because it really helps his campaign, even bought the ring for him and everything.

"I've never had a desire to be married." She gives me another shy smile, even though her statement feels like a stab in the heart, considering we are *actually* married. On paper, at least.

"My mother is at my dad's beck and call. What he likes, she likes. His good days are her good days. His bad moods are her bad moods. She's never had a life of her own. I don't want that for myself. I want a career and a life that I choose... for me," she confesses.

I cross an arm over my chest, using it as leverage for my other. I press my mouth into the back of my hand to mask my face.

I am obsessed with a woman who is terrified of relationships.

Fan-fucking-tastic.

"So, you see, Hud, this is a perfect setup. I can fake it for your coach, and you can help me get my parents off my back for a bit. We just have to promise each other we won't make it complicated with feelings during this little arrangement of ours. After that, we'll just have the paperwork to clean up the whole accidental marriage thing. It's a win-win for us both."

Fuck. That.

Not only did she eliminate a future with me, she called me "Hud", sentencing me to the goddamn friend zone.

Pushing this, pushing her, isn't going to work out well for me.

I have to keep this light, unless I want to keep seeing the back of her head.

"Okay. Cross my heart and hope to die. No complications," putting an X on my chest.

"Oh no, I don't like that. It's too morbid." She places her elbow on the counter and holds her pinky out to me. "Pinky promise."

"Pinky promise? I don't think I've pinky promised anyone since grade school, little red," I quip back with a chuckle.

"It's better than crossing your heart, hoping to die! Who came up with that, anyway?"

She's not wrong.

I slip my pinky in hers, my eyes bouncing back and forth between her eyes, lips, and our intertwined pinky promise that I know is impossible to uphold. There is no way I can stop myself from the feelings I have brewing inside me, and it's the first time I have no intention of keeping my word.

She releases our bond, and I realize how much I hate it when I'm not touching her.

"So, not only do you need me to attend this... what kind of event is it?" I don't think she said.

"My parents' wedding anniversary," she replies quickly.

My face flashes a pinch of shock before recovering. "Your *parents' wedding* anniversary?"

She just nods, biting into another strawberry, and the way her lips wrap around the base is ridiculously distracting.

"Well, you're going to owe me. Big time." I exaggerate the 'big' part.

"What? How so?" she whines a bit.

"Attending your parents' wedding anniversary *and* you need a place to stay for the next two weeks. That's two favors. The playing field is no longer even. Oh, how the tables have turned, Mrs. Byrnes," I say to her with a smile.

She rolls her eyes, shaking her head with a smile. She leans forward, crooking her finger at me. So, I lean in to meet her.

"For as long as you get to call me *Mrs. Byrnes*, we're even, Mr. Byrnes." Her whisper of mister and missus is playful and sounds so goddamn sexy.

She's right, though. I need the married title more than she needs me.

She's close enough that I can't help my eyes from peering down at her lips, desperate to kiss them. Instead, I place a gentle kiss on her cheek before pushing myself back up. "Alright then, Mrs. Byrnes, let's get you to work."

17

HUDSON

The day has gone by incredibly fast. I've spent it meeting the crew behind the team. *My* new team. The coaches, trainers, assistants, and, for me, specifically, the physical therapist for the team. Coach Raymer insisted he was the first person I met. I don't know if that was meant as a compliment to take care of my injury, or a slap in the face that I need to be babied about it.

Either way, I'm still grateful.

This is the second chance I've been waiting for. Timing couldn't be worse, with my current situation with Ember, but I can't help but think this was somehow fated for us.

Meeting her on the plane, then running into her at the strip club. One in a million.

Us separately moving to the same city after a drunken marriage in Vegas. One in a trillion.

I just hope fate isn't a tease. Because I want her. I want all of her.

I've spent the last half an hour setting up my locker, getting my gear ready. My athletes' locker is already displaying my last name, stationed next to our starting pitcher. His is stuffed full of his gear and a boatload of pictures and personalized cards from his kids.

I've brought in all my personal gear, and still, after all these years, I only have one picture that hangs in mine. A picture of me and my twin brothers playing ball together during high school. It's my favorite picture of the three of us. Not only is it a core memory for me, but it doesn't include Henry. Seeing him just induces thoughts of resentment and bitterness.

I hope one day I'll be able to get over that.

"Where's Henry?" Coach Raymer steps beside me as he glances at the one solo picture I just hung up.

"He had already graduated when this picture was taken." Keeping my reply generic.

"I mean, you have a picture of all your brothers, except for him. Is there animosity between the two of you because of your injury?"

"Nah, we're good. We just don't get to see each other much." The lie feels like razor blades on my lips.

There has always been tension between Henry and me over the years. He's the oldest, I'm the youngest. He spent our childhood making everything between us a competition and creating strain on our parents, making everything a fight or a challenge.

Oh, and the tiny, insignificant fact that he stole my ex-fiancé in college. Other than that, he's not so bad.

Our reunion when I was drafted to *his* team for my first year of pro ball was a match made in heaven for the team and everyone that followed the Byrnes brothers. The pitcher and the catcher, together again.

Until my injury happened.

Maybe one day I'll rid myself of the bitterness I'm holding. One day.

Coach just hums at my reply.

"I can't say it wouldn't be amazing to get the two of you together again." His eyebrows raise, turning his statement into a question that I refuse to answer.

I just hum back.

"So, what time is Ember coming by?" His question kicks up my heart rate a couple decimals.

"She said earlier she could come by around four-ish." I peek at my watch. "So, anytime now."

"Come by when she gets here. I have the keys in my office and the rest of the paperwork for you." He pats me on the shoulder and begins to make his way out of the locker room.

"Hey, Coach?" He stops and turns back to me. "Thank you," I say, sincerely.

He knows what I mean. Thank you for believing in me, trusting me, taking a risk, giving me a chance. Everything.

He nods.

<hr>

"COACH RAYMER, this is my wife, Ember," I introduce them as we walk into his office.

She holds her hand out to him as he stands, rounds his desk, then pulls her into a fatherly hug.

I try not to take it personally, but when we first met, I walked into his office, he gave me a strangers handshake, and told me to "sit".

Ember's smile is wide and absolutely stunning as she thanks him for having her here.

"So, you are the magical creature that tamed Burnsy here, huh?" He pulls her chair out for her to sit.

She glances at me, attempting to hide both a smile and a scowl.

"I suppose I did, sir."

"Oh, enough with the 'sir' stuff. Please call me John." My jaw slacks a bit at how easy going he is, and I can't help but chime in here.

"John...?" I clarify out loud. If someone asked me what his first name is, it would take me a moment to remember because everyone knows him as Coach or Coach Raymer.

"No, not you. She can call me John. You call me Coach." Great. My coach likes my wife better than he likes me.

They fall into conversation easily about random topics, and I just sit back and observe. I can't help but notice how she just... fits. I know a part of her is playing the part for me, but she is so likable, it's effortless for people to fall in love with her.

She's completely engaged in conversation with him, her hands are animated, and she's laughing. God, she's beautiful.

The more she smiles, the more the invisible band around my chest tightens with unknown anxiety. Our time is so limited. After this meeting, she'll probably never see Coach— John, internal eye roll—again. She'll work and find a place, and we'll end up going our separate ways. At least, that's how she probably envisions it.

Then later, I'll have to tell my team we're separated, and Coach Raymer will be incredibly disappointed in me. How come she has to be so damn likable?

We've had one day together, technically an overnight, and I already know I want more.

"I truly believe behind every good man is a great woman. That's clear here, isn't it, Burnsy?" he asks, turning to me, still smiling from an Ember high.

She looks over at me and mouths, *Burnsy*, with an adorable face.

"Absolutely, Coach. She is truly my better half," I reply, staring straight back at her.

I want to keep going. I want to say, I can't imagine my life without her. Can't imagine another day without her smile, her laugh, the sound of her voice or the touch of her skin. I never want to know what it feels like to go one day without talking to her. Instead, I smile at her and lean over the armrest of our chairs, kissing her on the temple, because I'll use any excuse to touch her.

Her body leans into me, naturally. Like she's finally letting loose and relaxing a little.

"I've been married for over thirty years. My wife made me the man I am today. Marriage is a partnership that too many young people take for granted and walk away from at the first hurdle." He is shuffling a few papers around his desk, grabbing a couple of pens out of their holder and pressing into the top, exposing the ink point.

"Giving up on your marriage is like giving up on your team, a commitment you devoted to yourself and others. When someone decides to take back vows, destroy promises and break bonds they've made, well, let's just say, I question the loyalty and values of someone who is coward enough to divorce."

Luckily, Coach is engrossed in the paperwork on his desk because Ember's eyes turn to the size of serving dishes as my mouth becomes its own sinkhole.

Jesus. I mean, that's pretty fucking judgmental. What if someone cheats? Or, like Seamus's parents, his mother was abused by her husband. That excuse for a human being drank himself half to death every night, and the nights he wasn't too far gone, he was strong enough, and sober enough, to beat her.

I agree, divorce is used too heavily these days, but there are reasons for a divorce.

Ember falls completely silent, turns her head just slightly in my direction, and peers at me through her periphery. I smile, even though I'm not sure she can actually see it. So, I reach over, grab her hand, and bring the knuckles that she was rubbing nervously against my lips, grazing a kiss over the peaks.

"Both our parents are great examples for us, Coach." I leave it at that in hopes it will end his current rant.

Fortunately, it does, and he slides the paperwork he was just shuffling around directly in front of us. He grabs two pens, laying one on either side of the paperwork, one for us each, which already feels like a separation I hate.

I grab mine and place it back in his pen holder. Then I grab hers and hold out for her to take from my palm. "Ladies first."

She purses her lips before a pierced smile crosses her face, then takes the pen between her thumb and pointer finger.

"Now, keep in mind, the leasehold rules are set. You are both required to occupy the condo together at all times. The purpose of these properties is for the team to live close to the stadium, but also close to the families." He weaves his fingers together, holding his own hand in front of the paperwork. "Ember, you know what you were getting into marrying a baseball player. His schedule is going to be incredibly invasive between practices and games. Plus, all the travel during the away games. It's good you'll have the other wives around, living in the condo, during those times. Also, we have a lot of events throughout the season. Charities, fundraisers, PR events, things we do together as a team. A family. I expect you both to attend together as often as possible for those events."

Well, shit. After her confession this morning, I might have to chain her to my bed now. I asked her to be a doting wife for a day. I had no idea Coach would be so adamant about the accountability of his players and their significant others.

My entire body is on the verge of a panic attack, and the lack of oxygen from holding my breath is making my hands tingle. I'm questioning whether or not I'm having an actual heart attack.

"I set this up like this to create camaraderie within the team and for the wives and girlfriends of our players, because I remember how difficult it was for my wife. I fully expect you to both be present and incorporate yourselves into the team. The wives and girlfriends often travel with us, and I fully promote that." Coach pauses, then looks directly at me. "I'm investing in you. I expect the same in return."

I look down at Ember's shoes, and thankfully, she's wearing high heels. I'd definitely be able to catch her if she physically started running. I glance up to see her appraising the pen, then peer down at the signature line of the document, then she swivels her neck as her eyes meet mine.

My heart rate is completely out of control. She could put down that pen and walk away. She has no obligation to me, to us, to any of this.

My eyes are begging a silent plea. *Please stay.*

I reach for her free hand, wrapping my pinky around hers.

Her eyes are so fucking sad. Like she already knows she's going to break my heart.

She looks at our pinkies dancing together, then her gaze returns to the pen, and with a short exhale, she leans forward to the desk. My stomach plummets to the floor when it looks like she is going to place the pen down, but instead, she presses the ink point to the paper and scribbles quickly, then hands the pen to me.

I take the pen out of her hand and quickly scribble my signature next to hers, my eyes on her the entire time.

"Thank you, Coach," I say, setting the pen down before we both stand together. "We'll get our things moved into the condo this weekend." He reaches out to shake my hand, eyeing us both. I pull her into me, wrapping my arm around her and kissing the top of her head.

"Take the weekend to get settled in and explore Seattle. Report back on Monday."

"Thank you, sir, will do," I reply, guiding Ember out of his office as I follow behind her. Each step fills me with relief as we get closer to exiting the stadium and into the parking lot.

The relief is short-lived, because the moment she closes the door to the passenger side of my truck, everything she was able to hold back comes out.

18

EMBER

"What the hell was that, Hudson?" I throw my hands over my face and push them back through my hair. "You told me you needed a wife for a day, one day! Not... not... signing up to be a forever baseball wife, following you around like a lost puppy."

"I didn't know it was going to go down like that. I had no idea he felt that way." He turns to face me, reaching his hand to grab mine, and I instantly yank it back.

His frustration is obvious, but it's quickly replaced with concern.

This is exactly why I didn't want to get involved in this. I feel stuck. Even the cab of his overly sized truck is closing in on me, and everything feels so goddamn small.

"Just drive. Please drive." I jam my finger into the window button, rolling the window down to get some air as Hudson faces forward, starts the truck, and pulls out of the parking lot.

As we exit, I see a couple of families on the sidewalk across the street, at what appears to be the condo that we will be living in. Two women are taking a selfie together. Their men are behind them, as they expertly try to move so the stadium is the backdrop behind them. One guy has a child on his shoulders, the other has one in each arm. They all squeeze together and smile as we pass by.

"Those guys are on the team," Hudson shares with me, his tone understated.

"I figured." I don't intend my reply to be so curt, but I feel so frustrated I don't bother to apologize for it when it does.

His confession this morning about everyone else's idea of his image and the injury he had pulled at my heartstrings. I was just trying to help him out, but I should have just said no. There are too many things that I'm trying to work on for myself.

I'm finally out from under my parents' grueling pestering about marriage and babies. Away from my friends, who judged me for wanting a life, a career of my own. Just to fall into a situation where I've agreed to be a housewife and worry more about someone else's future than my own.

So, why did I sign the papers? I signed the paper because I also lied to my parents about meeting Hudson. Even though they don't know I got married, the lie I told them led me here. And I couldn't let Hudson down or embarrass either one of us in front of his coach. His coach, who under normal circumstances would be a great guy, but right now, his upstanding, old-fashioned morals are the bane of my existence.

And because I feel like a goddamn pushover.

There is an underlying guilt that I shouldn't be so selfish, but I've just worked way too hard and fought for too damn long to not be. Staying with Hudson will require a lot of time and energy, and things that I never intended to focus on. I committed myself to my new role at XConnect—the dream job I've been waiting for—uprooted my life, lied to my family, all so I can create something for *me*. Something that I can call my own.

Now I just signed my life over to being the exact thing I have been trying to avoid.

The words my mother would always tell me repeat in my head. *Men hold the power, and it's our responsibility as women to support that so they can support us.*

I hated that. I hated when she reminded me that anytime I felt more ambition than she'd like, telling me I'd be better off finding a strong, wealthy man than a career.

I watch as Hudson grips the steering wheel, turning it wide as he pulls into a parking spot and kills the engine. I peek at the time, and it's been less than ten minutes since we left the stadium, realizing the drive was short in distance, but long in my head.

"Please say something." He turns to face me and his eyes plead with mine.

"I can't," I reply, and he huffs a short breath at my response.

He pulls his wallet out of his back pocket and hands me the keycard for the hotel room.

"I'll pick up some food at the restaurant and bring it upstairs for us. I'll meet you up there." Giving me a concerned look before he exits the driver's side and closes the door behind him. Taking a couple steps away, he stops, pauses, looks over his shoulder, then walks around the front of the truck.

It actually pisses me off how handsome he is. His dark brown hair is covered by a baseball cap, which somehow looks better on him than not. His joggers are snug, low on his waist, and the basic navy t-shirt he wears looks like it's tailored for his body. Could he look any fucking sexier?

He opens my door, stepping into it, blocking everything.

Reaching over, he clicks open the glove compartment. It pops down, displaying a folded, mustard yellow manila envelope.

He grabs it, lifting the top flap, and pulls out the paperwork inside, showing me the top of the front page.

Decree of Annulment.

"I had these prepared immediately after you left the hotel

room in Vegas." His chest lifts as he takes a deep breath, letting the exhale release slowly.

"I don't want you to feel stuck. I don't want you to do anything you don't want to do. But we know this situation can benefit us both." His tongue darts over his bottom lip, pulling it between his teeth, like he's a bit nervous about this proposal.

"If you want to sign these papers right now, we will. But it doesn't have to be as terrible as you're envisioning it to be. You have a life, a job, a career. I understand that, and Coach Raymer will understand that. That's your priority, and I fully support it. We both need something that we can benefit from right now, and that's all it needs to be. Plus, it would just be for the season." He places the palm of his hand over my cheek, and my body, my traitorous body, leans into it, like a comfort blanket.

Is he right? Could this work? Could we do this without me giving up on myself?

My mom sure couldn't.

I close my eyes and suck in a lengthy breath. When I reopen them, Hudson's stare is feral.

His dark lustful eyes boomerang between mine and my lips. His intense study causes my eyes to fall away from his, and they find the keycard that I'm twiddling with as I pull my bottom lip in with my teeth. It's a wasted attempt to shy away from him when he pinches his thumb and forefinger to my chin and returns my gaze to his; the collision is a perfect storm.

"Don't look at me like that." I challenge the lion behind this façade of a man.

"Like what?" he replies, with a tone as lecherous as his face.

"Like you did before you kissed me on that stage," I whisper.

His lips lift in a devilish smirk.

He slides the envelope on the top of the dash, then grabs the bill of his baseball cap and swivels it around his head, removing any obstruction from between the two of us.

And I take back what I questioned early.

Yes... he absolutely *can* look sexier.

He leans in slowly, nuzzling himself into the column of my neck, giving me a chaste kiss with his soft lips.

"You mean, when I couldn't keep my hands off you?" He places the palms of his hands on the tops of my thighs, trailing them all the way up to my hips.

"When you put a spell on me and nothing in this world could have stopped me from putting my lips on yours?" He yanks me forward so my center is flush with his, then he, softly, so fucking softly, presses his lips to mine. "Or anywhere else on this gorgeous body." He trails his lips over my jawline to the soft flesh under my ear. "Before, when I had a mind of my own and no idea that someone could make me feel so consumed and possessive, so weak and powerful."

Releasing my hip, his hand roams loosely over the top of my shirt, caressing me as his lips explore my neck, jaw, chin, collarbone. He kisses me in areas I've never been kissed before, that reach areas of my body I didn't know I had.

My hips act of their own accord and press into his. His groan is long and drawn out as his hips collide with mine, rolling together with perfect rhythm.

A distant honk and a male voice screaming from a drive by car pulls us back into reality.

It's so easy to get lost in him. Just like on the stage, when we got so lost in each other.

Pulling his hands away from my body, the distance is instant and a devastating relief.

His joggers don't do him any favors to hide his current state. Not only did I feel everything when he was pressing into me, but now he's packing what looks like a plumbing pipe between his legs.

He grunts as he pulls away from my neck and looks down at himself and his unavoidable erection, soundlessly chuckling.

"You might be the death of me." A tone as serious as it is playful.

Reaching over the dash, he grabs the envelope, placing it back in the front compartment, then flips it closed.

Holding out his hand to me, "Come on, little red. Let's go eat."

19

HUDSON

Bringing Ember to the restaurant was the only way I was going to keep my hands off her. I have absolutely no resistance in any part of my body when it comes to her.

The most dangerous being the goddamn beating organ in the middle of my chest, protected by a useless cage of taffy textured bones, that can't seem to think logically when it comes to her.

If I don't get my actions under control, I'll end up pushing her away.

I can see it written all over her face. She's teetering on the edge of running. I'm still shocked she's here with me now.

We're seated at a window table, facing each other. She's rubbing her hands together and picking at her nails nervously, so needless to say, when she wants to talk about the situation we're in, I'm shocked.

"I think we should figure this out." She meets my gaze, her gorgeous emerald eyes shining with meaning, and dare I say hope.

"I think so, too. What are you thinking?" I ask, happily giving her all the power I feel she needs.

"Maybe... it could work?" she says so quietly I barely hear it.

I sit up straighter with hope blooming in my chest.

"How long is the season?" she asks, looking down at her hands still kneading into each other.

"Officially... through September, pending playoffs," I reply, hesitantly, knowing how long that sounds.

Her eyes widen momentarily, but return to a normal size after she exhales a sizable breath.

"Okay, we live together for the season. That'll keep your coach off your back and my parents off mine. I'll go to the events you need me to be at, and you can come back home with me for my parents' anniversary." Her gaze is still down as she nods, as if she's trying to talk herself into it. I can't help but nod along.

"I will contribute to the rent. I won't be a charity case. I'll pay my half, and—"

"Ember," I interrupt.

"No, Hudson, that's a deal breaker for me," she insists.

I put my hands up in surrender, just in time for the food to arrive.

The waitress comes by and slides our dinner plates in front of us. When the season starts, I always mind my food and eat lean meats and veggies, so her seafood pasta looks far more appetizing than my grilled chicken and broccoli.

She picks up her fork, poking gently at the greens mixed in with the shrimp. She only looked my way to insist about making payments for the rent. Other than that, she's avoided all eye contact with me. She just continues to pick at her food, losing herself in the action. She's so unpredictable it has me on edge. At this point, I just need her to be comfortable, because I'll take her anyway I can get her.

"So, we do this. Live together. We can act like we are a

happily married couple until we divorce at the end of the season. In the meantime, we'll be... friends, you know, do our own thing."

Wait. What? That took a fucking turn I was not expecting.

"Friends?" I respond, disgustingly.

"Yeah, friends."

Uh, no. I don't fucking think so. I know I just said I would take her anyway I could get her, but are you kidding me?

Live with her and study every crevice of her body? Sleep next to her and not swallow her with my entire body? Walk with her on my arm, claiming her, without having her?

Hell no.

"Ember, we are not friends." Her eyes shoot up to mine. "We are way more than friends."

"I can't, Hudson." She nods incessantly, unnecessarily.

"Can't what?"

"You make my head all fuzzy when you touch me. I can't think straight, and that's bad for me. This has to be completely platonic for it to work for me." Her eyes are begging, pleading, in a desperation I can't understand. "We both have a lot we're working toward in our careers. That should be our main focus. So, this should be an easy, agreeable, business arrangement that benefits us both."

We both have a lot to focus on, and yes, we are infused with each other in moments of passion. So much that I understand exactly what she's saying. It's consuming, all-encompassing, and I can so easily get lost in her. But how can we ignore this?

I have no control over my motor functions as my head bobs automatically, agreeing with her. She's on the edge, almost ready to jump into this with me. My entire being, from the layers of my skin to the depths of my soul, agrees unanimously.

I guess I *will* take anything I can get.

"So, we do this... as friends?"

"Absolutely. Friends," I repeat, hating the way it sounds as it leaves my mouth.

She grants me a relieved smile that shines in her eyes. Like a load has been lifted and she can smile again without suffering.

Well, I'm wholly, fully, and entirely screwed, because I'll agree to anything for her with a smile like that.

20

EMBER

"I don't know about this." I appraise myself in the full body length mirror with a questioning look on my face and the same feeling in my stomach.

"You look fabulous, my friend. Gorgeous. Hudson is going to freak," Cruz replies from the corner of the closet, as he pulls out the shoes I bought specifically for this dress.

Cruz is Elena's assistant and pretty much knows everything about everything when it comes to Ford Enterprises and XConnect. Since we both work so closely with Elena, he's been my go-to for everything, and we became instant friends because, well, he's amazing.

Being that this is my first outing as *the wife*, I asked for Cruz's help, and to say I'm nervous is a complete understatement.

Sure, I've met his coach, who seemed to like me when we met, but I've only been able to attend a casual dinner with the team since then. It was actually a lot of fun. It was the first night that Hudson and I went out together as a *couple*. Fortunately, I spent most of the time meeting the other wives and girlfriends of the team, who were all easy going and fun. I connected with them easily, and I was surprised by how much we all had in common.

The only other event I missed because I've been so incredibly busy with work, in the best way possible.

We've taken strides for XConnect, one of many of Ford Enterprises' companies that Elena specifically hired me for.

XConnect is a platform that connects individuals for very specific things. "X" being the variable, plus connect, allows our users to choose who they are looking to get matched with. It can be as simple as looking for a book reading buddy or a workout partner, all the way to looking for specific sexual kinks.

One thing Elena did when she took over this portion of Ford Enterprises was separate out the sexual matchmaking side of XConnect and rebrand it as XConnect - Unleashed.

It was brilliant on her part, and that's the side that I get to focus on the most. It's been liberating, not only learning from her, but also creating ways to market this and put it out there.

Luckily, there is a team behind the scenes who thinks of the kinks and selections that are added to the platform. I would be totally useless for that, being that I had to Google half of them to know what they were. My main job: market the hell out of it and inspire the teams behind it with new, exciting, and creative ideas. *That*, I can do.

I've actually had an idea stirring in my head for a while, which I brought up to Cruz, since he's my new work bestie. He loved the idea and has been encouraging me to pitch the idea to Elena. I want to, but nerves fail me every time I've gotten close.

"Are you sure about this dress, Cruz? Is it too much? I've never been to a gala before, so I have no idea." I air-quote the word gala, because that's what it's been dubbed as. The Seattle

Smashers opening night gala, where all the players will be there to kick off the year and raise money for local charities. That's exactly how Hudson explained it to me.

Last weekend, after the first week of our new arrangement, he came home with a large pizza and we vegged out in the living room, just like we did the first night in the hotel room.

I can't say it didn't cross my mind to end it the same way that night did. Hudson is the most tempting eye candy, and this three thousand square foot condo feels tiny whenever he is in it. But our situation—yes, at my request—is friends only. It's just not as easy to maintain as I thought it would be.

Especially because he's used to showering naked in a locker room, which is an occupational hazard that rolls over into the house. So, needless to say, a naked, topless, freshly showered Hudson walking around the one bedroom that we have to share is unavoidable. And I swear he does it on purpose.

It has crossed my mind a time or two to do the same, just to see how he'll react.

"Em, seriously, put these shoes on your feet and duct tape over your mouth. A gala," he air quotes, mocking me, "is a glorified prom for adults. This dress needs to be attention grabbing and sexier than all git-up. It qualifies for both."

Well, he's not wrong. The satin hugs my upper body in a tailored fashion, all the way down to my waist, which then splays out into a blanket of shiny material, with a tempting split all the way up to the top of my leg. Every time I step forward, my leg is on full display for the world to see, and I swear my leg does not need that much attention. Somehow, the light seafoam green brings out both the red in my hair and the green in my eyes. Attention grabbing is yet another understatement.

"I'm trusting your fashion sense here." He side-eyes me with a credulous look. "I know, I know, as I should. But I'm going to hightail it out of there immediately if I'm overdressed, and you'll have Hudson to face if that is the case."

"Speaking of, he's waiting in the living room for you, and I don't feel like listening to this nonsense anymore. So, seriously, put on these shoes and chop chop, gorgeous." He places the shoes on the ground next to my feet, kisses me on the cheek, then saunters out of the room.

Note to self: he acts the exact same in a personal setting as his work setting. He's just as bossy and unbearable, in the best way possible, of course.

I can't help but smile and shake my head, as I take his advice internally and quiet the voices in my head that are creating the nervousness that I don't need tonight.

A beep from my phone draws my attention, and I pick it up from the charger, releasing the cord, and see it's Suzy.

Ugh, I've been so terrible about keeping in touch with everyone. Suzy and Dana both know about Vegas, being they were both there for the entire thing. They promised to keep the whole thing a secret until I could figure things out. Needless to say, they were shocked when I told them I had arrived in Seattle and Hudson was here.

Their decision to be supportive in my career endeavors is purely based on whatever mood they are in. Some days, they love my independence and have a "you go girl" attitude. Other days, they try to talk me into staying in Weston and marrying Elliot. They want me to have babies in the same age range as theirs.

Suzy: Are you ready to come home yet? We miss you. Double dates with Micah and Elliot are NOT the same.

Me: LOL. You mean you are the third wheel with the bromance besties now?

Suzy: …

Suzy: So, seriously, when are you coming home? Micah says Elliot spends way too much time with your brother and that your parents are asking a lot of questions.

UGH, why does she do this? She insists that I need to drop everything and get back with Elliot. Not always, just whenever the mood strikes her. Predicting if she's pro-Elliot or pro-career is as predictable as betting on a greyhound dog race.

Her now husband, Micah, and Elliot have been best friends for a long time. We used to go out all the time, but over the years, with my grueling class schedule and then after Elliot proposed and I broke everything off, a lot changed between all of us. Mostly due to my choices, which they all like to remind me of, blanketing me with thick layers of guilt whenever the mood strikes any of them.

I knew it was only a matter of time before my parents started questioning my extended absence. I've been able to placate my mother's incessant questions with me just needing some time for me. She berates me before she gives in, telling me to be ready to marry Elliot when I return home because, *'my father really needs it.'*

I hate that she doesn't support me, or even attempt to see it from my side, but when you only mirror the emotions of your significant other, you ignore glaring signs and want what they want instead of what you want or what's best for the other person.

Needless to say, they are just praying that this little Seattle rendezvous will wash the *rebel* out of my system before I come home and agree to a marriage with Elliot.

I don't have it in me to reply. I turn my phone on silent, then place it inside my clutch.

One final glance in the full-length mirror, as I press my palms to the front of my dress, flattening the fabric that's already all in perfect placement, thanks to Cruz.

"Okay, here we go," I whisper to myself.

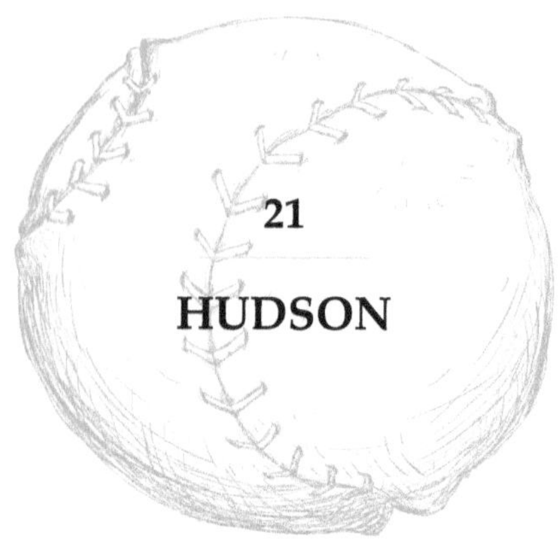

21

HUDSON

"Thanks for your help, Cruz." I wave as he makes his way to the door.

"Anytime. Ciao!" he calls out without looking back.

He's been around a lot these past couple of weeks for Ember, which I'm grateful for.

The front door clicks shut, which must have been synchronized with the bedroom door because I never heard Ember step out, until the angelic sound of her voice hits my ears.

"I'm ready."

And when I turn around, I am not ready.

My hand, with a mind of its own, lands on my chest. Why? Because it might fucking stop.

She's stunning, absolutely breathtaking. Typically, she wears minimal make-up, which suits her well due to her natural beauty. But tonight, her eyes have a dark, smoky look to them that contrasts the pale green color of her satin dress. Her gorgeous red hair flows over the tops of her shoulders onto her creamy, kissable skin.

"Ember, wow." My eyes widen and I finally breathe. "You

look... incredible." That doesn't do it justice, but I'm at a loss for words.

"Thank you," she replies shyly, as she bites the corner of that goddamn irresistible lip. "So do you. You look straight out of GQ magazine."

"Well, Cruz picked out the vest and bow tie, and now I see why he picked this color." I unbutton my jacket and pull open the lapels to show her the matching pale green, or seafoam green, as Cruz referred to it as, satin vest.

"It's perfect." Her smile is contagious as she takes a few steps toward me to feel the fabric.

She's even more beautiful up close, and now, the tropical scent that fills not only the space I'm standing in, but the space we live in every day, engulfs me instantly. It's a daily reminder she's still here, and I can never get enough of it.

"Alright, shall we go?" she asks.

"Yeah, but you are missing something."

She pats her neckline, testing for her necklace, which is there. Then she looks down at her tiny purse, her shoes, and back up to me. "I am?"

I pull a little black box out of my pocket and place it in my palm, presenting it to her. My close-lipped smile has more concern than I would like, but this part was inevitable.

"Your ring can only be 'getting sized' for so long." Which is what she has been telling everyone she works with. I think only Elena knows the real truth as to why she doesn't have one. And actually, come to think of it, Cruz has either figured it out or Elena told him the details of our situation.

Her questioning smile matches mine as she reaches for the box and pops it open.

"Oh my." Her breath hitches. "It's stunning."

"The most flawless diamond in the universe wouldn't compare to you," I pull the ring out and place the box down on the countertop of the kitchen island, "but it'll do."

I did tell her I was going to buy her a ring. That we had to in order to keep this charade going, to which she agreed. But kept insisting to just get her a plain band.

A plain band, my ass. I would have her wear the entire goddamn mine cave on her arm if I could.

"Hudson, this is too much," she replies.

"It's not enough." My fast reply makes her lips thin as they press together.

She splays out her fingers on her left hand, and I place the two karat, emerald-cut diamond ring at the tip and push slowly down her finger. It crosses over her knuckle and finally lands at the base, fitting perfectly.

I hold up my left hand, displaying the band I bought for myself. She mentioned buying one for me, but ultimately, she is doing this for me more than herself. So, I insisted I would grab us both simple bands. I just upgraded hers... slightly.

I lift my left hand to show her my palm and she mirrors it with her own, pressing them together. Our wedding bands connect together for the first time, and it feels just as right as it does foreign.

Her chest lifts as she inhales and releases a hefty breath, giving me a soft smile and a nod. "Okay, I'm ready."

I weave my hand into hers and smile as I lead her out through the front door.

"We've got this, little red."

22

EMBER

I had no idea what to expect when walking into the ballroom. Yes, ballroom. It looks like I time warped into some kind of mid century, European debutante ball and the setting feels the same. Except for the extravagant gowns and tuxedos that everyone is wearing. Those are modern, gorgeous, and colorful, and I have never been happier that I trusted Cruz on the dress he picked out for me.

Hudson hasn't left my side since we came in. I'm sure he senses my hesitation, since I've never done anything like this before, and he's been doting on me since we left home. It's been, well, perfect, actually. Even though this is his first time going to one of these with this team, he mentioned he's been to some in the past, so he's been at ease. Or at least it feels that way.

"Here's when all the high rollers come out," he leans in, whispering in my ear. "The team is going to get called up there. It's all just for looks, but we'll be up there while they offer up whatever they are auctioning to raise money for the foundation. Everyone starts throwing their paddles around and trying to outbid each other. Usually, it's fine, but sometimes you get two people who just can't stop and it's pretty humorous to watch."

I've only ever seen one of these on TV, in a movie, so this should be interesting.

Someone walks onto the stage, a gorgeous woman in a strapless red pantsuit with long, wavy brunette hair. Hopefully, she's just some kind of host for the hotel and doesn't work for the team, because, wow. I could see her being a distraction for all the guys.

"Good evening, everyone! I'm Bailey Lester, the Seattle Smashers public relations director, and we are beyond thrilled that you could all make it out tonight!" Her voice is much more enthusiastic than the look on my face, especially when she invites the players to step onto the stage and she greets each of them nonchalantly, except Hudson. With Hudson, she wraps her arms around his neck, pulling him down into a longer than usual hug.

I'm not typically a jealous person. Ever, actually. So, why the hell does she make me feel like a murderer in the making? Maybe she'll slip on that stupid red high heel and fall off the stage.

"Hey there," a voice, and a soft touch to the side of my arm, rips my gaze away from the stage.

The man now standing next to me is tall, as tall as Hudson. His sandy brown hair and blue eyes are light and friendly, and I smile in return. "Hi."

"Are you bidding tonight?" he asks, as his gaze trails down to my hand, seeing no paddle, but eyeing the elegant and quite sparkly ring on my finger, and I'm suddenly very happy that Hudson gave me the ring earlier tonight.

"Gosh, no." I huff out a giggle. "I've never even been to one of these before. I'm completely out of my element."

"You look like you fit right in." His eyes meet mine, and I

can't tell what is happening here. Is he just being friendly or is he trying to flirt? He feels familiar, like I've met him before.

"Have we met before?" I ask.

"No, I definitely would have remembered that." He grants me a friendly wink as he smiles, then tips back the rest of his glass.

"Would you like to grab another drink at the bar?" He nods to the empty glass in my hand, and when I look down, I realize I must have finished my champagne without realizing it.

"Actually, my husband is up there and I should probably wait," I reply back to him, pointing at Hudson on the stage.

"I know all the guys up there; it's all good. We can just sit down and get off our feet while they get through the auction." Since my feet are already killing me, that actually doesn't sound half bad, and this guy doesn't feel threatening.

"I'm Henry," he offers his hand, and I slide mine into it.

"Ember," I reply with a smile as we turn around and head toward the bar.

23

HUDSON

Some of the guys on the team thrive on events like this. I've never favored it one way or the other, but you can tell which ones love the attention and which ones couldn't care less. I'm definitely the latter.

I've always been more of a homebody, but now that I've spent the last couple of weeks coming home to a beautiful woman who likes the same, it's hard to want to do anything else.

There is only one reason we stand up here during the auction, and it's because people like to see the team and the players pay attention and congratulate the winning bidders. The foundation feels like it adds to the experience and we end up getting more money. That part I don't mind if it's raising money for the foundation that benefits the kids in the community. So, I easily play the part I need to.

Between bantering with the guys on stage and congratulating the winning bidders, I try to look out beyond the blinding lights that are spotlighted on the stage to find my girl. Looking out over the crowd, I find my gorgeous green-eyed beauty, who stands out amongst everyone out there like a beacon. It's been easy going these past couple of weeks. Completely platonic, unfortunately, but easy, and dare I say, blissful.

I've somehow managed not to cross over the friend zone boundary, which I'm both impressed by and pissed off at. But overall, we've done nothing but have a great time, enjoying each other's company while we talk about our day. It's been perfect. Except the night she referred to me as a roommate.

That was not perfect. It took everything in me to refrain from showing her all the ways I am not a fucking roommate. Again, impressing myself with my restraint.

The spotlights change for a brief moment, highlighting the last high bidder, and I'm able to see her with more clarity. Her smile is on full display and hypnotizing, and I squint to see who she's talking to.

What the fuck.

What the hell is Henry doing here? And what the hell is he doing talking to Ember?

Full panic laces through me. Panic, stress, anxiety. Jesus, I need to get her away from him. My fists clench and Callahan, our pitcher, who is standing next to me senses it immediately.

"What's up, man?" He leans in closer to me, trying to find my line of sight.

"My brother is here. He's talking to my wife," I say, between clenched teeth.

"And that's a problem because?" His question is clearly laced with confusion.

Because the last woman I had, he didn't hesitate to seduce, which ultimately led to her cheating on me with him before we called off our engagement. He proposed to her shortly after, then broke off the engagement a few months before the wedding date.

That's why that's a problem.

I don't say that because I never talk about that. That was in college, a long ass time ago, but I still don't talk about it.

I watch as they talk to each other, smiling loosely, like he doesn't have a care in the fucking world. That's probably because everything has come so easily for him, or maybe it's because he doesn't give a shit about who he hurts while going after whatever it is that he wants.

"She came after me. That's what happens when you can't keep your woman pleased, Hud," he tells me, like his actions didn't just tear my world apart.

"What the fuck were you thinking? You don't pursue your brother's fiancé. There's a basic moral code, and you fucking broke it, Henry!" I yell, practically spitting in his face.

My fists are balled and ready to swing, but I'm holding myself back with everything I have. He fucking slept with Veronica. And she slept with him. How did this even happen? How did I not see it coming? Probably because what brother, flesh and blood, would do that?

Henry, that's who. And clearly without remorse or guilt.

"Why would you do that? What the fuck did I ever do to you?" The asshole is actually smirking. Smirking.

"Sorry, bro, I really like her. We're going to see where this goes." He pats me on the shoulder, silently saying, 'no big deal—get 'em next time, Tiger', and turns to leave my room.

Fucking prick.

Henry has always had it out for me. He got all the attention, being the first born, then when the twins came along, that changed a lot. They got most of the attention, and I feel like, sometimes, he just lashes out at me, being I was the youngest and the last, and our parents knew that I was the final child. I'd like to give him the benefit of the doubt, being he had to grow up faster than any of us, but he's the most immature, self-centered person I've ever met.

It doesn't matter if it's school projects, baseball, or now, my girl, he feels entitled to take over anything that I take any liking to.

I've fucking had enough. Too many years of built up frustration explodes out of me.

I push him from behind, making him turn to face me, and punch him square in the face. His body stumbles backward into the wall, holding his broken nose.

"You fucking dick, you broke my nose!" He lunges forward, grabbing my shirt and swinging me back against the wall he just fell against. "I'm going to fucking kill you." He grabs my left hand, my catching hand, wrapping one hand around my pinky and ring finger and the other around my middle and pointer and tears them apart, sending a searing pain through the back of my hand.

"Ah, fuck!" I pull away as he reaches in again for the same hand.

The door to my room opens, and Grant comes barreling in, ripping us apart and throwing Henry across the room.

"What the fuck, you guys?" Grant creates a blockade between us.

"Hudson just can't keep his girl happy and he's pissed off about it."

I'm holding my catching hand, hunched over in pain. It's not broken, but it's definitely sprained.

Grant looks at me, confused, as Henry pushes himself off the ground, glaring at me like I've wronged him, as he walks through the doorway, leaving my room.

"I GOTTA GO," I say to Callahan and exit the stage.

24

EMBER

"Cheers." I gently collide my glass with Henry's while we sit at the bar right outside the auction area.

"So, what do you do?" he asks.

"I work for Ford Enterprises, for one of their subsidiary companies as Marketing Manager," I say, giddy, because it makes me feel proud to say that. Although, I never say XConnect specifically because if people assume it's the *Unleashed* side, they might be uncomfortable or get the wrong idea. "How about you?" I ask, returning his question.

"Baseball." He shrugs.

"Oh, are you part of the team? Why aren't you up there?" My brows pinch in confusion.

"Not for this team. I play for another team. I just know a couple guys here, so I thought I'd come by in support," he replies, taking a sip of the drink he ordered. There's a large ice sphere that peeks out over the top of the glass, making his plain bourbon drink much classier than it should be. He ordered me the same without even asking what I would like, and the sip I take makes me cringe.

"That's nice of you." I smile, then glance back at the stage.

Hudson is no longer on the stage, and I squint in confusion, looking around, my eyes bouncing from one side of the stage to the other. I slip off the barstool to stand, in an attempt to get a better view, which is futile, considering I was higher in a seated position.

"Who are you looking for?" Henry asks.

"Uh, my husband. He was just up there." I'm still peeking over the top of the crowd.

"I'm sure he's busy with the auction. Come sit back down." He places his hand around my elbow, attempting to grab my attention, and I look down at where his hand grips my arm. It's not hard or painful, just there.

In my periphery, I see, and feel, a large force walking up to us with purpose. Glancing in that direction, Hudson marches up to where I'm standing and wraps his arm around my waist, pulling me into him.

"What are you doing here, Henry?" The moment he says his name, it hits me. Henry. His brother, Henry. I remember he mentioned his name on the plane, but Hudson skimmed over his name and picture quickly before bringing up his twin brothers in more detail. Henry looks familiar because I've seen his picture before.

I don't remember Hudson saying anything in detail about Henry, but it's clear he is not happy to see him.

"*Henry?* Your brother, Henry?" The look on my face is as questionable as my tone.

Henry puts his hands up in surrender. "I was just talking with Ember here. I came to support my baby brother. Nothing more," he says, with a smile that feels far from genuine.

"Let me rephrase. Why are you talking to my wife?" Hudson's hand, the one that rests on my waist, clenches, and I can feel his entire body tense.

"Your wife? You don't say?" Henry looks between the two of

us. "Why wouldn't you tell me you got married? Do Mom and Dad know?"

"It's none of your fucking business. Why are you even here?"

"Relax, I came to support you. To congratulate you. I happened to run into Ember by coincidence," he replies, taking another swig of his drink.

"I doubt that." Hudson's reply is short and as bitter as that bourbon tastes.

"I really came by to say congrats. I fly back home in a few hours, and I was hoping to just catch up." His tone is reserved and steady, sounding authentic. He shoots down the rest of his drink, placing his glass down on the bar.

Hudson remains stoic, the scowl unchanged from the moment he greeted him.

"Okay, baby brother, you win." He looks over to me. "Ember, it was a pleasure to meet you." Holding his hand out. I slide mine into his for a friendly shake, still trying to figure out what the hell is going on. He turns my hand over, the back of my hand facing up, and places a kiss on the top. His eyes peer over to his 'baby brother' before Hudson yanks me back, ripping my hand from Henry's.

"Have a good flight," Hudson replies, as he swings me around and steers me away from Henry. We walk toward the patio doors of the ballroom, exiting into the outdoor garden area. The darkness rivals the mood we just left, but feels serene with just the moonlight shining over the groomed rose bushes and ivy that lines the perimeter.

He releases my waist, stepping forward, stopping in front of the large three-tier fountain, expertly placed in the center of the courtyard.

"What was that?" I ask, quietly, standing a few feet behind him.

He's leaning over the circular barrier of the fountain. He

would be clenching his fists if it weren't for the cement preventing his fingers from curling. I'm surprised the pressure doesn't break the hardened stone with how tense everything is. I've never seen him like this.

He looks at the water, studying his own reflection, before he stands to his full height and turns around to face me.

"Just do me a favor and stay away from him." His tone is calm and sounds like my Hudson again. But it's clear he's bothered.

"Why?" Which is the wrong thing to ask because it sounds like defiance. "I mean… what happened between you two?"

Placing his hands on his hips, he's uncomfortable, unsure.

"I was engaged—" He pauses and looks at me with concern, before quickly averting his gaze. I am a little shocked, but I remain impassive and just listen. "He said she came after him… but Henry, he… he always wants what someone else has. Specifically with me. He's done that our whole lives."

He kicks an invisible rock on the ground, his eyes avoiding me.

"They were engaged for a while after she left me. Until he got bored."

He runs his hands through his hair, weaving them behind his neck as he peers up to the sky.

"I'm so sorry," I reply genuinely. He's embarrassed, ashamed. And I can only imagine the self-doubt that someone would live with if their fiancé left them for their sibling.

"I didn't know he was your brother. He just said he knew the players. I just figured he was part of the team somehow." I step closer to him and reach around his shoulders, unhooking his stiff hands from his neck and placing them on my waist.

This is definitely crossing that line I drew out, but he's struggling. I can feel the hurt in his voice, and this is the only way I know how to comfort him.

Placing my hands over his face, I pull his nose down to meet mine. I'm engulfed by his familiar and comforting woodsy scent, mixed with the florals that surround us, and I can't stop myself from bringing his lips to mine. I know I shouldn't, but I want to make him feel better.

The agony he's feeling is like wildfire, spreading between the two of us, and this kiss is powerful enough to extinguish it.

I instantly melt into him as he pulls me in flush with his body. We swallow each other's moans as our tongues dance together in perfect rhythm with each other.

His hand trails up my arm and caresses my neck. Our kiss turns passionate as he palms my face, bringing us even closer together.

My heart and mind battle each other, and it's these moments that make me wonder if I could have both. The kind of relationship that allows for independence and a reliable comfort in someone else, without losing myself to that person. The kind of relationship that is highly improbable. The kind of relationship that scares the shit out of me because it increases my chances of turning out just like my mother.

His eyes are squeezed shut as I pull away, and I can feel him tense again. I press my nose back to his, telling him I'm not going anywhere and that I know he needs me right now.

"Take me home."

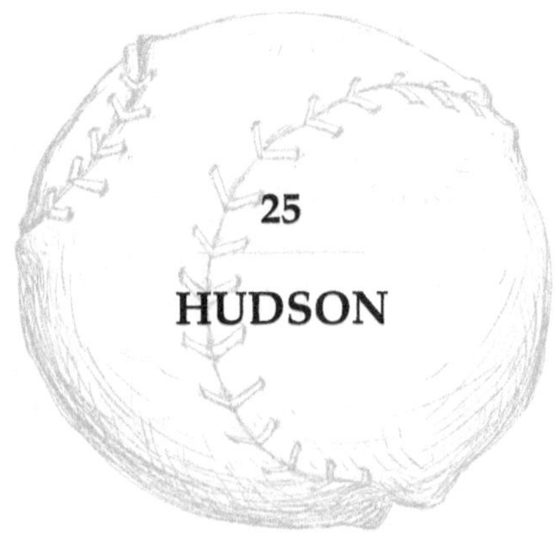

25

HUDSON

I haven't heard from my brother since we left the gala last week. I'm surprised, since he usually likes to instigate shit with me. I know he doesn't have Ember's contact information, and thankfully, Ember hates social media, so if he tries to find her, he won't be able to. Not easily, at least.

I'm probably overreacting, and I definitely overreacted when I saw him, but I couldn't help myself. The moment he came into view, standing next to her, it was like all the therapy I've done got tossed out the window and the only things that were left were rage and resentment.

That night, Ember comforted me in ways I didn't know she could. I think she surprised herself, too. She also opened up more than she wanted to because after, she shied away from me a little. Even though we didn't cross the friend line, other than that courtyard kiss that could have rivaled the most romantic movies, we went home together and she let me hold her, which I took advantage of, all night long.

She's definitely getting used to the idea of some kind of relationship, even though it's just an *arrangement,* in our case.

Maybe, that's just it. It's easier to view this as an agreement, and that makes it easier to disconnect.

Regardless, she has been opening up, and I'm thankful for that.

I've decided to let this continue to play out, in hopes she'll really see how great things could be before our time comes to an end. She can have everything she wants. And I want to give it to her.

The team leaves for our first stint of away games tonight, and I won't be back for almost two weeks. The schedule is going to get brutal from here on out. I'm excited to be traveling with the team, and this is an entirely different experience compared to the minors. I'm beyond excited to travel with the guys, play ball, and reclaim my worth, but can't say I'll miss my nights coming home to a certain redheaded siren. Especially Friday—my new favorite night of the week—designated as take out night, on which we always decide on pizza.

> Me: What are you up to, little red?

> Little Red: Thinking pizza alone sounds terrible.

> Me: That sounds a whole hell of a lot like, "I'll miss you, Hudson." :-)

> Little Red: Maybe ;) Sadly, I mentioned this to Cruz and he is trying to talk me into going out. Send help.

> Me: Good luck with that. No one stops him from getting what he wants.

> Little Red: I'm learning that about him.

Me: Still have your meeting with Elena today?

Little Red: I do, in 15 minutes. I'm so nervous.

Me: Don't be. It's a great idea, and she is going to love it.

Little Red: I hope so.

26

EMBER

Knock. Knock.

I tap my knuckles on the outside of Elena's door and look back at Cruz, who's giving me two thumbs up with a ridiculously large smile. Even with my nerves taking over all my bodily functions, I can't help but smile back at him.

"Come in," Elena calls out from somewhere behind her office door.

I take a deep breath and turn the handle, pushing it forward, and walk into her office.

"Good Afternoon," I announce with more confidence than I feel.

"Hey, Ember. How is everything going?" she returns with an ease I'm jealous of as she types on her keyboard.

"Great, it's really great," I reply. "Not only is this a dream job, but I'm learning so much from everyone."

"That's so great to hear." She closes her laptop and looks my way, giving me her full attention. "Cruz mentioned you had a couple ideas you wanted to run by me during our meeting today."

Damn him. He told her that in case I chickened out. Which has crossed my mind twice already since I walked in.

"Actually, yeah. I have some ideas that I thought might work in getting some more traction for XConnect. It's... unconventional. But, if we do it right, I think it could pay off."

A look of curiosity crosses over her face. "Really? Interesting. Tell me more."

I have been doing nothing but thinking of this idea for the last couple weeks, and the fact that she's giving me this chance to propose something new and different, I wanted to take it seriously. I open my portfolio and pull out two pieces of paper. One has a full floor plan mockup that I created, along with a detailed proposal, in a business plan format.

"We've run some surveys with our users, and there was a lot of feedback that people were hesitant to meet up because we have no way to truly scan for AI pictures or filtered pictures. Also, women are more and more reluctant to meet strangers these days. There are so many matchmaking platforms out there, and although our niche is a little more unique and aimed toward sexual pleasures, users are still hesitant."

She leans forward in her chair. "Okay, tell me what you're thinking. How do we combat that challenge?"

"Well..." clearing my throat, "I thought maybe we could bring a function to them. Sort of a set up meet and greet." I slide the floorplan sketch I made in front of her. The mockup has a full-scale club and bar, along with different rooms and areas in which people can meet. The layout is based on the layout of our website, directing our users to their desired kinks. Certain rooms designated for those who want to explore. I explain all of this in detail to Elena, referencing back to my business plan, detailed with membership programs, sign up options, and managing this event a couple of times a month.

"I feel like this may boost user engagement and allow for a safe space for people to meet. Member-only events, and we can theme them, depending on where we see the most traffic on the website." My mouth feels like quicksand as I swallow thickly, finishing my proposal.

"I know the cost of an on-site club is not ideal, clearly. But I think this will allow us to not only increase the base cost, but collect door fees as well. Also, if we're able to sell liquor, I have the liquor license permit process on that second page there, plus product sales at the venue. I truly believe it will pay itself off, and more importantly, promote our users to engage both in person and virtually. It's time we get our recent generations out from behind their computers and phones in a comfortable and safe environment."

She studies the plan; her eyes bounce between my business plan and side written notes, then the sketch. Back and forth.

I have no idea what she is thinking, and it's killing me.

"So, yeah, I thought it could be, XConnect - Unleashed Live or Live After Dark or even simply, XConnect - the club, some-thing catchy and—" She stands, straightening her blazer before grabbing the papers and rounding her desk.

"Follow me, please."

Shit.

I stand urgently, pacing her hurried steps. As we exit her office, I look over at a stunned Cruz. I shrug with raised eyebrows and continue following Elena.

There's only one office in this direction.

Christian Ford's office.

Double shit.

She knocks, an interesting patterned knock, and he quickly replies, "Come in."

Now, one of the things that Cruz shared with me, that some people know and some people think is rumored, is that, although Elena is married to Jake, they—as in her and her husband Jake—are also *with* Christian. I've never asked her about it, and I've only seen her and Mr. Ford in a business setting, where they were completely professional, but I do believe they live together. I'm so curious about it and would love to ask Elena about it one day.

"Ember has brought something to me that I felt you needed to urgently consider." She doesn't even say hi, she just bolts straight to his desk, placing the papers in front of him.

"Ember, please share with Christian what you shared with me." My eyes look between the two of them, and I swallow the boulder resting at the back of my throat before I go into the speech I practiced way too many times.

After I finish, a smirk crosses his face as he looks up at Elena then back to me.

"This is going to be incredibly costly," he responds. Which I knew. Why would we even consider doing something like this when you have an online platform and zero brick and mortar costs.

"I do realize that, sir. I truly feel like this can set us apart from the competition, and I do have a third leg to my business plan of renting out industrial space that will allow us to test this for a few months, like a pop-up event, before we—you—would invest in buying a building for it." My passion in this idea surpasses the nerves I feel, and not only do I sound confident, but I feel that way as well.

"I don't rent buildings, Mrs. Byrnes." The lopsided grin that rests on his face is one that tells me he knows my secret, which wouldn't surprise me, since Elena and Jake are aware of my situation. "I own far too many buildings that are doing way less than what this could potentially do. Elena, I assume you're on board with this?"

She looks my way, taking a momentary pause before looking back at Christian. "Yes, I think it's a great idea, and I think if anyone can put something like this together, she can."

Jesus, I thought I'd leave this meeting with tears of embarrassment at my idea, not tears from emotional destruction.

She believes in me. They believe in me.

"That's what I thought." The smile he returns to her is one that would burst my entire body into flames if Hudson looked at me that same way.

Christian steps out from behind his desk, and I have to take a minute to breathe. Not only from the high level of anxiety that I've been experiencing since the moment I stepped foot in Elena's office, but also from the power that exudes from Christian Ford. If what Cruz says about Elena and her relationship with both her husband, Jake, and Christian is true, wow. How does she handle them both? I was impressed with her from the moment I met her, but impressed is far beyond an understatement, at this point.

Christian stops a few feet shy of where I'm standing. He crosses his arms over his chest, then brings one hand to his face, wrapping it around his sharp jawline. He takes a moment to appraise me, and I surprisingly don't feel belittled or concerned. I feel ready. I believe in this proposal.

"The public won't see the perks of what we are offering for a venue like this. They will simply see it as us opening a sex club. I've been around long enough to know that some people in the community will eat us alive for pursuing something like this. There will be backlash, protesting. Also, we'll have nothing but red tape from the city regarding permits and approvals. Are you ready for something like that, Ember?"

I rise to my full height, standing taller. My chin automatically follows as I tip my head back to meet his gaze.

"I am."

"Good. Connect with Deitrich on security details for what we would need for a venue like this. Have Cruz start researching the existing floor plans to convert one of our downtown buildings."

Oh my god. They love it, and we're doing this.

Holy shit.

"Congratulations, Ember. This is a great idea, and you're taking the lead on this project. You'll get a commission of the sales for any event that we profit on. We'll work out those details later. For now, let's just get this ball rolling."

"Yes, sir," I reply, as I retreat from his office with a bounce in my step and a tenacious smile on my face. "Thank you, sir. I won't let you down."

I silently mouth a '*thank you*' to a beaming Elena as well before I exit his office and internally scream as I power walk to Cruz's desk and squeal out loud when I share the news with him.

"I freaking knew it! I knew they would love it. We really are going out tonight, because we have to celebrate."

I concede and agree because I couldn't be happier. The only thing that could make this better would be going home to share it with Hudson.

27

EMBER

"Okay, hold on. You've only had sex with two guys? In your entire life? And one of those guys is your husband?" Cruz asks me with a non-offensive judgment.

"Yes. So what? There is nothing wrong with that, Cruz!" I reply defensively, anyway.

"I am not saying that. My shock is coming from the fact that you are literally going to spearhead the opening of an actual sex club and you have hardly had any actual sex." He sips on his cocktail while giving me a smug side eye, because shit. He's right.

When I put that business plan together, it was easy for me to come up with the concept. That aspect of business and public relations comes so naturally to me. The floor plan took a little more energy, especially when I had to utilize the website as a guide for the sexual themes and kinks for the types of rooms I wanted to incorporate.

I did use Google, admittedly a little too much, in my research, and many of the topics definitely made me blush. But it also had me curious as well.

But Cruz is more than right. I can't do this without more experience. People are probably going to think I'm a joke, and I don't have the first clue about any of this. I mean, they won't know, right?

"Well, you're not wrong, but no one else needs to know that I don't have that much experience. This is a business venture, regardless of what kind of a club it is," I say with confidence. Fake it 'til you make it, right?

"No, E, no. Building out a sex club is different. The rooms need to be specific to very specific themes. The voyeur room needs all glass surrounding it, toys, certain things built into it. Maybe a spotlight and special lighting. The BDSM room should have restraints, other things that make it more ideal for doms and subs."

Clearly, Cruz knows a lot about this.

"I have you for that, don't I?" Plastering my most adorable smile at him.

"You are learning far too much from Elena, far too quickly, my friend," he says, which makes me happy to hear, since she's pretty much my idol. "Look, I can tell you all these things all day long. You are going to write it down in black and white and use that information like you studied it out of a textbook. You're wicked smart and super creative. But sex isn't black or white, there's a whole gray area out there that only hands-on experience can get you. You want to make this out of this world? You need true experience for that, girl."

Shit. He's right.

I'm totally in over my head. What was I thinking?

I don't know the first thing about any of this.

My shoulders deflate as I spin my drink around in circles on the bar table me and Cruz are sitting at. It's not far from the condo, which is a blessing because I am still relying on Uber when I can't get a ride from Cruz or Elena.

My parents offered to drive my car to Seattle then fly back

home, which I was shocked by. They were not supportive of my decision to stay here longer, especially long enough to need my car. In fact, during the first conversation, they berated me about Elliot and how *he* might feel. Insisted I wasn't seeing how selfish I've been. Which goes more in line with them always being more aware of his feelings than my own.

Either way, I was happy when my mom called back and offered to help. It will give me a chance to introduce Hudson to them before we fly back for the anniversary party, so it's easier when I drop the bomb that I'm permanently moving. Plus, saving me almost a week off to pick up my car is a godsend now that I have this project weighing on me.

The project that I'm now in full-blown panic mode over, thanks to my buddy Cruz here.

"Hey." Cruz slides his hand over my fidgeting ones, that continuously circle my glass on the tabletop. "You've got this. You just have to ask your faux husband for help."

I almost snap my own neck, whipping it in his direction. "You know?"

"Of course, I know. I know everything." He blinks excessively during his eye roll. "Faux or not, he can help. And why would you not want him to help you? Look at that man, all meaty and lickable."

"Cruz..." I whisper, like we shouldn't be talking about Hudson that way. But Cruz is totally on point... again.

"I'm serious, ask him. He'll help you."

My head falls into my hands as I ponder this idea. But who am I kidding? I'm going to need some sex lessons. Jesus, that sounds terrible.

"This is a really bad idea." My voice is muffled, trapped behind my palms.

"Oh, girl, you don't know me that well yet, but my ideas are always the best ideas."

An hour later, the alcohol is swimming through my body, making agreeing with Cruz far too easy and texting Hudson effortless.

> Me: I need to modify our arrangement.

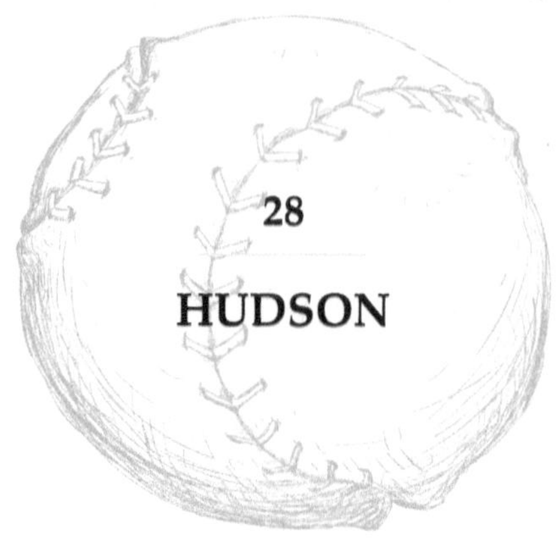

28

HUDSON

The nine games we played in the last twelve days were both exhilarating and exhausting. The minors schedule is not nearly as tiring. Also, the excitement of the press and crowd adds a whole other element.

It's been surreal.

We won all but one game, and Coach has been walking around with a pathetic, but contagious, grin permanently tattooed on his face. I've incorporated myself into the rotation, adding value to the team, and I've honestly never played better.

During the little off time I do have, I've thought about Ember. Not just her, but that text from two weeks ago that she's refused to elaborate on since.

Little Red: I need to modify our agreement

WHAT THE HELL does that mean?

When I first received that text, it was the middle of the

night, due to our time difference. So, when I finally responded, she was still sleeping. When she woke up the next day, she avoided the twenty questions I had to talk to me about it. I assume she had been drinking with Cruz and probably lost the courage to say anything more.

So, needless to say, I've been in a constant state of suffering since.

Modify it how?

So many ideas have flashed through my head about how she is wanting to modify it and all of them seem to end up with her gone and out of my life, and I have no clue as to how I've become so reliant on her presence. It's absolutely terrifying.

I pull into the garage and park in my designated spot. Ember's reserved spot next to it is still empty, due to her car still being in Missouri. She mentioned that her parents are driving it down and will arrive tomorrow with it. She also told me she was excited to get her car, but incredibly nervous about her parents being here.

What she has shared with me about them is not bad, per se. It just seems like they don't support her, or what she wants. They only support her when she makes her decisions based on what they want.

It'll be interesting to see how they react when she shares with them that, not only is she married, but she's working at one of the biggest companies in the U.S., and she's climbing the ladder faster than I can throw a baseball.

I'm so proud of everything she's accomplished in the short time she's been there. She told me that Christian and Elena liked her idea, but there were some stipulations that she was working on. Regardless, I know she'll work through those because she's made for this. Business, marketing, public relations. It all comes so naturally to her. And it's so goddamn sexy.

"Ember, you home?" I ask as I enter through the front door

because I didn't want to appear too needy and text her when I landed.

"Hey, in the kitchen," she yells back.

Hearing her voice makes the fluttering in my stomach go wild. How she can turn me into an excited teenager that easily is beyond me. Then her request and all the scenarios I have flash through my head, and my stomach is instantly a butterfly graveyard.

I turn the corner to the kitchen and see her pulling a pizza box out of the oven. She's dressed in leggings and an oversized Seattle Smashers shirt that's tied in a knot at her lower back. My—our—last name crosses over the back of it, and it takes everything in me not to claim her just like that shirt is.

Turning around to face me, an unavoidable smile crosses over my face at the sight of her. She smiles right back, biting her lower lip. "Hi, mister winning streak."

"You watched my games?" I ask as my eyes gaze into hers, and fuck, I've missed them.

"Of course, I did. I can't say you didn't scare the hell out of me when that guy came rounding third and your shortstop threw the ball to you just in time for him to barrel into you. I was yelling at the TV, cursing that guy to hell. But when the umpire called him out and you won the game, oh my god. I was screaming."

Her talking baseball does things to me that I have never felt before in my life. I might take her right here, right now, on this goddamn kitchen island.

"You should stop talking right now, because you recapping my baseball game is better than any dirty talk I can ever imagine. I'm not sure I'll be able to hold back." She tosses her head back and laughs and, Jesus, I've missed that, too.

"It's Friday," she replies, opening the pizza box she kept warm in the oven, steam rising from the inside, filling the room with the aroma of our Friday night favorite, which is just as comforting as the scent of her when I walked into the house.

I grab the box and head over to the couch, to continue our tradition. "Come on, little red. You have a lot of explaining to do."

"So, did they love your idea?" I ask, as I pull an olive off the slice of supreme pizza from the paper plate on my lap, tossing it into my mouth.

"Yeah, actually, they jumped on it immediately. They pretty much took any other responsibilities I had, dispersed them to others, and are having me spearhead opening this club."

I can't help but smile.

"It's been so crazy, Hudson. We've already located the building we are converting, applied for the permits, and hired contractors. I'm leading the marketing team to start putting this out there next week. It's all happening so fast; so much faster than I could have ever imagined. I guess that's what happens when you tell everyone your boss is Christian Ford."

"So, then, what are the stipulations you told me about?" That makes her pause.

"Well, it wasn't their stipulations, it was mine," she replies shyly.

"Does this have anything to do with the excruciating text message about modifying our agreement?" I ask.

Her head snaps my way. "Excruciating?" she repeats.

"Yes." I toss an olive at her. "About modifying our agreement and not telling me anything more for two long ass weeks." I half laugh, trying to keep it light.

"Well, I wanted to have the conversation in person." Her voice is light, too light.

Fuck.

I sit up, placing my plate on the coffee table in front of us.

"What's up?" I interlace my fingers together, placing my elbows on my legs, giving her my full attention.

"Well..." She sits up, sliding her plate on top of the closed pizza box, next to mine. Her fingers pinch her bottom lip, as if in deep thought. Then they move slightly, tugging on her top lip as she nibbles on the inside.

"Ember..." I pull her hand away from her face, keeping it held in mind. "Talk to me."

My heartbeat has kicked up a few notches. The pressure flowing through my veins rivals that of world famous geysers.

She's having a hard time verbalizing whatever is on her mind, and it's clearly been weighing on her.

"I..." She pauses, a long ass pause. Her lungs deflate with a long exhale that matches the descent of her shoulders. "I need sex lessons. I need you to give me sex lessons."

I physically choke on air.

Her wide eyes glare with concern for only a brief moment before they furrow in confusion.

After I catch my breath, I can't help but let out a chuckle.

"Don't laugh at me." She lets go of my hand.

"No, no. I almost died by choking on my own breath. I'm laughing at myself. But I can't say I'm not shocked." I reach for her hand again, pulling it close to me as I slide off the couch and place myself in front of her, so we're face to face.

I use my index finger to tilt her chin up, so her eyes meet mine. "Tell me more about these lessons."

The vulnerability in her eyes is like nothing I've seen. Ember has been a positive energy source, as powerful as the sun, since the moment I met her. Other than that moment on stage, where her nerves got the best of her, she's always been strong, confident, and assertive in what she wants.

"I mean, maybe not *lessons*, just experience. It's just... I know this could be a really great thing. This club. I feel it in my soul and down to the marrow of my bones. The business stuff I can do. I just need... help, in the other areas. I want to do it justice."

Jesus.

Her emotional mix of nerves and confidence marry each other in a way I've never seen before.

Could I *teach* her things about sex? Sure. Some things about certain sexual lifestyles I know enough about; the others we could figure out together. But spending the next, however long it takes, to get this building up and running, exploring her in ways no one else has.

Fuck.

This might destroy me. Just in time for her to leave me.

"I've only had one other partner, aside from you," she says.

Elliot.

An uncontrolled sound releases from my throat that sounds more like a territorial growl. It's unintentional, and I cover it up by clearing my throat before she continues.

"He hated oral sex—both ways." She tucks a loose strand behind her ear, biting nervously at the corner of her bottom lip. "He only liked to be on top, so when—"

"Mmhmm, I understand," I interrupt her so I don't need to continue to envision another man touching her, regardless of how bad it was.

Her eyes flicker up to me with a shy smile before returning her gaze back to her hands.

"So, my little red is going to open a sex club, but plot twist, hasn't had any sex."

"I've had sex," she counters back defensively.

"That wasn't sex." I lift from my kneeling position and wrap my hands around her hips, pulling her flush against me, crashing her lips to mine. She moans into my mouth, and I swallow the sound, claiming it just like I want to claim every-thing else about her.

Keeping my grip on her ass, I stand, and her legs naturally pretzel around me as I carry her into the bedroom.

"Lesson one starts now."

29

EMBER

Hudson carries me into the bedroom that now feels like a lion's den.

The moment I shared my request with him, curiosity and concern etched over his face, but it was quickly replaced with a lust I've only ever felt from him.

The sexual tension has always run naturally high between the two of us. There's no way either one of us can avoid it, but being away from each other for two weeks only poured gasoline on that already flaming inferno.

I feel it, he feels it, and I just gave this man free reign of all my sexual pleasures.

I can't say I regret that one bit.

He stops at the end of the bed and I unwrap myself from around him. Standing in front of him as he towers over me, my eyes trail up his chest, to his clenched jaw, as I see his tongue dart out to wet his lower lip. He stares at me behind hooded eyes, and his dark gaze turns every ounce of my body to liquid.

"I'm going to tease you, all night long, which will only be a sliver of the pain and suffering you put me through the last two weeks."

Okay, I might have some regrets.

Leaning down, he kisses me. His soft lips and gentle touch contradict the wildness behind his eyes. He steps back, one, two, three strides, and I instantly feel the glacial distance.

I stand there, as if on display, while he observes from a distance. His dark shadow is ominous in the corner and so goddamn seductive, I can't help but moan as pleasure begins to build in my core.

"Take off your clothes. Strip for me," his voice gravelly, somehow so desperate, yet so controlled.

And somehow, I easily comply.

I tuck my thumbs into the waistband of my leggings and bend forward, stepping out of them and kicking them aside. I reach behind my back to loosen the knot in my shirt, and when it splays open, I cross my arms over each other, reaching for the hem, and pull it over my head in one swoop, tossing it to the ground.

I stand there, exposed in the silence. Only the sound of my own breath can be heard until I see his silhouette move with a subtle zipping sound. He moves back another step, sitting down on the chair that's placed just a few feet from the bed. The moonlight shines through the small opening in the window, expertly casting light exactly where he is sitting.

He's watching me. His jeans splayed open at the center, hands on the armrest of the chair, stoic. Like a king, surveying his land.

"Touch yourself, Ember. Show me where you like to be touched."

Well, shit.

My pulse is racing, and I can feel my heartbeat in every corner of my body. Most prominently at the center of my core that causes my knees to buckle in where I'm standing.

I've never touched myself in front of anyone, ever. I get embarrassed touching myself when I'm alone.

I look down at my body, questioning everything we've talked about.

Questioning myself.

I can't do this. I can't even touch myself and feel comfortable. How am I supposed to talk to strangers or feel confident standing in—

"Ember, look at me." My eyes snap up to his, kicking myself out of the internal beating.

"Touch yourself with me." He pulls down the front of his boxers, exposing his hard cock. Wrapping his fingers around the tip, he strokes down the length as his hips pump up softly into his hand.

My jaw slacks into a small "o" as a gasp leaves my lips. My hips instantly match his movement, desperate for the same.

Jesus, how is that so sexy?

He pumps his hand over his length, slowly, twisting slightly as he reaches the tip.

My hand reaches up to my collarbone, my fingers digging into my own flesh, before it trails down to my hardened nipple. I moan as my fingertips graze the peak. They are so sensitive, shocks of ecstasy shotgun to my core.

I'm aching and wet, and not only do I want to please myself, but I want to please Hudson.

My eyes don't leave his, like I'm drawing strength from them.

I suck in a steady breath and sit back on the bed, then slowly spread my legs open.

A low animalistic growl comes from the voyeur in the corner, fueling my confidence.

I press my middle finger into my mouth, sucking it all the way down to the base of the knuckle, then trail my hand down my body until my fingertip slips between my slit, finding my hardened clit.

I whimper at the touch, biting my lip to keep my sounds reserved.

"Fuck." His moans vibrate through the air as if I can feel them on my body.

I don't know what I prefer, him watching me or me watching him.

He came home wearing his hat, which he removed after he set me down, so his hair is completely disheveled, matching the desperate rhythm in which he's stroking himself. His day-old shave is shadowed perfectly by the moonlight, highlighting his dark features.

I feel like his prey, and I'm desperate for it.

My finger brushes my clit at an agonizing pace. I toss my head back, unable to control the breathy moans. I keep going, stealing moments between staring at him and inspecting myself.

This is all so intimate and so... stimulating. I've never felt so nervous and excited at the same time.

"Oh, god..." My eyes are squeezed shut as the sensation of my building orgasm intensifies.

"Oh, no you don't." A loud thud causes my eyes to pop open in time to see Hudson rushing to me, hitting my hand away before I can come.

"What are you doing?" I say between heavy breaths.

"Sit on your hands," he says as his palms rest on the insides of my thighs, keeping my legs open.

"I don't want to." And the bastard just smiles.

"Sit on your hands, Ember."

I roll my eyes and listen, annoyed because I was so close.

"I told you, I'm not going to make this easy for you." He leans into me, placing a gentle kiss to my chin. His body lowers as his lips trail down my sternum. His tongue circles around my nipple expertly, avoiding the puckered tip as I gasp, shifting my chest, desperate for him to touch me there.

He continues down, his face parallel with my pussy, which provides me a bit of unease until he whispers, *"Beautiful,"* before blowing his warm breath over my center. The heat of his breath feels ice cold against my fevered pussy, and I jump at the sensation.

"Oh, fuck," I can't help but whine.

The pad of his finger grazes my clit; it's featherlight and excruciating. He stops, reaches up to softly pinch my nipple, and continues to alternate between these, teasing me, for minutes, hours, days.

"Please, Hudson," I beg. "Please."

He rises up from his kneeled position, meeting me face to face. "Now you know how desperate I've been for you." He presses his lips to mine, pulling my legs forward so our hips are flush together.

My wet pussy rubs against the underside of his cock that juts up to his abs, and I can't help but roll my hips against it.

"Fuck, that feels good," he groans, grabbing each side of my hips as I continue to rub over his cock. He's so thick and hard, and my body has a mind of its own, trying to take what it wants.

"I saw your birth control. Are you still taking it?" His voice is as desperate as my body.

I pull my bottom lip between my teeth and nod.

"Good. I want to feel all of you."

He leans back, placing his cock at my entrance. Pre-cum beads at the top, mixing with my arousal as he plunges into me, simultaneously pushing all the air out of my lungs. I gasp at the invasion. He feels so big, so perfect.

We moan in unison as he pistons in and out of me. My orgasm begins to build again. With each thrust, his cock gets harder, thicker, and it completely conquers me. "Hudson, it feels so good. It's never felt like this before," I whisper-whine, not understanding the sensations my body goes through when he's taking me like this, with nothing between us. It's foreign.

"This is exactly how you belong, little red. Raw, wet, and desperate for me, with my cum dripping down your leg and my name on your tongue."

Jesus, he's so dirty, and it turns me on even more.

My body and mind battle each other for sanity and control.

It's all encompassing and everything begins to mesh together.

"Hudson..." I gasp, squeezing my eyes shut as my fingers bite into his shoulders, and I erupt around him.

"That's my good girl. Come on my cock," he continues at a flawless rhythm. His breathing is rough and labored, and his cock grows impossibly hard.

I want to make him lose control, like I do when I'm with him. Make him desperate and begging for it.

I cup my hands over his jaw and gaze into his eyes. They're dark and wild, and just as desperate as I am.

"I want to feel you come inside me." I brave the words, because that's exactly what I want. His eyes flicker quickly as his lips part.

"Oh, fuck, Ember." His cock twitches then throbs inside of me, another foreign sensation that makes me feel... everything.

He leans forward, his arms on either side of my open legs, using any strength he has to hold himself up as his forehead meets my shoulder.

"I was holding out fine until you fucking said that. Why did you say that?" I giggle at the discovery that he likes my dirty talk as much as I like his.

I just shrug, the shyness overpowering me.

He lifts his head, his gaze searing through me with a fierceness I've only ever felt from him.

"We're going to discover all your kinks, my dirty girl, and I'm going to explore every inch of this gorgeous body while we do."

And I have a feeling he's going to completely ruin me in the process.

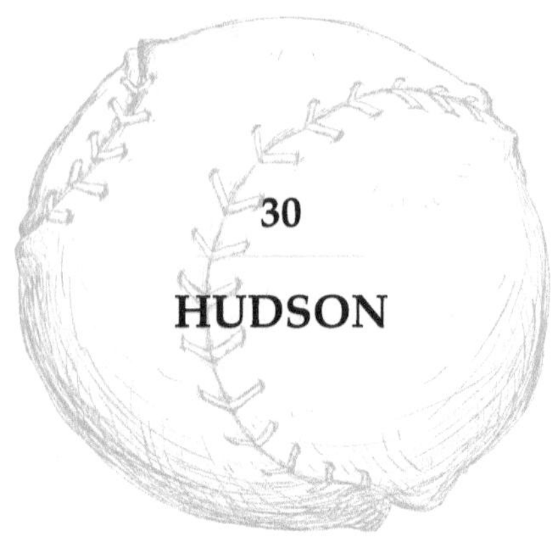

30

HUDSON

I enter the kitchen, where Ember sits at the table, going through her work notes. She sorts through some paperwork between typing on her laptop, with a piece of toast hanging out of her mouth. If she's not physically working on something for XConnect, she's researching something related to it.

She is the most hard-working, dedicated person I've ever met.

It's sexy as hell.

She's so focused she doesn't even hear me enter the kitchen while she plugs away, nibbling at her breakfast, but paying more attention to her work than her food.

I had only been gone for two weeks, but it felt longer—not only in time, but in the subtle changes that are shining through her. She's more confident, something that I think has to do with Elena, Cruz, and her current project. Maybe she's got a little glow from last night; I'd like to think it has something to do with me, too.

She has also lost a few pounds. Not much, but enough for me to notice, because hell, I notice everything about her.

I see now that she gets so involved in work, hyper-focused on whatever she is working on, that her food ends up just sitting there, and she probably skips way too many meals.

I can handle her dedication to her career, but not at the expense of her health.

"Your breakfast is getting cold," I remind her of the lone plate that's been pushed to the side.

"Oh, yeah. Thanks." She picks up her fork, stabbing a tiny strawberry, eats it, then returns the fork, and pushes the plate even further away.

A subconscious habit I'm going to have to break out of her.

Pouring myself a cup of coffee, I take a few sips, observing her before I slide into the seat next to her, placing my laptop on the table.

"Do you have a few minutes to research some other things?" I push my closed laptop closer to her and she eyes it suspiciously.

"Sure, like what?" she asks, glancing at me before shutting down her laptop.

"Open it up." I tip my chin at my computer.

Her brows furrow, and she gives me a curious look. Reaching for the device, she pulls it in front of her and opens the screen.

"Oh... my." Her voice a breathy whisper.

I smile as I watch her eyes bouncing between the sections of the screen. I observe deeply when she stops on one side, biting her lip, and her cheeks flush a bright shade of pink.

"Which one caught your attention?" But I already know the answer based on where her eyes are stalled.

I took the time this morning to pull up different videos with an array of kinks, things that I thought might interest her. Using a new window and placing each of them on different areas of the screen. I was curious as to the one that would catch her attention first and, as I guessed, her eyes zero'd exactly where I thought they would—the top left-hand side of the screen.

The night we spent together, after I steered her away from that shitty hotel she was trying to stay at, she took charge in a way I had never experienced with another woman. It was euphoric, seeing her take charge like she does in life, with how she dives into projects, her job, and anything else she puts her mind to.

I assumed lack of sexual experience caused her to shy away from doing more of what she desired, but I think nerves got the best of her, so she refrained from being open about what she really wanted.

So, I strategically placed a video of a woman blindfolded and tied to a bed in complete submission to a man who is clearly dominating her. Another video is the exact opposite. A man, blindfolded, restrained, allowing the woman to be in full control.

As I suspected, her head tilts to inspect the subdued man. Avoiding the submissive woman like it's the plague, she leans closer to the blindfolded man, angling her view as she appraises the stilled clip.

My lips lift up in a smirk at my observation and her blushing as she bites her lip.

Reaching over the keyboard, I tap the spacebar, and the video begins to play. She flinches back with a gasp as the woman crawls over her lover, caressing him softly at first, then wraps her hand around his cock and begins stroking and jerking as her lips lick the swollen tip.

My body has a mind of its own when I stand and step behind her. My hands rub up the sides of her arms and the touch rips her out of her trance. She stands, panicked, picks up her coffee mug, and walks around the kitchen island, setting her mug in the sink. She misjudges the depth, and the mug drops aggressively onto the steel, clanging against the ceramic.

"Shit!" she curses.

"Hey." I follow behind her.

She turns around to face me, her shoulders back, faking a confidence that doesn't match the flush in her cheeks.

"I wasn't... I wasn't looking at that one." She's trying to convince herself more than me.

"Yes, you were." I place my hand under the hem of her top, grazing my fingers over the soft skin of her stomach, wrapping my arm around her back and pulling her hips to mine.

She whimpers, feeling the hardness of my length against her belly button.

"But guys don't like that. They like to be in charge." She refuses to look at me, only allowing her gaze to protrude downward, in a shame that she shouldn't feel.

It didn't take long for me to realize she was sheltered her entire life, but I didn't realize until now how debilitating it has made her feel. The glass ceiling she was raised in is built of fortified metal and stone, and I have every intention of breaking it the fuck apart.

Tipping up her chin, I force her to look at me.

Our eyes sear into each other. The burning desire behind hers fuels mine.

"That guy doesn't." I angle her chin toward the video playing behind me. I can't see the man, but I can hear him. Boy, can I hear him. He's close, desperate, begging.

Her eyes flutter with her heavy breath, hearing the guttural, anguished sounds coming from the tiny speakers thunderously filling the silence between us.

"*You* like control." Her eyes wholly focused on the wretched man.

"I'd give it up for you." I trail my hand down her chest, over her pebbled nipples, and dip my fingers into her loose cotton shorts. Her arousal coats my fingers instantly, and we moan in unison.

I need more of her. God, I'm desperate for her, as much as that man in the video is desperate for the release his lover has withheld from him.

I switch places with Ember, placing her back against my chest. My body leans against the counter as I circle my arms around her and slide my fingers over her slit.

We can both see the screen. The man's hands are still tied to the bed, his lover edging him to the peak of his climax before stopping. He's begging, whining, and asking for release.

Ember grips me tightly, one hand clenching around my pant leg, her other around the back of my neck, holding on for dear life.

Her moans grow louder with his. It doesn't take a genius to see how much she likes to please more than be pleased herself. She can't take her eyes off him, and I can't take my eyes off her.

Would I give up control for her? Let her do whatever the hell comes to that gorgeous mind of hers?

Fuck, yes.

His moaning stops, and I glance up to find the woman walking around the bed, grabbing something from offscreen, then appearing again at the end of the bed. Ember's hips are rolling into my hand as she moans, my moans echoing her own. My hips dance with hers subconsciously, my cock needing something, anything.

The woman kneels onto the bed, placing herself between the man's legs. Pressing one hand to the inside of his thigh, his legs open, and a shiny plug appears in the palm of her other hand. My eyes are a permanent fixture on the blinded man. His eyes may be covered, but he knows damn well what's coming.

I should have done a better job of screening the fucking video, given the fact that I just told Ember I'd give up control for her. I've never had a plug up my ass, so I'm not quite sure how I, or she, feel about that.

It takes milliseconds to figure it out, when Ember's lips part and she whimpers along with the man as the plug invades the forbidden space.

I freeze, trying to focus on him—her—my own shocked response to the sexual act, which is surprisingly a whirlwind of sensation pooling at the base of my spine, ready to explode when Ember whispers, "Please, don't stop."

She tosses her head back against my chest as she moans through an explosive orgasm, timed perfectly with his.

Jesus, fuck.

That was hotter than I expected.

My cock is rock hard, and I need her. I need her so fucking bad.

Flipping her around, I grip her waist and lift her on top of the island. Pulling down the front of my sweatpants, my cock springs out and she reaches for it on instinct. Her delicate fingers wrap around the base, and she strokes her hand to the tip, feeling my hardened length under the soft skin, forcing a grunt from me of an immeasurable tone.

She feels so good. Everything she does feels so good.

I'm staring into her blazing green diamond eyes, that are as hooded as mine, and I'm desperate to taste her. Before I can crush my lips to hers, the ringing from our front door intercom chastises me, stopping both of us.

"Fuck," I whisper, leaning my forehead against hers, still unable to stop a smile from lifting at the side of my lips at the fact that she's opening up to me, that I get any part of her for even a tiny bit.

"Don't move." I kiss the tip of her nose, pull the waistband of my pants up, and walk to the intercom.

"Hello." I press the intercom button to the lobby desk.

"Mr. Byrnes, sir. There is someone here to see Mrs. Byrnes. He provided the name Robert Riley, which Mrs. Byrnes gave us yesterday, but upon checking his ID, it actually says Elliot Jones."

Giving myself a mini whiplash, I turn to look at Ember. Her widened eyes and suddenly pale face tell me she is just as shocked as I am to hear that.

She jumps off the counter, grabbing her zip up sweater laying over the top of the couch, and slips on her flip flops.

"I'll be right back." She reaches for the handle of the front door.

I place my hand over hers. "I'll come with you."

"No, I can handle this." She smiles. It's soft, unsure.

The worry behind her eyes is like a goddamn trumpet and just as chaotic as the music it makes. I'm confident she can handle it. I'm not confident she won't become a verbal punching bag in the process.

I purse my lips and allow my hand to slide off hers. "Okay."

31

EMBER

The rampant thoughts of bewilderment roll through me as fast as this elevator's descent. What the hell is he doing here? And where the hell are my parents?

With a ding, the doors glide open gracefully, and I step into the pristine lobby. The modern marble flooring and all white everything makes this place feel like pure luxury, which I am certain Elliot was not expecting.

I round the corner, where bright orange couches contrast the white walls against the black and white abstract art. Elliot stands in the center like an eyesore, completely out of place.

He turns, relief washing over him when he sees me, like I'm here against my will.

"What are *you* doing here?" My tone is far more aggressive than I intend, but I don't care.

"What are you doing *here*?" he repeats, waving his hand in big circles as a reference to this specific building.

"I don't have to answer you when you shouldn't even be here, Elliot. My parents told me they were dropping off my car. I should have known not to expect them to go out of their way for me, and send you here instead." The hurt I'm feeling comes out as anger. They couldn't do this for me. This one thing. Instead, they sent Elliot as a replacement, like they always have over the years. And his loyalty to them clearly outshines his loyalty to me. He didn't bother to text me or tell me what their plan was. He just went in on it with them.

"I came here for you. Because I wanted to see you, baby." He reaches for my hand, but I step back, out of his reach.

"Elliot, we broke up." I shouldn't have to remind him of the last time we saw each other.

"Em, you needed time. That's all."

The way he disregards me is just a subtle reminder of the way he treated me, always telling me what I needed.

He clears his throat, hesitating for a moment. "You're the only woman I want, and it doesn't make sense for us to be with anyone else. Your father needs this."

I can't help but cock my head at him in disgust. My father needs this. I spent most of my adult life with a guy because my parents wanted me to. I've never had a choice.

He continues, which is weird considering my facial expression is completely uninterested in whatever else he has to say, "We've been together forever, Em. You just got scared. I've given you space. I haven't called or texted you. We let you put yourself through school. Then all of a sudden you needed time," the air quotes with an eye roll, "and we gave that to you. What else do you want?"

He doesn't miss a beat in shaming me, probably following the Robert Riley manual of *how to make an obedient woman*. He discredits my goals and dreams, just like my parents always have. It makes me want to scream and rip out my own hair. Why does everyone feel like they know more about what I want than I do?

"Elliot, you've always chosen my parents over me. And right now, finally, I'm choosing me over everyone else. Call me selfish, I don't care. I told you that when you proposed and embarrassed me in front of everyone. I told you not to do that, and you did it, anyway."

He proposed in a way that wasn't a question. It was a command, a statement. Not giving me a voice, a choice, or an option, and everyone screamed and cheered before I could even open my mouth to respond. He proposed in public so I couldn't reject him, sliding the ring on my finger in front of everyone while I remained mute and stone cold. The ring felt like a jail around my soul the moment it glided past my knuckle.

Nothing like the exhilaration I felt when Hudson gave me his.

"Ember, you love me. You just felt confused. It's normal." He continues to push.

"I met someone," I reply in a whisper. Not because I'm ashamed, but because I don't want to be cruel.

"Yeah, your parents mentioned you've been staying with a friend, but I know you, Em. You just told them that so you could get away. You forget how well I know you, baby. You just needed time, but time's up." He takes a step toward me. "It's time to come home."

"She is home." Hudson's deep gravelly voice thunders through my body from behind me.

"Who are you?" Elliot tips his head to look behind me, although Hudson's colossal force is unavoidable in the now crowded space.

"Hudson Byrnes. Ember's husband." He stands next to me, and instead of wrapping his arm around my shoulder in ownership, his hand reaches down to my side, interlacing his fingers through mine, giving me both my own power and his strength at the same time.

Elliot's face falls. To the floor. Hard. He blinks, confused.

I feel... bad. I don't want to hurt him. He doesn't mean to

hurt me. He just has no idea how to let me have a voice of my own. He never has.

"Em..." He looks back at me, then down to my hand that reveals the two-carat emerald-cut diamond on the same finger he tried to claim. But not for himself, not for me, and certainly not for love. For him, it's ownership and image, all for the benefit of my father.

"Thanks for bringing her car. Do you need a ride to the airport?" Hudson asks, ending this unwelcome reunion.

"N-No..." His eyes glaring between me, Hudson, and the door. "No, I'm good." His voice decibels softer than ever before.

He steps forward, dangling the keys from his pointer finger before dropping them in my outstretched hand.

"So, I'll see ya, then?" He pauses, like I could possibly change my mind and step to his side.

"Bye, Elliot." I squeeze Hudson's hand. A silent thank you for helping me.

We watch Elliot retreat a few steps before turning around, giving us his back, and walking through the glass doors of the lobby onto the sidewalk and out of view.

I breathe for what feels like the first time since I stepped out of the elevators.

Realization hits me. It's not the first time, but the first time it sinks in to my core like an immovable root.

My parents truly don't give a shit about anything that has to do with any choice I want to make for myself. I thought maybe they just wanted to insist they think they know what's best for me, but it's deeper than that. They don't have any faith in me. Who I am. My choices.

And they don't care.

My heart feels like it's breaking, tearing into miniature fragments of dust that can never be repaired.

No matter what I do, I will never be good enough for them.

32

HUDSON

"Hudson, stop by my office before you head out, will you?"

"Will do, Coach," I reply, as I finish tying my shoe.

I remove my AirPods from my ears, which are currently blaring my pre and post music playlist, consisting of Green Day's entire arsenal of songs. I've done that my entire baseball career, and even though we don't win all the games, it seems to be my superstition, guaranteeing me an injury free game. Which is always a win.

Our team has been slaughtering it lately. We're on a winning streak, and it's a relief knowing that, not only am I contributing, but I'm a big factor in the standings with the teammates I've been lucky enough to play with.

Callahan and I can easily predict each other's moves on the field, like a color-coded chess board that only he and I can see. I know exactly what options we have, what direction we can go, and we're both headed on the same path every time. I've played with a lot of different people in my career, and he's been the easiest to fall into rhythm with. Other than my brother, of course. Which undoubtedly—regardless of our strained relationship—we somehow played like twin souls. We were practically unstoppable on the field.

"Good game, Burnsy." Callahan reaches his fist out. I bump it as I stand from the bench in front of my locker.

"You, too, man. You killed it today. How's your shoulder holding up?" I ask, as he holds the back of his arm, waving it around in a large circle.

"Great. At least my brain likes to think so. My body, that's a whole other story." He chuckles. "It's been a good run, and I love that I'm going out this year with a bang, thanks to you."

"Nah, it's teamwork. So, you're really going to wimp out on me, huh? You can stick it out for another, I don't know, five years, can't you?" I give him shit because I don't want him to leave, even though I know it's his time.

"Hell no, man. I'm going out on top." He pats my shoulder and heads out of the locker room. He's been pretty quiet about retiring, and I think, as much as he knows he needs to, he's not ready to accept it. When all you've ever done your whole life is one thing, then one day it's gone, who the hell are you anymore?

I can imagine the identity crisis he is feeling. I had a small taste of it after I was injured, and that made me hit rock bottom, even with the small hope that I could come back.

Grabbing my bag, I unscrew the lid of my protein shake and finish the rest before throwing it into the recycle bin on my way out of the locker room.

Coach Raymer's office is down the hall, but his door is closed, which is unusual.

I come to a halt in front of it, hearing muffled voices.

Tapping my knuckles on the thick wooden door, the chatter fades and Coach Raymer calls out, "Come in."

The shock that hits me as I open Coach's door halts me mid-step. My eyes meet Henry's, who is peering back at me over his shoulder as he sits across from Coach Raymer's desk, the same way I did the day I first met him.

Mine full of confusion, his full of confidence and excitement.

The panic spreads from my torso to the outstretches of my entire body, arriving at my trembling fingers and sandpaper throat at the same time. The worry and anger battle each other for a moment as I look between my brother and my coach.

"Hudson, come in." I look at my hand, still on the doorknob, and at my surroundings, realizing the invisible brick wall physically stopped me from stepping further into his office.

I step to the side and close the door, but stay planted where I'm at.

"Hey, brother, good game." He stands, walking toward me, holding out his hand in a high five handshake, and for the sake of appearances, I hold mine out. He slaps our palms together and pulls me in for a bro hug, patting me on the shoulder. I quickly step away from him and walk into the office to stand in front of Coach's desk.

"You asked to see me, sir?"

"I figured you knew your brother was here, considering he's going to be a free agent next year, and I'm looking for a replacement for Callahan next season." He looks between the two of us, sensing the tension. How can he not?

I knew the reason he was here the moment I saw him. I just didn't want to accept it, say it, or even consider that as a possibility. But Coach already is.

Coach continues, "The Byrnes brothers back together again. Wouldn't that be a match made in heaven?"

Hell. It would be hell.

"We were the best of the best, sir, back in our day. Man, it was a sight. Wasn't it, Hud?" Henry steps to my side, patting my shoulder again like a condescending asshole.

"That was a long time ago." My voice comes out dry.

"Well..." Coach clears his throat. "I just wanted to give you guys a moment to catch up before Henry flew back home. He's got a game tomorrow, so he wasn't staying long."

He never does, just comes barreling into my life, throwing my world upside down so I can drown in the shitstorm of emotions he brings out of me before leaving again.

"Have a good flight, Henry. I'll see you tomorrow, Coach." My reply is robotic at best. I've been programmed from years of unpredictable behavior from my brother. My entire body shuts down the moment I'm in the same space as him.

"Hold tight outside for me for a minute, Hudson, while I finish up here." I simply nod at him, then look over at Henry. I tip my chin up with a silent goodbye and half acknowledgement, hating that I have to do even that.

And waiting outside his office is just as painful. Is he making a deal with him? Is he really considering him for our team? *My* team. It's only a few months into the season, but we are a family now.

That reminds me of our trip next month to meet Ember's family. She's been even more stressed about it since Elliot showed up. To my surprise, she didn't talk to her parents about why they sent Elliot instead of coming themselves. She completely ignored the whole situation. I don't know why she stayed quiet instead of standing up for herself like she did with Elliot. Clearly, it's deeper than I realize. But so is the situation with me and Henry that I hardly speak about.

Finally, he steps out of the office, and Coach steps through the doorway, calling my name. It feels like he's leaving the principal's office at school and I'm the next one to get called in. I ignore him and keep my gaze on Coach as he steps back into his office.

I follow him in, shutting the door behind me, and he wastes no time.

"What's the deal with you guys?" Coach Raymer asks.

"Nothing." Literally nothing. We have no deal. No relationship. Nothing. He lost those rights a long time ago. And he ruined it time and time again, every time I gave him the benefit of the doubt.

"That wasn't nothing, Burnsy," he replies, and rightfully so.

"We haven't been the same, sir. Since everything happened."

"It was an accident, right?" he asks.

He doesn't know about Henry's engagement to my ex-fiancé. At least that wasn't all that public because we were so young back then. It was before Henry was the star professional player he is now. So I know he's talking about my injury.

I STARE BACK *at Henry on the pitcher's mound. We're up one run at the bottom of the ninth, and we can't risk anyone else getting on base. Our Coach almost took Henry out of the game after that double, but thankfully, I just stopped Leach from coming into home base with the last hit. Now we just have one player on second and we need another out.*

I eye him in a silent understanding. We both know what needs to happen. Reynolds is coming up to bat. Reynolds is calculated; he needs his pitches slow and steady. His reaction time is not as great as others, but he packs a power punch when he does nail it. I call out to Henry for a high fastball. We both know he needs to go top right because Reynolds doesn't hug his bat close to his body as he should. A high fastball will make him swing, but he'll miss.

I crouch down and call it out with my fingers, my mitt strategically placed exactly where I know Henry is throwing.

Henry stands tall, bringing his mitt to his pitching hand, looks over his shoulder at second base, then back to me. He shakes his head and his hand peers over his mitt, just barely enough for me to see his pointer finger and middle finger, separated, splayed over the top of the baseball.

Wait. Why is he holding it that way? That's not his fast-pitch grip.

He lifts his leg, whipping it up quickly before circling his shoulder and ripping the ball through the air. His stance is all off.

My reaction time is slow. The ball cannons through the air between the mound and home base. It flies like lightning, and I'm still thrown off by the moments before his pitch.

Before I can register, Reynolds is swinging. The ball misses both his bat and my mitt as it soars between us, crashing into my ankle, forcing me to fall backward as my entire body explodes in pain.

"Hudson?" Coach calls me back into the room.

"Honestly, sir. I don't know. I called a fastball. He threw a curveball. I wasn't ready. I should have been ready." I dip my chin, ashamed of myself, because I blame myself. I've always blamed myself.

"Pitchers aren't always able to throw perfectly," he replies.

"I know, Coach." His reply sounds like the broken record I've heard from everyone over the years. Placating me and protecting him. "I just don't know that I can trust him."

"Trust him, or trust yourself as a catcher with him?"

"Both, sir," I reply honestly.

He just nods.

"Great game today. I'll see you tomorrow."

And I'm excused.

I leave urgently, heading straight to my truck. The game is long over and most of the people have left the stadium. Only a few reporters linger outside. I never need to drive to the stadium, considering we all live across the street, but our tinted windows allow us some privacy and protection as we leave the stadium. I pull out of the garage, into the street, then turn quickly into our condo garage, parking in my normal spot.

Fuck.

Fuck.

Henry being a free agent next season allows any team that can afford him to offer him a contract. I can't imagine New York letting him go, but Henry plays hard-to-get really well, and he'll make any team he's considering battle it out for top dollar.

He doesn't want to play for Seattle, and his motivation is purely to make my life hell. And I still, to this day, have no idea why my brother goes out of his way to do that.

As I exit the truck, my lungs expand fully, taking in much needed air that's been restricted since the moment I saw Henry.

I was so lost in my own thoughts I didn't see Ember sitting in her car. She must have pulled up right before me.

"Hey." She exits her car, shutting her door behind her.

"Hey." I smile, because I can't not smile.

"You okay?" she asks, because she's gotten to know me far better than I ever expected.

"Perfect, now." I wrap my hand around the nape of her neck and pull her lips to mine. Her touch abolishes the stress, the worry, the anxiety. It evaporates everything except my desire for her and the smile behind my kiss.

Everything is perfect now.

"Good, because I met with the wholesale vendor for all the... products, err—accessories," a hint of uncertainty in her voice and a furrow in her brow as she tries to find the proper word to describe sex toys, "to purchase for the club, and I have a ton of questions."

She pops the trunk, and I peer inside to see a huge box of different styles of sex toys. Dildos, vibrators, whips, cuffs. An array of colors, textures, and designs.

My brows take up all the space on my forehead, and I'm quite speechless.

"The construction will be finished by the end of next week. I'll need to tell her what we need for each room by then."

Speechless no more.

"Well, looks like we have some homework, little red."

33

HUDSON

"What the hell is this?" Ember asks with more excitement than I've ever seen. I barely placed the box on the bed before she opened the top and pulled out an all black, rubber toy with about a half foot of ropey looking balls over its length and a really stretchy circular section at the top.

My eyes bulge out of my head at the realization that it's a scorpion tail cock ring.

She's whipping it around, placing the length of it through the cock ring and pulling it together like it's some kind of rubber rope tie.

She's so focused she doesn't realize she's eyeing the damn thing like a Rubix cube, and her tongue is slightly peering out over her bottom lip; she bites on it as deep as she's concentrating.

I chuckle to myself, palming my face.

I realize instantly the rubber texture is deceiving when it hits the back side of my hand and whips the other side of my face, before it hits the floor with a thud.

"Please tell me that slipped and you didn't throw a sex toy at my face." I look at her completely dumbfounded.

"Don't laugh at me." There's a shy smile behind her accusation.

I hold my hands out. "No, God, no. I'm laughing because you probably think that toy is for you." I point at it, still taking its place on the floor, where it probably belongs. Well, there or in the furthest depths of hell, I haven't decided yet.

She eyes it with a furrow in her brow as she tries to consider what else it could be for.

I bend down and grab it by the tail, my attempt to alpha this device into submission, which is not possible considering what it could do to me.

"This," I pull on the circle section and stretch it wide, "is a cock ring. It goes around the man's cock and over the balls to restrict blood flow."

"Oh my god, wouldn't that hurt? Why would you do that?"

I chuckle. "I wouldn't do that. You would do that... to me." She pulls her bottom lip into between her teeth.

"And this..." holding the cock ring in place, I pull the tail back and under, "would go... well, up the butt. My butt." I hit the button at the base of the tail and the damn thing starts vibrating. Of course it vibrates.

She releases that damn gorgeous lip she was biting and it forms a small "O".

"Have you ever, um..."

"No, to either," I reply quickly to avoid her having to ask. "You use a cock ring to make yourself harder, bigger."

"Well... you don't *need* that."

Now it's my turn to blush, then all the blood flow goes straight to my cock.

"I don't need it, but do you want it?" I ask, taking a step toward her.

She steps back.

I take another step.

The flush in her cheeks tells me yes. But I know she'll never ask for it.

"I mean, for research purposes. We might have to, you know, see if it works," I add.

I have a hard time hiding my smile. I haven't ever wanted to use a cock ring, and I have never had anything up my ass. I can't say I've ever gone out of my way to try it or fantasized about it, but I'm not against it, either. Not for her.

"I mean, you're right. We definitely need to find the best products for the club. I could make you an honorary member for your service." The playfulness behind her eyes is fucking addicting, especially with lust swimming in them.

Okay, she likes to joke when nervous. Noted.

I reach behind my neck, pulling my shirt off, and I push down the waistband of my joggers, leaving me only in my boxers.

I couldn't be happier that I showered at the stadium after the game and I don't need to ruin the moment by stopping where we're going. I can tell she's nervous, but I want her to take the role she wants, which I know holds more dominance than she has the confidence for right now.

She wore a loose flowy baby pink dress today and she looks fucking gorgeous, but I need to see her. Maybe that's my own need for comfort speaking.

I reach behind her and pull the zipper all the way down to her low back. It falls and pools at her feet, leaving her in just a black bra and black lace panties and those goddamn high heels. With her high, tight ponytail, it instantly gives her a dominating look without even trying.

How she goes from innocent to filthy in a matter of seconds, I have no idea.

"Lie back," she whispers, biting her lip.

There's my girl.

My cock swells instantly.

I sit down on the bed, pressing into it, and pull myself back to lie flat on the bed. My cock is surprisingly—and not surprisingly—hard. Very hard.

I don't know if it's because I know what's going to take place and I'm more excited than I realize or because it's just what Ember does to me.

She grabs lube from inside the box, ripping the plastic seal at the top before popping it open.

"You want the cock ring to stay in place, so don't use too much lube on the ring, just enough to get it on and off." She nods, that bottom lips still tucked in her teeth.

"But lube the hell out of the bottom part." She giggles and lifts her eyes to mine. Fuck, the desire licking through them is burning through me.

"I may have watched a video or two on this. Well, not with this thing." She waves the scorpion tail around in a circle. "The woman I watched used a dildo. I got through most of it before I had to make myself come." Another shy smirk crosses her gorgeous face, and I'm realizing I like this more powerful and assertive Ember.

The thought of her masturbating to this. Let's just say I don't need the cock ring to help retain the blood flow to that area.

She grabs a small towel before placing her knees on the end of the bed, crawling next to me. The anxiety builds as she gets closer, but she places the toy down on the towel, then uses her fingernails to trace the tattoos over my arm and chest.

"Did you know, I love these?" she states, eyeing the ink over my body.

I didn't know that, but now I will cover every fucking inch of myself in them if she loves them so much.

Her fingers trail down my upper leg and back up, over my

hips and pelvic bone, just under my belly button, making rounds over and over again.

She's a goddamn tease, and it feels incredible.

She places herself between my legs and leans down, licking the pre-cum off the tip of my cock.

"Mmmm, I love that, too." She is going to be the death of me.

Opening her mouth, she takes my cock over her tongue and sucks, taking me to the back of her throat, bobbing up and down.

"You look perfect on your knees with my cock in your mouth." My words encourage her, and she takes me even deeper, forcing another groan out of me. The heat of her mouth engulfs me completely.

How she can make me feel so weak so quickly is something I'll never understand.

She continues to move up and down on my cock, taking as much of my length as she can, and keeps going for what feels like a goddamn hour. My moans are closer together, heavier. My breath is labored, and I won't tell her to stop, but I don't know how much longer I can hold out.

I don't need to say anything because she can easily read me, so she stops, just holding the tip of my cock in her mouth, and I whine at the edging. Needing more, but not wanting it to stop at the same time.

"Jesus," I grunt, gripping the bed sheets because I was so close. "You're a goddamn tease." I stare up at the ceiling, squeezing my eyes closed.

I feel a rush of cold air hit my engorged crown as she releases it from her mouth, then just as urgently, the tightness and pressure fill my cock as she places the ring over it, landing at the base, then pulls the rest over my balls.

"Oh... fuck." The pressure is insane. Not painful, but not

pleasurable, just there. I can feel how hard my cock is, and Christ, it's throbbing.

She wraps her lips back around the tip, licking at the thinned, hardened crown, and I look down to see her watching me, her eyes full of hunger and unrelenting desire.

I tense at the sensation of her finger rubbing over my back hole. It's wet and soft, and I can't decipher everything I'm feeling, due to the sensory overload. Her finger pierces through the tight ring, and she reminds me to breathe, so I inhale deeply, forcing myself to relax.

As I requested, she lubed everything really well, so her finger slips in with just a little pressure, and it feels... good. Way too good, actually. I moan through the intrusion, louder than I'd like to admit.

She sits back, watching as her finger thrusts in and out of me. Her nipples look like diamonds piercing through her bra and her jade eyes dark with curiosity, and so goddamn beautiful.

Pre-cum leaks out of my incredibly hard cock. It drips down the side, and she leans down to lap it up, like she needs it to survive.

"Ember, please let me do something to you." She just shakes her head, back and forth, mesmerized by the movement of her fingers and the hardness of my cock.

She hits a sensitive spot with the pad of her finger and more pre-cum leaks out, uncontrollably, like nothing I've ever experienced.

"Fuck. Fuck." I throw my head back against the mattress, pushing the back of my head into it as my hands grip the side of the sheets.

I can't stand this; I need to do something. I'm fucking desperate. I reach for her, and her body, like a magnet to my hand, slides back, so I reach for my cock. My fucking red, hard, throbbing cock, but she slaps my hand away.

"I will tie your hands up if you don't leave them at your sides." Her tone is as even as her finger thrusting.

Who the hell is this girl and what has she done with Ember?

I grip the sheets more; the harder I grip the more pre-cum leaks out. Or maybe it's the opposite.

"Jesus, Ember," I beg. Begging for her to understand the torture I'm feeling. It's the most pleasurable fucking torture I've ever experienced in my entire life.

She removes her finger and I suddenly feel empty. The pleasure still pulses through me, just not as intensely, and I want nothing more than to have it back.

"Ember, I need you." I need you more than you'll ever know. Here for this and in my life. I need all of her.

I lift my head to look at her, and she's focused back on my center, tilting her head as I feel pressure again and a bigger sensation pushing into me.

"Oh, fuck. Yes." Christ, did I just say yes?

The pressure goes deeper this time. It feels fuller... better.

She leans down, wrapping her lips around my cock again, before forcing her face down to the base. Taking me so goddamn deep.

I realize it was a distraction when a buzzing sound turns on and the toy begins to vibrate.

Moans tremble from my core uncontrollably, just like my leaking cock.

Ember pops her lips off my cock, inspecting me like artwork she's making.

She continues to run her fingers over my body. The back of her fingers brush over my abs and graze my cock, then down over my balls, between my legs, and back up. Wrapping her hand around my hardened cock, giving it a stroke and then releasing me, just to repeat these teasing movements, over and over again.

"God, your cock is so hard and you have so much pre-cum.

This is so sexy, Hudson." She pinches her nipple over the fabric of her bra, and I can see her rolling her hips between my legs.

More pre-cum leaks out of the tip at just the sight of her pleasing herself like that, and a bolt of pleasure spikes through me.

She forces herself to stop and places her hands over my legs, just caressing me with her fingers as she eyes my center. She's watching me, allowing me intense pleasure, but not letting me get to the point of climax.

"Ember, I need to come. Please do something." I beg with both my words and my eyes, as I stare at her bewildered, lustful face inspecting my cock, like she's studying me.

Her desperate eyes peer up at mine, and she must see the torment in them. "Fuck," she whispers to herself before she wraps her hand around my cock. She gives me one gentle tug from base to tip, then releases again.

"P... Please, don't stop," I stutter, throwing my head back and squeezing my eyes shut. I don't know how much longer I can hold out. I take in a long, drawn out breath and open my eyes to tell her that.

She's closing the lid to the lube bottle, placing it down on the towel, then grabs a small black device, pressing a button on the center.

The tail fucking obliterates me. The vibration changes, and it's so deep and so fucking good.

An animalistic groan expresses from my body, and I have no idea where it comes from. My vision starts to blur and I'm seeing fireworks behind my eyes. The sensation is so over-whelming my brain battles between wanting the tortuous feeling to stop and keep going.

Ember's hand wraps around my needy cock. The heat of it engulfs the coolness of the lube in her hand as she strokes me from base to tip, the tempo matching the jolting of the vibra-tion, and cum sprays out of the tip with each tug. My eyes widen at the sight because my climax hasn't quite peaked, but I'm shooting cum.

It's as if my thoughts reflect my body's actions. My orgasm hits me full force, like a goddamn freight train with no brakes.

I have no control.

"Ember, I'm... I'm coming." My abs tighten and toes curl, and my entire body convulses, as my release sprays fucking everywhere.

At my peak, the climax was so goddamn powerful, and the sensation trailed on for longer than I expected. She just gave me the hardest and longest orgasm I've ever felt in my life. Was it the undivided attention, the butt play, or just Ember? I'm confused and overwhelmed by the realization that I loved that more than just the act of sex itself.

I'm thankful Ember turned off the vibration so I don't have to beg her to stop it. I've literally just spent the entire time lying here, begging her for more and to stop, going back and forth every other second. Jesus, I sounded confused and so desperate.

My head falls deeper into the mattress as I turn my cheek to face her. Her face is completely flushed. Nipples completely erect behind that lace bra, her fingers biting into her thighs like she is trying to prevent from touching herself, and she's nibbling on that gorgeous lip of hers.

The shyness Ember leans toward is coming back, and it's one of the things I find the most attractive about her. She has this perfect balance of a bashful reserve and a bold confidence in moments of desire.

My cock twitches.

It should be dead.

I reach down, gently removing the tail and ring with a slight grimace, and sit up, taking the towel and toy with me. I wipe myself off with the towel before tossing both into the sink in our bathroom and stalk back to her, still kneeling on the bed.

Her face is looking away, at a space in the corner of the room. Her eyes are far away, dazed in her own thoughts. I lean into the bed, putting one hand and one knee down in front of her as I place my fingers on her chin to turn her face toward mine.

She's still looking down, hiding the shame of whatever she's thinking. I've realized she does this, like no one has ever given her permission to be in charge or be okay with something she likes. She's trained to retreat within herself and quiet her voice when she likes something she thinks she shouldn't.

That's going to fucking stop.

"You've never looked sexier." I kiss her neck. "Then you did just now." I kiss her jaw. "You made me come," I kiss her ear, "harder than I ever have in my entire life."

Her eyes flicker my way, and I lean in to kiss the corner of her lips. "I hope you liked it because we definitely have to do that again."

Her hands wrap around my face, turning it to press her lips to mine. Like I just gave her permission to kiss me with unruly passion.

She leans back on the bed, taking me with her, and thank god, because I'm not even close to done with her yet.

34

EMBER

I woke up this morning, my phone treating me like I am a scandalous celebrity with news no one but paparazzi cares about.

Mom: You got married?! Your father is furious. WE are furious!

Mom: Stop ignoring my calls.

Cody: Mom and Dad are pissed. I can't believe you got married, Em. What the hell?

Mom: Ember, I am so disappointed in you. What were you thinking?

Dana: Cat's out of the bag. I don't know who said what, but the whole town knows you got drunk married in Vegas. Including your parents...

Mom: Ember, you need to call me so we can figure this out. You can still get this annulled.

Mom: It's time to come home now.

Dana: Suzy slipped and they know you got a job, too. That went over well. Don't be mad at her. She was trying to defend you and it just came out.

Mom: Elliot has been waiting. How could you do that to him?

Cody: Have you been brainwashed? This is so not you. What's going on?

Mom: You call me immediately!

Dana: Okay, for real. Elliot's been acting weird. And your parents are on another level.

Mom: The whole town's talking about this, Ember. How could you embarrass us with reckless behavior? This is over now. Call me.

I reread through the plethora of text messages from my mom, brother, and Dana, and as much as I've dreaded this moment, I'm relieved it's out in the open. Timing is bittersweet with the trip back home this weekend. It'll be like choosing to fly into Hell, but at least they know I won't be staying.

I can only assume Elliot was the one who finally told them. I didn't race after him when he was here, and now that he knows where I stand, I just need to make my parents understand how I feel and what I'm doing. I'm permanently moving to Seattle. I'm with Hudson, albeit temporary for us, but they don't need to know that.

Another text message pops through and I dread looking at it, but like a car crash, I can't turn away. A smile instantly tugs on my lips when I see it's Hudson.

Hudson: Are we still going to check out the building before our flight?

Me: Yup! So excited to show you everything!

Hudson: Can't wait ;) Pick you up at 2?

Me: Perfect.

"So, Hudson has been helping you with your sexual research, huh?" Cruz shocks me with his question as he walks into my office with our morning coffee.

Why have espresso when you can just have a shot of Cruz?

"What makes you say that?" I ask, trying to hide my blush.

"It's obvious you are totally getting laid, like a lot," he replies. "You try to hide it, but I'm sort of a professional at smelling sex from a mile away."

I scrunch up my nose.

"Figuratively, of course, silly girl." Batting a hand at me.

Sexual research. Well, you can say that. You can say it's been a lot of that. The only nights in the past month that we haven't *researched* were the days he was gone for his away games. And even then, the dirty and flirty text messages leave us both in a major state of need the moment he comes home.

I've never enjoyed sex as much as I have with him, and it's sort of an addiction at this point. I might need an intervention and to check myself in somewhere.

Of course, it's for research, I tell myself. The logical side of my brain says it's needing as much information on these products to make an informed decision.

My body, my traitorous body, needs something else.

I keep telling her she's delusional, but like a damn addict, she can't keep her hands off Hudson.

The first day I brought home that box was the day something shifted between us.

I have never been given the sort of freedom that he has given to me. No one has made me feel as comfortable as he has, giving me a confidence I've never felt before, to be who I feel like I am naturally. He adds something powerful to my life, and a part of me is terrified of what happens if it's gone.

That reliance scares me, and I've felt like ending this thing between us more often than I'd like to admit. But somehow, he still keeps me grounded. Everyone does, actually.

For the first time in my life, I feel like I have my own friends that aren't somehow controlled by my family. As much as Suzy and Dana are friends, their parents are best friends with my parents, so a friendship was just expected of us.

The entire Smashers team hangs out daily; if not at the field for games or practices, at the condo for family game nights. And as domestic as it all is, it doesn't feel like how Weston felt to me—all-consuming and restrictive. It feels like how happiness should feel.

There are moments I get a bit lost in it all, so I just have to keep reminding myself we are just helping each other out. We're over halfway through the season now, and next year, I won't be living in the condo. I'll have to find a place of my own.

"Fine, you got me. I'm experimenting with my fake husband," I admit.

"Oh, you dirty whore. Tell me more," he quips back instantly.

In the past month, we've used pretty much every sample product that the vendor gave me, and it's probably shameful to admit that I liked, well, everything.

So, I'm probably a nymphomaniac now.

Of course, I love when I control Hudson's orgasms, and the shyness that was there before is now replaced with confidence and courage. It's easy because he makes it easy.

That's by far my favorite.

We also experimented with some more BDSM style toys. I didn't love that as much. I loved the control, yes. I didn't like the pain aspect that came with it. Hudson was completely relieved by that realization. I did enjoy tying him up, though.

So, what have I realized in the last month?

I like control, but not pain—giving or receiving. I love teasing. I love his orgasms more than my own, but when he reigns over me, possessively, after I've edged him for as long as I think he can handle, that's another favorite.

He's wild and uncontrollable. A savage side takes over that I also crave.

So, in true libra fashion, I'm indecisive as hell. I love being in control of him, yet also love being controlled.

Strange, I know.

We're both finding out things about ourselves and each other that we didn't expect. It's liberating.

"I'm not giving the details of my sex life, Cruz."

"Your fake sex life." I can't help but roll my eyes at his reply. "Just give me the fake details."

"Your wit is over the top this morning. Did you have a quad shot in your coffee?" I ask, evading his questioning.

"Nope, this is just me. Stop avoiding it." He smiles.

Ugh, he's annoyingly adorable. Both in his persistence and his looks. His dark hair is thick and always styled perfectly. The black-rimmed glasses that he always wears give him a Clark Kent look, especially with that perfectly shaved, sharp jawline. The Latin side of him is starting to show now that it's summer and we get a tad bit of sun during these months. A rarity for us in the Pacific Northwest.

"Did you get a tan?" I ask.

"Oh, wow, okay, professional dodgeball player today, I see. I'll be at my desk with all your reports and details for the completion of the construction—that I'm handling while you're gone this weekend at your parents' party. Which I wasn't invited to, by the way. So, when you want to go over those, I'll hand them over... *after* I get a spicy story."

"Cruz," I yell at him as he saunters out of my office. "That's blackmail."

"No, no, it's more like extortion. But, like, barely. Let me know when you're ready."

I need those reports, like, this morning.

"Hudson literally made me pass out from an orgasm," I spit out and instantly want to retrieve it.

He flips around, a full one-eighty degree U-turn, on the ball of his foot, so eloquently he should have been a ballerina.

"That freaking devil. The quiet ones are always so dirty. How? Details?"

"Oh, god." I press my palms into my face.

I've learned to be comfortable with Hudson, but talking about everything with someone else is entirely new. I need to get used to it, being that I'll have to do that when the club opens.

"So, he had me wear this remote control vibrator," I whisper as he slides back into the chair in front of my desk. "Like, all day, around the house, and even when we went out to lunch." I lean in closer, whispering lower. "He almost made me come when we were at the restaurant."

His jaw slacks. "You dirty girl, that's so hot."

"So, needless to say, by the time we got back home, neither of us could wait any longer. He fucked me for so long and drew out my orgasm to the point that, when I finally came, I just blacked out." I bite the corner of my lip. A little embarrassed that I'm admitting all this to Cruz, but feeling a little sexual freedom at the same time.

"You need to make your fake husband become your real husband. You know he wants it."

Panic sears through me instantly with his words. My

mother flashes in my mind; the years of *service* to my father. Like he's her own personal religion. God, I don't want that. I don't want everything to revolve around the man in my life and marriage. Yet, lately, it's just been Hudson and me living in our own world.

Suddenly, it's like everything nearby is closing in on me. Even the air feels claustrophobic.

Breathe.

"You okay? You're sheet white," Cruz asks as he tilts his head, looking at me.

I inhale, close my eyes, and physically envision a wide open space, then exhale and release the heaviness in my chest.

It takes only a few seconds to reel myself in before I get my bearings again.

"Oh, yeah, good. I just don't have any desire to be married long term. We're only helping each other out. It's a simple arrangement," I tell him, avoiding his gaze, because I know he'll see right through me. "So, do you have those reports?"

"Sure," he replies cautiously, "I'll bring them in," he stands slowly then pauses for a moment as I side eye him, still avoiding his gaze, before he turns to exit.

"Em..." I stop mindlessly shifting benign accessories on my desk and peer up to where he is standing. I stare at his shoes and expertly steer clear of his gaze.

"It's okay to let go of people that don't bring you peace and allow in those who do. Family is what we create for ourselves sometimes. It might not always be what we envision for ourselves, but if it protects our peace, well, it's worth... everything."

His statement forces me to look at him, and the sincerity in his face is blinding. He's not just giving me advice based on some old Chinese proverb out of a daily desk calendar or a self-help book he has read. This is raw emotion, love and loss, based on life experiences, for him. I open my mouth to reply, but stop at the interruption of knocking.

Tap. Tap.

I tilt my head to look behind Cruz. Christian and Elena step through the doorway, and my spine instantly perks up. I stand as they enter my office, because what the hell do I do? They never come to my office.

"Good morning." Confusion laces my greeting.

Christian smiles, that gorgeous smile he gives when he's trying to make you feel comfortable. Elena's smile is directed straight at me, with some kind of look I can't quite read.

Her eyes flicker toward the doorway behind her, and another man I've never met comes through.

I put my best smile on and round my desk. My spine still ramrod straight and chin held high, exuding the confidence I've gained with every meeting, appointment, and conversation I've had since I started here. As the unknown man walks through the door, my jaw slacks slightly in recognition of who this man is.

His short black hair and dark skin contrast his bright golden eyes. There is a kindness to them, like he's always smiling, without actually smiling.

"Morning, Ember. We're just showing Corbin Maren around while he's here. He is the—"

"Director for Ford Enterprises, East Coast operations," I excitedly interrupt Elena as I hold my hand out toward him. "Yes, I know. It's great to meet you."

His eyes light up in surprise at the fact that I know who he is. I know who everyone is. I studied everything about Ford Enterprises when I applied here.

A blinding smile crosses his face when he slips his hand into mine and gives me a kind handshake.

Christian turns to me. "I'm glad you weren't in a meeting this morning—"

"She was, but I guess I'm leaving since I'm invisible here until one of you needs work done."

Christian grants Cruz a 'you know what I meant' look, with a slight smirk and head shake before Corbin interjects.

"Ah, you must be Cruz." Corbin holds his hand out to him. Another kind smile, but this one with a bit more humor behind it, because, well, Cruz does that to you.

Cruz stalls for a brief moment, sliding his hand into Corbin's. He's looking down at their hands, Corbin's completely engulfing Cruz's, before glancing back up to his face. Cruz's usual smile fading into a tight-lipped grin before clearing his throat. I don't think I've ever seen Cruz shy before. "Great to meet you, sir." His voice a notch over a whisper. Then he peers over to me. "I'll be at my desk."

He looks between the three of us, avoiding Corbin, before leaving.

Corbin's gaze consumes Cruz as he leaves the office before blinking a few times, then finally turns back to me. "Mrs. Byrnes, I've heard you are leading the XConnect club project?"

"I am," I say proudly. "It's going well, and we should be ready for opening night in about six weeks. We're going to announce the opening date here in the next," I bounce my head back and forth and purse my lips, as I peer over at Elena, "week or so?" It's a question because Elena has been guiding me through that process to make sure I nail down a proper opening night based on the timeline for everything we need to finish.

"Yes, we're aiming for the last weekend of next month, and we're planning a soft opening and masquerade ball," she replies with effortless confidence.

"I'd love to check it out. Will you send me an invite?" Corbin asks.

"Of course, definitely," I reply, unable to read his expression on whether or not he wants to inspect or support opening night.

Corbin continues to lead the conversation, asking so many different questions about the idea of the club, how the memberships will work, and questions about the city's approval. His questions are never ending and have me feeling on edge.

The confident woman that I've grown into is telling herself he's asking questions because he's curious. The girl from Weston, Missouri is trying to make an appearance to remind me I'm nothing special and not capable.

We continue chatting about the project and a few details before he thanks me for my time and they leave.

The tightness in my shoulders releases, and I slouch slightly forward. All the tension in my body visibly diminishes the moment my door closes. I can lead my peers and teams easily, but the moment my bosses walk in the door, I swear I'm a gibbering mess. Like they are going to see through my scam and finally realize they hired someone completely unqualified to complete this project or work for this company. Someone not worthy of learning from someone as amazing as Elena or grow into something similar to her, while finding my own version of myself. To do something special with my life and create something that I can be proud of. Instead, they probably all see a little girl, with more ambition than wit, who will fail at anything she attempts.

Or maybe that's just my parents' voices floating around in my head, reminding me I'm good for nothing. Reminding me to stop trying to be something I'm not.

And now, I feel like I'm not only faking my marriage, but lying to myself about everything.

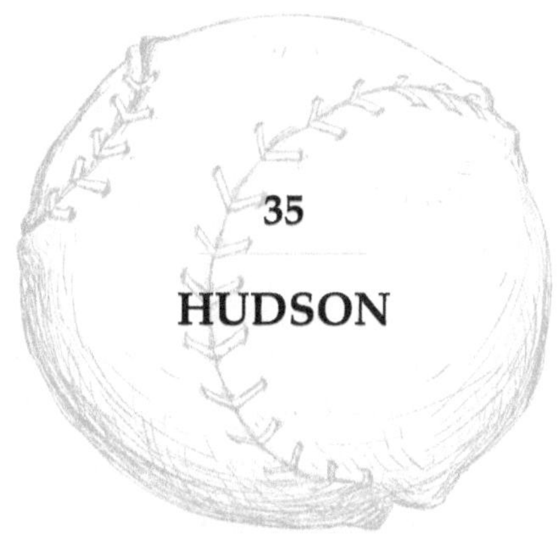

35

HUDSON

Even though Ember has her car now, I still find every excuse to drive her to work. Today's excuse was the fact we are flying out to her hometown for her parents' wedding anniversary this weekend, and she wanted to stop by the XConnect building for a walk through before heading out.

She's been here every day, multiple times a day, over the course of the last few weeks. Creating every detail as she goes along, using all the information she's researched both online and, my personal favorite, in our bedroom. The intense rubbing of her thumbs over her fingers is a direct sign of how nervous she is to show me what she's been doing, and I have no doubt I'm going to be so impressed.

"It's not fully completed yet. There are still some rooms that need finishing touches. We're missing the art shipments from overseas for rooms two, six, and ten. The paint we used for the main hall was too dark, so I had to order a cooler tone, which we're still waiting for. Mostly, it's decor delays since we built most of the devices and furniture in each room. The lobby is still missing the table and chairs I ordered from this small business that I knew would take longer than it would if I went with a bigger company, but the design was just so perfect, so we're still waiting for that. And..." She's so nervous about showing me, and it's adorable, but so unnecessary. I reach over and press my fingertips between her fingers, weaving our hands together. That accomplishes both me touching her and stopping her from chafing the skin off her palm.

"I know it's not fully done yet, and I'm excited that you're sharing this with me earlier than anyone else. I mean, honorary member perks, right?" A shy blush bites at her cheeks.

As we come up on the building, I turn on my blinker to turn into the parking lot. There are a handful of people lined up on the sidewalk that surround the lot. They are holding signs and screaming at passing cars.

"NO TO PORNO!" "SAVE OUR NEIGHBORHOOD!" "PROTECT OUR CHILDREN!" "SEX CLUBS ARE THE DOORWAY TO HELL." "THEY WANT OUR DAUGHTERS."

"There she is!" The crowd points at the front windshield of my truck, then they begin to pound on the side of it, chanting profanities as we pass through. "Whore." "How do you sleep at night?" "Do you believe in God? Repent your sins!"

I pull in quickly and park around the corner of the building so my car is not exposed in the front.

"What the hell, Ember? How long have you been dealing with that?" I ask, putting the truck in park. I glance back, and they stay on the sidewalk, never crossing over to the private property, but I'm still relieved to see there is a security guard parked near the entrance.

"The city posted the notice two weeks ago. It only took a day for them to start camping out there. They figured out who I was pretty quickly because, well, I'm here a lot." She grants me a tight smile and a shrug that tells me they don't bother her.

It fucking bothers me.

She peers out the windows, doing a full three-sixty view of

her surrounding area. Seeing no one here, she grabs the keys out of her purse and reaches for the door handle. At least she's mindful of her surroundings.

"Come on. I can't wait for you to see," she says excitedly, jumping out of the truck.

As we walk up to the expansive, heavy double doors, she slides the key into the door, at the same time entering an extensively long numbered password on a keypad next to it. A dense thud echoes behind the door and she pushes it open, allowing us entry.

There's a lengthy desk expertly placed at the front, blocking entrance, except for the two openings on each side of the floor to ceiling frosted glass backdrop with a large bold lettering, 'XConnect Live' embedded in the glass.

"This is going to be a waterfall." She points to the glass. "The way the water will flow, you'll still be able to see the words through it. We haven't finalized the official name of the club yet, but we wanted to keep the interior website related, so we decided on that for this display. We turned it on the other day and it looks so good. " Her voice is laced with giddy excitement. I can't help but smile.

We pass through what will inevitably be the check in area and move into the open lobby area. Even though it's incredibly expansive and there are still some ladders and other paint buckets lying around, it's immediately welcoming. A fresh modern feel with a comfort only she can bring.

There is a large circular bar, surrounded by bar stools, that is perfectly placed in the middle of the room. The glass and modern design matches the ambiance of the entire lobby.

"We will have high tables placed throughout with some leather seating that trails along the outer wall." She walks through, waving her arm in the direction of what she's showing me. She points toward an arched doorway leading into another open area. "That is going to be *The Chat Room*."

I see a deep yellow stick figure figurine next to the doorway that looks like he's taking a large stride.

"Isn't that the old AOL Chat Room symbol?" I ask.

"Yes, exactly! The whole room is designed around the original chat rooms, like a tribute. Even the signage leading into it is going to resemble the old school AOL Chat Room design, along with other memorabilia from those days. It'll be the designated members' meet and greet area, which—you know —was the whole purpose of this project—to bring people together." She smiles, staring at the open space, pride behind her eyes, still inspecting for perfection.

"My favorite part is..." we step through the archway and the original voice from AOL chat chants *'Welcome'* through the speakers, with the sound of a door opening when we walk into it, followed by the sound of a door closing when we step out of it, "...that."

I smile from ear to ear, feeling so nostalgic. She wasn't even born around the time that was around, but to bring that in here, it speaks to generations of people. Even the younger generation knows about dial up and original chat rooms.

"Ember, that's so freaking cool."

She grabs my hand, practically skipping, urgently passing through to the next area.

Pointing to the left behind, there's a blocked off hallway that leads to a staircase. "That's the staff area."

Now she leads us to the right. "Down that hallway are the private rooms that people can reserve for a night. We're still detailing each one, and the room names will correspond with the theme."

"Ember, this is... amazing. All of it. Seriously, I hope you're so fucking proud of yourself."

She can't contain her smile as she bites her lip at my praise. Jesus, she's gorgeous.

Being inside these walls is like an adrenaline shot of erotica to your bloodstream, and with Ember alone, it isn't helping.

I lean forward, sliding my hands into hers, and lure her body into mine. And because this place is a goddamn aphrodisiac, and I swear she must have pumped Ember scented pheromones into the ventilation system, I kiss her. My palm holds her cheek, and I pull her as close to me as possible. It's deep and passionate, and it's everything.

We pause for an awkward moment, because we don't typically kiss without sex being involved, but I just couldn't fucking help myself. She must see how much I want her, more than just for these so-called sex lessons we've been doing. It's grown into something more, something undeniable.

She blinks quickly and nibbles on that bottom lip again before stepping out of my embrace.

"Come on, you haven't seen the best part." She grabs my hand again, leading me in the opposite direction of the private rooms.

"This is the Voyeur Room." A blush crosses her cheeks. And I see it because I know this is probably a favorite of hers.

We walk up to horizontal bars that align an outer area, and I walk closer to see that it's a reverse loft style set up. I peer over the top and there is a stage centered below us, with stadium seating in a half circle around the middle. I can see everything from this view, and it's brilliant. Anyone standing here, at any location, will have an unobstructed view of the performance, along with anyone in the seating that descends below.

"We have private rooms this way for exhibitionist couples that want to perform. There are three rooms in total, each with their own eccentric taste. The glass is made of this thermochromic glass that can darken with the press of a button and become tinted from the inside out. It'll allow for immediate privacy if someone needs it. The glass cost a fortune, but I think it was worth every penny."

She leads me through a curtained area, and there are floor to ceiling windows peering into rooms that mirror that of a standard bedroom. Except these are adorned with overhead lights, horizontal metal bars that line the room, and an over-sized plush bed with bed posts that raise to the ceiling.

The next room looks similar, but with a human sized "X" attached to one wall. Buckles and clips hang from the ends of the taunting letter.

We continue to the final room as I trail right behind Ember, still studying all the gadgets in the second room, when Ember gasps and comes to a dead stop, and I run directly into her back, almost toppling over her.

My eyes follow her line of sight to see Jake behind the glass.

Jake is standing, leaning up against the side wall, his pants are unzipped and splayed open. His fully erect cock is gripped tightly in his hand as he gives himself long, languid strokes. He is completely hypnotized by the view on the bed. Like synchronized swimmers, both Ember and I crane our necks further to see Elena, blindfolded and tied to the bed, with Christian's head between her spread legs.

36

EMBER

"**S**hit!" I whisper-yell, airplaning my arm out as I push us back blindly. We hit the back wall and both of us instinctively stand stick straight, him pressing hard against the wall and me molding into him. Neither one of us moves. We're both frozen icicles melting into the barrier, preventing us from our escape.

"What the hell are they doing here?" Hudson asks, without even trying to move his lips.

Christian and Elena come often. Well, Elena does. If Christian comes, Dietrich drops him off in his blacked-out SUV, so no one can see who it is. That's probably why we didn't see any other cars outside. Plus, I told them I was leaving early today for my flight. They probably thought I left already.

I shrug, whispering, "I don't know," in dramatic fashion.

I look around, knowing it's probably safe to move because we dimmed this area for that reason. We didn't want the performers seeing hordes of people looking in, but it's still risky to get caught here.

My neck is tilted in the direction of the green, lit up Exit sign. The neon green rays shine brightly, symbolizing more

221

than just a simple sign. It's screaming, *green means go* and get the hell out of there, but instead, I stare out of the corner of my eyes, unable to look away from the three of them.

My cheeks heat at the sight of them together. Arousal builds in my core, and I press my hands behind me to grip the wall for support. Instead of finding the wall, my hands land on Hudson's leg and I grip the cotton of his joggers tightly between my fingers.

Hudson, sensing both my anxiety and nerves, wraps one arm around my shoulder and the other around my waist, fully enclosing me in his embrace. I melt even further into him and remain still.

"We should go, one at a time, as quietly as possible," I tell Hudson, while attempting to convince myself.

"We could... but I don't think you want to." Hudson's voice is soft, like butter, as his hand trails down the front of my sternum, finding the hem of my shirt and then sweeps back up to the peak of my breast. His finger dips into the cup of my bra, pulling it down, easily finding my taut nipple as he pinches his fingers around it. Shockwaves blast to my core, causing my breath to hitch, and I groan at the incredible sensation.

My hips rock into him as if they have a mind of their own, and his breath catches against the shell of my ear.

"Don't make a sound." His velvet voice is both desperate and demanding.

I nod passively without glancing up at him. I just keep my eyes forward, afraid to move even my eyeballs from one side to another.

Jake is now fully naked. Every muscle in his body is tight and hard, matching the mouthwatering lust in his eyes. He continues to move his hand slowly over his entire length, teasing himself from the base to the tip, as he surveys his wife and Christian on the bed.

Hudson's finger dips into the front of my skirt and under my thong. I barely register his finger is there until he swipes the pad of his middle finger down my wet slit, and we moan together at the sensation.

"Fuck," he breathes into my ear, at the same time I say, "Oh god."

"Jesus, you're so goddamn wet, little red."

His finger begins to move at a flawless pace, spreading my arousal over my clit. I moan louder, unable to control my voice box any longer.

Fortunately, Elena's sounds override my own as she begs Christian to make her come.

"Not yet, baby," Jake calls out before pushing himself off the wall as he begins to prowl toward the bed.

The sight makes my pulse pound so hard I can feel it in my throat, and a deeper desire tingles all over my skin.

Watching porn is nothing like seeing this in person. Everything is so raw. I don't know if it's because I know this trio, making this scene so sexy and sensual, but I've never been turned on like I am now.

And Hudson can sense every ounce of it. He presses his hips into me, and I feel his just the same. His cock is impossibly hard behind his pants, the cotton feeling like trace paper as his length presses against my ass.

Jake places one knee into the bed, dipping the side enough that Elena's head turns in that direction. Still blindfolded, he positions the crown of his head against her lips, and Christian peers up, briefly pausing feasting on her as he tells her to take Jake's cock. "Open your mouth, baby. Show him how much you love his cock."

Jake's hand grips the headboard while he holds himself over her, her lips spread open, inviting him in, and he thrusts into her mouth. His cock slides over her tongue and down her throat easily. He throws his head back and hisses into the air as he pauses for a moment, holding her head all the way against the base of his cock, before he begins to move in and out. His thrusting becomes harsher, more erratic, all while praising her.

Christian continues to devour her, consuming her with his tongue. Her muffled and desperate sounds escape from around Jake's cock as he completely impales her mouth.

"Do you like watching them?" Hudson whispers in my ear, trailing kisses down my neckline. I tilt to the side to give him better access and nod.

My body is completely engulfed by his. His arm, still wrapped around my chest, gives one of his hands full access to play with my nipple, while the other terrorizes my pussy in the best way possible. It's so good, I need more.

"Hudson, more. I need more," I whimper. "I'm so close." And by the way Elena's moans are rising, so is she.

Hudson's growl in my ear mirrors the intensity of how hard he squeezes me, so I'm even more flush with his body. Rolling his hips against my back, he's as needy as I am.

Jake's cock leaves Elena's mouth with a pop as she tosses her head back on the pillow. Her back arches off the bed, and the whimpering moans and desperate pleas of all three of them create a soundtrack that is sending me careening to the edge.

"Oh, God. Christian, don't stop," Elena begs. "Jake, I'm gonna come."

"That's it, baby, come for us," Jake demands, as he strokes his cock.

My orgasm rises with hers, and the cadence Hudson's finger is unleashing on me is my undoing. I squeeze my lips together, groaning through my orgasm as it rips through me at the same time as Elena's. Hudson covers my mouth, pulling my head back to his shoulder as his hips roll into me.

"You're so fucking beautiful when you come," Hudson whispers, his voice laced with a desperation I've never heard before.

My body liquefies against him. I'm completely boneless, making the not-so-boneless appendage currently residing at the small of my back very apparent. My hips naturally roll into his, searching for more. The cotton covering him is thin enough to feel the hard ridge of his crown, but thick enough to cause a barrier that irritates me.

"Pull your pants down." My tone is far less desperate than it was a few seconds ago. It's turned raspy and demanding; I barely recognize it. Hudson's head tilts down to look at me. Even though my head still rests on his shoulder and my eyes are closed, I sense his surprise.

Blinking my eyes open, I turn to meet his, and lust pools behind those dark inky irises with a fierce anguish. They're nearly black.

He looks through the glass again, assuring himself they aren't getting ready to leave. By the looks of Christian undressing, they are far from it. And by the fire that's blazing behind Hudson's eyes as they return to mine, neither are we.

"Whatever they do to her, I'm doing to you." He pulls the waistband of his pants down, and his cock juts out against my back, feeling like a dangerous sin. All I can do is nod my approval because right now, he can do whatever the hell he wants to my body.

We're two deviant voyeurs, hiding our misdeeds in a dark corner. We shouldn't keep watching, we should stop this, but I can't keep my eyes off them.

I reach behind my back and wrap my fingers around Hudson's length at the same time he lifts my skirt above my waist. The cool air that hits my core sends shivers over my entire body. I grip his cock like I need it to survive, because right now, I do. Moisture from the tip of his cock paints my low back as I stroke him from base to tip.

A tortured huff floats over my ear before he bites into my shoulder, firm enough for me to flinch, while sending shock waves to my pussy.

Movement through the glass catches my eye as Jake releases

Elena's restraints, and Christian now sits on the side of the bed, completely naked and hard, everywhere. His body looks like it's made of granite. In fact, the entire scene is painted like a van Gogh masterpiece. The beauty of their bodies, not just in their sculpture, but their energy, is unlike anything I've ever seen. They move together like they are one.

Elena crawls over Christian, effortlessly floating one leg over his body, and straddles his hips. His cock looks like a pony wall between their bodies before Elena lifts her body, sliding herself onto it. Their agonized moans of relief as he fills her fill the room with a tenor that rips straight through me.

The sight distracts me enough that I didn't anticipate Hudson's sudden movement. He releases the arm that was wrapped around my body, grips my waist, and lifts me up as he squats back onto the wall. He lowers, angling himself at my entrance, and slides into me just as urgently as Christian did to Elena.

"Oh, fuck." We echo each other as I plead, beg, and cry, filling our small space with whispered wanton words.

My hands search around to find something to support this position, but his hold on me is solid, secure, just like I always feel when I'm with him. Even with the security, I still feel the need to help support myself. I press into his thighs, then try to wrap one behind his shoulder, but he stops my fidgeting, smacks my hand away, then faces me forward again to keep my view on the room.

"I can do this all fucking day."

Well... there are definite perks to getting railed by a professional catcher.

"We're not leaving this wall until you come on my cock."

Hudson's words send lightning strikes to my nerve endings. And the look on Jake's face as Christian pistons into Elena lights them on fire. Jake takes a few steps back, reaching into a bag on the chair, and pulls out something small enough to fit in the palm of his hand.

He wraps his hand around his cock, sliding it up and down the shaft, as he returns to his previous spot. But this time takes a few extra strides, placing him right behind Elena and between Christian's legs.

What is he doing?

Fondling the item in his hand, which I now recognize is lube, he flicks it open with his thumb and turns it over, pouring the liquid onto his palm. Trailing the back of his finger down her spine, he continues all the way down in between her ass, cupping underneath. All motion stops as she tosses her head back, and Christian nibbles at her chin.

"Are you ready, baby?" Jake's voice is hoarse, but still loud enough for both of us to hear.

Elena nods as his hand dips further down, swiping down her middle, before pushing a curved digit inside her. Synchronized moans fill the room, each one of them reeling from it.

I can't help but clench as my walls contract against Hudson's hard cock that's been punishing me at a tempo my brain can't even comprehend.

"Jesus, Ember. Fuck." Hudson feels it, too.

Jake's hand steadies, as he pulls back and reaches for the lube again, refilling his palm, then massaging it over the crown of his head and down his cock. He steps forward, crouching slightly.

Oh my god. Oh... my god. Oh. *My*. God!

He is going to fuck her. In. The. Ass.

While Christian is fucking her pussy.

It's not going to fit.

Holy shit.

She won't survive.

My eyes widen as I peer over my shoulder at Hudson. His

focus is on them as well, shock-filled lust covering his face, just like mine.

A tiny twist of his neck has his dark orbs now staring into mine. His cock throbs inside of me, and I can feel how much he loves all of this.

"You're so goddamn lucky I don't have two cocks." He smirks.

"Would you like that?" I ask, unsure of how to say it. "Taking me like that?"

"I'd rather grow another dick just to cut it off after than share you with anyone. But if that's something you want, I want to be the one to give it to you," he states with ease. "I want to give you everything you need," he finishes with a whisper.

Elena's guttural moan breaks our gaze. Jake's cock is half way inside her. His thrusts are slow and calculated as he gently moves her hair behind her ear and whispers into it. Christian is completely still. His forehead rests at her breastbone, jaw slacked, with a pinched expression. He's suffering and enjoying every minute of it.

"More, Jake. More," Elena begs.

"Mmmm, fuck." Jake pushes deeper, his cock completely disappearing between them. All three moan in unison, like practiced choreography, but by the look of their flushed skin and stalled movements, they've never done this before.

"Christ, baby. I can feel his cock inside you," Jake grits through clenched teeth.

"Please don't move yet. Don't fucking move," Christian begs at the same time Hudson pinches my nipple and I release an uncontrollable whimper that Hudson catches with his palm, covering my mouth and pulling me flush against his chest.

I roll my hips over the throne that Hudson has set me on, bouncing on his cock with a new sense of urgency running through my veins. My orgasm builds as his cock grows impossibly hard.

"I can't wait any longer. Fuck me. Please, fuck me," Elena demands while Jake and Christian cross a look at each other and begin slowly moving in and out of her.

A mixed tape of growls, pleas, and praises ascends from the glass room into an explosion of pure sin, bringing my orgasm front and center. I clench around Hudson's throbbing cock as his release barrels through him. My muffled pleas of ecstasy escape between his fingers that invade my mouth as Hudson grips me tighter, working through his own climax.

The three of them are still on a pleasure high, asking for more, begging and pleading. Statements of need and lust all mix together and echo through the room, but I can only hear Hudson's heady voice in my ear.

"I'll never get enough of this. I'll never get enough of you."

37

HUDSON

We managed to sneak out of the club undetected after the most intense sex session I've ever experienced. The orgasm high lingered over half the flight, then a slight tinge of guilt settled in, realizing I spied on my best friend DP'ing his wife with their significant other. I have no idea how I'm going to tell him, or if ever, but it was still the hottest goddamn thing I've ever witnessed. It wasn't the scene that made it so unbelievable, but the sexy woman seated next to me in yet another emergency exit aisle.

It feels like we've come full circle at this point, with everything we've experienced in the short amount of time we've been together. We're over halfway through our *agreement*. I hide my internal eye roll, saying the words in my head. Even though things are nowhere near what they were like in the beginning, a part of me is still terrified she'll find any excuse to end this at the end of our *business arrangement,* when there is no, and I mean no good fucking reason to stop.

I'm going to lay everything out on the table this weekend. I don't want to wait for her to make plans to go anywhere else but with me. At this point, there's no other option for me. She's it. She's everything.

The plane taxis and we exit with our luggage and head straight to the car rental place. The hotel isn't far, thank god, because my legs feel like I lit them on fire after running a double marathon.

I told her I could squat like that all day, but I don't typically wall squat while impaling the most gorgeous redhead with my cock, bouncing incessantly while attempting to control an orgasm.

Needless to say, I'm glad I don't have a game for a few days because I now need to recover from the brutal beating I put them through.

Worth every fucking minute, though.

"I love hotels with you," she says as we walk into the one we've reserved for the weekend. "It reminds me of when we met." She smiles at me with a shyness I only see when she gets vulnerable.

I want to take advantage of this moment to tell her how much I feel the same, tell her how much I don't want this to be fake anymore. *It's never been fake for me.* But I pause too long, unsure of my words.

"I'm going to shower. I am filthy." She gives me an astute look, like it's my fault.

It is, but still, the nerve.

"Think we can just sleep in and then do absolutely nothing until the party tomorrow?" she asks.

"I think that's the best idea you've ever had." Agreeing with her wholeheartedly as I unknowingly rub my quad muscles by instinct.

"Before we go to bed, I'll give you a massage. Your legs need it." She turns around, walking to the bathroom, carrying toiletries in her hand and way too much self-satisfaction in the other.

"All day, little red. I could have done that all day," I yell out with a smile, making sure she can hear me before walking through the bathroom door.

She uh-hms me, then shuts the door.

I don't just love hotels with you. I love everything with you.

PULLING up to the driveway in front of a mammoth-sized colonial house, there are cars lined up along the long circular driveway, already doubling up since we passed through the gate. It was an advanced level Tetris game trying to find a spot to park. Ember hasn't talked much about her family life or specifically her home, so I'm surprised to discover her family is royalty in this small town, being that the entire town appears to be here at their party.

The house must be five thousand square feet, on multiple acres of land. It's surrounded by lush green trees and a wrought iron gate. Having their party here makes total sense, since it feels equivalent to driving up to Buckingham Palace, Midwest style, and I'm certain no place in town could come close to competing with this.

Ember shared that her father has been the mayor of this town and dedicated to the town and the local counties heavily over their years here. In most towns, a mayor doesn't have much pull in the grand scheme of things. But based on what I'm hearing, her parents are deeply involved in the political scene, both locally and statewide, and he uses his connections wisely.

Her parents, well, father, specifically, paid for all her brother's educations, and they contributed nothing for her. That was irritating enough. Now knowing she grew up like this and she had to pay her own way through college. Well, that just pisses me off.

Her eyes look vacantly at the house with a pained appearance in them. I know this moment has been weighing on her. For a while, I thought it was introducing me to her family, but after she shared with me the text messages she received, I realized a couple of things.

One, Elliot is deeply embedded in her family and wants her back. Two, they don't care about anything else except getting her back home to live a mediocre life that she doesn't want.

Neither one of those is happening today or ever.

"Are you doing okay?"

She blinks and turns to look at me, opening her mouth to reply, but closing it quickly. Instead of using words, she grants me a thin-lipped smile and nods before shifting her gaze back to the house.

The silence between us is deafening. We've been living in our own world, and it's really been just the two of us in this so-called fake relationship. We've been able to ignore almost everything else around us, and it's been literal heaven.

Sitting outside her parents' house is a reality check I don't think either one of us is ready for. If they are anything like I think they are, they will manipulate her into coming back home or making her feel guilty enough to give up on everything she wants to make them, or Elliot, happy.

Again, not fucking happening.

I exit the car and round the front of it, my attempt to distract Ember from the monstrosity in front of us. Opening her door, I hold out my hand to guide her out of the car.

"You know, we probably need safe words here."

Her neck snaps in my direction. "What?" she replies, confused.

"Yeah, you know. If you need an escape." I tilt my chin up at the house.

Her mouth turns down with a slight eyebrow raise in realization that it's not a bad idea.

"So, if you need a quick getaway, what are you going to tell me?" I slide my hand behind the small of her back, pulling her close to me, hovering my lips over hers.

"Big Red," she whispers.

"And what about you? What's yours... if you need to get the hell out of there?" She tries to hide the crack in her voice, but she's worried.

Wrapping my pinky around hers. "Nothing, and I mean nothing, will scare me off from you, little red."

———

So, yeah... we were completely in our own world until the moment we walked under those pillars, which now seem more like overly sized prison bars.

Far from humid, the house still feels stuffy and claustrophobic. Dressed up like a home, decorated with both modern vibes and vintage touches, elegant antiques and expensive rugs that make you feel guilty walking on. It's cluttered with everything but love.

A few people walk through the house and linger in the kitchen as we walk through to the patio and through the French doors into the backyard where the party is.

String lights line the multiple canopies that surround a staged dance floor, with a few people already dancing to 80s music blaring from the speakers strategically placed throughout the open space.

There are men and women dressed in penguin suits carrying trays of beer, wine, champagne, and hors d'oeuvres.

Fucking really?

I get the celebration, and I am all for celebrating love. But this event probably cost more than the education that Ember struggled for five years to pay for herself, which just builds the bitterness I have for her parents even deeper into my gut.

"There are my parents." She points to a couple, standing stiffly next to each other, talking to a small group of people their age. "And those guys, they are my brothers." The guys standing around the bar, taking shots. She points to each one. "The oldest, he's Robert Jr., but he goes by Bobby, and that's Benson, and Cody."

She's been so reserved about her family, and whenever I ask questions, she keeps her answers vague. They seem like fun guys; guys I would get along with typically. I tell myself not to be bitter about the way they've allowed their parents to treat her, because it's not their fault, but damn, it's hard to disconnect from that.

"Benson and Cody are married with kids." Her head nods over to the two women sitting, talking quietly, as one holds one child and the other holds another around the same age, while a third child runs around the table with an airplane in his hand.

"Shall we go say hi?" she asks, her eyes fixed on her parents.

"I'm just following your lead, little red."

"Ember!" Benson calls through the backyard, excited as he jogs toward us, perfectly timed with the transition from the last song, so the room was quiet enough for everyone to hear and turn to look in our direction.

They all act like Ember has come back from the dead, whispering and looking around.

I know she didn't tell her parents she was moving, and led them—and apparently the whole town—to believe that she was just taking an extended break and spending some time in Seattle. So, I guess for her to be gone for months and come back married is odd. But wow, the judgment swims through the air like maple syrup.

Benson picks up Ember, and she lets out a slight squeal, as he spins her around in a tight hug. He's clearly happy to see her, and she's happy to see him. She must feel the same about Benson that I do about Grant.

Setting her down, he reaches his hand out to me. "I'm Benson. And I'm a Seattle fan, but don't tell my dad."

"Hudson. Great to meet you, and your secret is safe with me." Our grips match each other as we meet eye to eye. We measure each other up and instantly, there's a kindred spirit, a silent but mutual understanding.

We're both on Team Ember.

Since that's settled, I move on to the other two brothers that trail up leisurely behind Benson. Cody first introduces himself and we shake. It's kind enough, but he's skeptical.

Bobby stands a football field away, appraising us all. I reach out to shake his hand, and he tilts his chin at me, giving me the only acknowledgment he feels like I deserve.

The internal debate to punch his smug face crosses my mind. If it were Seamus, that's probably what he would do, but I do recognize that he's Ember's older brother and I am giving him the benefit of the doubt that he's just being protective of her and not controlling.

"Bobby..." Ember's eye roll can be seen from space.

"Come on, let's go say hi to my parents." Ember grabs my hand and leads me further into the backyard. She's taking charge, and I fucking love when she stands up for herself.

"Nice to meet you guys."

As we walk toward her parents, they stiffen more, if that's even possible. We're here celebrating their thirty years of love and devotion, yet they don't even look like they like each other, much less love each other.

There is always a distinct look of a politician. Ember's father exudes this energy loud enough to be heard across the entire state of Missouri. It stiffens the air around us and blankets everything with complete revulsion. It matches the scowl on his face, which is so hard a divot appears between his brows deeper than a moon crater, and his jaw is as tight as a TSA guard. Jesus, forget liking each other; there is no love or happiness seeing his gorgeous, successful, driven daughter. It's like he's disgusted that she purely exists.

I always assumed Ember would look exactly like her mother, and they look alike, but different. Her platinum hair is harshly dyed and as dry as a tumbleweed. She holds herself like a queen in an all white jumpsuit, and her eyes are nothing like the jade gems I gaze into in Ember. Her confidence is a stark contrast to the moments when Ember is confident. Her mother's comes with an extra large side of superiority and an excess of arrogance.

They don't hug her or kiss her. They don't even smile at her.

"Mom, Dad, this is Hudson. Hudson, these are my parents, Esther and Robert Riley." Her voice is tight as she introduces me.

"You always introduce me first, young lady," he scolds her immediately before turning to me.

"Good evening." I'd say it's great to meet you, but it's not. Keeping that thought to myself, I hold my right hand out to Robert. He switches the grip on his drink into his shaking hand, and I stand similarly to how I stood with his mini me, Bobby Jr., blankly holding my hand out that he refuses to shake.

Esther reaches over and slides her hand into mine to take the focus off her husband. "It's a few months too late to introduce yourself, don't you think?" Esther replies as she quickly shakes my hand out of obligation, then lets it go.

"I understand what you must think, but I am very committed to your daughter," I reply, with more truth than I can admit to Ember. I'd stay *fake* married to her for life, if that's what she needed.

He completely ignores me, looking straight at Ember. "You said you needed some time away. You weren't supposed to run off and ruin your life. You are done acting like a lovesick teenager, do you understand me? You are staying home, that's final."

"Dad," Ember whispers, looking around.

Esther says nothing, just staring at Ember with laser focus, scolding her silently.

"How could you be so careless and stupid?" he replies. Calling her stupid eases off his tongue like it's as automatic as breathing. Ember's shoulders deflate and her gaze turns downward to her feet, like it typically does the moment she internally starts scolding herself, and I see exactly where this behavior comes from.

"Enough of this." I pull Ember into me and step back, turning around and walking away from the pending nuclear bomb that the situation holds.

I glance back to Robert taking a sip of his drink and her mother smiling, checking her surroundings, making sure no one heard. Both act like nothing is wrong. When everything is fucking wrong.

How can they treat her with such disregard? They haven't seen her in months and showed no excitement that she's home.

When my gaze returns to Ember's, her eyes are filled with tears that she fights to hold back. We turn the corner into a private, secluded area of the backyard. She is still gazing down, shamed, humiliated, and fucking broken.

I pull her chin up to look at me. A tear escapes, floating down her cheek, and I watch it trail away from her gorgeous emerald eyes. The ones I've seen light up with so much love and excitement for the new life she is building for herself, but are now extinguished of the brilliance they normally beam.

The anger I have felt since all of this has come to light is boiling over. It takes everything in me to refrain from stealing her away from here and never allowing her to look back.

"I just wish they would be more understanding. I wish the things that I did, the things I work so hard to accomplish, would make them proud." Her voice breaks, like her shattered spirit, barely loud enough for me to hear her.

"Your mom didn't say anything," I state, factually but questionably.

"She doesn't, she never does. Like I said, whatever my dad wants, she wants." That irritates me. She literally has no one in her corner. Except maybe Benson, but it seems like no one really stands up to her parents.

"We don't have to stay. We can do whatever you want," I remind her.

"No, I need to stay. You can go. I can just Uber back to the hotel."

Oh, fuck that.

"If you think I'm leaving you here after that display of complete fuckery, you have lost your goddamn mind." I am never leaving her alone with them. If they say shit like that to her in front of me, I can't even imagine what they would say privately. I pull her close and she melts into me. I revel in the feeling that she's no longer running and finally letting me be whatever she needs me to be.

"I think maybe we should show them a recap of our wedding night. I can request some *112* from the DJ, and he can play *Anywhere* for us so we can show Elliot what a real Vegas show looks like?"

"Oh my god, don't you dare." She pulls away to look at me, showing me how serious she is, but with a hint of a smile behind her eyes.

"Okay, okay. I'll behave." I chuckle, before I lean in to whisper in her ear and show her how serious I am.

"Unless I see Elliot come near you... then I will claim you in front of him and burn the vision of us into his thick skull, and I don't care who sees."

38

EMBER

The excitement of the night tapered off after the initial introductions, and I'm thankful that it's been quiet and uneventful since then. My father has walked around like he owns the town, which he pretty much does, and my mother acts as if they are happy, loving and doting on him at his every whim. Smiling like the matriarch she is.

I was mortified by the way my dad spoke to me. I mean, it's nothing out of the norm, but in front of Hudson, who has never seen me at my weakest—for him to witness that was humiliating. As withdrawn as I've been with my relationship with my family, he knew to expect some pushback, but full-blown berating... I realize now how unfair it was for me to ask him to come here.

Although we were able to get some quality time with Benson and Cody, who also took time to get to know Hudson a little, which I'm grateful for. Bobby, of course, stayed at a distance—attached at the hip as usual with Elliot—stealing glances our way, in which Hudson would become a walking PDA poster. Eventually, it just became fun to tease from afar. Admittedly, I've always liked watching, but being on display for your ex, while your new, sexy, fake husband teases you, well, I'm not against exploring some exhibitionism, apparently.

"I have to use the restroom." Placing my hand on Hudson's arm as I stand, he mirrors my movement to follow me.

"No, it's okay. Stay here and get to know Benson and Cody better. I'll be super quick."

"I don't want you walking around by yourself," he insists.

"It's my parents' house. Seriously, everyone is engrossed in the party. It's fine." I stand on my tippy toes to kiss him on the cheek, except he turns toward me, catching his lips to mine. Running one hand behind the nape of my neck and the other holding me upright at my waist, giving zero shits that he's devouring me in front of my brothers.

"I couldn't help myself," he whispers over my lips as I float back down to earth.

"Dude..." Cody whines out as he gives Hudson a smack on the arm as I walk away. I can't hide my smile. The fact that they are getting along makes my heart soar. My parents may not appreciate or support my decisions, but Benson has always been my biggest cheerleader. And Cody plays Switzerland more often than not, but when he knows something isn't fair, he does have my back.

I enter the house through the patio doors and walk down the hall of my childhood home. It's as empty as I remember it feeling when I was little.

Things usually feel bigger and scarier when you are a child. The ocean feels enormous and overwhelming, horror movies are more terrifying. Bugs were bigger, and the unknown was just frightening.

But this home, somehow it feels bigger and more grandiose than ever. It's like it's had to expand with the ego of my parents. They have always been a staple in our small town, but over time, it's grown into something where they feel more powerful and superior to others. It feels as if, the more self-important they feel to the general population, the less love they have to share with their family.

And as I stare at the pictures on the wall, they feel just as vacant. Taken as a boilerplate, and placed strategically on the wall out of duty and obligation to make a home a home.

I know they love us, especially my brothers. God, we know they love them. A majority of the pictures, except a select few, are all of my older brothers. There is a small age gap between me and my brothers, since my parents had me late and I was unexpected. Still, the lack of my presence in the pictures only accentuates how exiled I have felt my entire life.

It's a far cry from how Hudson has made me feel from the moment he came into mine.

I exit the bathroom and hear the distant noises from the crowd and muffled music throughout the house. The DJ is getting a little rowdier as the night goes on. The music is louder and the songs are a bit more risqué than earlier, which I assume is from the excess amount of alcohol being dispersed like dinner mints.

Before I round the corner back outside, elevated voices catch my attention, preventing me from taking another step.

"You need to get control of this situation."

"I will, Robert. I promise. Please don't be upset."

"Upset? Upset? I'm not upset, I'm fucking embarrassed, Esther. She's humiliating this family and making us look like low class pathetic losers. I'm announcing my campaign soon. If she continues this shit, it'll ruin my chances."

"I will fix this. I'll... fix it. I will."

"The only reason I didn't leave you when she was born was to protect my fucking image. I wasn't going to be humiliated by your indiscretion then, and I won't be now, Esther. Get your daughter under control or I will throw you out with nothing, like I should have twenty-four years ago."

Oh my god. The words are barely registering. There is a

heaviness in the middle of my chest, the air is weighing on me like immovable bricks. I can't catch my breath.

What indiscretion?

They are embarrassed of me.

I am a disgrace to him, to both of them.

My father isn't really my father.

I don't hear the footsteps approaching over repeating words in my head, so I freeze at the sight of my parents turning the corner, staring down at me, as I catch my panicked breath.

My mother looks at my father with wide-eyes and a fear within them that I've never seen before.

"What did you hear?" my father asks through gritted teeth.

My voice box is broken. The words don't come out when I try to speak. I have been swimming upstream for years, fighting to be heard, to feel important to this family. And today, I am truly speechless. All the years of feeling insignificant, having my dreams and desires overshadowed by their own, muting me. They've finally succeeded.

My father grabs my shoulders and pushes me up against the wall. The impact knocks what little oxygen that is left out of my body.

"You will say nothing of this, Ember. Nothing!"

I stare into his eyes blankly. The only thing that shines clearly through the fogginess is the deranged madness behind them. He cares about nothing except his image. I don't need to see my mother's eyes to know they would mirror his own. Except hers would be terrified. Terrified to lose everything she's worked so hard to portray. The luxury, the life, the opulence of wealth and status.

"Ember!" He shakes me and slams me back against the wall, attempting to snap me out of my mental comatose. "I will not have your whore mother and her bastard child make me look bad in my own goddamn town. Do you understand that?"

I remain silent. My body is unable to respond, lacking any

understanding of all that has unfolded. My gaze returns to the floor, as it usually does in the presence of my father.

With one of his hands still pressing me against the wall, he begins to raise the other. I look up just in time for the back of his hand to connect with the side of my face, and the sensation is splintering. A thousand needles explode on my face, and the pressure behind my eyes forces them shut. A metallic taste explodes in my mouth, and I'm instantly stupefied.

Suddenly, the force that was holding me up is gone, and I collapse to the floor. My father is tackled to the ground. Hudson's size favors him as he hovers over my father, holding him down, swinging his arm, as his fist collides with my father's face over and over, like a video on a constant loop.

Benson comes to my side, inspecting me. His face is blurred as I can barely see him from behind my soggy eyes. A fog outlines the surroundings behind him, and nothing is clear.

"Ember! Ember, are you okay?" Benson cups my cheeks, turning my face to the side as he cringes at the sight.

"Fuck," he whispers to himself.

"Hudson!" Cody's voice screams through the invisible fog in the air. He's saying more, but sounds like a muffled white noise, or maybe that's just the ringing in my ears.

Cody bearhugs Hudson, trapping his flailing arms, and yanks him off of my father, who's curled up with his arms over his face, also screaming inaudible words. My father's legs kick at Hudson while Cody pulls him away, but Cody turns his body between them and gets struck with the bottom of my father's pristine Oxfords, right in the middle of his back. He grunts and falls forward, releasing Hudson as they both tumble to the ground.

I blink slowly. My eyelids are filled with lead and the sounds are deafening. Everything is so loud, but somehow dulled.

Cody's arm wraps behind his back as his face winces in pain.

Hudson crawls to me, cradling me in his arms. My body melts into his like a perfectly fitting comfort blanket.

With my face nuzzled into Hudson's chest, I hear Bobby before I see him. He's helping my father, attempting to pull him away, but my father is having none of that and he is challenging everyone now.

His voice is laced with so much hate and anger. He's usually uninterested, arrogant, and condescending, but always controlled. This is now the voice of a frantic, terrified man that is being exposed, and the lack of control is killing him.

"Get your hands off me," he shouts. I turn my neck enough to see him circling his arm to snuff off Bobby's grasp, then press his hands to Bobby's chest, pushing him away but still egging him on with words.

"You want to fight me, boy?"

"Dad, stop!" Bobby's hands are up in surrender.

"You fucking pussy." Disgust drips from his words like a loose faucet as he lunges at Bobby.

"Bobby!" Elliot's voice cracks as he rounds the corner, then comes to an instant stop. His eyes bounce around the room, landing on mine. A look of sorrow passes over his face before he turns to look at my father and Bobby.

"And you—" My father points at Elliot. "Stay the fuck away from my son. You're never welcome here again."

What? What the hell did he just say? A pinched look crosses my face as I look between them.

Bobby and Elliot share a silent look between each other that screams louder than any words could.

"I love him, Dad," Bobby shares quietly, but loud enough for everyone to hear.

"And I love him, Mr. Riley," Elliot responds urgently, supporting Bobby in his admission.

"No, you don't. My son is not gay!" he clamors, saliva misting over the air between them.

How long has that been a secret? I wonder how many others know about them? And how many others know about *me*. As usual, I feel alienated and completely in the dark.

"That's why you've been bribing me—forcing me on Ember all these years, right? To marry your daughter and forget about your son because Missouri can't have a governor with a *"gay"* son." Elliot looks down at me, his shoulders slouch as he passes me a pained look. "I won't hide it anymore. I'm sorry, Em."

He faked *everything* with me.

The truth should shock me and rip me to my core. My father used me to protect his image even further. He thinks if Elliot married me, it would force Elliot and Bobby away from each other. No, instead, they would have had a lifelong affair, hiding themselves from the world and deceiving me, all for the benefit of my father. If I loved Elliot, that would destroy me. But, at this point, it doesn't matter. They've all already done that.

Hudson's hold squeezes tighter, like he needs to hold me to keep me grounded, to keep me present and lucid.

Bobby's gaze dips in shame, and I realize for the first time that's not just my reaction to my father, it's all of ours. I've always seen him as the strongest of us all, the favorite to my father, but it's a mask. My father has built us to be ashamed of ourselves, and Bobby is no different.

"You are fucking done." He pushes Elliot out of his way. "And you," he turns to face my mother, "you fucking whore. When I'm done with you. You'll be nothing, you'll have nothing again." Her arms are wrapped around the front of her frail body, completely frazzled with tear-stained cheeks and labored breaths.

"Robert, you promised," she begs.

"Years of putting up with her presence, and the entire time,

she's been a toxin bleeding through this family. It disgusts me."
He rubs the back of his hand over his bloody nose, then spits
on the ground near my feet.

Closing my eyes, I turn into Hudson. I can't face them. I
can't face any of them.

I am an "*it*", the illegitimate child out of an affair my mother
had. No wonder he hates me so much and my mother
resents me.

I've always felt alone. That's not a new emotion in my
world, but never have I felt so distant and estranged because
I've never truly belonged anywhere. The small amount of
worth I held on to has dissipated to non-existent dust.

My throat is dry as sandpaper, and although my words are a
breath of a whisper, they blare through to Hudson like a siren.

"Red... big red."

39

HUDSON

The moment the words floated from her lips, a switch flipped. I tucked one arm under Ember's leg and wrapped the other around her back, lifting her off the ground and away from that torture chamber. An extravagant hallway painted with her childhood pictures, a mirage of lies, while they spewed the worst insults any human could to another.

My blood still boils, and I've never wanted to murder someone in cold blood like I do him. Still thinking of all the ways I could do that while I drive us away from the place she has always known as home, knowing she will never return, I know I need to do something for her.

Other than the safe word she used, she hasn't said anything. She's retreated within herself, just like she would when we first met.

My mind works in overdrive as I try to think of things that will help, and my original thought is still at the forefront of my mind. She needs to know she has a home. In me. In us. There are people that will love her unconditionally.

I pull over to the side of the road, pick up my phone, and

look up flights to get the hell out of here. There's one, one goddamn flight tonight.

I look around at our surroundings, knowing it's a stretch to get there, being that we need to go back to the hotel to get our things and to the airport, but I'm damn well going to fucking try. Turning back to Ember, she's dazing out the window, and I don't even think she's realized we've stopped. It's like she's petrified, and I have no idea how she's going to come back from something like this. And if she does, if she'll ever be the same.

STILL, she has said nothing. Not a word when we got to the airport, checked in for the flight, boarded the plane, got the rental car, or pulled up here to my parents' house. She doesn't even know what state we are in.

It's late, well after midnight. And even though my parents are typically in bed by now, the light is on and I'm guessing my mom waited up after I texted her all the details of what happened.

This is a gamble, but if anyone can make you feel loved, it's my mother.

"Ember, we're here." She shifts her gaze to me, then back at the house. A furrow in her brow tells me she's confused as to where we are, but doesn't ask questions. She just reaches for the door handle, mimicking that of a zombie as she exits the car.

As we enter the house, the aroma of freshly baked goods and cinnamon spice invades my senses, and I hope it brings the same comfort to Ember as it does to me.

My mother lies on the couch with a blanket draped over herself, fast asleep. Tiptoeing past her so we don't wake her, I lead Ember upstairs to my old room, and walking into it, like I do every time I visit, is an instant recollection of the past.

Filled with more baseball memorabilia than one person should have, pictures of classic cars, and an embarrassingly large Green Day poster, the room is still completely intact from the day I moved out.

Ember sits on the bed, and I crouch down to remove her shoes. She glances around the room but remains expressionless, either unaware of where we are or completely aware and still unable to speak.

"You need to get some rest," I say to her, cupping her cheeks as I seek to gain some sort of recognition from her. Something to rip her out of her current state.

Her eyes, her gorgeous jade eyes, usually filled with an ocean of fearlessness and a spark that you can feel, are completely empty of all color and existence.

"Ember," I whisper, pressing my forehead to hers. "I'm so fucking sorry."

I don't know what else to say. I just need her to speak, react, cry, scream, something. God knows I want to.

She peels away from me, feeling instantly a light-year away, and shifts her gaze toward the bed, eyeing the pillow and blanket, before crawling into a fetal position onto it. I clench my fists, envisioning the complete destruction of her father yet hold back any other reaction, knowing that is not what she needs right now.

Covering her with the blanket, I kiss her temple and give her the space I know she needs, and head back downstairs.

My mother must have heard us pass through. Not surprising, it's the same trait she had when my brothers and I were kids, hearing and seeing everything. She silently walks up and gives me a hug only a mother can give, that instantly tries to strip away stress and pain.

"How is she doing?" she asks, cutting to the chase.

"I'm not sure." I round my palm around the back of my neck, feeling stiff from both the plane and the madness of today. "I don't know what to do. She hasn't said a word since everything happened."

"She just needs some time, honey."

"I don't know. What happened tonight, it's life changing for someone. And the things her *father* said to her…" I shake my head, disgusted by the revolting things that came out of his mouth. "I'm worried." I look upstairs like I can still see her. God knows, I can feel her, always everywhere.

I've talked to my mom a lot about Ember over the last few months. She knows the details of how we met, ended up married after a weekend and living together because it favored us both. What she doesn't know is how deeply I've fallen for her. How I want nothing more than for Ember to see what our relationship really is. Something so real I can taste it, every fucking day.

"You're worried because you love her," my mom responds with an ease I'm jealous of. She says it out loud as easily as breathing.

I turn my head in her direction, again not surprised she can read right through everything.

It's an arrangement, so the likelihood of Ember feeling the same, regardless of the time we've spent together, is, unfortunately, unlikely. Especially for a woman who's built walls around herself thicker than Fort Knox and especially after tonight.

"I'm going to bed. You need to get some rest, too." She places her hand on my shoulder. "There's nothing more we can give for today. Let's start again tomorrow." Her smile is bigger this time as she feeds me the statement she's repeated frequently over my lifetime.

I trek back upstairs, anxious to get back to Ember, secretly hoping she's still awake so I can be selfish and talk with her, but praying she has fallen asleep.

Her heavy but steady breath tells me she's passed out, and I instantly feel relief.

I can't imagine the incessant thoughts rolling through her head. Her father's words on repeat through her mind like a virus, questioning her worth with every syllable.

I crawl into bed and curl myself up next to her as I watch her chest rise and fall in a peaceful rhythm. I wish more than anything she felt peace and want nothing more than to give it to her.

The promises she makes for herself, for us, always revolve around holding back, not taking things too far. I'm tired of holding back, faking it, pretending what I feel for her isn't real. I've never experienced something so goddamn real.

But after what happened to her tonight, I'm terrified I've lost her forever.

40

EMBER

I wake up feeling the same hungover sensation I did when I woke up next to Hudson in Vegas. Except this one is not alcohol induced, it's my father induced, or at least who I thought was my father. I've decided, right here and now, that a hangover from pure emotional destruction is definitely far worse than a hangover induced by any liquid poison.

I don't recall how we got to wherever we currently are. My mind was muddied and dazed last night, and I completely shut down. That's never happened to me before. I've always been able to control my emotions, my reactions to exciting things as well as negative. I'm not quite the master of the poker face, but I know how to wear a mask to camouflage my true sentiments.

Last night was an exception.

The mask was ripped off and torn to shreds by the people who are supposed to love me the most.

I'm not sure why I'm surprised; they have always treated me like the red-headed stepchild.

Shit.

I am, in literal terms, the red-headed stepchild. To my father, at least.

I think I always knew. Deep down. I just refused to accept it. My brothers, none of them have any inkling of my same coloring, in either hair color or skin tone. They always treated me differently than my brothers. And the way my mother would look at me, the scowl behind her eyes, the hate behind her voice. It was dripping with resentment, and no matter what I did, nothing made it better.

My heart feels as if it's been drained, leaving a faint pulse, just enough to keep me alive to suffer.

What will my brothers think or feel about me? Will they want to have anything to do with me? It's clear my parents don't. Definitely not my *stepfather,* and my mother... well, she'll do whatever he tells her. It's sickening, and the bile that sits at the back of my throat threatens to make an appearance.

I swallow down the bitterness and attempt to push the nausea aside.

The lost little girl in me wants her family, regardless of how they treated me.

The warrior in me wants to fight back, get revenge, show them who I can be, all while giving them the middle finger.

Instead, protecting myself and constructing a wall, like the professional bricklayer I've become, feels most natural. Easiest.

All I know is, I never want to feel this way again. Ever.

My briny eyes blink fully open, and I squint at the throbbing from behind my eyeballs.

Jesus. That hurts.

A large poster covers the wall. It's light blue, with drawings of people and cartoon dogs all around a nuclear eruption exploding in the middle, with the words "Green Day" coming out of the clouds. I instantly recognize it as one of the band's album covers.

The poster next to it is of the Goo Goo Dolls, and some other classic car pictures surround that.

Where the hell am I?

My eyes widen and my pulse picks up. Please note, for the record, an emotional hangover will cause memory loss, just like a regular one.

My pulse calms as my arm brushes against Hudson, lying shirtless in bed next to me. The steady rise and fall of his chest is a dead giveaway he's in a deep slumber.

I rise slowly, due to the full body ache, centering heaviest in the middle of my chest, and circle the room. A shelf in the corner, above a desk, catches my attention. There's only a small amount of light coming through the window, forcing me to squint to see the photos.

Hudson with his brothers, a similar picture like the one he showed me on the plane. Hudson with his parents, wearing a green graduation cap and gown. His mother is a timeless beauty, and he's a spitting image of his father, both beaming with proud smiles ear to ear.

I have a selfie on my phone from my graduation. I thought it was the only one I was going to get until Cody and Benson surprised me by coming. I almost cried when I saw them show up for me. Two was better than none.

More photos of his family and a larger one on the end of five guys. Picking it up for closer inspection, I recognize all of them. They are lined up, arms draping over each other, bonded together and all smiles.

Jake is on the far left, and a blush heats my cheeks as I recall how I saw him at the club the other day. He's older now than in this picture, but the same strong essence of power he broadcasts naturally is there, clear as day. The tallest of them all, Kobi, I think is his name, next to him with Dane. They are the only ones not looking at the camera, instead looking at each other, laughing like something happened right before the picture snapped. On the right side, Seamus and Hudson, in all his handsome glory, smiling in a way that I've only seen when he's with his friends.

The corner of my lip lifts and my eyes soften, something that I've been unable to prevent whenever Hudson is involved, but the heaviness in my chest wipes that away, and the hard ridges that I wear like armor returns.

Placing the frame down, I glance back at Hudson. There's a nightstand next to his side of the bed with a small frameless photo leaning against the lamp. I pad a few light steps in that direction and pick it up, then stand in front of the window to see it better.

It's me. From the opening night gala.

I'm in the green dress that Cruz picked out for me, my hair pulled over one shoulder as I look to the side, smiling widely at something someone was saying. I can't even recall when he took this. I never even knew he took this.

"It's a good luck charm." Hudson's voice startles me, and I jump-turn to face him.

"Well... actually, at first I just wanted to feel you next to me, whenever I was away at my games. So, I placed it on my nightstand next to my bed. Then, that first stint of games, we won all but one game." He smiles, pushing himself up to a seated position on the bed. "The game we lost, your picture had fallen off the nightstand the night before. I woke up in the morning and it was facing down on the floor, so now it's a superstition. If I don't have it..." He runs his hand through his disheveled bed head hair. "If you're not there... everything feels off."

He looks up at me with a tight smile, lifting his eyebrows at his confession. He tosses off the sheets and stands, wearing nothing but his boxer briefs and a field full of smooth skin and ropes of muscles. He closes the distance between us and lifts my chin, shifting my eyes away from the picture and directly into his.

"There isn't anything in my life that feels absolute, unless it's with you."

"Oh," I breathe out, my lips barely moving, feeling paralyzed and confused.

"You know, you say *'Oh'* a lot." He nods, answering my silent expression. "Whenever you are surprised about something." He leans in close to me and tucks a rebellious strand of hair behind my ear. "You say *'right'* whenever you have to accept something that you can no longer avoid, and you say *'I can't'*, instead of no, because you have spent your entire life pleasing people and don't like saying no."

Right.

"When you're nervous, you bite the corner of your bottom lip. This side," he brushes his thumb over the left side, "and you stick your tongue out on this side," he moves his thumb over to the right, "when you're hyper-focused on something."

Well, shit.

My broken heart cracks a little more at the realization of how well he knows my ticks. Or maybe it's attempting to repair itself, but my heart doesn't know the difference between breaking and healing, knowing that an open heart leads to a broken one.

"People see you Ember; the ones that matter do." His words speak volumes, even though they were hardly a whisper.

Wet cotton balls form in my throat with the density of the air and dryness in my mouth, mixed with that heavy ache in my chest, and it's difficult to breathe. My thoughts evaporate between my brain and tongue, and I'm unable to form any words. His statement leads to a conversation that I'm just not ready for.

"Well, you are an observant one, Mr. Byrnes." I smile, keeping it as light as possible.

His brow furrows and I step around him, avoiding any scrutinizing, and place the picture back on the table.

"We're at my parents' house." He steps into sweatpants and pulls a shirt over his head. "I didn't know where to go, but I knew we couldn't stay there, so coming home just sort of happened."

"Makes sense." I nod in agreement. Home is a comfort to him, so I can totally understand why this is the first place he thought of. I wish I felt the same.

"I just need a few minutes. I'll meet you down there?" He nods, kisses my temple, and disappears, closing the door softly behind him.

My purse sits on the corner of his desk, and I reach inside to grab my phone.

No missed calls. No text messages.

Nothing.

Not even my brothers.

I've walked through my entire life feeling like I'm on an island, fending for myself. Nothing but my thoughts, ideas, and goals to motivate me. I reveled in the solidarity because it made me feel strong.

But for the first time, I feel so alone, and it makes me feel so weak.

"I DON'T KNOW if or when they will ever tour again. They just so happen to be here today, when you randomly come out of the blue. When mom told me last night you were on your way, I called my guy and got front row tickets. It's like a miraculous divine intervention for you to finally see them!"

I stand at the base of the stairs, tucked around the corner from behind the kitchen. The smell of perfectly cooked bacon permeates the air, and it smells like I'm in the best breakfast diner in the city instead of someone's home.

My stomach was anxious to get to the kitchen, but I slowed instantly when I heard another man's voice talking with Hudson, realizing pretty quickly it's one of his brothers.

"Grant, this is amazing, but try to sell them or something. I can't go. I'm not comfortable taking Ember with everything that's happened."

"Okay, hear me out. From what little you told me, that's all kinds of jacked up shit what happened last night, but this is a once in a lifetime opportunity. It's fucking Green Day. You know, your favorite band, like ever of all time."

Hudson has mentioned this before, and I've seen his playlist for his workouts and game days. There's a mix of all kinds of different hype music, but his favorite 90s punk band takes up a majority of it. He told me his mom thinks he should have been born in an earlier generation with his love for 80s and 90s music, specifically punk rock. He prefers to listen to that than current pop or anything else.

I enjoy my share of that genre. I can lip sync a couple of Green Day songs, and Blink-182 had some good ones, but they were way before my time. Some days I feel like Hudson half lives for their lyrics.

His brother is right, this is a once in a lifetime opportunity.

Plus, getting lost in music sounds like an amazing distraction today.

I caution my steps and round the corner, and both Hudson and Grant crane their necks in my direction, stopping any further conversation. Hudson slaps the envelope onto Grant's chest, giving him back what I assume are the tickets and a pointed look.

"Good Morning, Ember." Hudson's mother, who I have only talked to on the phone with Hudson, smiles at me, setting down the towel she was drying her hands with, and opens her arms as she walks toward me.

"Good Morning." A genuine smile grows on my face as she embraces me in a cozy hug.

"I hope you're hungry," she says, walking back to the stove.

"I could definitely eat," I reply, looking over at Hudson, then turn to Grant. "Hi, I'm Ember." I give a shy wave.

Grant lunges at me, wrapping me in a hug as he picks me up and twirls me around.

"Dude..." Hudson says.

Grant is definitely a playful one, and it makes me giggle.

"Can't help it, I'm a hugger." He shrugs after he sets me down.

"Me too." My laugh still lingering.

I step up to the breakfast bar, lifting one leg on the barstool as I push myself onto the seat.

"What are you guys up to?" I ask, as Hudson slides a cup of coffee my way.

"Nothing much," Hudson quips quickly before Grant can say anything.

"That's interesting," I sip my coffee, "because it sort of sounded like you were trying to cock block me from going to a concert today?" Grant's eyebrow ticks up with the corner of his mouth, and Hudson's jaw slacks as his eyes glance over his shoulder back at his mom.

Christ. The woman literally just hugged me and I completely forgot she was in the room. A blush of embarrassment forms on my cheeks for inappropriate use of the word cock in front of her. Jesus, my recent job requirement of the use of any and all sexual innuendos is wearing off into real life way too easy and far too uncensored.

"I apologize, Mrs. Byrnes." Palming my face.

"Oh, no need to apologize, my dear. I'm glad someone is trying to talk some sense into my son." That makes me smile.

"Hey, I was trying to," Grant whines to all of us. That makes me smile, too, and damn, it feels good.

Hudson's fixed stare doesn't leave mine.

His brows pinch together ever so slightly, as he mouths, "You sure?"

The look of vulnerability kills me. Other than asking me for that one favor earlier this year—you know, that little favor of being his wife—he's literally asked me for nothing and done everything for me. A part of me feels like he has catered to me because of guilt, that I agreed to stay married to him, but I've realized... that's just Hudson.

He gives and hardly ever takes. He wants my happiness more than his own. He would never force me to go to this concert, no matter how much he wants to go himself, nor would he even consider leaving me alone for it.

I want nothing more than to go with him. His happiness will definitely feed mine. And I think we both need that today.

"Oh, we're going. My only requirement is breakfast and I'm all in."

"Yesssssssss!" Grant's arms fly over his head then slap Hudson on the back so hard he winces.

The smile that forms on Hudson's face after, though, it's worth its weight in gold.

41

HUDSON

Tonight has been the epitome of perfection.

This was after the flawless day we spent with my parents and Grant, all of them getting to know Ember, and it was the happiest I've felt in, well, as long as I can remember. My favorite people getting to know this woman that's consumed every bit of my soul.

Bringing her here was a risk. The stark contrast between our families could have brought on bad memories or feelings of envy and anger. My goal was to show her how many people care about her. I need her to see that, and I think it has.

She seemed to be handling the situation with her parents with ease. She laughed and held a conversation with Grant and my parents like she's been a part of this family all along. We spent the day talking about my childhood, what she's doing at XConnect, slightly censored for my parents, of course. Overall, being completely void of all negative emotion when it came to what happened last night, but that's in line with exactly what she's always done. Masked her emotions, putting a veil over a so-called weakness.

And I know she's still a fucking emotional marathon

runner. I wouldn't bet against her putting her running shoes back on at this point. So, needless to say, I've felt the need to stay close to her. For both myself, and just to make sure she doesn't finally break down.

Last night, she closed herself off and hardly remembers any of it. But she has yet to truly fall apart, and I can't imagine she's not on the brink of that. I don't want to risk not being around if —when—that finally happens.

Ember has been wrapped in my arms all night. We've been on the front line for every single song Green Day has played on stage. At some point, Billie Joe Armstrong's saliva or sweat, I'm not sure which, landed on my arm and I didn't give two shits about it. I was listening to my favorite band perform live, with my favorite girl by my side.

Every time I've looked down at her, a smile graced her gorgeous face, like she was eating the lyrics in, just as much as I do every time I hear one of their songs.

Their songs were evenly spread out over the night, between slow and fast-paced ones, each of which just fell in line with each other. We shifted between jumping up and down, screaming the lyrics, to swaying together with her in my arms, depending on whatever song was played. I was surprised to see how many she knew, which just solidified the whole 'she's fated for me' feeling even more.

At the end of the night, Billie Joe left the stage for only a brief moment after finishing with *Good Riddance*—which I appreciate now more than ever after meeting Ember's parents. The crowd started chanting for an encore over and over. Of course, he came wandering back on stage, with a barstool in one hand and his guitar in the other.

After he sits down, he strums a few chords, then the familiar rhythm of my favorite song starts to play.

It's pure acoustic and different from any other rendition I've ever heard.

. . .

I walk a lonely road
The only one that I have ever known
Don't know where it goes
But it's home to me, and I walk alone

I walk this empty street
On the boulevard of Broken Dreams
Where the city sleeps
And I'm the only one, I walk alone
I walk alone, I walk alone.

THEIR SONGS, specifically this one, got me through the toughest times of my life. After Veronica, after my injury, through so many issues with Henry. I soak in the lyrics and enjoy them for what they are to me now. What they've meant to me.

My shadow's the only one that walks beside me
My shallow heart's the only thing that's beating
Sometimes, I wish someone out there will find me
Til then, I walk alone.

I'm walking down the line
That divides me somewhere in my mind
On the borderline
Of the edge, and where I walk alone.

Read between the lines
What's fucked up, and everything's alright
Check my vital signs

To know I'm still alive, and I walk alone

Ember's body stiffens and stops moving with mine. As I glance down at her, her chin is tilted toward her chest, her gaze directly on the floor.

"Ember." She doesn't look up.

My feet shuffle faster than my brain can even keep up as I move myself in front of her. Cupping her cheeks, I force her to look up at me.

And the sight destroys me.

Tears pool over her emerald eyes before streaming down her cheeks. Pinched brows and a pained expression that I can feel radiating from her like a beacon.

"I'm all alone now." Her voice is cracked and broken.

"Fuck. Ember." I pull her into me, holding her close.

I knew it was a matter of time.

I had no idea it would be now.

She's grieving the loss of her family, something I can't even comprehend. Especially considering they are still living and breathing, yet they choose to disregard her like trash. I can't imagine the hopelessness she feels, and how much she is questioning everything in her life.

"Shit," I whisper under my breath.

I look around. We're completely surrounded by hordes of people, holding up their lighters or phones displaying their camera light. Everyone's sole attention is on the stage.

Seeing only one route, I place her arms around my neck and pull her into me. Gripping her hips and wrapping her legs around me, her body hugs to mine with vigor. Squeezing me as if she'll lose herself otherwise.

I trail the front of the stage to the side of the venue,

following the row of lights to the lit up exit sign, and barrel through the emergency exit.

The warm summer night air wraps around us as I carry her in the direction of the pickup area. I'm thankful we decided to Uber instead of driving so I don't have to let her go, and even more grateful that there is a taxi waiting on the side of the curb so we don't need to wait for a ride share.

Swinging the door open, I shift Ember's leg to one side of my body and slide in with her on my lap. She's shaking, her body hiccuping between the gasps of air she is taking between her tears.

"Ember..."

She tucks her face into my neck, avoiding my gaze.

So I squeeze harder, holding her as close to me as possible, and tell her the only truths I know.

"You're not alone. You're never going to be alone."

I pause, holding my breath.

"I love you. I love you so fucking much."

42

EMBER

This whole emotional hangover thing is shit. Considering I typically ignore my deep-rooted feelings, two days in a row of emotional breakdowns is a record I never intend to break again.

Between Hudson and Green Day, I swear the combination triggered a face-to-face meeting of all the feelings I've spent years teaching myself to ignore. Now, here they are, flashing like the Las Vegas strip lights, bright and on display for the whole world to see.

I know exactly what that entire breakdown came from. Not my parents or the way they talked to me. Frankly, I'm used to that. It didn't feel any harsher than how they've treated me since I was a kid. And at this point, in the famous words of Green Day, *Good Riddance.*

My brothers, though. They have always been my lifeline. Whenever I was drowning, grasping at straws, Benson and Cody were there. Bobby strives too much for my father's approval to have really had my back, but I see now how desperately he needed his approval. Terrified that his sexuality would exile him from the family.

He has only had a handful of girlfriends over the years but never pursued any of them seriously. He's been best friends with Elliot for years, yet he was never fully supportive of my relationship with him. I wonder how I never saw it before.

His secret relationship with Elliot had to have been going on for years. The fact that my father knew about them, yet still forced Elliot to pursue me, makes me nauseous. Elliot was hungry for a career in politics, and I know he felt like my dad could help him get there. So I can only assume my *stepfather* used that to his advantage.

Telling Elliot to stop being gay—like it's a choice. Forcing him to choose a career over his love for Bobby and using me to hide it all. It's sickening.

What Elliot and I had wasn't intimate or passionate. We were more friends than anything else, great friends, actually, and it all makes sense now. I avoided sex because of my lack of desire for it, specifically with him. But for Elliot, if he's gay and loves my brother, of course he would have avoided it with me.

The times we did, it ended up being out of obligation. Like it was something we had to do because we were in a relationship, and it had been too long or one of us felt guilty.

God, he must have been repulsed by doing anything sexual with me.

Then there's the mental hurdle of having sex with his boyfriend's sister out of fear of threats from our father. No wonder he never wanted oral sex and just turned the lights off during sex. I palm my face, embarrassed. I feel nauseous just thinking about it. I can only imagine that's exactly how Elliot felt when doing anything with me.

I'm disgusted that Bobby and Elliot used me in that way. They allowed my father to do that, knowing how much it was going to hurt everyone involved, and the sadness I feel easily warps into anger, toggling back and forth between feeling bad for them and being so fucking pissed off I can't see straight.

I want to say this is all my father, but they made their choice, too.

I don't want to see or talk to either one of them, at least until I manage my feelings on everything. But Benson and Cody, the fact they haven't called or reached out to me. I don't know if they don't want anything to do with me now or if it's something driven by my—I shake my head. Robert, his name is Robert. Not my father. He's been far removed as my father, in literal terms, and in all the ways someone should be a father, and he's never deserved that title.

I wish I would have been stronger before.

The fear he has ingrained in everyone around us, all for whatever benefit suits him.

God, it's revolting.

I wonder what I might be missing with Benson and Cody. If they've been hiding something in order to avoid his wrath. It kills me that those two haven't reached out to me. That was really the sole reason for my breakdown last night. I don't want to lose everything I've ever known, but those two, they mean so much to me.

My heart aches in my chest. The heaviness that's been lingering there for the past two days hasn't lightened up.

I'm terrified it never will.

My chest is tender from the last two days, from the constant anxiety, and my heart seeps of pure agony. I've never been so aware of the fact that I have one until these past few days. Stabbing pain hits me with every beat as I recall the images of all of their faces.

I never want to feel this way again, which forces my mind to go to Hudson and how I've come to rely on his support. It's just another thing I risk losing, especially knowing what we have is temporary.

I need to push back on what we're doing. I should probably start looking for a place, since we only have a few months until the season is over. The team is doing so well, I think he'll get an offer for a longer contract, and he won't need the title we hold any longer.

My phone buzzes on the nightstand next to Hudson's empty side of the bed. He already went downstairs, and I've been clinging to the comfort of the bed this morning, even though I told him I'd be down in a few minutes.

I suppose I can't avoid life all together today.

I reach across the pillow, picking up the phone. A slight twinge of disappointment blankets me when it's not one of my brothers, but I can't help but smile when I see Cruz's name on the screen. He programmed a picture of us as his contact picture; a selfie I took when we had lunch in the courtyard a couple months ago. My smile is beaming while his chin rests on my shoulder with his tongue sticking out.

I swipe to answer and put him on speaker.

"Hey, Cruz."

"Oh my god, she lives."

I chuckle. "You can't get rid of me that easily."

"Elena told me that Hudson called and you guys needed to stay an extra day. Everything okay?"

I pause, debating if I should share the details with him, but decide on waiting until we're together and I can formulate my words and thoughts better.

"Totally. I just needed another day to work through some family stuff." It's not far from the truth.

"Good, I'm glad to hear that, because Daddy Maverick has been working hard and everything is ready for you to come home."

I giggle at his self given Top Gun nickname. "Cruz Thomas," I call him by his full name, as if to scold him, "you only call yourself Daddy Maverick after a night of actually *being* daddy Maverick. Are you staying out of trouble?"

"Of course not. Why would I do that?" He starts to tell me a story, but I flash back to him saying everything was ready for me to come home.

"Wait. What do you mean, everything is ready?" I interrupt him and grab my leggings, stepping into them, pulling them over my hips.

"Fine. I guess I'll finish that story later, miss interrupter of the year. The final delivery arrived early on Saturday, and I had the team work over the weekend getting the rooms finished. The city just came and signed off on it... on everything." I can hear his smug ass smile through the speaker.

"Are you kidding me? And I missed it!?" I squeal.

"Don't freak out. It's not like you missed the birth of your first born or something."

"Yes, yes, this is just like that, Cruz." His analogy is an accurate one.

I rip my newly purchased Green Day shirt over my head, battling my conflicting emotions. Angry I missed the final sign off, but freaking the hell out that everything is ready.

"Well, I couldn't turn him away when he was here, so... Surprise, it's official!" he sing-songs.

"Oh my god." Picking up the phone, I take it off speaker and put the phone up to my ear. "I can't believe it," I breathe into the phone.

"I know, it's crazy. You should be so freaking proud of yourself."

I can't help but smile. My heart is beating out of my chest. I'm frantic, pacing back and forth, like I don't know what to do with myself.

Using my shoulder to hold the phone, I grab my hair, wrapping it around my hand and into a messy bun on my head.

"Teamwork, my friend. Amazingly perfect teamwork," I tell Cruz.

"Oh, I know." He doesn't hesitate. "So, Christian wants a meeting with the entire team. You're back tomorrow?"

"Yes, we fly back later today, so I'll be back in the office tomorrow." And I can't wait.

There will be a few outstanding things we'll need to get done, but knowing the club is officially signed off on and we can open... I can't believe it. I'm bouncing as I'm pacing around the room.

"Perfect. I'll plug it in your calendar. Also, we have a morning coffee meeting because Daddy Maverick met someone over the weekend that I need to give you all the details on, and I think I'll need to test out one of the rooms before we open." I blush at the comment, and a rush of excitement hits my core at the memory of Elena, Christian, and Jake.

"Cruz..." I warn, because it might appear to be a question from Cruz, but Daddy Maverick does what he wants.

"See you mañana!" He hangs up before I can tell him no, so he can break the rules without guilt. I shake my head and smile as I plop the phone down on the bed.

I can't believe it. My excitement is overwhelming and my mind is racing with all the things we need to do for the opening.

I can't wait to tell Hudson.

I slip my feet into flip-flops and race downstairs.

"Hudson, the city signed off on the club! XConnect Live is going to open for business!" I exaggerate the last part excitedly with my arms in the air, gyrating my hips as I turn the corner into the kitchen.

I stop dead in my tracks and my smile falls. Hudson's jaw is tense and his fists are clenched as he stands in front of Henry, engrossed in a competitive stare-down. Henry, not nearly as menacing, turns to look at me, donning the usual arrogant smile he wears.

"XConnect has a club now?"

43

EMBER

The flight back to Seattle is the most amazing experience I've ever had on a plane, being that Hudson booked first-class tickets. Apparently, the whole last-minute flight to his parents' house put us in a small coach seat on the plane, in which Hudson still has trauma over, and a stiff neck, so he upgraded our flight home since he has a game tomorrow that he needs to be ready for.

Needless to say, I am not complaining about our seating arrangement.

It's comfortable, spacious, and now I have no idea how I'll ever go back to coach. They even gave us champagne, blankets, and pillows when we got on board.

As giddy as I've been with the experience, Hudson has been a little reserved. Henry showing up at his parents' house has him spiraling, and I can only assume it's because Henry wants to get traded to Hudson's team.

There had been so much animosity between the two that before we left, I decided to pull Henry aside and tell him exactly what he needs to do. Leave Hudson the fuck alone or grovel like he should have years ago and beg for his fucking forgiveness.

It will take an act of Congress because of what Henry did, but he insisted he really is trying to make amends with his brother, even though every time he comes around, he just succeeds in throwing more fuel to the fire. Henry feeds too much into Hudson's anger, egging him on, like he can't help himself. Reluctantly, giving him the benefit of the doubt that he hasn't earned yet, I gave him a couple of tips and a few threats to try to resolve this ongoing war between the two of them.

Hudson's eyes are closed and his head is leaned back against the headrest, giving me a wide open opportunity to gawk at him. And damn, he looks edible.

He decided against a hat today, which is rare. His thick, brown hair falls haphazardly over his forehead, and the stubble growing on his jawline is thicker than usual, since he hasn't shaved since we left Seattle.

He opted for a light blue v-neck shirt, which is plainer than all git up, but it's snug against his chest and arms, fitting like a tailor-made glove, looking like a GQ model.

Feeling brave, I shake out the folded blanket the flight attendant handed to me and lift the armrest that separates us. I snuggle into Hudson's side, and he lifts his arm, allowing me to cuddle closer to his chest.

The comfortable scent that engulfs me is his and only his. Fresh linen that I want to wrap myself in and always that subtle hint of cinnamon. Like it's embedded in his skin.

I cover us both with the blanket as I sneak my hand underneath, trailing my hand down the front of his torso. I circle my hand a few times before moving farther south, just above the waistband of his pants. Fortunately, he wore joggers, and the elastic band makes everything easily accessible.

He shifts slightly in his seat, his head still pressed against the seat, and I peer up to see him attempting to smother a smile.

"What are you doing, little red?" His voice is low and raspy.

"Nothing."

"Doesn't seem like nothing." He lifts his head to look between his legs, then at me.

"Shhhhh." Peering up at him with my 'oh so innocent' eyes.

He sneaks a glance around the plane. The seats are set wider apart, which works in our favor. There are two men in the aisle next to us. The man closest to us sleeps with a neck pillow suffocating him and his mouth gaped wide open.

The man closest to the window is focused on his laptop, watching a movie with headphones snug to his ears.

Hudson is still looking in that direction when I tuck my hand into the waistband of his pants and wrap my fingers around his hard length.

He releases a short grunt before stifling it and presses his head back onto the top of the seat. He's closing his eyes like he's trying to sleep, and I'm cuddled into his chest like I'm using him for a pillow.

The arm that is draped around me tenses, and he clenches the back of my shirt into his fist as I pump my hand up and down over his cock. Moving slowly under the blanket, I grip the crown as I stroke it from base to tip. Wetness falls over my thumb and finger as pre-cum leaks out of the tip, and I wish more than anything I could get on my knees in front of him and take him in my mouth.

Lifting my head, I peer over to the seat in front of me to see if the bathroom is vacant. Not that we'd fit, but maybe, just maybe, we could try. It's terrible timing as I catch the attention of the flight attendant walking past.

"Can I get you anything, my dear?" Hudson's eyes fly open and he looks at her, then me.

"N-no, I'm all good. Thank you." My voice catches in my throat.

She smiles and continues to pass us.

Hudson's eyes meet mine. "You are going to get us in trouble," he warns, his voice stern but husky.

I bite my lip and release his cock, moving my hand further between his legs so my fingertips graze his balls, cupping them and massaging them in my hands, before gripping the base of his cock and tugging upward again.

His eyes roll back as he squeezes them shut, his mouth slacks open quickly before he slams his lips together as tightly as his eyes. He presses into my hand with a deep grunt that vibrates through my ear that rests on his chest.

"Ember—" A warning or a plea?

I'm going with a plea.

I continue long languid strokes, feeling his body tense with each one. His chest heaves with shorter but heavier breaths. I love teasing him, edging him, making him earn his orgasm, but right now, I want him to completely fall apart and allow it all to happen naturally.

I know he thinks I'm going to stop, since I usually do, but I keep going. I pick up the pace, and my grip tightens around his cock.

The hand resting on the armrest clutches the corner, his knuckles whiten at the intensity of his grip. The same for the hand that's resting behind my back. He moves lower and grabs the side of my hip, like he needs it to hold him down.

"Ember... Ember. Stop." He glances down at me with wide eyes and a warning.

"Eyes on me, baby," I say with a smirk, feeding him the same statement he has fed to me when I'm out of control. I crane my neck, stretching it so my lips graze over his parted ones.

From the outside, we look like a loving couple cuddling

under a blanket, kissing each other softly. In reality, this man is about to lose all control and explode all over my hand, a secret only we know, just like everything else we've done since we've become *us*.

"Come for me and don't take your eyes away from mine," I tell him, as his lids flutter over his midnight-colored orbs, every stroke pooling them deeper with need. But he listens, his gaze never strays. Releasing his grip on the armrest, he cups my cheek, pulling my forehead to his, whispering over my lips.

"Fuck, fuck, goddammit. What the hell are you doing to me?" His breath hitches. "Fuck, I'm gonna come," he grits, as silently as possible, through his teeth. My hair falls over the side of my face, and his fingers wrap around the strands, using them to pull himself even closer to me.

God, this is so sexy, watching him lose control and fall apart. All for me.

A growl leaves his chest, sending lightning bolts to my core. His hips buck and his cock throbs in my hand, then cum spills into my hand and drenches the pocket of fabric blanketing him.

Forcing him to hold back his moans, but keeping his eyes on mine, is the sexiest thing I've ever witnessed. His body, desperate and hiding, while his eyes tell me everything.

He told me he loved me last night. I remember it vividly, as clear as the lust in his eyes right now. I've tried to ignore what he confessed because there was a chance he said it out of pity. Out of obligation or guilt. Just to make me feel better in a shitty situation.

But the look in his eyes now, as they strip away all my reservations of whatever this is we have.

I feel naked.

Everything is so raw, so real, and there is no faking the pain behind his eyes.

He loves me.

It scares the shit out of me.
And he knows it.

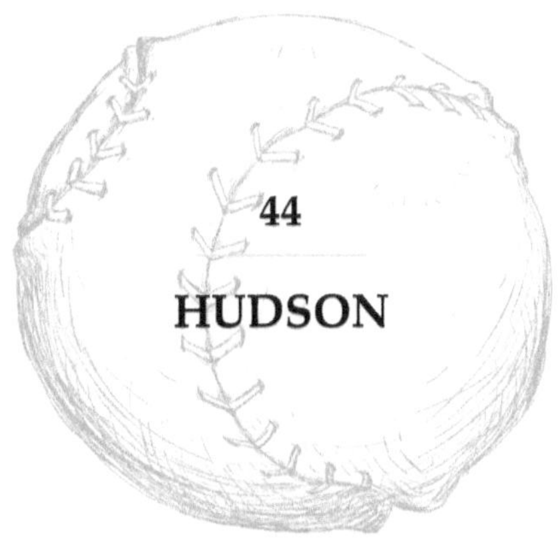

44

HUDSON

"How was your time with Ember's family?" Coach asks, as we retreat to the locker room from the field.

"I gotta be honest. They are total shit people, Coach. I'm shocked that someone as amazing as Ember could come from the family that I visited this weekend," I tell Coach as I remove my hat and run my fingers through my hair.

As of yesterday, her brothers still haven't reached out, and neither have her so-called friends. The rage I feel about how all of that went down has been weighing on me since the moment we left.

I didn't do enough damage to Robert Riley when I had the chance. A fleeting thought that I haven't been able to get over, causing moments of regret. Although I know there is nothing I can do physically to hurt him enough to do the sort of destruction I dream about.

So, instead, I have Seamus digging into him. Because what are best friends with Top Secret security clearance for?

"Well, if it's any consolation, I hope she's found a family in us. We sure have found one in you guys." My eyebrows hit my hairline as my neck jerks back with the sincerity behind his comment.

"She has, sir. We both have." A lie and a truth. I have. I have found a home in her and with my team. I can't, with certainty, say she feels the same. My chest tightens at the thought.

If I've learned anything about her, it's that she strives for something I don't know that I can ever give her. She's been dying to prove herself to her parents for so many years. After last weekend, I can only imagine now she feels like she has completely lost her identity. Knowing she doesn't have to impress anyone but herself. She finally has full control of her life and doesn't need to let anyone's approval allow her to make her decisions.

But she's never had that kind of freedom, and who knows how she'll respond to it.

"It's not official yet, so I shouldn't say anything..." Coach's statement rips me away from my thoughts. He looks to the left and right to check our surroundings.

My breath stalls as I wait for him to continue. His hands are on his hips, which leaves me with no clue, since that's his semi-permanent stance whenever he shares any kind of news. In fact, if they build a monument for him, it would be this exact stance.

"Sir?" I encourage him to say freaking something.

"We're working up a contract for you, Byrnes. I'm telling you now because I don't want you to get any ideas about talking to other teams. Technically, you're free to go anywhere when the season is over, but we want you to stay with us." I'm taken aback.

I force out a breath, and I stifle a smile. I wasn't expecting that at all.

"Wow, Coach. Thank you," spills out from me, and I have to urge to hug him, but he's the furthest thing from a hugger.

"I'm pushing for a five-year contract. We probably have to build in a trade option after three, but that's my goal."

I nod, smiling, but my smile drops instantly when he mentions the next topic.

"About your brother—"

My gaze snaps to him. Jesus, don't say it. If they are signing him, too, that would potentially be five long, dreadful years with my jackass brother. Him taunting me, making my life miserable. I swear he thrives on it.

"We are considering offering him a contract. He's expensive, but we're losing Callahan next year and he's exactly what we need. I have to know if that can work. Having the Byrnes brothers back together could make us unstoppable. Whatever troubled history you guys have, you gotta squash it, son." He places his hand on my shoulder. His brows are pinched together, like it hurts him to ask. Because he knows. He might not know all the details of everything that happened, but he knows I would have to climb Mount Everest to get over the trauma he's caused me in the past.

"I told you before that wild pitch could have been an accident, and I think it was. But he ruined my career and had no remorse whatsoever. He stole my fiancé, then left her after a couple months. He's just not a good man. I have no idea how long it'll take me to forgive him."

I place my hands on my hips, mocking his stance, because I don't know what else to do with them. Looking down, I gently kick nothing on the floor.

I chipmunk my cheeks and exhale.

"You gave me an opportunity, and I'm grateful for that. I don't want to go anywhere else." Especially knowing that Ember is here, and she's making a name for herself at Ford. "I'll stay with you... with or without my brother." I hate saying it. I fucking hate it.

He grants me a look of sympathy, but he's proud, too. He

stays silent, only granting me a stiff nod before pressing his lips in a tight line, then slaps my shoulder and heads down the hall to his office.

I can do this. I just have to find it in my heart to resolve the past with my brother. Maybe Ember is right, maybe he's been trying so hard these past few months to rekindle our relationship and make up for his mistakes.

She said, "*Forgiveness does not change the past, but it can enhance your future.*"

Maybe there is some truth to that. I hope so.

45

EMBER

"All the rooms are completed. I am debating about changing the theme of room six. It doesn't have the same feel as the others. Other than that, the private rooms are ready." I'm standing at the front of the main conference room. The PowerPoint I created is only a display to show the entire team, including Elena and Christian, the final layout for the club.

"The voyeur stage just needs backstage curtains installed, and I am waiting for our updated AOL logo for *the Chat Room* entrance." Cruz writes down the items we're pending because he tracks everything, and I swear nothing gets past him. Smiling when he looks back at me, giving me a thumbs up.

I told him how nervous I was about this presentation, being that it's literally in front of half the executive staff of the company. But I know this club inside and out, so the moment I stepped up here, I knew exactly what I needed to say. It's been the easiest presentation I've ever done, and I'm giddy with excitement. In fact, I can't stop smiling like an idiot.

"On Saturday, both the app and the website will announce the soft opening date and allow members to upgrade their membership in order to purchase tickets. I suspect we will have, at minimum, a thirty percent increase of our existing members upgrading and an additional five percent of new sign ups. We've paid minimal for public marketing, to avoid negative press, but with our social media profiles and current member base, I think this will be substantial growth for the initial opening, and within a year, I suspect our numbers will triple." Christian peers over at Elena. Her lips are turned up in a semi-permanent grin as well.

"Lastly, we'll have double the security we would typically have on staff. I've tasked Dietrich," I look over at Christian's head of security, sitting next to him at the table, "with building a team for opening night. He can give us the details as we get closer to the opening, but we will be bringing on an outside security vendor for placement, both outside and inside, to ensure the protestors don't scare away the clientele and we don't have anyone enter the club that shouldn't."

Over the last few months, we've had a lot of *incidents*—people spraying graffiti on the exterior of the building or trying to start fires. We've always had security in the parking lot, which has prevented some vandalism but last week, while I was away, a small group of protestors tried to break inside, so we've increased our twenty-four-hour security as we've gotten closer to the opening date.

It will die down eventually, but until then, I'm doing everything in my power to protect what we've built. Just because they don't agree with the lifestyle that others have, doesn't give them a right to destroy it. We have consensual loving adults with open sexuality. What gives these protestors a right to say they can't express themselves in open and honest ways? Their beliefs are beyond unreasonable, and I hate that they throw out such hate and violence. Those actions force people to hide their true desires from others, feeding their own guilt, making them feel like they are not normal for what they need. I know because I've spent my life pushing those desires into a black box, hiding it from everyone.

Until Hudson. Until his support allowed me the permission I needed to tell him what I desired. And he did everything in his power to bring all of those to life.

"I'll email out an agenda for opening night and everyone's tasks for the week leading up to it. Does anyone have any questions?" I glance around the room at all the executives, seeing everyone excited and humming words of praise and encouragement.

Cruz raises his unusually long arm straight in the air, pushing it as far as possible to the ceiling, like I'm going to ignore him if he doesn't.

I smile and point at him. "Yes, Cruz."

"I have a great idea for room six's theme," he shares enthusiastically, as Cruz normally does.

"Oh, yeah? Give it to me," I reply, shifting the papers in front of me, so I can look at the specs for room six, even though I have them memorized.

"Well, I think we're missing the boat with the people who have a food fetish. So I suggest we stock it with things we know that group of people like. Whip cream, strawberries, chocolate syrup... cucumbers. You know, stuff like that. We can call it something fun, like Flavor Fantasies or Edible Euphoria, or ooh, ooh, Culinary Playground." Cruz wiggles his eyebrows, but stops and cranes his neck back when he sees my wide-eyed expression.

I side eye over to Christian, who is pinching the bridge of his nose while Elena just giggles, looking at her folded hands on the table.

Another executive is nodding, like it's the best idea since sliced bread.

"What?" His arms are splayed out, palms face up, confused at my expression.

"Okay... wow... um, great idea in theory. Love those room names. But uhhh, we'd be taking on a bit too much liability with potential..." I pause, picking my words wisely, "infections," I say, softly.

And fuck it. I have to say it.

"Plus, cucumbers belong in salads, not vaginas." I shrug at Cruz.

Cruz's shoulders slouch with a dramatic eye roll.

"Alright, any other questions?" I ask the room.

"Yes, I'd like a minute." Christian stands up from his seat at the head of the table, buttoning his suit jacket, stoic and serious, as usual. It's a hard contrast from the desperate man I saw at the club behind that glass wall completely falling apart for Elena and Jake. My cheeks flush, which is great timing to make me appear shy instead of turned on.

I smile and pull my seat out to sit next to Cruz, who is currently giving me the stank eye from turning down his idea. "Great names. Icky idea. Who wants to clean that?" I whisper.

"Who wants to clean *any* of the rooms?" Cocking his head to the side.

So, yeah, he's got a point there.

"It's necessary to recognize Cruz and the support he's provided throughout this project." Cruz stands halfway, taking a small bow with a smile, eating up the praise in a way I'm envious of. "Necessary, but clearly not needed." It's the first smile that's crossed Christian's face and, of course, only Cruz can bring out the playful side of him during a business meeting.

"The entire team really came together on this one, but I'd like to take a moment to recognize Ember for the outstanding job she has done running this project. She came to me with this idea only a few months ago, and I'm truly shocked and incredibly pleased it's come to fruition effortlessly. Even though it was far from that." He meets my gaze and grants me a proud smile. I press my lips together, unsure of how to reply to his praise. He continues circling the table.

"Every detail was well thought out, planned, and you did a stellar job building this from the ground up. There is just one thing that doesn't fit."

My face falls. What? What doesn't fit? His eyes flick to mine, studying me. Like he's trying to tread lightly.

My confidence sways with his words, my mother's face flashes behind my eyes, and I question everything instantly. My thoughts run rampant before I squeeze my eyes shut, stopping the stampede of nonsense.

Fuck that. I may not have the most sexual experience. I may be young compared to this group. But I fit. I fit here.

I steel my spine and open my mouth to defend myself, but Christian continues.

"*XConnect Live.* Yes, we're bringing the app to life. In all literal terms. But after some thought, another name fits better, so I went ahead and filed the updated name with the city and worked directly with the contractor to create the proper signage for the building."

He fucking did what? I mean, I know it's his company, but he didn't even tell me.

He steps to the corner of the room, where a poster board is on a display stand, draped with a white cotton overlay. I noticed it there when I came in, but figured it was for something else.

He grips the corner of the white drape. "Ember, you came to us, brand new to the corporate world, but with an ambition I have never seen in anyone. I can't express how happy I am that you chose to work here." His eyes soften as he looks back at me, and I furrow my brows, a bit confused as I nervously bite the corner of my face off.

He continues, "The definition of *ember* according to the dictionary is, *'a small piece of glowing coal or wood in a dying fire.'* In my eyes, you have already revived XConnect in ways I never predicted with this brave idea, bringing something that was potentially dying back to life. It's only fitting that the club be named after that drive and motivation. After you." He slips off the sheet, revealing the poster, which is a sketch mock-up of the front of the building, my building, that I've seen day in and day out.

AFTERBURN is beautifully displayed over the front of it.

My hands cover my mouth, that falls uncontrollably.

Everyone claps, cheering, while Cruz shoulder bumps me. Christian and Elena smile at me.

I can't believe it. Tears flood my eyes and I'm utterly speechless. My hands tremble from nerves, from excitement and happiness, and I have no idea how to navigate through all the different emotions rifling through my body.

"I don't know what to say." My voice splintered from the boulder in the back of my throat. "Thank you."

"You deserve it, Ember."

46

EMBER

I can't believe that just happened. I walk back into my office, placing the mess of papers on my desk, before plopping down in my chair. My blood pressure is skyrocketing from all the excitement pumping through my veins, and I'm riding a high that I've never experienced before.

For someone like Christian Ford to be proud of what I've done is a validation I never knew I could experience.

He named his club... after me. Tears pool at the corners of my eyes again, and although I hate the defiance of my own emotions. I smile at their persistence.

I want to scream from the rooftop, but to avoid being a total psycho, I reach for my phone to call Hudson.

The floor swallows me whole when I see my mother's name, with multiple missed calls and a few text messages.

As usual, her timing is impeccable, always on the sidelines ready to bring me down after I've been lifted up.

My thumb hovers over the screen, unable to tap to view. I'm too afraid to see what she has to say. I pause a moment and tell myself that no matter what she says, it doesn't matter. She can say the worst, most vile words, and it won't be anything I haven't heard. Or she can say the kindest, sweetest testimony to attempt to revive our relationship and I won't believe her.

She berated me all my life, resented me for *years*, for a choice *she* made. She hated my existence because of the toxic and dysfunctional relationship it created between her and *her husband*. I didn't create that. I did nothing wrong, and she blamed me, taking all her indiscretions out on me.

My entire life.

The more my father despised me, the worse he treated her, I inherited the brunt of.

So, if it doesn't matter, I should just delete it. Swipe left and delete her messages. Then block her.

But, like her, I suppose I also inherited a glutton for punishment. I tap on the screen, bringing up the messages.

Mom: You are a disgrace to this family.

Mom: Not that I need to tell you, but never return here. Ever. This town needs Robert, and you nearly tarnished his reputation and ruined everything. Luckily, no one other than your brothers saw the chaos you created here. And we've taken care of that.

What the hell does that mean? She's taken care of my brothers. It feels like an elephant is sitting on my chest. How can she force them to stay away from me? I guess if they are ashamed of me, too, it's an easy choice to make.

My vision blurs over the letters on my screen as tears threaten again. The kind only my mother can bring on. Pure emotional loneliness and the feeling of worthlessness begin to slip down my cheek. I squeeze my eyes shut, allowing the waterfall of emotions to shed so I can wash myself of this, of her.

Opening my eyes, the words are still fuzzy but clearer than

before, and I see her final text. I give myself a strong, steady breath.

> Mom: You are dead to me. To all of us.

And, I'm done.

Taking the choice in my own hands for the first time in my life, I click on her contact name and block her number. The flush of relief is instant.

I should have done that a long fucking time ago.

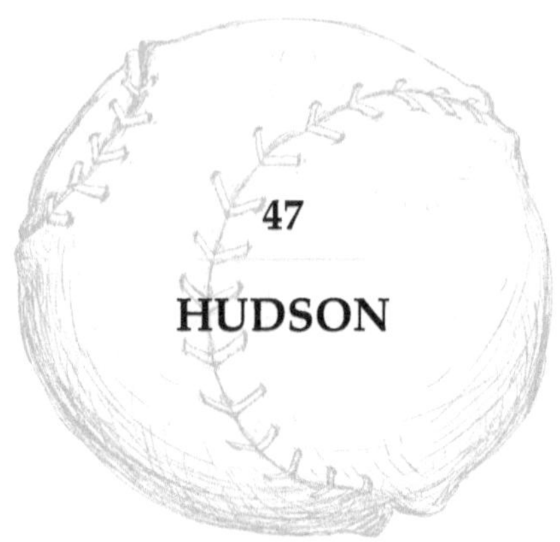

47

HUDSON

"**Y**es, you have to wear the mask, Hudson. It's a masquerade party!" Cruz declares, as he adjusts his own mask in the mirror of my bathroom.

Cruz's date fell through, which he has expressed his disdain about more times tonight than baseball games I've played this season. Since my date, the queen of the club, had to be at the club early, I agreed to go with Cruz so he didn't have to show up alone.

I wasn't all that concerned about who I showed up with, other than that I would have preferred the gorgeous redhead that is my current obsession on my arm. But Jake just messaged me and said the media was swarming outside the club.

We've nearly clinched a playoff spot, and knowing they are there snapping pictures of anyone coming in might draw some unwanted attention that I'm certain Coach would not appreciate.

Actually, these masks are a good idea.

"Do you have another one that covers more of my face?" I shift the mask that covers my forehead, eyes, and nose. It's black, with rose gold colored lines embossed over the front and the top cut out in a fashion that resembles a king's crown.

"Oh, hell no. I had those specially made to match Ember's. You are wearing *that* one." He steps out of the bathroom. Cruz always looks good in pretty much anything he wears, be it casual or black tie. But tonight, he belongs on a high fashion runway.

His charcoal suit is tailored to his body, a purple satin vest that matches a purple bow tie that only he could pull off. His mask matches himself—black, white and purple designed throughout—one side of the mask flares out over the top of his head, and I couldn't envision a better look for him.

I look down at myself, straightening my tux. I didn't opt for anything, since I let Cruz dress me to match Ember. I've never worn all black everything. It's definitely not my style, but I don't hate it. Black tux, black shirt, black vest, black tie. It's very John Wick.

I take one more look at myself in the mirror, running my hands through my newly styled hair that I just had cut earlier today.

With the black suit, mask, my new haircut, and slight stubble I decided not to shave today, I wonder if Ember will even recognize me.

I know I won't miss her.

My eyes find her in any room she's in, like they are drawn to wherever she is.

I didn't get to see the dress on her, but I did see it on its hanger when she left earlier today. She is beautiful in anything she wears, but that dress already looked sexy as shit on that goddamn hanger. She's going to bring that to life when she slips it on, just like she does everything else she touches.

I know that she's been busy with the club, but I also know she's been pulling away slowly. It's been gradual, but the same fleeting feelings I had when I first met her have returned. She's been preparing herself to run. Except this time, I know she feels like it's time because the season is almost over and she's protecting herself.

I hate that I feel like I'm already losing her. Which is why I never told her of the five-year contract that Coach told me about. I couldn't bring myself to tell her that option was on the table, for fear she would leave earlier than the end of the season.

I want her to decide to stay... for me. For us.

I know I have to confess everything to her. I have to risk it all to keep her. I just haven't had the guts to bring it up yet.

"Are you ready to head out?" I ask Cruz as I walk out of my room.

"I've been waiting for your lagging ass," Cruz replies, his ass plopped on top of my kitchen island, like he owns the place.

"Get your ass off the table where I eat." I wave my hand at him.

"Ember sits here all the time," he fights back, not moving.

"Her ass is welcome there," I reply with a smile, because her ass is welcome anywhere.

"Ugh, fine." He pushes himself off, landing on his feet.

"Am I driving?" I assume I am, so I'm already reaching for my keys.

"Oh, hell no. There is a limo waiting for us downstairs. I expensed it." He shrugs, heading out the front door I'm holding open for him. "Ember might be the queen of this club, but I am, by default, its prince, and a prince arrives in style, baby."

Jesus, I'm arriving at a very public event in a limo with Cruz. I chuckle at the prospect of the media headlines. "This should be fun," I whisper to myself, following behind a very excited Cruz.

THE SPECTACLE outside of the club is completely out of control. The police have an area blocked off, where protestors are chanting and holding signs. Nothing I know they didn't expect, but the sight is still pretty jarring.

These people are taking time out of their life to protest, in such a violent way, what others do with their bodies and their choices in their sexuality. I just can't justify that.

We pull up to the front of the club, and the building is lit up from top to bottom. Spotlights shine from the ground up, over the building, and criss-cross on the front, bringing attention to the all capital letters, AFTERBURN, in a deep red. A white back-light snakes around the back of the letters, bringing more life to it. Again, just like Ember.

I can't help but smile seeing all of this come together, all because she had one idea and a big vision, with an even bigger ambition.

Cruz exits the limo first, his arms flying straight to the sky, waving at everyone outside. There is some media here, but no one famous is showing up other than some social media influencers. Or I guess, perhaps some famous people, but I'm sure their intention is like mine. Anonymity, or as much as possible.

Fortunately, Cruz is an attention whore, and they don't pay much attention to me, as I slink out behind him, walking straight to the front door of the club.

Seamus, who is part of one of two teams hired to run security for the event, is at the front.

He typically doesn't do private events like this one, but when Ember told Dietrich she knew him, he agreed to do it as a favor for her, for me, knowing the potential crowd it would draw with how much protesting was going on.

He's not wearing a mask, but he's in all black like me. His dark hair is a tad longer than the last time I saw him, but he is completely clean shaven, wearing a scowl that would scare off a lion.

I walk up, holding out my hand as we slap them together with a quick chest bump hug and pat on the shoulder. His death stare as he surveys the crowd doesn't falter, even during our bro hug, and he grabs the large brass handle to the door, pulling it open for me to enter.

"There's a lot going on here with the crowd." He nods into the building. "I'll catch up with you later."

He seems a bit on edge, as his eyes bounce in every direction. I can't imagine how difficult it is to try to keep order. Especially with some of the protestors and monitoring who is trying to get in the building.

I nod and give him a quick salute as I walk through the door. Cruz follows right behind me.

The environmental change is instant. Like walking through a portal into another dimension. Once the door shuts, the media crowd shouting for pictures and protestors disappear, and the music from the entrance of the dimly lit club scales itself.

It mixes with the sound of the floor to ceiling waterfall that sits behind a welcome desk. The "XConnect Live" appears through the middle of the flowing water, and the name of the club, in big bold, over the top.

There are two people at the front who check our IDs and hand us glasses of champagne.

"Feel free to walk around and explore for yourself. Anyone with a red mask with glowing "X" on it is an employee. You can ask for anything you might need. If you're here to meet someone from the app, you are welcome to wait in the *Chat Room*."

"Thank you." Cruz downs his champagne like a shot, then hands it back to her. "I'll have another, Jasmine." He lifts his mask and winks.

"Oh my god, Cruz. I didn't recognize you, otherwise I wouldn't have been so professional." She blushes as she leans in, giving him a kiss on the cheek, and gives him another glass.

"Thanks, baby," he replies, with another wink.

Cruz is gay, right? Maybe he's bi. I have no idea now. That whole interaction just confused me.

I instantly forget about it when I round the corner of the waterfall and see the vast open space of the main area of the club.

Ember's vision coming to life is truly unbelievable. It has the same bones from when I saw it a few weeks ago, but with the ambient lighting and music bringing the entire space to life, it's surreal. The centrally located bar, mirrored with glass and up-lighting, gives birth to the club spreading throughout the entire area. It's full of people; some standing around the high tables that surround the bar, others that are seated around it.

My eyes hone in on one guy leaning against the corner of the bar. He's wearing a mask, but I'd recognize that stiff, arrogant body language even if I were blindfolded.

Henry stands sipping his whiskey, taking in the people all around the room.

You've got to be fucking kidding me. I knew the moment he found out he would do his research. He's way too resourceful when he has an agenda that he's blinded by.

I have no idea what he's up to, what his intentions are, or what he decided to show up here for, but I refuse to let him get to me. I spent far too many years allowing him to ruin moments like these.

As if he knew I was here, he glances over in my direction, smiles as he lifts his drink in a distant toast, with a quick dip of his chin, then turns around.

The usual Henry would already be heading in my direction, trying to rile me up. But he seems uninterested. Which is bizarre.

Taking Ember's advice, I'm going to give him the benefit of

the doubt. He's trying to turn a new leaf, rekindle the volatile relationship that has defined us our whole life.

Forgiveness starts with a choice, and I'm choosing to do that. But later.

Right now, I have a gorgeous wife to find.

I glance around the room again, taking in the vision that Ember has brought to life and the people here enjoying it. I'm not surprised when my eye catches a rose gold mask in the crowd, and I don't need the confirmation of her gorgeous cinnamon hair or emerald eyes that peer through the disguise to know it's her.

As if she can sense my presence as well, she turns my direction. A smile crawls over her face that she doesn't even attempt to conceal, and it makes my heart swell to the size of a fucking watermelon.

Jesus, she does *everything* to me.

I told her once I loved her, and I meant it. But it was in a moment that diminished the seriousness behind it. She never said anything, and I was too much of a pussy to tell her how serious I was in fear of her running.

I have to tell her how I feel tonight. Our *arrangement* needs to end, because that was built on fake feelings and a need of benefit for us both. Neither of which matter anymore.

The only thing that matters is my future with Ember, our future together. And I won't leave here tonight without telling her exactly how I feel.

48

EMBER

I didn't have to see him to know he was here. I sensed him, like I always do when he finds me. This time, when my eyes meet his, there is something deeper behind them. Like he's drowning and he's silently asking me to pull him up.

There was a shift after we returned from his parents' house. He's been a little more reserved, like he's trying not to push anything too much. I think he's being sensitive to the emotional roller coaster I've been on the last few weeks. My brothers did end up reaching out to me. Well, Benson and Cody did, claiming my mother and Robert are doing everything in their power to maintain their status.

According to Cody, Robert Riley will be running for governor, and my recent rebellion of leaving home and running off with a stranger from a drunken Vegas marriage was completely unacceptable for his image. His oldest son being gay is completely unacceptable, and he's attempting to win over Cody and Benson to try to appear *normal* to the voters of Missouri.

They failed at that attempt, being that Cody and Benson told me last night they decided to list their homes for sale and move. Cody's company is willing to transfer him to their

Houston operation, and Benson works remotely, so he can work from anywhere.

I completely broke down and told them how much it hurt me. Neither one reached out those first few days after everything happened, and that left some underlying trauma. I felt so alone, and I never want to feel like the people I care most about can so easily disregard me.

Regardless, I know how challenging and persuasive my parents can be. So, I told them I would come visit when they got settled in Houston, and that would give us a reason to visit Hudson's parents again.

Hudson overheard me say that last night while on FaceTime with them, and he craned his neck back in shock. I realized it probably wouldn't be for a couple of months, which is after the baseball season is over, so I can understand his surprise. I quickly backtracked, trying to pull back my words, but I just ended up looking like a blubbering idiot.

I was also still reeling through the conversation with Kari from the night before. Kari is Derek Callahan's wife, and Hudson's closest teammate. She's probably the closest friend I have here, which saddens me because Callahan is retiring this year and she won't be part of the team anymore.

But neither will I.

The thought has been weighing on me, and I've found myself pushing away from, well, everyone. Including Hudson, and I feel like it's better that way.

Especially after Kari told me that the owner and Coach Raymer are going to offer Hudson a contract. She said she didn't know anything else, other than it was being negotiated and that Hudson was aware it was coming. He loves the team, loves Seattle, and it's been such a pipe dream for something like this to happen. I'm shocked he didn't share it with me the moment he heard.

It is something personal to him that doesn't involve me after the season, but I guess I just saw myself as someone he could confide in.

Now that the club is open and I'll have some time off, I'm going to start looking for a place and plan a move out date. I think it's truly for the best, at this point, before things get messier than they already are. We've blurred so many lines it's hard to see any of them now.

I uncomfortably shift my weight in my way too tall heels and excuse myself from the couple that came up to introduce themselves to me. They flew in from California for the opening, being avid in the lifestyle. They were excited to be here, at what they called the club's maiden voyage.

Shaking their hands, "Thank you for coming. It was so great to meet you guys." I step in the direction of the bar and glance back over in Hudson's direction. Like a hawk, his eyes are still on me, watching my every move. I smother a smile and dip my head down with a shyness only he can pull out of me. How one man can make me retreat into myself in the most timid way, but bring out such a powerful woman in the bedroom, I'll never know.

Goosebumps swarm over my skin as I continue my way across the room.

He looks fucking edible. All black everything, and even though he blends in with the dim room, you can't miss his presence. It's colossal and demanding, and I'm drawn to him in every way.

I stop at the bar, placing my empty champagne glass on the bar top, which is instantly replaced by a full one thanks to the amazing bar staff that we've hired for the club.

I take a sip, peering over in his direction again. Still he fucking stares, with a smirk only I know. This man.

I shake my head and smile behind the long flute of my champagne glass.

Oh, fuck it. This whole long distance teasing has gone on

long enough. I find my inner tigress and turn in his direction, allowing the mask to give me assertive confidence.

I feel like I'm floating in his direction as I take him in from head to toe.

He has one hand on the stem of his glass and one hand in his pocket. Seductively taking a sip while staring at me through the mask that makes him look like a king.

"Ember!" My name floats through the air from behind me, ripping my gaze from his.

I turn to see Elena. Even with her mask, you can't miss her luscious blonde hair and bright blue eyes, especially with her arms interlaced in the arms of two incredibly handsome men beside her.

"Hi!" I say with genuine happiness. She throws her arm out for a hug and I lean in for it. "You did this. You *created* this," she whispers in my ear before she pulls back and looks at me, holding my hands in hers. "I hope you are proud of yourself, Ember. This is truly amazing."

I can't help but smile at her praise.

"It really is," Jake replies. Leaning in, he kisses me on the cheek. Christian does the same on the other side, and I can't say that it didn't send some shockwaves everywhere. I wonder, for a brief moment, what it would be like to be shared between two men, but when I glance back at Hudson and see his Grim Reaper death stare, I quickly extinguish that thought. And what the hell am I thinking? I can hardly handle Hudson alone.

"Thank you." I say sincerely. "Thank you for believing in me."

"Easiest decision I've ever made," Christian replies with a smile behind his mask that covers a majority of his face, but the kindness behind his eyes say more than enough.

"Do you remember Corbin?" He holds his hand out next to me. I turn enough to open a space for Corbin to step up next to me.

"Yes, good evening, Mr. Maren." I smile, because you can't not smile at Corbin Maren. He places his hand at the small of my back and grants me a kiss on each cheek.

"Ember, this is very impressive. I was congratulating Christian, but he confessed he had nothing to do with this and you were the mastermind here." Corbin's compliment has me blushing a deep shade of red, and I'm more than thankful for the mask that covers my cheeks.

"This was the perfect marriage of teamwork, sir." I idle on the description of perfect marriage, and my eyes focus on Hudson, who stands in my periphery behind Corbin. I swallow thickly as he studies us. I continue, "Christian and Elena took a chance on this idea, and if it weren't for Cruz, none of this would have happened."

"I love your modesty. It's a great leadership quality," he compliments again, then turns to Christian. "Christian could learn a lot from you," he quips.

"You're fired," Christian replies sternly, then chuckles, and that loosens the mood a bit.

Christian and Jake open up a bit and banter back and forth. Elena and Corbin chime in, sharing a few stories, and it's a few minutes of easy going conversation.

"So, Ember," Corbin takes advantage of a brief pause in our conversation, "I have a director position available in our Manhattan office, and although I had to do some major groveling, Christian gave me permission to extend an offer to you to come visit the teams and see if that is something you would be interested in."

I lose my footing, even though I'm literally standing still, and my heel falls from underneath me. Corbin reaches out, catching my forearm and helps balance me.

God, how embarrassing.

"Oh, wow," is all that I can come up with.

He glances over at Christian as I turn to Elena. Jake stares at her as she stares at me. They know my situation with Hudson, and I can tell it's as awkward as it should be.

"Corbin informed us one of his directors is retiring, and when he brought up his interest in you, I wanted to pay you the same respect I would want from my boss." Elena looks over at Christian. "I would always want to be given the opportunity to make the choice." She smiles at me, knowing what all this means.

She continues, "For the record, we don't want you to go, and I know you might not want to move. But I didn't think it was fair to not afford you the option to make that decision for yourself."

Jake shifts uncomfortably, clenching his jaw, as he looks in another direction, avoiding my gaze all together. He clearly doesn't agree with Elena on this.

Corbin isn't privy to my entire relationship dilemma, so I'm not sure what he's thinking, but I know he is very interested in having me join his team.

"Have you been to New York?" Corbin asks.

"No. I've been wanting to plan a vacation there, and it's been a bucket list dream to work in Manhattan one day," I confess, which feeds Corbin's sales pitch.

"Come visit for a week, get to know the teams, the area, and you'll have a better feeling about everything after you spend some time in the city. If anything, you get the vacation you've wanted, and then you can make a truly authentic decision." This is why Corbin runs the entire east coast. He can sell you on just about anything.

"You know, I can't pass that opportunity up," I reply to Corbin as he smiles at my resolve.

"I know it's a big decision, but ultimately, I would like you to mock what you did here. Creating a club like this one, but in Manhattan—" I glance around, knowing how much energy and effort I put into this, and wonder first if I can do it again.

Second, do I want to? This feels like my baby, and Seattle feels like... home. "That would be the first of many projects in your new role as Director."

I glance between the four of them, their eyes studying me behind their masks, and it feels so surreal. There are multiple goals being checked off here, and I've only ever dreamed of coming together like the perfect storm, which is creating a tsunami of emotions.

I can't pass up this chance. New York City. Director. The beginning of a life I can call my own. Not ruled by the desire to please anyone else, including the parents that never wanted me, that never even cared about me.

I touch my neck, the pulse point at the base of my throat that Hudson loves to kiss, knowing if I say yes to this, I have to give up something I've come to rely on. A small panic filters through me. Relying on that makes me more like my mother than I want to be.

I never want to be like her.

I steel my spine and lift my chin, showing the confidence I've gained. The confidence in this position and myself, that Elena has pulled from me in ways that only she could inspire. The confidence it takes to make hard choices and do hard things.

Finding my best conference room smile, "When would you like me there?"

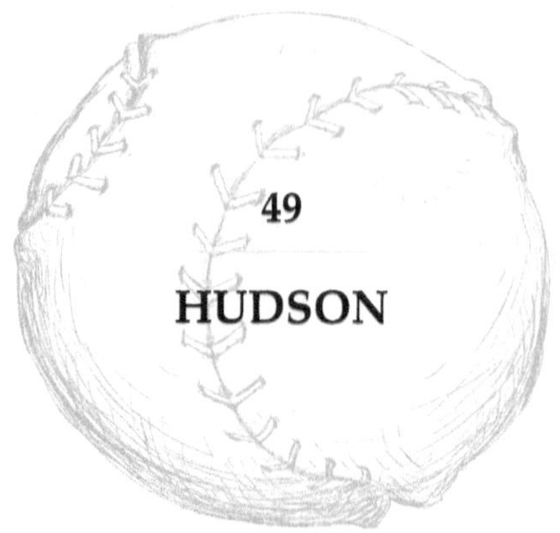

49

HUDSON

I watch Ember from across the room, marveling at how gorgeous she is. She fits in everywhere, yet stands out like one of the seven world wonders.

Elena, Jake, and Christian caught her attention when she was heading my direction, but then whoever this new guy is joined their conversation and hasn't seen his way out yet.

I don't recognize him with his mask, but I don't think I would even if he didn't have one on. He's as tall as Christian and just as broad. His dark mask blends with his skin tone, and his light eyes shine through his mask with a kindness that can't be faked.

Ember knows him. I can see it in her body language. She's comfortable with him, and he's a bit overly excited with their conversation. Especially when I see him reach in and touch her arm once, then again, but this time grazing her low back as he points to something on the wall. I can't tell if it's platonic friend-liness or if I am going to jail for committing a murder tonight.

"Cruz, who's the guy Ember is talking to?" I nod in their direction.

Cruz shifts his gaze toward the bar, stalls for a brief

moment, and although the music is loud, I can hear a distinct hitch in his breath.

Clearing his throat, "Corbin Maren. He runs Christian's east coast operations." Taking a sip of his champagne, he clears his throat for a second time.

"Hey, I think I see someone I know. I'm gonna go... over there." He points in the opposite direction and shuffles off.

Weird.

I down the rest of my drink and place it on the tray of one of the wait staff walking by, grabbing two fresh ones. Ember's glass is nearly empty, and I've had enough distance from her for the night.

I only get one step in her direction before someone runs directly into the right side of me. I drop one of the flutes as it crashes to the ground, and the woman stumbles over her feet, her dress getting caught in her heel as she reaches for something to prevent her fall. She grips both my arms as I try to balance both her and the drink.

"Are you okay?" I drop my gaze to meet hers, and she looks up at me, then behind her, like she's being chased. "Miss?" I say again.

She's wearing a sheer all white dress with a matching white mask, her olive skin and black hair a stark contrast to the brightness of her outfit in the dim room.

"I'm so sorry, thank you. Thank you for catching me." She stands up straight, running her hands down the front of her dress, removing the bunching that occurred from her almost fall.

She looks behind her again, then back to me. "Sorry again... sorry," she apologizes profusely, then continues to speed walk past me.

I'm a bit shocked by the encounter and just watch her dash through the lobby and toward the front entrance.

"Okaaay," I whisper under my breath as I inspect myself to

make sure I didn't get any champagne on my suit. A staff member walks up next to me and hands me a towel, then begins to clean up the mess that spilled on the floor.

"My apologies, sir. Let me get this cleaned up."

I use the towel to wipe off my hands and pat him on the shoulder.

"Thank you," I reply, taking another step toward Ember. My eyes navigate back to where she was, but before I can find her through the crowd, Seamus appears out of fucking nowhere.

"Did you see her?" There's an urgency in his tone.

"Who?" I grip his arms, holding him back as his eyes bounce all over the room behind me.

"Me—" He cuts himself off. "The woman, the woman in white?" He's speaking so fast, as his eyes flicker everywhere but at mine.

What the hell? Seamus is the epitome of control. He is not in control.

"Shay, what's going on, man?" I ask.

"Did she pass through here?" He finally looks me dead in the eye. It makes me flinch back.

"Yes, she was heading to the front door. I think she left." My eyes look at the front door, searching for her, even though I know she's long gone now.

"Shit." He moves around me, racing toward the door.

I turn, taking a few steps to follow him, but stop and watch him disappear as he rounds the waterfall that separates the room from the exit. Placing my hand on my hips, I chipmunk my cheeks while exhaling.

He's on some kind of mission. Maybe she stole something from one of the rooms or snuck in.

Deciding that's a lost cause, I turn back and trek over to the group standing in a circle still chatting, but I don't see Ember.

"Hudson." Elena's soft voice greets me as she leans in, giving me a chaste kiss on the cheek. Christian and I have become closer over the past few months, with some of the company events I've attended with Ember. He holds out his hand, and we pull each other in for one of those semi-professional bro hugs.

I glance over at Jake, and he nods at me, taking a drink of his whiskey, acting weird as fuck.

"Hudson, this is Corbin Maren. He runs my east coast operations," Christian introduces me, and I hold out my hand.

"Hudson Byrnes. Great to meet you," I reply, still unsure if it's really great to meet him or if I need to crush his hand for putting it on Ember's back.

"Hudson Byrnes, as in the Smashers' new all-star catcher?" He squints, attempting to get a better idea of who is behind the mask.

My lip turns up and my chest fills with a bit of pride. A half a second away from Tarzan, beating my chest in front of him.

"The one and only." With a bit more confidence than I would usually reply.

"Also, Ember's husband," Jake grits out, annoyed, side-eyeing Christian and Elena.

What the hell is his problem?

"Oh, wow, how did I miss that? I didn't put two and two together," he replies in awe. "Ember is something special."

Yes. Yes, she is. I sip my drink, dipping my head and flicking my eyebrow in a silent agreement with him.

"I'm thrilled she agreed to come to New York."

As an impulse, my drink shoots out of my mouth, spraying back in the glass chute.

"What?" I look around at my three friends, all staring at me with looks of shame, guilt, and pain etched over their faces.

Corbin, living with too much excitement, doesn't read the fucking room and continues.

"Yes, the director position in our Manhattan office. She's perfect for what I'm looking for. She's—"

He pulls his phone out of his jacket pocket and looks down with a curious look, "Excuse me for just a moment," and steps out of the circle to a secluded area of the club.

My gaze jumps between all of them again. I am torn between a mix of emotions. How am I just fucking hearing of this right now? She doesn't need my permission to do anything. I know this. I fucking know this. But they could have paid me a tad bit of respect and told me that was on the fucking table.

"Was no one going to say fucking anything to me?" I finally break the silence.

"Corbin just asked us earlier today if he could talk to her about it tonight," Elena replies softly, defensively.

"And what? He slides in, offers her the job of her dreams, and she fucking says yes without a second thought. What are you going to tell me next, that she's leaving tomorrow?"

"Tomorrow night." I practically snap my neck to look at Christian. "Just for a week to check—" I toss my hand up, stopping him, to avoid hearing anymore bullshit from his mouth.

I know what 'a week' looks like to Ember. That's exactly how long she told her parents she was going to visit Seattle. That's a goddamn excuse for her to permanently run.

"You knew about this?" My death stare falls on Jake.

I've told him how I feel about her, he knows. They all do.

The scowl has yet to leave his face as his eyes shift to Christian and Elena.

"Yeah... yeah, I knew." His eyes avoid me.

"This is fucking bullshit." Leaving the circle of non-fucking trust, I slam my glass down at the nearest table and leave to look for Ember.

New York might be her dream, but she's mine, and now that I've had a taste of a life together, I can't let her go. I won't.

I pull out my phone and text Cruz.

Me: I need a key to one of the private rooms.

Cruz: Oooh ;-) Okay

Cruz: Oh, wait. It's for you and Ember, right? If not, I'm telling. My loyalty is to her, not you. Sorry.

Me: Cruz…

Cruz: Okay, meet me outside the Chat Room.

50

EMBER

I watch my chest rise and fall in my reflection as the vision of myself darkens the longer I stare at myself. I've seen myself fade in and out, my lazy eyelids performing half blinks, bringing a tad more light to just fade over again.

I know I've been hiding out here too long and it's time to go back to the party, but I haven't been able to talk myself into it. I have to tell Hudson what just happened, and I'm not sure it's in my heart to say it.

Do I want to go to New York? Yes, absolutely. It's everything I've ever wanted. Everything I've worked toward.

Do I want to leave Hudson? My face scrunches up all on its own, and I toss my head back and forth. The season isn't over yet, but he's proven himself by now. Plus, this was all supposed to be temporary, but the loss of him feels... catastrophic.

"Fuck." I hate that he's branded himself inside me. I hate that choosing one over the other doesn't ease the guilt I feel in either direction.

But I knew instantly when Corbin asked me. I knew that I would say yes. Just like I know now; the chances of this New York visit going from one week to permanent is as predictable as the sunrise. We know it happens, we can see it coming and there's no stopping it.

Because, as hard as it will be to say goodbye to Hudson, I can't resent him for staying somewhere when I had a chance to follow my dreams.

I grab my purse from the top of the sink and take one more look at myself in the mirror, giving myself a nod. Like one of me needs to approve my own decision.

Exiting the bathroom, I walk down the narrow hallway. I'm on the second floor, which is just a small loft area with a few rooms. Our offices, break room, and private bathrooms, reserved for staff only.

The artwork I picked out lines the wall between each of the doors, and my favorite one hangs at the end of the hallway before the corner to the stairs. It's a pencil drawing of two people in bed, tangled into each other in such a way it's hard to see where one ends and the other begins.

It's majestic.

The moment I saw it, it was like witnessing two soulmates finding each other, loving each other, sexually, sensually. In all the ways that two people should.

And just as the thoughts of soulmates come to mind, a shadow appears at the bottom of the stairs, and I don't need to turn in that direction to know who it is.

51

EMBER

Hudson finds me, like he usually does, and his stare sears through me. I've never felt so conflicted, and the look in his eyes tells me he knows it.

He walks up the stairs with the same determination in his eyes I saw when we first met.

Holding out his hand, "Come on."

I squint, looking between his outstretched palm and his face, questioning him silently.

"I have a surprise for you." He reaches his hand closer to me.

I slide mine into it, and he leads me down the stairs, past the voyeur rooms. I peek over at the corner we were stuck in as we watched Jake, Elena, and Christian, and the reminder provides a flutter to my core.

He stops in front of room six, scanning the keycard as it beeps and allows us to enter. I quirk up a smile.

"Cruz gave me a key, but made it clear his loyalty still stands with you. Just in case you were concerned." He smiles at me, tossing the key on the table closest to the door.

We step into the room, and it looks the same as when I inspected it earlier tonight.

The large king-sized bed, with bondage posts on each corner, sits against the wall in the middle of the room. Other than some floggers, handcuffs, and a few other toys, the shelves are bare. Only a tripod sits in the corner, for anyone who wants to record themselves with their own video equipment.

We never decided on a theme for this room, so we left it as basic as possible and didn't plan to give it any attention until after the soft opening of the club.

Hudson walks to the center of the room, shrugging off his jacket, and hangs it over a chair. Loosening his tie, he pulls it over his head and sheds a few of the buttons from his all black ensemble. Including the cuffs of his shirt that he rolls up over his forearms, and fuck me, he's gorgeous.

I shift my stance, sucking my bottom lip in between my teeth. Everything about him is appetizing.

The look in his eye tonight is fierce, like he has something to prove. Yet, he paces, like he's digging for something.

He's both in full control and completely lost, and I feel like I'm witnessing a battle of will between the two in real time.

But I can tell he's holding back, and I know what I need to do.

I push the straps of my dress down over my shoulders, and the silk fabric floats down off my body with ease. It pools at my feet and I take one step out of it, then bring my other foot forward. Standing closer to him in just my heels and mask.

His eyes flicker as he grazes his tongue over his lips, and his eyes trail my body from head to toe.

"Lie down on the bed." His gravelly voice is a low tenor in the already too quiet room.

I step forward without challenge, my arm skims over the front of his body as I pass by. Turning around, I sit down and scooch myself back toward the middle of the bed.

He grabs the wrist and ankle cuffs expertly placed next to the bed, then comes back and stands in front of me.

He's quiet, reserved. Not like Hudson.

Wrapping his fingers gently around my ankle, he straps the cuffs to each one, then does the same to my wrists.

He pauses for a minute, glancing up at the restraints on the bedposts.

"Hudson..." I dip my head so his eyes can find mine.

"Tell me you want this," he says, still avoiding my eyes.

"Tell me you want me," he clarifies. "Because if I strap you to this bed, I don't think I'll ever be able to let you go."

I squint, confused at the softness of his voice, with the intensity of his body language.

He looks up, a fire burning in his eyes that sears my skin, giving me goosebumps everywhere.

He needs something. I can't tell what, but I'm more than willing to give it to him.

I hold out my wrists.

Giving him permission.

Giving him control.

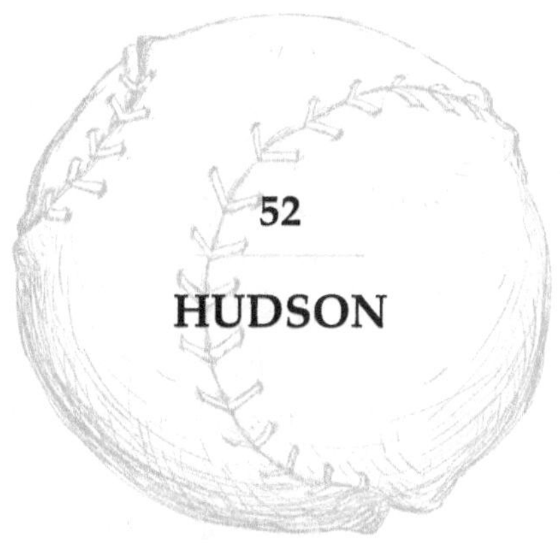

52

HUDSON

I warned her I wouldn't be able to let her go, and she's giving herself to me, anyway. I wish it meant more than it does.

I knew the moment I saw her at the top of the stairs she had made her decision. Her eyes give her emotions away, and it's like she's already saying goodbye.

I've always known that whatever it is that she's searching for, whatever validation she needs, is something I'll never be able to provide. Because regardless of how special what we have is, she wants something completely different.

So, tonight, tonight I'll attempt to etch myself into her soul like she has in mine.

Grabbing her hands, I push them back over her head and clip both of the cuffs into the hooks of the bedposts.

Pulling her legs down to the corners of the bed, I do the same to her ankles, so she is spread eagle in front of me. On display and completely at my mercy.

I unbutton the rest of my shirt, untuck it from my pants, and shimmy my shoulders out of it, tossing it on the chair with my jacket.

Her eyes follow me around the room, and she nibbles on the corner of her lip. She's nervous, probably from my own unpredictable energy.

I honestly don't even trust myself. I meant it when I said I'll never let her go. I don't know that I'll be able to unclip her out of those restraints when I'm done with her.

There are a handful of sex toys, all of which have been in our bedroom and half of them we've already tested and played with. We've experimented so much with each other, discovering things that neither one of us even knew about ourselves, much less what each other liked.

I've never had the openness and honesty in any relationship than I have with her, and it fucking kills me that she doesn't feel the same. Actually, she has to. I refuse to think that she doesn't feel the same. She has to know how special this is.

I glance back over to her and decide I don't want to use anything. I want it to be just me and her tonight.

Placing my hands on either side of her head, trapping her between me and the bed, I hover my lips over hers.

"I don't want any other name, other than mine, to leave these lips. Not God or Jesus. It's Hudson or *husband*. Do you understand?"

She nods softly.

I slap the peak of her breast, and she gasps as her nipple puckers under the sting.

"Try again."

"Yes... husband," she replies in a breathy whisper.

"Fffuck." I huff out a long exhale as my cock thickens. This is a terrible idea. It's already torturous.

I round the bed, kneeling in front of her, taking in every inch of her creamy skin and gorgeous display. Her red hair is splayed out, like a wild mane over the top of the bed, and her toes are curling without me even touching her.

"Spread your legs." She inches them closer to the sides of the bed, and her glistening pussy comes into view.

"Already wet for me, my wife?" Her breath hitches at the absence of her nickname, replaced with the title I so desperately want her to keep. Which is exactly why I'll call her that all night.

I graze my lips over her ankles, kissing up her calves and behind her knees. Licking all the way up her inner thighs and right over the top of her pelvic bone, teasing everywhere except where I know she needs it.

I reach up and pinch her nipples, earning me a gasp and moan as her back arches off the bed, pressing her pussy closer to my face, so I flick my tongue over her clit.

"Oh, God." Her hips fall to the bed, and I slap her pussy, stinging her exposed clit.

"What did you say?"

"Hudson. Hudson," she says frantically.

"Good girl."

She moans, biting her lip. I think she likes that.

I float my lips over her pussy, blowing air through my pursed lips. Her hips lift, and I think she likes that, too.

A part of me wants to do just this all night long. Tease her until she relents. But the other savage side of me just can't hold back any longer.

I lick through her slit, then suck on her clit. Flattening my tongue with each pass, continuing that same punishing pace and tempo, over and over again.

"Fuck. Oh my god, that feels so good."

I lift my head, spank her pussy again, her clit even more swollen and needy, and I suck it between my lips to cool the stinging sensation.

"Jesus, fuck," she breathes out.

Is she ever going to learn? I silently laugh, hiding my smirk when I lift my head up to look at her. Her eyes are squeezed shut, and she doesn't even realize she said it again.

I smack her pussy again, before putting my mouth back on her.

"Hudson... husband, my husband!"

I hum into her pussy as she chants my name and title like she fucking needs it to survive.

Just like I need her.

The vibration of my humming rewards me with guttural moans, and she's so fucking close. I use the tip of my tongue to massage her clit in rapid movements, knowing this is what she likes, and how I get her to fall apart every time.

Her body starts to tremble, and her arms and legs pull on the restraints.

"Please, don't stop," she begs.

I keep my pace. Her body jerks and her chest heaves as she moans, and the sight of her falling apart for me will forever be burned into my mind. It took her so long to stop running, to stay still with me, so when she's here with me, letting go, I relish every fucking minute of it.

"Oh, God..." she screams again.

I rear back and slap again, this time harder, knowing it's what she needs to push her over the edge.

"Fuck, I'm gonna come."

"Say it," I growl into her pussy.

"Hudson, please..."

"That's my wife." The words vibrate over her pussy, and she falls apart, screaming my name.

53

EMBER

Hudson's dominating me tonight, in every way possible. Taking control of my body, my mind, and even the words I say.

I've never referred to him as "*husband*" before, and it's like he is training me to love it. Rewarding me with pleasure every time I chant it for him.

The orgasm high lingers longer than usual as he strips off his pants and slides himself over the top of my body, our chests melting into each other. His hard cock is wedged between us as I roll my hips up and down over the length.

I'm still harnessed to the bed and desperate for more of him, like usual, so I use what little space I have to move and rub my clit over the backside of the swollen tip.

His face is pressed into mine, with his jaw slacked, hanging on to his last thread of power as I continue to rock my hips over his. He's squeezing his eyes closed, like it's painful to look at me.

"I need you." He nuzzles into my neck as he rears his hips back and pushes his cock deep inside me.

I whimper as he fills me inch by inch because, no matter

how many times I've had him, it still feels like getting impaled by a semi truck. Knocking the wind out of me for a brief moment until the pleasure completely takes over.

He pushes into his hands, hovering our faces over each other, pressing his forehead into mine. It's different than anything I've felt from him before.

His movements are slow and calculated, spending time surveying my body with his eyes, fingers, and his tongue, not missing claiming an inch. The entire time, he pushes in and out of me at a flawless, excruciating pace.

"You feel so goddamn good," he admits, his tone demanding and desperate.

"I want to keep you here forever." He pistons deeper into me with a groan.

"Say you're mine." Pumping into me again. I moan at the invasion and his words.

"Say you're fucking mine." He pushes into me harder, grabbing my hair to pull my face flush with his, forcing me to look deep into his now jet-black eyes. "Everything, all of it. Tell me you're mine."

"I'm yours..." I confess, because it's the truth. I have had no control over my body when it comes to Hudson, and it's been that way from the moment he touched me. But now, my heart, my back stabbing heart, betrays me, no matter how hard I've fought to keep it from him. "I'm yours... always."

He growls into my neck, cursing through his orgasm as it plows through him and into me. I clench around him, and my teeth bite into his shoulder as I moan through my own.

Falling into me, his body covers me wholly, and I welcome the weight. I can hide behind it, hide for a moment longer in a world where it's just me and him.

Our breathing slows, and the only sound is the soft whisper of air that moves between us as we come back to reality.

The air around us thickens. The silence thunders. It's

louder than all the words he said tonight, the ones that play on a constant loop, repeating in my head.

"*Husband.*" "*Wife.*" "*I need you.*" "*Say you're mine.*"

There was a softness about him tonight, hidden behind the aggression of his body language. He made love to me tonight while claiming me at the same time, and it's nothing like anything that I've experienced from him before. It was both love and hate, pain and pleasure battling each other, landing us in a post sex world of confusion. It's only after I hear the words he says next that I realize what this was for him, for us. A goodbye.

"I know about New York."

54

HUDSON

A silent and awkward car ride brought us home last night. She didn't say anything more about my confession of knowing about New York, because neither one of us was ready for it.

It resulted with us in bed; her completely passed out from exhaustion, and me restless and wide fucking awake.

The nerves trickled through every inch of my body, robbing my ability to relax, and my mind reeled through so many thoughts, emotions, and scenarios, reliving our entire relationship over the span of the night.

I love her, and the thought of losing her is eating me like a flesh-eating parasite from the inside out.

Yesterday, before the party, Coach called and asked me to meet him this morning, and knowing it was about signing me was bittersweet. It's everything I've ever wanted for my career, but it keeps me here, three thousand miles away from her.

So, now, I'm returning home after my meeting with him, feeling even more conflicted than before.

Up until now, it's just been talk, rumors of signing me, but this morning, they made an official offer.

Five years. He was even able to turn the non-negotiable trade agreement after three years into an optional one, allowing me the right to choose if I want to be traded.

It's a no-brainer situation. Other than the fact that there is still a consideration of an offer to my brother to come on as pitcher next season. As much as I'm trying to regain some trust there, I think I need more than a few months of an offseason to get there.

Regardless, it's what I've been waiting for, and there's nothing that should persuade me to turn it down. Except a walking, living, breathing, intoxicating redhead that I would follow to the edge of the universe if she asked me to.

My first response to Coach Raymer was, *"I'll think about it."*

That took him completely by surprise, as it should. So, I finally confessed to him.

Everything.

Vegas, the wedding, keeping up the fake marriage, and what everything has turned into leading up to her decision to take this position in New York.

He was more understanding than I deserve, but now he's worried that I won't stay. But I have to stay. So why didn't I fucking sign?

I WALK through the front door of our condo, and the quietness that fills the room tells me that Ember is still sleeping. It's not surprising, considering the week she had leading up to the massively successful opening of the club and, well, our extracurriculars in room six last night.

I walk into the kitchen and press the brew function on the coffee pot, then grab a couple of mugs down from the cabinet.

The click of the bedroom door handle rings through the

silence, followed by the soft patter of Ember's bare feet coming down the hall.

"Hey," she greets me softly, holding the corners of the comforter that's draped around her like a suit of armor.

"Hey." I smile, because I don't want her to feel like she needs to walk on eggshells. And I can't help but smile whenever she's around me.

"Where'd you go?" She leans into the barstool, pushing herself up to sit on it.

"I had a meeting with Coach Raymer." I pour her coffee into a mug and slide it her way. "He wanted to talk about a potential contract."

Her eyebrows lift and her lips quirk up. "Really?" she says with genuine excitement.

I huff out a small chuckle and nod. "Yeah, it's a good offer. I have to think about it."

I peer at her over my coffee mug, taking a sip of the warm intoxicating liquid. She does the same, and her eyes roll to the back of her head with a moan.

"Wow, I think that challenges some orgasms I've given you." I wiggle my eyebrows, attempting to lighten the mood.

"I'm not sure that's possible." The corners of her lips quirk up behind her mug, giving me a knowing look.

We have a lot of those between us. Things just we know about each other. I love knowing I hold her secrets, desires, the side that she hasn't shown to anyone else.

That's mine.

The floating sensation in my stomach drops, making my chest tighten when I think of her giving that to anyone else.

A pregnant pause passes between us, and I don't want to wait any longer. Sleep evaded me all night as I fought with myself, the battle to fight for her to stay or completely let her go.

When I saw her at the top of the stairs last night, the

moment my eyes connected with hers, I felt her pain, like some silent connection, rebounding between the two of us like morse code, yet avoiding a conversation about it like we don't speak the language.

The conflict of wanting something so badly, but feeling guilty because of the hurt it will cause when we both want something so completely different.

My desire for her to stay, and her desire to take the next step in her career, doesn't keep us together on that path.

I want to take the pain of her being forced to make that decision away. I never want to cause her that kind of suffering, but the excruciating pain exploding behind my rib cage won't allow me to give up that easily.

Knowing I need to rip my heart out of my chest and expose it to her in order to try to keep her is worth the risk.

"I walked onto that plane, lost, aimlessly wandering through a meaningless life. Then there you were." I can't help but smile. "Two hours later, I stepped off that plane, alive, with only a first name and a memory of a woman I somehow fell instantly in love with."

Her breath hitches at my confession.

"Every inch of who I am—from the surface of my skin to the depths of my soul—loves you. I love you with everything I have. I love the life we've built, the friends we've made, the experiences we've had. Nothing about what we've had has been *fake* for me. None of it."

She curls the comforter closer together, tightening it around her body.

"I can't offer you New York, at least, not right now. I can't give you what you need in your career, and I'm fucking pissed there's nothing I can do to change that." My hands run through my hair, attempting to grab the rampant thoughts streaming through my mind. I take a steady, deep breath to continue my fight.

"You can have both. You can have a career and a life and... us. It doesn't have to be one or the other. I never want to hold you back, ever, but I have to fight for this. I can't not fight for you to stay... with me." My words are more rushed now, coming out as a plea, a desperate demand.

I didn't have a speech prepared, but it sure came out like one.

"Hudson—"

"Stay." I interrupt her before she can say anything more, and I stare straight through her, even though she's dodging my gaze. "Stay with me."

She glances around the room nervously. Her eyes are glossed over and shiny, and as much as I don't want her to resent me for staying, the selfish part of me would rather live with that than live without her. Even though I know how wrong that is.

Her chest lifts as she sits taller in her chair. There's a slight tilt in her chin and an invisible wall constructed within the blink of an eye.

"I can't." She swallows thickly, like the truth of her wanting this, wanting us, sits at the top of her throat and she refuses to let it surface.

My heart fucking shatters.

As if there is an anchor on my neck, my weighted head falls forward and I close my eyes painfully, wanting to say so much more. A tight band forms around my chest, killing the air from my lungs, along with the desire to keep fighting.

I step over to the side of the island, open the top drawer, and pull out the manila envelope that I stuffed in there this morning. I had it tucked away in my desk for months, hoping it never saw the light of day. But I retrieved it this morning and signed it, knowing I would be powerless to do it in front of her.

Her eyes widen as she sees it, and I know she knows exactly what it is.

I grip it tightly in my fingertips, not wanting to give it up.

"Fuck," I whisper to myself. Scolding myself. Blaming myself.

I walk around the island, cupping her face urgently, hauling her lips to mine. She kisses me back with just as much urgency and silent tears streaming down her cheek. The salty liquid crawls over our lips and hits my tongue. I can't help but moan into her to avoid more petitioning and desperate begging for her to change her mind.

Reluctantly, I pull back, resting my nose on hers, keeping my eyes closed. If I look at her, it will destroy me, and if I don't stop, I'll never fucking stop.

"I can't watch you leave." With my head down, ashamed and disappointed in myself that I couldn't do more, be more for her, I place the envelope in her hands, containing both the signed papers and my bleeding heart.

"I love you." Giving her one final kiss before I tear myself away, I step around her as a gaping hole bursts through my heart.

55

HUDSON

I walk out the front door and keep moving so I don't turn back. Reaching the elevator, I step in and go down to the lobby.

My mind reels between mixed emotions of anger and sadness. I'm proud of her, so fucking proud. I really am. But why did they need to offer her that job? I'm pissed at everyone, when it's no one's fault but this fucked up circumstance.

The elevator doors open, and I'm surprised when Henry is standing on the other side of it.

I glance around, looking for anyone else, but it's just him.

"Hey." He was shocked to see me here, even though he's in my fucking building.

"Hi," comes out as a question.

He places his hands in his pockets, showing a timid side I rarely see.

"I came by to see if you wanted to get some breakfast," he asks with some foreign sound of vulnerability in his tone.

I pause for a moment, hearing the questions that Ember has asked a few times over the past couple of months.

Does he deserve my forgiveness? No.

Is it more pain for me to carry than anyone else? Yes.

The only way we can move forward is by my actions, my choice. Granting him forgiveness is step one, before I can even begin with trust.

"Sure," I say without much enthusiasm, as I step out the elevator and nod my head at the front door. "But you're buying."

WE MAGICALLY MAKE it to whatever restaurant my legs navigated us to, feeling unsure of how we actually got here. My mind has wandered in a million different directions, all of which ended in a daydream, trapped in a blanket of cinnamon hair and lost in jade-colored eyes. One where she chooses me, chooses us.

But the ache in my chest is my new reality, and I realize my daydreams are hallucinations that will quickly drive me to the brink of insanity. I still don't want to give them up.

"What are you doing here, Henry?" I cut to the chase. I'm tired, emotionally drained, and I'm over whatever shit he's constantly trying to pull.

He twirls his cup of coffee on the table, and it's the first time I think I've ever seen him nervous.

His eyes are all over the place, bouncing between his cup, the waitress, me, back to his cup.

"Henry, I don't have time—"

"I fucked up, Hud. I fucked up, and I'm sorry." My eyebrows hit my hairline, and I just stare. In all my life, not once has Henry ever admitted fault. To anything.

He peers up at me, searching for something. Acceptance maybe, understanding? But I'm still fucking speechless.

His long exhale is the only thing I hear between the silence that engulfs our small space.

"I remember when Mom told me I was going to be a big brother. She said I was being upgraded to a double big brother because she was pregnant with the twins. Up until then, it was only me and Mom and Dad. Then, after they were born, I felt like I never saw Mom at all. She was so overwhelmed with Grant and Graham. Dad really stepped up, and we got a lot closer." A tight-lipped smile crosses his face at the mention of our father.

My father and I are, well, we're decent. I've always been closer to my mother, and Henry closer to our father. The twins are close with both, but incredibly independent of our parents because they've always had each other.

"Then you came along and they became massively outnumbered. I was older, so I was left alone a lot. They relied on me to walk or bike home if they couldn't figure out how to get all of us to our practices or games. Tutored myself through school because keeping my grades up to keep playing ball was an enormous struggle. I cheated a lot. Did whatever I had to." His regretful eyes reach mine, like he's never confessed that to anyone.

"I lashed out at everyone, you specifically. Then you proposed to Veronica, and all attention was on you again. I was talking to different teams, looking at getting drafted, but the excitement of it all was buried under your engagement." He palms the nape of his neck and takes another deep breath.

"I look back on it now and, fuck, it was so stupid and immature. I could give you excuse after excuse, but it doesn't matter. I just fucked up everything for you, and I'm sorry."

Wow. *Wow.*

"The pitch..." He rubs his forehead, resting his head in his palms before sitting upright again. "I was out to prove I was better than you. I was jealous that the team wanted you so quickly after you came up, and I had been there for years, making a name for myself."

"How is that any different than what is happening right now, with my team?" I interrupt.

"Let me finish." He puts up his hand in a small surrender.

"You called that pitch and I didn't want to listen. I wanted to be the one to tell Coach that I made the call and struck him out. I wanted it to be about me for once, just one time. But you have to know that pitch was a complete fucking accident, Hudson. You have to know." His voice is more urgent now.

"You never fucking apologized to me. Not fucking once, Henry," I fight back.

"I know." His fingers tremble slightly as they press into his eyelids.

"I was embarrassed that my mistake cost you everything. And I knew you would hate me forever. I'm grasping at straws here; I know I am. I'm just asking for a chance to earn your trust."

Do I believe him? I do. Sadly. My toxic trait is loving too much and forgiving too easily, then allowing myself to get hurt, wondering why the hell that would happen to me. Although, with Henry, I've never even given him the opportunity.

He's been going home every month to my parents' house for the past couple years, making sure to be present with them. He's been actively trying to talk to me, but I've pushed him away time and time again, not allowing him to get a say in otherwise.

It was only recently that I even considered it—because of Ember.

Forgiveness allows you to let go, so you can stop carrying the burden of someone else's actions.

Maybe that's how she handled everything that happened to her so well. Sure, she's a professional at hide and seek with her heart and has superior emotional intelligence, but she doesn't live in the past or allow it to control her future.

Fuck, I miss her already.

"Is this about getting on the team?" I ask, abruptly.

"I got an offer this morning after you left the stadium. I met with Coach Raymer as well," he confesses, "but if you tell me not to sign it, I won't. I mean," he runs his hands through his hair nervously, "I can't sign it until after the season is over, but I do want to make a commitment to a team. I only have a few more years left, if that, and I want us to play together. We'd have the same schedule, could visit Mom and Dad. They could easily make it to our games. Sort of like old times."

I squint, confused. Like I don't know my own big brother. He's sentimental and a big teddy bear. But, in reality, I guess I really don't know him at all. I've never tried to really know him.

"Are you going through a midlife crisis, brother?" That earns me a chuckle.

"Maybe..." He pauses. "But it was probably the life altering conversation your wife threw at me when you guys were at Mom and Dad's."

Just the mention of my wife perks up my spine.

"She, somehow all at the same time, put the fear of God, the devil, and her own wrath—which is scarier than both of the former, by the way—if I didn't get my shit together and spend my life earning back your trust. No matter what it took."

I can't hold back my smile, envisioning my little red spitting threats at a man, my brother, over a foot taller than she is and three quarters his size. All for me.

It slips instantly as I glance down at the face of my watch. The second hand struggles to move, attempting to move, flickering but staying in place, and I wonder if it's powered by my heart.

Maybe she's still packing. Maybe she's stalling for me to come home. Maybe she's already gone.

"She's quite perfect for you." My brother's words snap my eyes in his direction.

He's smiling as he takes a sip of his coffee, but it fades when he recognizes the look of despair as I begin to panic, knowing I've really lost her.

"What's going on?" he asks.

Annnnd. The flood gates open.

"She's gone," I say, flatly. "She got promoted, and she's moving to New York. Today."

"Oh." His response brings me an unwelcome flashback of when I asked her out on that plane. Shocked, a little embarrassed maybe, that someone would ask her out. I remember the flush in her cheeks and the shy twitch of her full lips. The way she breathed those words as she tucked her hair behind her ear.

Then the following reply, *"I can't."* The same one she fed me today when I begged her to stay.

I suppose it was always meant to be this way, something I continued to fight for too long. Risking my heart for the inevitable outcome. Battling something that was never in my favor to begin with.

"Are you sure that you guys—"

"Don't," I interrupt him because that's the last thing I need right now. Hope.

I can't talk about her right now. It hurts too fucking much.

The waitress steps to our table and slides our plates in front of us, giving me the reprieve I need.

"Let's eat. Then let's go see Coach Raymer," I say curtly, as he studies me briefly, then gives me a tight-lipped smile. He's probably torn between the excitement that we're on a road to recovery or wondering if I'll completely flip out at any given moment.

I need to accept that Seattle will be my permanent home for the next five years, and the worst part of that is being haunted by the memory of knowing what it was like with her here. Knowing nothing will fill that void.

I finish my egg white omelet, and Henry inhales his blueberry pancakes and overly large side of eggs and bacon. He's always had a huge appetite and faster metabolism than anyone I've ever met.

He keeps his end of the bargain and pays the bill before we leave, a good first step in the whole trust department, then we start our walk over to the stadium.

It's early enough on Sunday morning that the fog still sits low on the horizon, and the somberness that lingers in the air matches my mood.

They say Seattle is one of the most depressing cities in the world due to the lack of sunlight and the adverse effect that has on your mental health. Interesting that since Ember came into my life, in Seattle, I've been the happiest I've ever been, yet this morning, I can completely relate to Seattle statistics.

She brought her own light, combating the Seattle gray. Now, it all feels empty.

"Are you ready?" Henry asks, as we pause to look up at the stadium from the main entrance.

I take a moment to marvel at the stadium, as if I were a spectator coming to see a game, like I was so many times before.

This is my new *permanent* home.

I turn to look at my brother, freeing myself of the resentment I've been carrying for too long. All because one little siren came into my life and made me realize the power of letting go.

"Ready."

***

"I can't tell you how excited I am for next season," Coach Raymer says, as I finish signing the last signature line on my contract.

"Me too," I reply with a smile, because I am happy. At least, that's what I keep telling myself.

Henry left to go help the athletic trainer with some field equipment while I was signing, so I'm taking advantage of the private moment. "Thank you for your understanding this morning, too, sir."

He pauses for a minute and sits back in his chair. His back rests against the tall plush leather backing and inspects me like he does when he's pondering how to say something.

It's something I realized about Coach when he debates about his approach. He's so calculated, knowing how important the delivery is when sharing any type of news with one of his players.

"You know, Hudson, my wife had her masters and attempted to work in every city we transferred to. She didn't have to work, and I reminded her of that all the time. After the third move, she realized she couldn't settle into a company and decided to stop trying. I was relieved, but she was frustrated because I didn't understand her desire to work when she didn't have to." He leans forward, folding his hands into each other.

"She resented me, she got depressed, lost purpose in her life, and it was hard on us for a while. Then she left me."

I just about fracture my neck, snapping my eyes up to look at him. If I know anything about Coach, it's his undying love for his wife. I had no idea that, at some point in their marriage, she left him, or that they had any kind of trouble at all.

"I gave her some time, knowing she needed that. At that time, we only had another month left in the season, and it was the worst fucking month of my life. After that, I decided I would give up everything to get her back. I'd leave baseball, stay home and take care of the kids. Whatever she needed me to do, because my career wasn't worth losing her over."

My eyes widen in curiosity. Even though I already know they are still together, I ask, "So, what happened?"

"I showed up at the house, groveling, begging. Confessed my eternal love. Continued to beg. She laughed. She actually laughed at me, Hudson." He shakes his head with a smile at the memory.

"She needed time to find herself, her worth. She identified as a strong, independent working mother and put herself through school to get there. When we got married and started moving all over for my job, it stripped away her identity. She didn't want to leave me, she wanted to find herself again, and me forcing myself to stay away from her gave her the space she needed to discover that. During that month, she started working on a foundation that she was able to dedicate her time to that she could do from anywhere we lived, and it brought her purpose."

As much as his story is endearing, Ember isn't lost. She knows what she wants. And it still ends with her in New York and me in Seattle.

"And you lived happily ever after?" I ask with a thin-lipped smile.

"Give her time. You both are young. Maybe it's just not the right time for the two of you. That doesn't mean it can't be later."

"Anytime is the right time with her, at least for me."

"Are you sure you want me to have this?" He holds up the contract, exchanging a look between me and the paper shredder next to his desk.

I pause, debating what my life would be like. And I would give it all up, if I actually thought she wanted to be followed.

"Yes, I belong here."

He gives me a long, very questionable slow nod, agreeing with a sad smile.

I hate it.

"Don't lose—"

"Hope?" I interrupt, standing up because I can't seem to exit fast enough now. I made my decision, signed the divorce papers, signed my contract, and signed them both with ink from my bleeding heart. The last thing I need is fucking hope to carry with me day in and day out, knowing the end result.

"Hope is what guides us through the darkest of times," he says, with far too much... hope.

Walking to the door, I grip the handle and swing it open, pausing through the walkway that started this whole endeavor, and I take a minute to think back on all the moments in between.

Pulling what's left of my optimism, praying that when I walk through this door, my memories fade and I live in a world without the torment of hope because it'll kill what little is left of me.

"Hope destroys the strongest men."

56

EMBER

My eyes squint as I peer out of the small airplane window, watching the clouds float like pillows covering the world below us. The dark shadow of the plane glides over the bright cotton candy clouds, carrying me and everything I own in two medium-sized suitcases, exactly the same as earlier this year when I arrived.

It seems like time changes everything and nothing at the same time. Considering the only difference is the additional baggage of a broken heart I had no intention of getting.

I spent the day packing my bag, gathering up everything from the place I've called home, and yes, I opted to bring everything. Because this opportunity means everything, and as conflicted as my feelings are, I want this.

I never expected Hudson to brand himself into me like he did. So, I allowed myself the afternoon to wallow at the finale of my self-inflicted decision, but I promised myself to leave that behind before getting on the plane.

Yet, here I sit, pondering every single decision I've ever made.

I've been working toward something like this for so long.

Five years of crawling my way to a degree, being berated for my choices, day in and day out. Questioning my worth due to the awful, disgusting words spewed from the mouths of the people that were supposed to love me the most. I struggled too much for too long to allow myself to stop.

Right?

I shake my head, questioning my own confusion.

Corbin comes through to the main cabin area, which I haven't been able to appreciate enough.

Plush white leather seats scale each side of the plane. The beige and blue earth tones make the petite space of the private plane feel open and light. It's so welcoming, yet I feel like I belong somewhere else.

There's a small bar at the back and what appears to be a bedroom in the back with a full ensuite bathroom, shower included.

It's a luxury I've never experienced, and as prestigious as it feels, my heart lurches at the thought of missing another first class experience with Hudson.

I half smile at the memory of that experience. He had to make an excuse as to why he wanted to purchase the airplane's blanket because we both felt too awkward leaving it behind.

The TV bracketed to the front wall flickers on, catching my attention. It's a national news channel spewing meaningless information about the weather and other probably biased news reports favoring whatever politician is paying them the most at the moment.

Corbin sets the remote down on the table in between us, sliding into the chair next to me.

"So, Mr. Maren, tell me about some of your current projects," I ask, turning my chair to face him so I can get lost in work instead of my dubious thoughts.

We talk about a few of his passion projects and some other things that he's been working on, a charity that clearly means a lot to him, and the potential of what we could do with an XConnect club in Manhattan.

"There's a lot more competition with the types of clubs that are in Manhattan versus what is in Seattle, but I think if we could get an idea of what these other clubs are missing, that's something we could tap into," I respond with an ease, knowing exactly what to expect in order to see where we need to start.

A smile tugs at his lips. "I'm very excited to see what you will do running our teams."

Glancing over at the two pieces of luggage, more than what someone would typically pack for a week, he tips his chin at them, and that makes me peer over at them.

"Is that for a week, or were you planning ahead?" he asks.

I steel my spine, cauterizing my decision by permanently melding them to my bones.

"I'll be staying. Indefinitely." My body language shows more confidence than the crack in my voice did. "I think we should get started right away, capitalize on the excitement of the west coast club by announcing a new one on the east coast." Again, my normal excitement is dulled by my conflicted heart.

I exchange a look with him, as his eyes flicker between me, my luggage, and my hands, which are uncontrollably picking at my nail beds.

"Hmm." His reply is curt.

Just keep going. You are a professional at your job and a professional at hiding your feelings. This is just another day.

"Does Ford own any buildings with upcoming renewals on their leases, or would we need to look into getting a real estate agent to purchase one?" I divert my energy back to a conversation I'm comfortable with.

"We'll have plenty of time to figure that stuff out tomorrow. Tell me about you." He twists in his chair to face mine, giving me even more of his undivided attention.

And suddenly, my chair is a stage, the heat of his stare like a blinding spotlight.

Tell me about you.

I pause. Way too long, I pause.

"Well, I love marketing and I'm good at my job." I smile with a shy confidence. I hate talking about myself, but that much is true.

"I already know that." He smiles kindly, sensing my nerves. "What do you do for fun? What makes Ember, Ember?"

Fun? What do I do for fun?

Well. Shit.

I do a lot of things for fun.

Experiment with sex toys with my fake husband. Eat pizza on Friday nights and go to Sunday morning matinees—again with my fake husband. Talk baseball with a group of supportive women, even though my baseball talk consists of the bare basic language. Play charades with my fake husband's family and laugh until our cheeks hurt.

"I love crossword puzzles and reading." Another long ass, awkward pause passing between us. God, I'm so boring. Crossword puzzles and reading? I might as well tell him I like to crochet and watch infomercials.

"Baseball. I like watching baseball," I spit out, recalling how much I've fallen in love with the game this past season.

"Ah, yes. I had the pleasure of meeting your husband at the party on Saturday." Just the mention of the word husband makes my pulse kick up another beat.

I force a smile and try to think of something else to say.

His eyes drift down to where my nervous hands are placed over my lap. My fingers promoted themselves from picking at the nail beds to rubbing the skin off at the base of my ring finger that now sits bare, since I left the ring on the kitchen island.

I didn't feel comfortable taking it.

I also couldn't bring myself to sign the papers.

So, I left the ring and took the papers, leaving nothing else behind. Like I had to erase myself from the existence of our home.

"I couldn't help but notice you're no longer wearing your ring," he mentions, as a statement. I think. Not a question. But it probably deserves an answer that I'm struggling to come up with.

"We—I—I mean... It's complicated?" Well, ain't that the truth?

"I'm not going anywhere," he replies with a compassionate smile, as his eyes bounce around the cabin of the plane.

Right.

We have another few hours left in the flight, and there's no really avoiding this.

"He's been offered a contract with the Smashers, and I want to go to New York. It's something I've always dreamed of for myself." I anxiously tuck my hair behind my ear, then flip the front of my hair over to the side, ruining said tuck.

I need a haircut. Hudson got a haircut before the opening, and Jesus, he looked mouth watering when he showed up in his tux. My mind is all over the place, wandering, and I wonder how long it will take to stop wandering back to him.

Probably never.

I hate it. I hate feeling so torn.

"We're just on two different paths right now." I leave it at that.

Factually, that is the truth.

I don't need to tell him about Vegas or why we stayed married or that I have divorce papers burning a hole in my carry-on the size of his home state.

I glance out of the window again, seeing the infinite ombre sky.

Flying at dusk is exquisite.

For a brief time, you can see the world as a universal whole. Dark and light battling each other in a limitless landscape.

The extreme palate change of the horizon is telling, as we fly into the darkness of the east, leaving behind the radiant setting sun that creates an ocean of pink and orange in the west.

It mocks me.

And because the world is cruel, lightning strikes in the dark sky, like I'm flying toward further agony. By choice.

"I was once on two different paths with my ex." Corbin's confession catches my attention, and I turn back to him, now realizing he was studying me that entire time.

"Really? What happened?" I ask curiously.

He presses his palms into his seat as he shifts forward, then recrosses his legs. Sitting back, like he has to get comfortable for this.

Naturally, I lean into my armrest and give him my full attention.

"We met in college. Both graduated the same year, and when I got a job at Ford, we moved to New York together. He didn't want to move to New York. He loved Georgia and wanted to stay there, but moved for me, for us." Corbin's smile was brief with that memory, like he was recalling the conversation they had when his ex chose him.

"I climbed my way up. The company was expanding quickly. The growth was exponential, and work became more and more demanding, but I was good at it, and it became my full focus." He weaves his fingers together, holding his own hand in his lap, his fingertips pressing aggressively into the base of his knuckles.

"He wanted to adopt and have kids. I wasn't against this, but adoption is incredibly hard to accomplish for any two people, especially two gay men. We spent a couple of years trying. Well, he did. My focus was still on work while his focus was...

well, on that path." He gives me a light smile, using my own analogy.

"He found a woman that was willing to donate an egg and be our surrogate. After a few rounds of IVF, she became pregnant, but we lost the baby at fourteen weeks." A heavy breath falls from his lips as his shoulders deflate. I want to run and hug him. God, how horrible.

"I lost myself in work to hide the anguish, instead of getting lost in him. He became extremely depressed, and we couldn't get ourselves aligned again. The years of living in a place he didn't want to live, working toward something but constantly feeling defeated, weighed too much on him. I loved him. I loved him so much. But I used my job as a crutch because it was easier to drown myself in work. One day, he had enough and moved back to Georgia."

At some point in his story, my hand moved to cover my chest, which still rests there. Like I need it to hold in my heart.

"I'm so sorry." My words are raspy and broken. Corbin's so kind and happy. There is such a kindness behind his eyes all the time. I would have never assumed he would have gone through so much pain. But I guess that's the thing, you never know what pain someone is hiding.

"I don't regret any decision I've ever made in life..." I flinch at his statement. How can someone not regret anything in life? I regret what I pick for lunch some days. "But I regret letting him walk out that door and out of my life. I regret being too stubborn to follow him. I regret not fighting for him." He leans forward, his hazel eyes burning a passion so bright, like he's trying to inspire a room full of people and it's not just him and I. "A *job* will always be available for people like us. But the *one*," he holds up his pointer finger, "that supports you unconditionally, loves you unconditionally, that will weather the storm with you. That's irreplaceable."

My mother spent years berating me, insisting marriage—

and only marriage—was the right path. That our job as women was to stand behind a man, let him make the money and do whatever he needs. I fought this because that never felt right. I never wanted to rely on a man to take care of me financially, chain me to a monthly allowance, and be at whatever beck and call he needed.

It sounded like a prison, not a partnership. Never once did she ever talk about marriage *and* love. Not like Corbin just did.

I was raised to believe they aren't the same thing. But that's so far from the truth.

The fear that's been ingrained in me by my mother was always because I never wanted to be put down or shadowed by a man. I never wanted a life she described.

But that's not the life that Hudson and I would have. I don't fear loving him. I fear the life my mother said I would have with a marriage.

But she never talked about *love*.

I was never taught how to love.

And I never even felt loved. Until Hudson.

I'm lost in my dazed confusion when the anchor from the news channel catches my attention.

"Robert Riley, running candidate for Governor of the State of Missouri, is being arrested for fraud, misuse of public funds, and tax evasion." I gasp as my jaw drops. The video clips over to him being walked out of his home—my childhood home—with his arms cuffed behind his back. He's glancing between all the cameras, yelling at them from a distance. "I'm innocent of all charges. My life, my entire life, I've spent serving the public, and my first priority has always been my commitment to this community and my state. That's all that's ever mattered. I am innocent," he states one last time, as the police officer places his hand on Robert's head to guide him into a police vehicle. My mother is in the background with her hands covering her face, in a complete breakdown, tears streaming down her face with dramatic sobs.

She is shaking her head at the people standing around her, probably claiming her innocence along with his.

The video scrolls over to the reporter standing at the wrought iron gates of the house. "Robert Riley has made no official comment at this time, but CI Special Agent Teddy Wong of the Internal Revenue Service stated this investigation is ongoing and they will not take his crimes lightly. They intend to prosecute him to the full extent of the law on all charges, current and forthcoming. That's all for now. Back to you, Angela."

They quickly move on to the next story.

Karma.

"Everything okay?" Corbin asks, as he shifts his chair toward the TV, then back at me.

I can't help but recap what he was screaming at the reporters.

"My first priority has always been my commitment to this community and my state. That's all that's ever mattered."

It's like a bolt of lightning that hits me when I realize that I'm no better than my so-called father. Prioritizing a job over everything else. I've spent so much time avoiding everything my mother was trying to force on me, I ended up turning out exactly like him instead.

Shit.

I glance back up at the TV. They've quickly moved on, because Robert Riley is now old news, then at Corbin, whose brows are pinched in concern.

"Respectfully, sir. I think I've made a mistake."

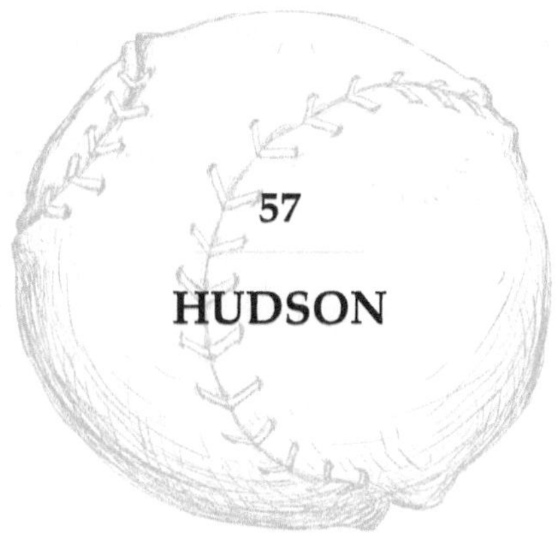

57

HUDSON

I hide in the dugout, stewing on the fact that Coach benched me at the top of the third inning, knowing after playing the first two that I wasn't going to pull through and get my shit together.

The team figured out quickly that Ember was gone because rumors spread way too fast, especially when the entire team lives in the same building. Someone must have seen Ember leaving with her luggage and either talked to her or Coach confirming my newly soon-to-be divorced status with the team.

And I know there is commentary happening by the sports-casters because there are too many cameras pointed in my direction as I sit as far in the corner of the dugout as possible, scowling at the fence line.

They are either talking about my shit performance or my five-year contract, wondering why the hell the Smashers would sign a complete joke of a catcher after the last two innings.

Yesterday, after signing my contract, I should have been on cloud nine. Calling my friends and family to celebrate. Instead, I found myself leaning on that *hope* that Coach insisted I hang on to, only to be disappointed by an empty house wiped completely clean of her.

She took everything she brought with her, but left my goddamn ring, making reality hit even harder.

She didn't sign the papers. In fact, I couldn't even find them. I assume she took them with her, wanting to read through them to make sure I'm not screwing her over, which just pissed me off even further. Even though that's exactly what anyone should do.

I was restless the entire day, moving between slamming things around the house to breaking down in the kitchen when something would remind me of her.

She made her decision so goddamn fast. There was no consideration of me, of us. How could I have been so invested, so enamored with her, and it was that fucking one-sided, but she cried when I was putting my heart and entire fucking soul on the table for her? At first, I thought she could change her mind, but after all this time, I still just got, *"I can't."*

The game is finally over, and thankfully, we won. No thanks to me.

I'm the first to storm out of the dugout and into the locker room, the polar opposite of my normal behavior, which is being the last on the field, talking the guys up as they head out of the dugout.

I just need to get the fuck out of here.

This feels eerily similar to how I felt after my injury. Lost in myself and just thinking of ways to forget. If I drank enough that night in Vegas to remember only pieces of the first night with her, I sure as hell can do that to forget everything else.

I ignore the guys patting me on the back, muttering inaudible words because they're probably just not sure what the hell to say to me, and pop my AirPods in.

Green Day plays instantly, *Good Riddance (Time of your life),* and I'd like to punch karma in the face.

What was once something that got me through the toughest times of my life, is now painful fucking memories, and I'm terrified the only thing that would ever pull me out of this is her.

"Fuck!" I rip the AirPods out of my ears and kick the bottom of my locker before resting my forehead on it.

A hand rests on my shoulder, and I turn to see Callahan, giving me the saddest face in history, and I hate it.

"Hey, man." He squints painfully at me. "It'll be okay."

"How?" I ask, because I'd like to know in what fucking universe it's going to be okay if she's not with me.

"I don't know." He shakes his head. At least he's fucking honest.

"Want me to come by tonight? We can hang out for a bit?" I shake my head, not needing any more pity than I'm already putting on myself.

"Nah, I'm good." I am not good.

I'm surprised Coach hasn't called me into his office yet, but I suppose he's giving me a bit more leeway than I deserve. I have to get my shit together.

Callahan just pats my shoulder, feeds me that tight-lipped, pathetic, sad smile, and walks off.

I finish getting dressed and walk out of the locker room. I avoid any areas with scroungy reporters, even though I know they are here to talk to me about the new contract. But I'm just not ready to talk about how excited I am to be here, to stay here, when I feel like my soul is on the other side of the country.

By an act of Congress, I'm able to get in my truck and back to the condo without being detected, and when I walk into the lobby, Arthur greets me with his same bubbly, professional smile.

At least his voice isn't dripping with pity.

"Good evening, Mr. Byrnes. This came for you today, sir." I

glance up and my heart drops when I see him holding the manila envelope I gave to Ember yesterday.

My feet stop moving as I stand in place, staring at the envelope like a ticking time bomb. If I don't reach out and grab it, does it really exist?

But I do, and it feels substantially heavier than it did yesterday. Like paper bricks weighing heaviest on my heart, and I would rather just burn these fucking papers and pretend they never existed.

"Thanks, Arthur," is all I can muster as I continue to the elevator.

Getting up to the apartment feels like an eternity, because the last thing I want to do is walk into an empty home, especially after she's wiped herself clean of it.

Maybe I should move. Everything is too fresh. Too much. And when I walk into the vast space of nothing, it still fucking smells like her.

Tropical sunset and citrus. I close my eyes and take a deep breath because pretty soon that'll fade, adding additional torment, because as much as I want this scent every day, it'll drive me insane to keep it.

Placing my keys and wallet on the side table, I kick off my shoes a little aggressively before padding to the kitchen. I reach in the fridge and grab a beer, probably one of many, which just adds to my pain and suffering, knowing I don't want to lean on alcohol but need something to take the edge off.

I daydream of tossing the manila envelope off the balcony and watching the papers fly into the wind, but instead, I uncontrollably scream, "Fuck!" and throw it against the side wall.

It lands with an odd thud. It should have fluttered loosely to the ground. It landed like it holds an imbalance of weight and there's a rock on one side.

I glare over at it, wondering if it actually might be a ticking time bomb, and walk up to it slowly, like it might be.

I squat down, picking it up, and pinch the metal tabs upright to open the flap. Sure enough, there are papers in there, but there's something else at the bottom. I turn it upside down and hold my hand out to catch what's sliding out.

A Big Red gum pack lands haphazardly in my palm. I shake my head as I stand up and place the envelope on the table. The gum pack is beat up, weathered on the sides, and the flap is bent in a few places.

Squinting, I flip it over once, then again, and open the flap. Mini Tic Tac Toe games align the inside flap, the ones from the flight we met on. Everything is identical to that first day we met, with the exception of three little words on the bottom right. They're not the same three words I said to her before she left.

Hers are even better.

"*I choose you.*"

Smiling but confused, I flip over the gum pack again for some other hidden message. I tear out the gum pieces that are stiff as metal and stale as day old popcorn—still nothing.

Pulling out the divorce papers that I nauseously, and reluctantly, signed two days ago, with my heart beating out of my chest, I inspect her signature lines, but they remain unsigned. Instead, they now have big large red X's over the top of them.

A chuckle pumps out of my chest, and happiness radiates every crevice of my body.

I close my eyes and tip my head back, smiling ear to ear, practically hearing those words leaving her lips.

I choose you.

"That look fits you better. So much more than that scowl you had when you walked in."

I'm shocked and questioning my sanity.

I crane my neck around the kitchen island and take one step toward the living room.

It's as if all the air deflates from my body as I drink her in.

Standing in our home, gorgeous as ever, with a beaming smile on her face and both suitcases at her feet.

"What can I say? I only have this look when I know you're mine." She bites down on her bottom lip and tucks her hair behind her ear, like she does when nerves get the best of her.

"Are you mine?" I ask, rubbing the nape of my neck, pinching myself at the same time.

I can see her chest expand, like she needs air.

"Wait, I don't mean that in some possessive, controlling way. I mean that in the 'I love you so fucking much and I will do whatever it takes to work this out between us' way. I want to be a part of giving you everything you dream of, not holding you back. I want—"

"I know," she interrupts, beyond calm.

"That's it?" I ask, so fucking confused.

"Well, it took a few hours, a view from thirty thousand feet in the air, and one conversation with the right person, to realize the mistake I was making. It was sort of a perfect storm of epiphanies." She smiles, that gorgeous glowing smile of hers.

"I also saw a news article, about my parents," she tilts her head to the side, eyeing me deeper, "and somehow, I think a divine intervention by the name of Seamus Matthews had something to do with that." Giving me a knowing look.

My eyebrows reach my forehead as I put my hands up in surrender. I open my mouth, unsure if I'm going to defend myself or deny yet.

"I don't want to know, and I don't care," she adds.

My hands fall to my sides. *Thank fucking god.*

"I'm a little slow on the whole relationship slash love thing. So it may have taken me longer to get here, but this is my home, *you* are my home, and... I love you. I just didn't know how to say it before, but I love you so much."

"Fuck." A smile beams out of my chest, and my legs instantly stalk over to her. I grab her, one hand cupping her face and the other gripping her waist so tightly I swear I'll never let go.

"You're really here?" I ask, between kissing her lips, chin, jaw, anywhere my lips lead. My eyes are squeezed painfully shut, afraid if I open them she'll be gone.

"I'm here for as long as you'll have me." She tilts her head back, giving me more access to the column of her neck as I trace lips over her creamy skin.

"Forever, little red, forever. And that's not long enough." I pick her up as she wraps her legs around my waist. Nothing is stopping me now that she's in my arms, back in our home, and the turn of events in the last few minutes has my mind spinning and body desperate to reclaim every part of her.

I carry her down the hallway and into our room. "I hope you slept on the plane."

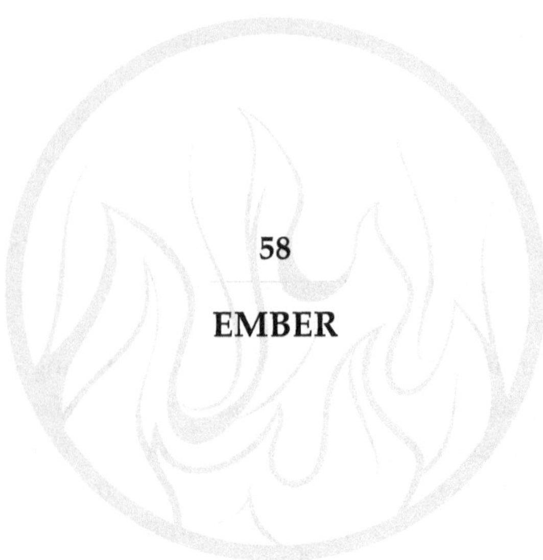

58

EMBER

"I need you." His words are desperate, in a way I've never heard. It just solidifies my reasoning for telling Corbin that I couldn't take the job and had too much more I needed to do here. Not just with Ford, XConnect, and Afterburn, but the most important part of my future. The man who desperately *needs* me. This man. The one who has loved me so unconditionally that I was blind to for too damn long.

Saying *"I choose you"* was quite literally that. Because I will always make choosing him a priority, like he's chosen me.

He's always been the most respectful gentleman, even in bed, when he takes control and dominates my body. But tonight, he's unleashed. I can feel it in the way his fingertips latch onto my body as his hands roam every inch of me.

Buttons fly everywhere as he tears the front of my top open and pulls the cups of my bra down over my breasts. Pushing them up even further, giving his mouth closer access to my hardened nipples.

I gasp as his lips pucker around the firm tips, and I roll my hips into him in response.

"I don't care what job you get, where you go, or what you

want to do. We're in this together. Do you understand?" He stops kissing me to cup both my cheeks. His soft but inky eyes gaze into me, and his playful tone is replaced by something grave.

I nod, knowing he'll never allow me to run ever again.

"Words, little red. I need your words."

"Y-Yes, I understand." Still nodding.

His lips trail down the middle of my chest, taking each nipple again, one at a time, then lower, as his tongue circles around my belly button. He tucks his hands in the waistband of my leggings and tugs them down my legs. There's nothing soft and sensual about him right now. As he stands, he circles me, like a shark eyeing his prey, before he stops in front of my nightstand.

Pressing his lips together in a thin line as he exchanges looks between me and the nightstand. Those sexy, seductive lips turn up in a lopsided, sardonic smile as he leans down and hovers over me.

"Do you remember what I said when we watched Elena at the club with Jake and Christian?" he whispers over the shell of my ear.

How could I forget?

"What they do to her, I do to you."

"Yes." My voice is unsteady and breathy, torn between feeding the monster or fighting it.

"Are you ready for that, little red? Are you ready for your husband to claim you like no other man has or ever will?" He bites down on the soft flesh of my neck, and my breath catches in my throat as I groan.

"Yes," I reply, too goddamn fast.

He grunts with a mixture of approval and satisfaction.

Grabbing my ankles, he spins my body to the side, flips me over, then kneels between my legs. I feel so exposed and vulnerable, and I love the power he holds over me. Because it doesn't feel like power, it feels like strength. Like it moves between us both whenever we're together.

Opening the side table, he pops the top of a lubricant container and cold liquid drips down between my cheeks as his finger trails down the center. I flinch on instinct as he runs his finger over the tight hole, all the way down to my entrance, and back up again.

"You were made for me." He tells me, as I press into my palms and glance over my shoulder at him. The fire in his eyes is still there; the burning desire seems like it never fades. But right now, in this moment, there is an appreciation, lust, love, respect, all rolled into one intoxicating expression.

His gaze meets mine, and he presses into his knees, lifting himself up. His chest presses against my back and he cups my face with one hand, kissing me forcefully, then cups my pussy with the other, rubbing slow circles around my clit. I choke out a moan, loving the balance of his vigorous kiss and tender touches.

I have no idea what to expect from him right now or where his fingers will go. The anticipation is both excruciating and so fucking erotic.

"Please," I whimper, and I have no clue what I'm asking for.

He presses two fingers at the entrance of my pussy. "Say that again."

"Please," I repeat, louder and more urgently.

Then he pushes his fingers into my pussy, sliding in as my arousal coats his fingers.

I bite my lip and pull away from his kiss, pressing my forehead against the bed, feeling the pleasure of his fingers all the way down to my curled toes.

"You're dripping for me." He hums, pleased. "Or are you desperate to feel my cock buried in your tight ass?"

He curls his fingers in me and I groan, unable to reply with a proper response. And the truth is, I'm so desperate for him to have me the way no one else has. To feel him in a part of my body I never thought I'd give to anyone. To see him fall apart as he claims that part of me.

"I want it. I want it so bad." I give in to him.

He withdraws his fingers and trails them up the middle of my ass, mixing my arousal with the lube still covering my hole.

My cheeks flush with embarrassment as he sits back, watching his fingers move back and forth, circling the tight ring. "You're so goddamn beautiful." Comforting me in a way only he knows how.

It eases my tension as he presses one taut finger into my back hole, and my fingers instantly grip the bed sheets as I moan into them. The initial intrusion stings, lighting me on fire. He moves his finger in a soft, tender motion, and I feel the sudden need for more.

"More," I beg, lifting my head to look back at him. His gaze as he looks between my ass and face is feral. Dire. His jaw is slacked, and he's squeezing my hip forcefully with his free hand. "I need more."

"Fuck." His voice drips with a wanton desire as he sits up, trailing his finger all the way out, only to replace it with two, and I hiss and moan, all garbled up into inaudible words, and I still need more.

He increases his tempo, picking a steady pace that has my mouth watering for more. I'm desperate for him.

"Hudson, I swear if you don't fuck—" His free hand rears back and smacks my ass.

Hard.

I flinch, and my jaw drops. We haven't ever played this game before, and I'm shocked.

I glance back at him, and the smile donning his face, glowing from ear to ear, tells me he's thoroughly enjoying this.

"Here is the way I see it, little red. You were gone for thirty-two hours, so I get the same amount of time. You're going to repay me my thirty-two hours of pain and suffering, by giving me your pleasure. Any way I fucking want." His fingers still push in and out of me with every syllable. Doing exactly what he said. Taking my pleasure.

I need more. I want more. I'm so close, and I don't think I should be. He has two simple fingers in my ass and I'm on the verge of selling myself to the devil for an orgasm.

I continue to groan and beg for more when his fingers slip out and my breath catches in my throat. I look over my shoulder, and he's standing now, unzipping his pants and finally freeing his engorged cock. It's so hard, the pink skin is thinned, and he grips himself tightly as his jaw clenches through his gaze.

He quickly coats himself in lube and uses his hand to spread it from base to tip. He looks fucking edible.

"Are you ready, baby?" I better be, because I don't think he'll wait any longer or hold back once he's there.

"So ready. More than ready," I reply, my voice husky, almost unrecognizable.

He lines himself up and presses the crown of his cock against my hole. Pushing in slowly, and my ass swallows the tip. His cock is so much bigger than what was just in there, and the burn is deeper, harder. Bottomless, indescribable stinging runs through every nerve in my body as he continues to push into me, until his hips are flush with mine.

"Ahhhh." I bite the bed sheets, suppressing my groan.

He leans forward, pressing his lips against my shoulders, biting the flesh, balancing the pain, and it feels better. Wrapping his hand around my hair, he pulls my head back, gently enough to run our bodies flush with each other as his lips graze my ear.

"You are so fucking tight, little red. This body was fucking made for me. Tell me, say it." His voice is strained, shaky. I smile through the subsiding pain, knowing I have just as much power here as he does.

"This body was built for you, husband, and I'm all yours."

"Fuck. Goddammit, Ember." He rears his hips back gently and then pushes into me again. The sensation that had me breathless moments ago is now replaced with an indescribable pleasure.

Holding my hair like a rein, he continues to move his hips in and out, stealing the pleasure from me like he promised. His free hand wraps around the front of my waist, and his fingers pad my clit, moving up and down in the same motion as his body. We've moving together in one fluid motion, and it feels like magic.

Like everything we've done together.

He finds a steady pace, matching the rhythm of his fingers, as he draws himself in and out of me.

"Hudson, I'm gonna come. Please..." Asking, praying, begging with every ounce of my being. "Please don't stop."

My entire body explodes from the inside out, and everything begins to tingle. His cock stretches me full, his fingers perform some supernatural movement on my clit, and I come harder than I ever have. My pussy throbs, forcing my ass to uncontrollably clench around him, and that pushes him over the edge.

"Ember. Jesus..." His words fade off into grunts, groans, and other curses, and I love seeing him fall apart.

I fall, spreading myself on the bed, as he falls on top of me.

Our breathing is labored, but I can't help but let out a giggle in my post orgasm high.

It's been a whirlwind of a day since I left here yesterday, and after the anxiety of the last thirty-two hours—since someone was clearly counting—I finally feel like I can breathe, even though Hudson literally just stole my breath away.

His chest flutters behind me slightly as he chuckles, pulling himself out of me and falling down on the bed next to me.

"I did not see my night ending like this," he says, all smiles, as he tucks my well-fucked hair behind my ear to expose my face. "Thank you for coming back to me." The softness in his eyes shines of gratefulness and love.

"I should have never left." Because it's the truth. I should have stayed the moment he asked.

"Well, I still have thirty-one hours of my reimbursement time left. I'll be taking advantage of every single minute."

My jaw drops. "Oh no, I don't think so. It does not work that way, mister." I shake my head.

He rolls over on top of me, hovering his lips over mine.

"Fine. Then I'll just have to take forever."

I lean up to bring our lips together in a tender kiss.

Then hold my hand out between us, pinky up.

"Promise?"

He wraps his pinky with mine, all smiles.

"Promise."

EPILOGUE
HUDSON

"To the coolest World Series champion I've ever known," Seamus cheers as we click the necks of our beer bottles together.

We're celebrating at Afterburn, because what better way to celebrate than at the place my wife literally created?

After turning down the position in New York, Corbin decided he didn't want to miss the chance of having her be a part of the project he envisioned for the New York club. So, both he and Christian offered her an Assistant Director position where she oversees the management of Afterburn and its growth, along with taking the lead on the project in New York, with her and Cruz flying in between. I've gone with her a few times since the start of the offseason, and the entire situation couldn't have worked out better.

She gets her dream job, and I get my girl. Win, win.

The Afterburn bar is open nightly, but only for meet and greets. Since the opening of the club, the XConnect - Unleashed platform has skyrocketed, and it drives a ton of business to the bar almost every night.

The theme rooms are also open nightly, and Ember and I have taken to visiting often, during and after business hours.

There are shows on the weekends and special events nights a couple times a month.

Which is the reason Seamus told me he was moving here. Because the venue needed to contract high-level security on the special event nights and weekends. Ember asked Seamus if he and his team were interested.

I told her he would never agree, and like a total dick, he proved me wrong. Agreeing almost instantly when she asked.

"So, what's the real reason you're moving here?" I ask, calling him out on moving here so drastically.

"Your *wife* drives a tough bargain." His reply is simple, but I call bullshit.

"Bullshit. You wouldn't move here unless it was calculated, purposeful, and you had the entire thing mapped out in your head. What's really going on?"

"I don't need to work and only take jobs when I feel like it. This is one of those times." He shrugs, sipping his beer, looking around the venue and not at me.

"Double bullshit," I say again. He's never been an emotional guy, nor has he ever needed to be around us guys. So, as much as I would like to say it's about Jake or me and his freedom to move anywhere at his leisure...

It's not.

He's like a hermit crab, in almost everything, and doesn't need to be around anyone, so I know his ass isn't moving here for us.

"Does it have anything to do with that woman in white?" I side eye him over my beer to test his reaction because, let's be real, the guy is an ex-SEAL and a government-trained killer.

He didn't expect me to say that, and I can tell when a small, almost insignificant, twitch happens between his brows and his

Adam's apple bobs, but he quickly takes a swig of his drink to cover it up.

"What woman?" he replies, with zero intonation and zilch in the eye contact area, too.

I laugh and shake my head.

"Nevermind. I'm glad you're here, brother." I might have three biological brothers, but he doesn't have any, and he might as well be my fourth.

I pat his shoulder right as my phone buzzes on my side of the table. Glancing at it, a message from Ember pops up.

Little Red: Room 2 - now.

"I GOTTA RUN. What time does the moving truck get here tomorrow?" I told Seamus I'd help him move his stuff in. He got a place about five minutes away from me and Ember.

"About ten. I'll text you, fucker. Now go get laid or whatever kinky shit you're going to do in room two." I want to bitch slap the smug look off his face.

Instead, I smile and salute him with my middle finger.

And since I enjoy being married to my wife, my legs road-runner straight to room two to avoid keeping her waiting. The door is cracked open, and I peek in before opening the door all the way and stepping in.

I close and lock it, then I flinch as something covers my eyes and the sensation of fabric hugs against my temple and the back of my head. Reaching up to touch it, it's a satin blindfold, and I'm completely in the dark. I tilt my head back to peek through the bottom, but even with that, there's no light coming through.

"Ember. I can't see anything." I reach my arms out and

hands wrap around my wrists, guiding me forward in a rush. I feel myself panic, stumbling forward as I try to use all my other senses to take in my surroundings.

I get spun around and pushed back against a wall, and like an idiot, I try to look over my shoulder like I can actually see something. One hand gets pulled to one side, something cold hugs my wrist, and the sound of metal on metal zips through the room. The same happens too quickly on the other side, and now I'm strapped to what I know to be a bondage cross, with both arms completely immobilized.

I pull on the restraints, which is futile, because I'm definitely not going anywhere.

"Ember," I call out, because I can't sense her anywhere around me. The silence in the room is uncomfortable, and I hate that I haven't even heard her voice.

A soft sweep of air grazes the exposed skin of my face, and I can feel her close. Fingertips trail the front of my shirt, and a slight cool breeze brushes past my chest and abs as the shirt is splayed open.

Her hands continue to my belt, unlatching the buckle and unbuttoning my pants, then she tugs the denim down, taking my shoes and socks with it.

My already hard cock tents behind my boxers and I'm fully exposed. It's nothing new, how fast she can turn me on, but the uncertainty of my surroundings has me on edge.

"Ember, baby. I need to hear your voice." Because what if I walked into the wrong fucking room? *It was door number two, right?* Now I'm second guessing myself. "Ember, say something." Uncertainty laces the tone of my voice.

Fingers curl into the waistband of my boxers, which get pulled down, and my cock bounces out as I feel the fabric pool at my feet.

"Ember, seriously, fucking say something." I'm pulling on the cuffs, trying to pull myself away from the board I'm currently chained to, revisiting every moment since I stepped through the door.

Hot breath coats the crown of my cock, as a hand wraps around the base, and I stall. Panic surges through my body, but before I can say anything more, hot wet lips wrap around the tip and both hands move around to grip my ass, pushing my cock all the way to the back of her throat.

"Ah, fuck!" I throw my head back, drowning in the pleasure of her mouth. I know it's hers. Because it's fucking incredible, it's always incredible. But no matter how sure I am, I'm still running on pure apprehension and fear.

Her head bobs back and forth, using her hands to pull my hips closer as she fucks her face with my cock.

She's relentless tonight. And completely unstoppable in my current status, being chained to the wall. She continues, her pace flawless, taking me all the way down to the back of her throat, gagging slightly before releasing, just to repeat over and over again.

"Jesus, Ember, please," I plead, because I need confirmation. I need to hear her. "Say something." My voice is unsteady as I attempt to prevent myself from coming, begging, downright begging.

She pops off the tip, and I shudder at the loss. Fuck, I was so close. I could have come if I wasn't holding back from the stress of the unknown and my anxiety getting the best of me.

Lips suck in my bottom lip that's slacked, as I try to catch my breath, and she kisses me, pulling my head down to meet hers. Her tropical and citrus scent wafts over me, and I instantly feel at ease.

She pulls away gently and smiles over my mouth.

"You are never doing that again. I feel like I'm having a heart attack." I huff out a breath and my head hits the back-board, relieved. But only a little, because I'm still restrained and completely at the mercy of my currently psychotic wife.

"What if it wasn't me? You didn't even try to kick me away," she asks, as she walks away, opening a drawer, tsking.

The dominant Ember, that comes out of her when she's feeling strong and confident, is a fucking sight to be seen. I wish I could see her right now.

"I didn't want to hurt you," I reply. "Take off my blindfold."

"No."

The sound of a plastic snap grabs my attention, and I naturally turn my head in that direction, but I'm not even certain where it came from until fingers graze past my balls and cold liquid is brushed between my cheeks.

"What the fuck!" My hips jerk forward. "Ember, what are you doing?"

"What does it feel like I'm doing?" I hear her self-satisfied smile.

She's Satan. My wife is Satan.

Just then, Satan steps between my legs, presses a cold tip to my back hole, and pushes in slowly. She wraps her hand around the base of my cock and tugs forward, granting me both pleasure and pain, and she continues to push what feels like a goddamn light post in me.

"Emb—" I'm interrupted by my own moaning as my ass swallows the plug to the base.

She continues to stroke my cock, moving my hips slightly and making the plug move just enough to make me mewl at the sensation.

I move and attempt to shift my stance, but quickly realize it just prods at my prostate and sends uncontrollable shockwaves to my cock, pushing pre-cum out of the tip.

I feel completely out of control.

And just when I think I can't drown anymore, she wraps her lips around my cock and takes me down her throat again.

"Fuck, fuckkk..." My voice is cavernous and desperate.

I was close before, but now—now I'm on the precipice of shooting myself into another galaxy.

Her pace is perfect, her mouth is hot and wet, and with every bob of her neck and shift in my legs, the plug rubs against my prostate, careening me closer to an orgasm.

"I'm so close... I'm gonna come."

She fucking stops. Everything.

I grunt, pushing my hips forward, asking for more.

"Ember," I'm begging again. "Please don't fucking stop."

She snaps something on my left wrist, and it falls to my side, then does the same with the right. My arms tingle from the position change, but I lift them to my face. Pulling the blindfold back over my head, and it falls to the floor.

The room is dimmed, but it still takes my eyes a moment to adjust as I squint and glance around.

Ember's standing a few feet away, taking slow and calculated steps backward, biting her lip with that smile I could hear through my blindfold.

"You can fuck me. But you have to leave that in." She dips her chin and eyes my ass. "And if you don't make me come first, I get thirty-two hours of whatever I want to do to you."

Oh, this little hellion.

I step forward in her direction, and instantly regret it when the plug rubs my prostate and stops me in my tracks. My jaw drops, and I have to huff out a steady breath.

She's already sitting on the bed, with her legs spread open, just fucking waiting for me, and I'm standing here trying to prevent pre-ejaculation from just walking.

I grab my cock and squeeze hard as I take another slow step, then another. Feeding myself enough pain to get through the pleasure of walking.

I have no idea how I'm going to get through fucking her long enough to make her come before me. But she did say I *could* fuck her, not that I *had* to.

So, I drop to my knees in front of her and palm her sternum, pushing her back against the bed, and swipe my tongue through her slit.

Her moaning makes me clench, and again, a stab to the prostate, and pre-cum leaks out of my cock.

"Goddammit, woman. You are going to be the death of me," I say, between licking and sucking her clit as I glance up, and she's pinching her nipples.

Her red hair is splayed out over the bed, and her strawberry lips are as flush as her cheeks as she groans and chants my name.

I begin to hear the trembling in her voice and her legs share the same demise, shaking under my hands.

Staying as still as possible, I lick and suck while holding her arms down at her sides. She's writhing underneath me as her moans get louder and louder.

I want her as wretched as I am.

Sitting up from my kneeling position, I line myself up, tapping the crown of my cock on her clit and rubbing it through her pussy. She's fucking soaking and so ready.

"Beg me. Beg me for my cock." I press the tip at her entrance and wait.

Her head lifts off the bed, and her gorgeous emerald eyes, as dark as the deepest parts of the ocean, meet mine. A smirk tips the corner of her lips, and I realize immediately how much of a fool I am to think she'd give in to me tonight.

She wraps her legs around my waist, pressing her heels into my ass pulling me into her, giving herself what she needs and giving that evil plug a deeper nudge.

I bite my lip, and one hand falls to the bed. Holding myself up with it, I piston into her, while thumbing her clit with the other, clinging on to as much determination as I can.

Her determination is on full display, not giving me a hint of how close she could be.

"Fuck." My whisper is defeated. She's hell bent on winning that goddamn thirty-two hours, and I'm taking the losing train to Orgasmville.

I'm about to give in, but her pussy flutters around me, and she finally moans so loud it comes from the depths of her chest as she throws her head back against the bed. This little minx was holding out, trying to stay quiet on me. I thrust into her harder as she comes around my cock, and the faster movement rubs the plug in perfect rhythm, and I fucking explode.

Everything around me goes dark and my vision blurs. Bits of fluorescents flash behind my eyelids and all over the room as I blink them open to watch Ember ride out her high.

I catch my breath and reach down to pull out the plug that doesn't feel nearly as good coming out as it does going in. I throw it on the ground, because, well, I'm mad at it. For the amount of control it had over me.

Then look over at the woman that will never cease to amaze me. The woman who caught my attention from the moment I laid eyes on her, and the woman she's becoming. I love every single experience we've been through together, and after the stunt she pulled tonight, I have no doubt she'll keep me on my toes—and probably cuffed to a chair.

EXTENDED EPILOGUE
HUDSON

"That's the last of it," Seamus calls from the inside of the truck as I take the last box into the house he's going to call home for however long he decides.

It's exactly him, in that it's small, quaint, and not big and flashy. It's a modest three bedroom, two bath home on a small cul-de-sac, which is hard to find near the downtown Seattle area. Houses like these rarely come up for sale. In fact, I don't think it was, but he made some insane off-market offer to the homeowner to buy it.

Not surprising, considering whatever Seamus wants, he gets.

The truck is backed into the driveway, and I trail the side of it, taking a few garbage bags to the trash can that's placed by the side fence.

Just as we're finishing up, the next-door neighbor pulls into their driveway, turns off the car, and steps out of the driver's side of the car. "Hi, are you moving in?"

She's roughly my age, long dark hair and olive skin. She looks like she could be Kobi's sister, making me believe she's Japanese and something else, or maybe Hawaiian.

Either way, she looks way too familiar.

"No, my friend—" I point at the truck and side-eye a look inside of it. Seamus's back is ramrod straight against the side closest to us, hiding.

This motherfucker is hiding.

He is waving his hand, not looking at me. Still hiding.

Hum.

"My friend is moving in, but he... went to the... store." I turn back to look at her again. I'm a terrible liar, so *'store'* comes out like a question instead of a statement.

"Oh, bummer. I'll have to introduce myself another time."

"You look familiar. Do I know you?" I ask, because it's bugging me. I know I've seen her before.

Her brows pinch together as she inspects me, giving me an honest review before saying, "No, I don't think so."

She pulls one side of her jacket off her arm then shrugs off the other, leaving her in only a white tank top and denim shorts.

Oh, shit.

I palm my face to hide my expression as the flashback hits me.

The woman in white.

THANK YOU FOR READING

I hope you enjoyed Hudson and Ember's story as much as I enjoyed writing it!

I am a self-published author. If you loved this book, please consider taking the time to leave a review as it helps me tremendously!

www.berlinwick.com
Please sign up for my newsletter to keep up to date on my upcoming releases and receive exclusive content!

ACKNOWLEDGMENTS

As usual, with any book I write, it wouldn't be possible without the support of my amazing husband. He encourages me to read, write, better myself everyday and allows me to follow a passion I never knew I had. I love the hell out of you. You are one of the good ones and I'm so happy you're stuck with me.

To my "Angelina", even though you didn't want to read my books in fear of hating them, I still love you. Your support means so, so much!

Nicole, my "PP", my sounding board. Thank you for allowing me to talk your ear off about every random ass plot idea I have. I absolutely adore you.

Sarah, for editing all my horrible grammatical errors that shouldn't be written by a grown woman. Thank you for making me look like I know what I'm doing.

Kelly, my IG book bestie and beta reading extraordinaire. I am so grateful for your support and encouragement. Thank you for taking on the role of Hawkeye for this manuscript.

Chloe del Rey, you are so darn talented. I feel so lucky to have met you. You were truly the first author I connected with while writing my first book and helped guide me more than you know. I'm truly grateful for all your feedback and honesty, and our friendship!

To all the ARC readers that took the time to fit this in and review, your support means everything. ARC readers help indie authors so much and you are so appreciated!!

Lastly, you the reader, the Goodreads reviewer, the social

media poster, the romance lover. By sharing your thoughts, ideas, reviews, and love for the book, you help spread the word and grow us in so many ways. We would not be able to share our stories without you.

THANK YOU!

ALSO BY BERLIN WICK

<u>Elena, Jake & Christian's Story - The Secrets We Hide</u>

Creating our fantasy jars filled with love notes of our secret desires was a way to revive the monotonous routine that had become our marriage.

But pulling that little piece of paper with my husband's most desired secret was a shock I wasn't prepared for.

To watch my wife

I never knew that he was a voyeur.

I didn't realize he had a hunger to witness another man give me pleasure.

And I had no idea I would like it as much as I did.

Meeting the perfect man to fulfill this desire was easy.

Having him take me in the corner of a dark club while my husband watched was surprisingly simple.

Running into the sexy stranger in a meeting with a new client the next day—extremely problematic.

Especially because I never told him I was married. Especially because a desire still burns for both him and for my husband.

And the secrets we hide could destroy us all.

ABOUT THE AUTHOR

Berlin was raised in a tiny town in North Idaho who moved to the Bay Area, California, at the age of eighteen, where she still resides with her husband and two boys. Her bucket list items include skydiving, attending the Oscars, becoming a New York Time best-selling author, and cruising the world for retirement. She loves writing and reading, ANY and ALL kinds of romance novels, and loves engaging in the booksta community. You can find her most active on Instagram!

9 798990 627321